ROOTLESS

Krystle Zara Appiah is a British-Ghanaian writer, editor and screenwriter based in London. She has a degree in literature and creative writing from the University of Kent. In 2020, she was one of forty writers selected for the London Library's Emerging Writers Programme. *Rootless* is her debut novel.

ROOTLESS

KRYSTLE ZARA APPIAH

THE BOROUGH PRESS

The Borough Press
An imprint of HarperCollins*Publishers* Ltd
1 London Bridge Street
London SE1 9GF

www.harpercollins.co.uk

HarperCollins*Publishers*
Macken House, 39/40 Mayor Street Upper,
Dublin 1, D01 C9W8, Ireland

First published by HarperCollins*Publishers* 2023
1

A catalogue record for this book is available from the British Library

Hardback ISBN: 978-0-00-852883-6
Trade Paperback ISBN: 978-0-00-852884-3

This novel is entirely a work of fiction.
The names, characters and incidents portrayed in it are
the work of the author's imagination. Any resemblance to
actual persons, living or dead, events or localities is
entirely coincidental.

Typeset in Meridien by Palimpsest Book Production Ltd, Falkirk, Stirlingshire

Printed and bound in the UK using 100% Renewable
Electricity by CPI Group (UK) Ltd

For my mum, who loves fiercely and deeply always.

Marriage is like a groundnut. You have to crack it to see what is inside.

Ghanaian proverb

PART ONE

Five Months Before

Sam knows he is too late even as he sprints back from the station. He runs the whole way, phone clenched in his fist, the early afternoon sun at his back. His lungs are seizing in his chest by the time he crashes into the stairwell. He takes the stairs two at a time and, panting loudly, calls Efe's name as he staggers into the flat. Nothing is out of place. Maybe he's overreacting. *She has to be here somewhere,* he thinks as he moves from room to room, peers around corners, behind the bathroom door. He throws open the airing cupboard and stares at the hoover and dust-covered pots of paint. The last room he checks is their bedroom. The door sits open and ominous at the end of the hall. Here he finds gaps everywhere: bare hangers, three pairs of shoes gone, a drawer cracked open as if she'd left in a hurry, her favourite necklace glinting on the dresser.

Sam doubles over. Suddenly the air is warm and sludgy. The room swims. He feels like a small child, waking up groggy and alone in a ghost-filled house. He checks his phone again, scans through the stream of messages he's fired out, but there's still no reply from Efe. All his calls go to voicemail. The £1300 payment to British Airways is still pending. Then he thinks of Olivia and panic floods his system anew. He fumbles with his mobile, calls the childminder and mutters, 'Pick up, pick up, pick up' until she does.

'Hello.'

'Is Olivia there?' Sam says.

'Of course. Is everything o—?'

'Let me speak to her,' he interrupts. There's a brief scuffling sound as the phone changes hands; then Sam hears Liv on the line. His legs soften as he listens to the four-year-old sway to her words, the soft 'p' sounds and the wobbly 't's. He sinks to the floor. Unaware, Liv chats happily about Bear-Bear, seamlessly picking up their conversation from hours earlier. Sam lets his eyes close and smiles. 'See you soon. I love you. Be a good girl,' he says, then adds, 'I'm coming to pick you up, okay? Put Miss Bea back on the phone.' After the call, Sam lowers his face into his hands. He waits for the ringing in his ears to stop and the flecks of dancing light to scatter; then he summons up all the energy he has, to face the aftermath.

Later, when Sam returns to the flat with Liv, he holds his breath as she pauses in the hallway, looks both ways, first into the living room, then into the kitchen. Even in her absence, Efe is everywhere. Olivia gives him a curious look. 'Where's Mummy?' she asks.

'Out. She'll be back soon,' Sam says. He too believes these words. No need to worry Liv. No matter what happens between him and Efe, they always find their way back to each other. He just needs to give her time. All he has to do is wait.

Sam settles Liv in the living room, glances at the clock and sees it's early, not quite 3 p.m. 'Want some juice?' he asks and returns with juice and buttered crackers.

In the quiet of the kitchen he listens to the voicemail again. It was hard to make out at first because of the cars hurtling past in the background. Sam had listened to it three times, struggling to make sense of the words, before he'd finally understood that she'd gone. She'd told no one, only called her sister minutes before she'd boarded the plane and her sister had called him. After the beep there's a three-second pause before Serwaa realises it's recording and speaks. 'Hey, Sam, it's me,' she says. 'Can you let Efe know I got her message? Her phone's going to voicemail, so if you're with her, just tell her it's fine. I'll be there when she lands. I hope things are good.'

All afternoon Sam makes phone calls. Most are to Efe, even though he knows she's somewhere high above Europe or the Sahara, more miles threading between them with each passing second. He calls Serwaa too. His movements are mechanical. He hangs up, waits a few minutes and redials. He doesn't let himself think or stop.

'Daddy?' Sam turns to find Olivia standing in the doorway. She looks at him warily, his brave and curious four-year-old, and Sam's sure she can tell something is off. He takes a deep breath and fills his voice with false cheer.

'Need something?'

'I'm hungry,' Liv says, a half-second before her stomach rumbles.

'Oh.' Sam's eyes move to the clock. Hours have passed. Outside the sky is a dim grey. 'Let's get you some dinner,' Sam says and digs around in the fridge. He finds rice but no stew, pulls out a bag of fish fingers and frozen peas iced to the back of the freezer, but can't find chips. In the end, he feeds Liv cheese on toast and nudges her back in the direction of the TV.

Just before 10 p.m. the shrill sound of the buzzer pierces the flat. Sam lowers Liv into her bed, still dressed, teeth unbrushed, and races back into the hallway.

'Efe?' he says into the intercom.

'Phoebe.'

Sam doesn't remember calling his sister but is relieved to hear her voice over the static-filled line. He buzzes her in. A minute later she's standing on the welcome mat, pulling him into a hug. The tan blazer and the faint scent of rum on her skin tell him she's come straight from a work event.

'I got your message,' she says. 'Have you heard anything?'

'Nothing.' Sam steps to the side as she strides into the living room, dumps her blazer on the nearest armchair.

'But her plane landed, right?'

'Two hours ago according to Google. I'm pretty sure her phone was on around nine, but now it's going straight to voicemail.' Sam pushes past the clamminess in his throat, tries to play it down. 'But that could be anything. Maybe the battery died or she lost it or something.'

Phoebe gives him a look. 'Do you actually believe that?'

Sam doesn't answer. He flicks his phone screen on. Still nothing. Another part of his mind is combing through memories of the last few months. He thinks back to how happy they were on New Year's Eve: somehow separated at a party at 11.59 but making a mad dash to find each other just before the clock struck midnight; how nothing was amiss at last month's family dinner, everyone gathered around the table at Sam's dad's place, trading stories over a takeaway like normal. Maybe she had been quieter than usual during their day trip to Brighton, staring out the window as they crawled back to the city in bank holiday traffic. Sam hadn't thought much of it at the time. They'd all been tired. Liv had slept for most of the drive. He needs to think harder and see something he missed. Something they all missed.

Across the room, Phoebe sighs loudly and begins pacing. 'I can't believe you're not more freaked out.'

'I know where she is. I don't know why she won't talk to me, but at least I know she's . . . safe.'

'How could she leave the country and not say anything? Are you sure she wasn't mad about something?'

'No,' Sam says softly, despite the thought that bubbles to the surface. 'We're good. Really good.'

Phoebe shakes her head. 'Who does that? Who books a flight and leaves?'

Sam groans, and puddles into the sofa and puts a hand to his throbbing temples. He sits there for a few moments, his face cupped in his hands, before he hears Phoebe's footsteps nearing, feels her hand squeeze his shoulder.

His voice comes out quiet, shaky. 'I just want to talk to her – figure out what's going on. I don't know what she's thinking.'

Above him, Phoebe replies, 'Then you have to do something. Go after her or something.'

'This isn't a movie, Pheebs. I thought you were here to help.'

'I am helping,' she says. 'Do you really think sitting here like this is working?'

Sam comes to with his face buried in the musty sofa, head hidden beneath a cushion, his first thought of Efe. Five days have passed since he last saw his wife. He thinks back to the last time he saw her: straight-backed at the dining table, one knee pulled up under her chin, her gaze fixed on the middle distance. He'd watched long ribbons of steam curl up from her mug and peter out into nothing. Her face was dewy with heat; her twists pulled back by a satin headscarf. Sam had paused, palming a warm cup of coffee and just stood there, looking at her. A long drawn-out moment had passed before she lifted the mug to her lips and drank.

The conversation that followed was normal. Still, over the last four days, Sam's replayed it in his mind and sifted through her words for hidden meanings. He remembers chatting about work, Phoebe, deciding who'd take Liv to the child-minder's house. He'd made a comment about the tea she'd been drinking – more of a non-comment, a dumb question really. He'd expected her to nod and agree. Instead, she'd said nothing, only stared at him, like she didn't recognise him, like it was the furthest thing from her mind, so Sam had let it go, regretted saying anything at all. Six hours later she was gone.

Sam flops over onto his back, feels the heaviness in his sand-filled head. Through thin curtains, he sees the sky is a watered-down navy. His phone is already in his hand. Blue-white light skewers the darkness. He squints at the screen, scrolls past the endless stream of notifications, emails, WhatsApp messages, hoping for something from her. Over the last five days, he's listened to the voicemail message thirty-seven times, memorised it, wallowed in it. He checks flight prices hourly, logs into their joint bank account and does mental gymnastics. Even if he borrows money, he has both the plane ticket and expedited visa to consider so it'll be tight.

Sam sighs and wipes the trail of dried saliva from his cheek. He tells himself it'll be fine. Any moment now she'll walk in. Swinging his legs down to the floor, he shuffles from the sofa into the hallway, a hand kneading away at the crick in his neck. He stops at Liv's room and stands with his bare toes on the threshold. The curtains are drawn, but he can make out the powder-pink walls, the semi-circle of teddy bears holding council by the bookcase. Olivia is the small mound bunched up in the top corner of her big-girl bed. She stirs, twists deeper into the covers, then settles.

It's Saturday. Sam has a photoshoot on Monday. He has some engagement photos to edit. If Efe isn't back by then, he'll have to cancel the job or figure what to do with Olivia. Maybe Aunty Dora could watch her for a few hours. Or Phoebe. Maybe his dad. Sam pushes the thought away. *She'll be here*, he reminds himself and tamps down the dread rising up in him. He doesn't let himself waver. He tries calling Efe before he showers, calls after he's dressed, and a third time as he pours his first coffee of the day. He leaves short, effi-cient messages like, 'Please call me when you get this. I just want to know you're okay.' No longer the rambling voicemails when all of this was brand new and he was reeling. He calls at odd times, tries to catch her off-guard. He imagines her just waking, mistakenly answering the phone. Then she'd have to talk to him.

Olivia will be up soon. A whole day stretches ahead of him, full of hours where he'll have to keep their daughter entertained and answer questions he doesn't have answers for yet. Sam swallows and tries Serwaa's number. He isn't expecting her to pick up and almost drops his phone when she answers on the fourth ring. Still stunned, Sam rushes in, pounces while she's still uttering a hello.

'Serwaa?'

'Sam, hi,' she says.

'Is Efe there? Can I speak to her?' Sam can hear the desperate lurch in his voice.

'She's resting.'

'Is she okay? What's going on? Is it something to do—'

'I can't. She needs to be the one to—'

'Put her on the phone. That's all I'm asking. Please.'

Sam hears the hitch in her breath. Two moments of hesitation, then she mutters a hurried apology. Her voice drops to a low whisper; she's still apologising as she hangs up. The call lasts seventeen seconds. Afterwards, Sam presses his palms into the counter and resists the urge to throw his phone at the wall. Something sharp and hot flares in him. They have a life together. A family. Sam breathes out a long, tired breath. He looks down at the phone in his hands, the British Airways banner still blinking at the top of the webpage. Through the thicket, a single thought crystallises. He knows what he has to do.

SEPTEMBER 1997

Nineteen Years Before

The first thing Efe notices is that the sky is closer here. As the plane begins its descent into the outer lands of the sprawling city, she can feel it pressed upon her shoulders. It follows her down as they come in for a bumpy landing and hovers just out of arm's reach, but every so often it dips down and brushes the top of Efe's head. It makes the city feel cramped. It awakens and unsettles the feeling rumbling in the bottom of her stomach.

The feeling had begun when Maame made the announcement: the girls would be going to London to stay with Aunty Dora and would finish up their schooling there. Whatever the feeling was, it had held on lightly over the whirlwind summer break, filled with goodbye parties and capped off with tearful farewells and long hugs with her parents, before she'd taken her sister's hand (because her mum said she had to), and together they'd boarded a plane heading for Heathrow.

Serwaa rouses from sleep reluctantly. 'We're here?' she asks, squinting out the window.

'Yes.'

People jump out of their seats before the overhead sign pings. The cabin fills with restless energy that only eases when the doors open. The girls have to fight to stay together through the surge of people pushing out into the London air. They wait in long snaking lines for their papers to be checked, collect their bags, and when they step out into the slick, bright airport, Aunty Dora is waiting just like Maame and Paa said she would be.

'*Adjei!* Is that you? Look at how grown you are, my girls.' She beams, pulls them both into a back-breaking hug.

It has been years, but the girls would have recognised her anywhere. She stands a half-head taller than Efe. Each time she smiles, full lips part to reveal clustered-together teeth and a faint dimple appears on one cheek. She looks like a slimmer version of Maame, shades lighter thanks to the mild British summers.

'Okay, does anyone need the toilet? The drive is far.' Still smiling, she scoops up one of the heavier bags, clamps a hand around Serwaa's shoulders and leads the way across the huge glass atrium. Efe walks behind them, dragging her suitcase over polished floors so shiny she can see her blurry outline reflected back.

On the way into the city the girls say very little. The quiet car ride is filled with the sounds of BBC breakfast radio. It makes Efe think of Paa, who listens to it every morning without fail. He lives a life underscored by dreary weather reports, A3 traffic jams and the latest news from four and a half thousand miles away, and Efe imagines him listening now, mindlessly fiddling with the chain on his glasses and staring off into space at something only he can see. She presses back into the seat and pretends she is beside him in his office, watching the light dance across the piles of books overflowing from their bookcases, dust settling on their sun-faded spines. When the daydream begins to dim at the edges, she tightens her grip on her seatbelt, turns her face to the window and watches the rows of identical houses slip past.

The house is called a flat. It is one of many houses stacked on top of each other and stuffed into a bland concrete shell. Throughout the day footsteps slap on the council-approved tiles and the lift grumbles as it drags itself up and down twelve floors, just behind the living room wall. That is when it works; the girls will soon learn that it is out of order more often than not. And for the days and weeks it doesn't work, they will climb five flights in a bare concrete stairwell that is perpetually cold and damp.

Maame had warned them that in London there is very little space and that people live on top of each other, but they were not expecting this. They have never been in a house so small. To them home is a building with an excess of rooms. Back home, Maame has a sitting room specifically for entertaining important guests, her prized possession a hand-carved cabinet filled with gold-rimmed serving dishes that are barely used but cleaned often should they ever be needed. This will take some adjusting to.

'I'm sorry it's not much,' Aunty says as she gives them the tour. She waves a hand towards mismatched furniture stuffed in cramped rooms, wallpaper that is brown and floral, its uppermost corners darkened with damp. The girls smile politely. The bathroom, kitchen and living room all branch off a narrow windowless hallway, where light fights with darkness.

'And this one is yours.' Aunty smiles and swings the last door open. Miraculously, she's managed to squash bunk beds, a desk, chair and wardrobe into the tiny space.

Serwaa's face turns towards the bottom bunk, eyes widening at the school uniforms laid out. 'Are those for us?' She rushes into the room and snatches up a dark blue jumper, runs her hands over a crisp blue shirt. 'Ɛyɛ fɛ.'

'The other ones are for you, Efe.' Aunty smiles encouragingly.

Efe, crossing the room in four measured steps, can feel jittery anticipation brewing in her. Black polyester skirts. Plain white shirts. It's like something she'd wear to a funeral – a far cry from the golden shirts and dark brown pinafores she's left back home, in her actual wardrobe, in a bedroom so big she'd never be able to reach out and touch opposite walls at once.

'What do you think?' Aunty murmurs.

Efe turns and gives Aunty a small smile and says thank you, just like she has been taught.

The school is disappointing. After a fifty-five-minute journey by bus, they arrive at a place sapped of colour: a cluster of stunted two-floor buildings and an expanse of grey tarmac, so unlike her old school with its sprawling yard, well-maintained tan-and-brown-painted buildings, surrounded by deep, green trees. She thinks of the friends she left behind. Efe tries not to let her heart sink. But again, the sky dips and the feeling rumbles within her.

Aunty Dora hurries the girls towards the reception, the only building with glistening yellow lights. The three of them squeeze onto a beige sofa meant for two, avoiding springs that press through the worn fabric. The headteacher arrives for their 8 a.m. meeting at 8.09, out of breath, with damp rings at his armpits.

'Mrs Ansah, I'm so sorry to keep you waiting. Come in,' he says.

Aunty Dora, Efe and Serwaa follow him into an office. Efe sits, noticing the phone blinking with unanswered messages. One red light turns to two, then three, as the headteacher rattles on about optimal class size, expected workload, state-of-the-art study facilities and top-notch anti-bullying measures.

'I think that's everything,' the headteacher says, fifteen minutes later, as he rises from his seat. 'It was very nice to meet you, Mrs Ansah.'

'Ms,' Aunty Dora corrects.

'Right.' He nods furiously and glances at his watch. 'I'll ask Mrs Andrews to walk Efe and Serwaa to their tutor groups.' Coming out of his mouth their names sound like 'Effie' and 'Sarah', but no one bothers to correct him.

Aunty stands and turns to the girls. She straightens Serwaa's collar, runs a hand over Efe's neat braids. 'Take care of each other, *wa te*?'

Efe nods. 'Okay,' Aunty sighs. 'I'll be back late. There's rice and stew in the fridge. Call me if you need anything. The number for my workplace is on the fridge.'

Back in reception, a slim woman in a grey skirt and kitten heels introduces herself and begins the tour. 'You can see from your maps that classrooms are split between A block, B and C. A is for years 7–9, B is 10 and 11 and C is sixth form. This –' she pauses outside the door marked A07 and glances at Serwaa – 'is your classroom.'

Inside, awkward pre-teens are clustered around lockers, showing off new stationery and summer hairstyles. There's a brief, reassuring squeezing of hands, then Serwaa unhooks her fingers from her sister's and strides in before Efe can say, 'See you later.'

Mrs Andrews turns on her heel and leads Efe down another long corridor; already the route is jumbling in Efe's mind, like cables stuffed in a drawer.

'That's the sixth form common room. You can study or relax during your free periods. And the library's just through those double doors. We've got brand new computers, now with Windows 95 and the worldwide web. Everything you need to know is available at the click of a button.' She chuckles to herself.

Efe can feel students pressing all around her. It has been years since she last saw such a mix of people all in one place, so many white faces amongst the black and brown. For the most part, they are tall, taller than she is, their uniform tight in places that Efe's isn't, sloppy where hers is neat and crease-free. Their loud conversations almost drown out Mrs Andrews, but all Efe can focus on is the straining in her chest, her heart lurching like an animal caught in a trap, and the sudden heat in her feet, the blood pooling there, her body prepared to take flight. Efe fights the urge to run back and find her sister. She's been in the UK for less than a week. *This is all too soon*, she thinks, trying to swallow down the panic swelling in her chest.

'Are you okay, dear?' Mrs Andrews asks, retracing her steps to where Efe has frozen with her back against a wall.

Efe is shaking, tears brimming, panic rioting through her veins. But she nods, not trusting herself to speak. They climb a flight of stairs. Upstairs, the corridors are emptier, students are beginning to disappear into classrooms.

'And here we are. C12 with Mr Summers. Come back to reception if you need anything else.'

Efe mutters a thank you even though she knows she will never find her way back. She gathers her courage and marches into the classroom before she has a chance to think twice, slides into a seat at the back, where she has a good view of every other student in the room. Her welcome brochure is clasped like a shield across her chest as she watches the other students trickle in, hoping no one will notice her.

It's a slow crawl towards 3.30. At the end of the day, Efe waits for Serwaa at the agreed spot. She retrieves the piece of paper and reads and rereads Aunty's instructions, memorises the hand-drawn map while hordes of teenagers pass by. When Serwaa finally arrives, she is surrounded by a gaggle of twelve-year-old girls, girls with crinkly blonde hair and wavy brown ponytails. They spend several minutes hugging and saying their goodbyes. Only when they are out of the gates does Serwaa look up and see Efe.

Serwaa smells different. She talks the whole way home, matching her stride to Efe's and trailing her fingers along the dense green hedges as they walk towards the emptying bus stop. On the 87 bus, Serwaa talks about the friends she made and how delighted her teachers were to meet her. She is still speaking when they enter the flat and the phone rings. Maame's timing is impeccable.

'Hello?' Efe says.

'Aye, Efe, is that you?'

'Mum, hi,' Efe says. The line fizzes.

Serwaa appears at Efe's shoulder. She tilts her ear towards the phone, her bag abandoned in the open doorway. 'I want to speak to her,' she hisses.

Efe rolls her eyes and moves the phone to her other hand. Maame's voice crackles.

'I miss you girls. Is your aunty taking good care of you?'

'We miss you too. And yeah, Aunty Dora's doing great.'

'Oh good. Good. Have you eaten?' Maame asks.

'We're about to. We just got back.'

'Oh, okay.' The line fizzes again. Efe only catches part of whatever Maame says. She presses the phone closer to her ear. 'What was that?' she asks.

'I said, how was school? How was your first day?'

Four and a half thousand miles is not enough to stop the weight of that question pummelling into Efe. She hesitates. She could mention that even with a map she got lost and was late for both her Chemistry and Business Studies classes, or maybe she could talk about how she'd spent most of fifth period fighting back tears and struggling to follow along because the feeling had rioted inside her, quickened her heartbeat and made it impossible for her to catch her breath – but Maame's voice had wavered. The phone feels heavy in Efe's hand, and in the end she says, 'Fine. It was fine.'

'Did you make friends?'

'Some,' she lies.

'And the teachers?'

'They're nice.'

'Good, good.' Maame practically exhales the words and Efe can hear the light *ting* of jangling bracelets. She pictures Maame raising a hand to wipe relieved tears from her eyes. Maame clears her throat, her voice light now. 'Don't forget that your cousin goes to that same school. You remember Aunty Justine? It's her daughter, Abbey.'

A vague recollection comes to mind. It has been eight, maybe ten years, and Efe remembers Aunty Justine as a thin woman, who spent some years in Ghana after two decades parading down catwalks, but Abbey – Abbey she remembers clearly. They are only months apart in age, but somehow Abbey had always seemed much older, cooler, charming everyone with stories about her life in the UK and boasting about places she'd travelled to. Between the ages of seven and fourteen, Abbey had made annual trips to Ghana. Every summer, she spent a few weeks in Accra before scuttling off to her father's village, somewhere in the northern region. Efe only saw her for a week or two each year, witnessed her thin limbs grow soft and pudgy, her light skin darken to a deep, radiant bronze. By night Efe watched through the curtains as the neighbourhood boys found reason after feeble reason to stop by again and again, just to catch a glimpse of her.

'Let me call Justine today,' Maame says, almost to herself. 'Abbey's such a nice girl. It will be good for the two of you to be friends.'

'Okay.'

'Is Serwaa there?'

'Yeah, she's here. I'll just—' Efe begins to move the phone away, then catches something else.

'And Efe . . .'

'Yes, Mum?'

'Be good.'

It is a Friday, four days into the autumn term, when Efe steps out of the toilets and hears someone call her name. It cuts through the steady current of teenage conversations; before she has the chance to react, Abbey's body collides with hers.

'Oh my gosh, Efe! I've been looking all over for you!' Abbey exclaims. 'Your mum called and told my mum that

17

you and Serwaa go here now – and here you are! How crazy is that?'

'Abbey, hi,' Efe says, relieved to see a familiar face. All week she's longed to be anywhere but here, wanted to be back in Ghana with her friends and her old, familiar life. Instead, she's stayed silent and kept her head down, only answering questions when called upon – and even then, always caught off-guard, her voice coming out rushed and frantic. She spends every hour in school trying not to draw too much attention to herself, certain the moment she does something bad will happen.

'I just can't believe you're here,' Abbey says, still smiling.

It's been two years since Efe saw Abbey last; she is leaner now, a half-head taller, her eyebrows plucked to near oblivion, an even white-toothed smile where silver braces used to be.

'What are you doing after fifth? A group of us are going round to Serena's. Wanna join?' Abbey asks.

'After fifth?' Efe reaches into a pocket and unfolds her timetable. 'I have General Studies lesson six.'

'No one goes to those. Come with.'

Efe hesitates. 'I have to meet Serwaa at three thirty.'

'Fine.' Abbey shrugs. 'I've got to go but let's do something this weekend, 'kay?' And with that Abbey spins on her heel and saunters off.

Over the weeks that follow, Efe sees Abbey at regular intervals. She pops up in the common room during Efe's frees or whisks her away from the library in the post-lunch lull. Sometimes they sign themselves out and go off campus, drift in and out of shops along the high street or catch a bus to the nearest mall. She introduces Efe to her friends: boys with frosted tips, girls with crimped hair who peek at her from behind *Mizz*, *Sugar* and other glossy magazines to say hi. Abbey seems to know everyone. Efe grows more comfortable. She stops trying to slip through school undetected and starts daring to be a part of something. To her, Abbey's presence is a life-raft, sweeping in to carry Efe up and out to calm waters. With each introduction and warm welcome, Efe feels her terror dissipating. There are too many names for Efe to remember, yet she feels her world expanding, her shiny newness wearing away. A few times a week, they head straight home with Serwaa, and the three of them meander through the after-school hours watching *Sister, Sister, Kenan and Kel* and *Moesha*, flicking through the channels until Aunty Dora comes home.

Halfway through term, the week of Abbey's seventeenth birthday, they head to the cinema. It's a Saturday and Abbey arrives at the flat, fresh from her dance class, her relaxed hair pulled back in a ponytail that brushes her shoulders, a plaid minidress just visible under an oversized denim jacket. She's dressed like she walked off a photo-shoot, right down to the dark eyeliner and black choker coiled around her neck. Eyes trail her from the bus stop to the mall, and later as they take the escalators up to the cinema Efe catches their reflections side by side. She can just about see similarities in their wider than average eyes, the flare of their nostrils, but everything about Abbey's face is slim, sharp and angular where Efe's is soft and full. Nate is hovering near the counter when the girls arrive, his coat wedged in the crook of his arm. Efe watches as they hug, then linger with Abbey's head nuzzling into the gap beneath his chin.

'You look great,' Nate says in a voice that sounds heavy with sleep.

'Just something I threw together. You remember my cousin Efe, right?'

'Absolutely, hi.' He nods in her direction.

Efe has only met this boy a handful of times, but she's heard from friends of Abbey that they've dated and broken up at least six times since they were fourteen. When asked, all Abbey had said on the topic was that she and Nate have that 'Cory-and-Topanga, will-they-won't-they vibe', so confident in her coaching of Efe and sure she didn't need to explain any further. And she didn't.

Efe looks at Nate closely. Aside from the light brown curls that droop over his brow and the slightly lazy eye, he looks like he could be in one of the boyband posters on Abbey's wall. And now Efe sees them together – Abbey still gripping his arm – Efe can think of nothing worse than ninety minutes squished into the seat beside them, while they do whatever they can get away with in a dark cinema.

Somewhere behind Efe, a voice says, 'Happy birthday, Abbey,' and the trio turn to welcome the new arrival.

'You made it,' Abbey says, breaking into a wide smile. 'Sam, this is my cousin Efe. She just moved here. Efe, this is Sam. He used to go to our school, but now he's over at St Stephen's trying to be the next Fresh Prince. That's why he *never* hangs out any more.'

'I do hang out.'

Abbey folds her arms across her chest. 'Name one time.'

Sam shrugs. 'I'm here now.'

'Welcome back, man,' Nate says and reaches across to clap a hand on Sam's shoulder. 'It's been forever.'

Sam returns the gesture, smiling broadly. 'Too long. What, you stopped going to the barbers now I'm not there to go with you?'

Nate laughs, his head dipping back and pulling Abbey closer. 'What can I say? The ladies dig it.'

'Ladies?' Abbey pipes up.

'One lady. This lady.'

As the laughter dies down, Sam catches Efe's eye and smiles. Something about him feels familiar and different, all at once. He looks like a mix of several boys Efe went to school with: tall and slim, with the same recognisably Ghanaian features on deep mahogany skin, a blunt jawline and a sprouting of patchy facial hair. A month from now she'll learn that she is only partly right. 'Just on my mum's side. My dad was adopted, so we don't know for sure,' he'll say.

They join the queue for snacks. Sam leans towards her and says, 'So you're new?' and, before Efe can answer, Abbey peers over her shoulder and interjects. 'She's been here since September.'

'All right,' he says, a light laugh in his voice. 'I get it. I've been MIA. All I do is go to school and work.'

'What are you studying?' Efe asks.

'Econ, Double Science, Politics and Art.'

'Art?'

'Yeah,' Sam replies. A self-conscious hand moves to his nape. 'Well, photography mostly. I take photos.'

Inside the screen, the girls sit in the middle. Abbey curls round the armrest and presses into Nate. His arm rests behind her shoulder blades, fingertips graze her chest. On Efe's other side is Sam, an oversized tub of popcorn wedged between them, the buttery scent wafting.

'Want some?' he whispers.

She nods, takes a handful and allows herself to relax into her seat. She whispers a thanks just as the lights dip and darkness cocoons. Later, they blink as they re-emerge buttery-fingered in a rain-speckled world. The sun has set and stark yellow street lamps illuminate the street in fragments. Abbey reaches into her pocket and half sighs, half grunts. 'I should get back. My mum has paged me, like, five times.' She turns to Efe. 'Want to share a ride?'

Efe glances at the taxis idling nearby and thinks of the coins jammed into her pocket. Abbey's house is twenty minutes away at least, to the west where houses are larger, rooms are high-ceilinged and spacious. The taxi fare will be immense. It will cost more than she has to get back. 'I'll just take the bus,' she says.

'Call me when you get home,' Abbey says.

'My dad's picking me up in ten,' Nate says, then heads back into the cinema. Efe and Sam smile awkwardly, then make their way across the car park.

'Did you like the film?' Sam asks. He walks with his hands deep in his pockets and every few steps his eyes dart over to her.

'Nate and Abbey were . . . distracting. And I missed something near the end,' Efe says. 'What was the deal with the tunnels?'

'You want me to spoil it for you?'

'The end is always the best bit. If I could skip to the end and watch it first I would.'

'Nah, that sounds like cheating to me.'

'So you won't tell me?'

'No,' he laughs. 'We'll have to go back and see it again.'

Efe bites down on the smile lifting her lips. Her fingers find the end of her sleeve and tug. Two light pulls. 'Yeah, cool,' she says. They stop at the bus stop. The cold seeps into their shoes and Sam curls his lips inward, runs a finger over the timetable and groans.

'What?' Efe asks.

'I think we just missed one, maybe five minutes ago – unless it's late.' Both pairs of eyes stare down the road, a ribbon of grey tarmac stretched out under a midnight sky. Efe takes a closer look at the timetable. They're so close now their coats brush past each other with a rustle and a whisper.

'They're every thirty minutes now.' Efe crosses her arms over her chest, thinking of the long winding route home if she walks. She has lived here for almost two months, but in that moment she isn't even sure she'd be able to pick out the block of flats if she saw it on the horizon.

Ten minutes pass. Sam suggests they walk up to the station where there are other buses they can catch. They chat easily as they walk. It begins to drizzle. They dip their heads as the wind starts to stir. Then a bus thunders past, already a blur of red up ahead. Their heads snap towards each other in the instant before they begin to run. They are the last to board, damp, erupting in fits of laughter and squeezing into a double seat, the fabric worn and frayed beneath them. The bus lurches forward.

Efe remembers to press the bell as they near her stop. She and Sam step back out into the yellowy glow of street lamps, the smell of rain filling the estate. Aunty Dora's block stands like a giant in the centre.

'Which one's yours?' Efe asks as she loops her scarf around her neck.

'Oh, I live by the hospital,' Sam replies.

'The hospital,' Efe repeats in confusion. 'Didn't we go past that four stops ago?'

'Five.' Sam nods.

'Why didn't you get off?'

'Making sure you got home okay. Which one is yours?'

'That one.' Efe points to the mellow giant, a block of grey concrete covered in warm, yellow windows. 'We're on the fifth floor,' she adds though she isn't sure why. She wants to say something else, whatever she needs to say to keep him here a little longer.

'Cool,' Sam says. They look to their shoes. Nearby a cat yowls.

Sam nods. 'I'm gonna head now.'

'See you next time,' Efe says.

'See you then.'

Efe watches as Sam walks away, hands shoved in his pockets, shoulders raised against the wind.

Eighteen Years Before

Sam is at work, blue-polo-shirted, slotting returned videos back onto the shelves when Nate drops by. It's a quiet afternoon. Only a few people are browsing beneath fake spiders dangling from plastic webs. Nate makes his way over, and Sam's gaze returns to the stock list. He already knows why Nate is here.

'Tell me you're coming to this party,' Nate says.

'You know it's not my thing.'

'Come on.' Nate groans and rests a hand in the empty slot beside *Flubber*. 'Don't be like that. What time do you get off work?'

Sam rolls his eyes and puts the clipboard down. Through the half-opened door he can see his manager in the back room, feet propped up on the desk, comic book in hand. Sam's only an hour into his shift, but he's pretty sure he could leave early if he wanted to. 'Ten,' he says.

'That's fine. Come after,' Nate says. 'I need my wingman.'

'What?' Sam's eyebrows come together. 'Have you and Abbey broken up again?'

'You know what she's like: happy one moment, pissed off at me the next.'

'She always has a reason to be pissed off. What did you do?'

Nate shifts his gaze away. 'Nothing—'

'Bro.'

24

'Nothing . . . She's just mad 'cause I've been talking to Portia.'

'Are you kidding?'

'I can't cut off every girl who has a thing for me just because Abbey hates them. That's basically the whole school,' he says, grinning.

Sam rolls his eyes and pushes the trolley of videos further up the aisle. He knows Nate is joking, but sometimes Sam can hardly believe this is the same freckled, droopy-eyed kid he met at the start of Year 8. Back then they'd been amongst the shortest in their year group; two gawking twelve-year-old boys with backpacks nearly as large as they were; wearing scuffed-up trainers that were explicitly banned under the uniform policy; both recently made motherless. During the previous summer, Nate's mum had been bested by an inoperable cancer that had silently burrowed through her brain for years. Sam's mum was simply gone, exiting stage left like she was an actress who'd taken her final bow, or worse, like she was a figment of Sam's imagination. The previous year they hadn't been friends, but that September, still adjusting to their losses, they had common ground.

Nate is still close behind when Sam picks up the next stack of videos.

'Please, man. It's one night. I need you there.'

'You should just call Abbey.'

'Or you can come to the party, be my wingman and I can talk to her in person.'

Sam looks towards the till, where a family of four hover beside a ghoulish display. He feels Nate's hand on his shoulder.

'Don't make me beg.'

Sam sighs. 'What's the address?' Over his shoulder he calls, 'Be with you in one minute,' while Nate scribbles it down.

'I owe you big time.' Nate beams. 'Oh, and you're gonna need a costume.'

*

The address leads Sam to a road thirty minutes away. The houses on either side are large, identical terraced houses with tall bay windows. The party's in full swing. He can hear the music even before he crosses the road. Strobe lights flash in foggy windows. He bounds up the front steps and knocks. The bass thunders through the floorboards and gold-framed paintings tremble on the walls. He peers into a vast living room, squinting into the thick haze as he tries to make out the faces behind masks and make-up. The centre of the room has been turned into a makeshift dance floor, much of the furniture pushed up against the walls. Sam skirts around the sweaty bodies. A chandelier sways gently above their heads. He's almost finished a loop of the living room, and is just beginning to wonder if he can slip out unnoticed, when a hand shoots into the air and Nate waves him over.

Sam makes his way to Nate, pushing deeper into the party. On the other side of French doors, he finds a high-ceilinged kitchen. His gaze moves upwards from the tall, white cabinets to the elaborate filigreed cornices. He's never been anywhere this fancy. Clusters of people fill the dim kitchen. He recognises some from his old school, nodding an acknowledgement as he edges past and finally reaches Nate. His mouth drops open the moment he sees the banana-yellow suit and green-painted face. He chokes on a laugh.

Nate's face falls. 'Where's your costume?'

'Me? What are you wearing?' The guys on either side of Nate chuckle.

'I'm The Mask. Everyone loves The Mask.' Nate looks worried for a moment, then he runs his hand over the plas-ticky material and shakes it off. 'Who're you supposed to be?'

'Myself. You told me about this party five hours ago.'

Nate grumbles and hands over his sunglasses. 'Here. Now you're Men in Black.'

Sam looks down at the faded jeans and black jumper he's pulled over his work polo. He shrugs and slides them on. 'Whose house is this?'

'Toyin. Her parents are lawyers or barristers or something.' Nate tilts his head towards the girl in angel wings and a white minidress, wining with a vampire.

'Rah, that's what I wanna do.'

'Of course you do.'

At the drinks table, Sam roots through the overturned plastic cups and half-empty bottles of alcohol and fizzy drinks. He tips some Sunny Delight into what he hopes is a clean cup. Beside him, Nate bobs his head to the music and scopes out the room.

'Hey, it's Portia.'

Sam's head whips round. He clamps a hand on Nate's shoulder. 'Don't even – you're here for Abbey, remember?'

Nate bites down on the corner of his lip, sneaks another look across the room. 'And I am. I'll be one minute.'

Sam doesn't have a chance to reply before Nate cuts his way through the crowd. Alone now, Sam takes a sip of his drink and lets his eyes follow the flow of people moving from room to room. Two girls break away from the dancing mass and Sam watches them slink through the crowd then pop up beside him at the drinks table. The genie in purple satin tilts a bottle of vodka to the light, swirls the last drops into her cup. She reaches for the lemonade, looks up and notices Sam.

'Look who it is!' Abbey squeals, leaning in for a hug.

'Hey,' Sam chuckles. 'You should talk to Nate. He's real—' She holds up a palm and Sam lapses into silence.

'Don't try it. Nate's dead to me. I don't wanna think about him tonight.'

A cat slides into the space beside her, and it takes Sam a moment to recognise Efe beneath the cat ears, face paint and glitter. He brightens at the sight of her.

'Why didn't you dress up?' she shout-asks over the music.

'I did.' Sam slides on his sunglasses. 'Men in Black.'

'That must be the low-budget edition.'

'Straight to video.'

They laugh.

'What you drinking?' Abbey asks, reaching for Sam's cup. She places a small pill on her tongue and takes a large gulp of Sam's drink. Efe's eyes flick up to Sam and he realises she's holding a second pill.

'Want in?'

'No, do you think that's—'

She places the pill on her tongue and chases it with a drink. 'Ooh, Sunny D.' She smiles. 'Don't look at me like that.' Efe throws her head back and laughs. The song changes. Mary J. Blige croons through the speaker. Somewhere nearby people whoop. The dancers slow.

'I love this song!' Abbey says, loops an arm through Efe's and drags her back to the dance floor. Efe's dark skin looks glossy under the pulsing lights. She glows green, purple and red in turn, her braids bouncing at her shoulders. She's wearing a dress that looks like something Abbey would pick out: high-necked and short, every inch covered in sequins. Every time she looks his way, Sam feels a smile pucker at the corner of his lips.

Hours pass. Midnight comes and goes. Sam chats to class-mates he hasn't seen in over a year. All this time he's been consumed by school, work, extra-curricular stuff to make his Oxbridge application shine, and now he's finally sent it off, he can relax. Eventually, Sam graces the dance floor with a few self-conscious moves, his cup held aloft. By the time the third song ends, the beginning of a headache thrums above his eyebrow. He isn't sure if it's because of the lingering smoke or the thudding bass. He breaks away and heads out the back door, takes a deep breath of chilled night air, then another until he begins to feel better. In the dark, the garden looks never-ending. He feels drowsy now, considers climbing down the steps and curling up in the grass.

Through the glass doors he can see a Power Ranger chatting to Mr T. Beside them, a genie is making out with The Mask, the two of them pressed up against the fridge. *So Nate and Abbey figured things out*, Sam thinks, wondering how long he's been out here. Two girls dressed as Spice Girls wander outside, passing a joint between them. He decides to head back inside. He moves towards Abbey and shouts over the music. 'Where's Efe?' he asks.

'Bathroom.'

Sam feels the weight of all those drinks on his bladder. He squeezes through the people pressed on either side of the hallway. Cigarette smoke lingers in the air outside the bathroom. He runs his tongue along his teeth, mumbles the rap to 'Ghetto Supastar'. The song's almost over when he hears voices on the other side.

'Get off me!' Efe yells.

Then a male voice shouts, 'Relax!'

Sam pounds on the door. 'Efe?'

'Kinda busy,' the male voice calls.

Sam jiggles the handle. There's a yelp and a loud clatter on the other side. Sam feels the thrum of blood in his ears and his adrenaline spiking. He rams the door with his shoulder. Twice. Takes a step back and kicks until the lock gives way. The shower curtain's been ripped from its railing and they're tangled up in it, bodies heaped in the tub. Efe's arms pinwheel, connect with the boy's nose.

'Bitch!' he yells. His head comes round too slowly. Sam already has him up against a wall, the boy's collar held tight in his fist. The bridge of his nose is turning a deep aubergine, the colour blooming as blood trickles out between clenched fingers. He blinks back tears.

'Chill,' he says, panicking. 'She was game.'

'What is wrong with you? She said no.' In his peripheral vision, Sam can see faces crowded in the doorway.

He hasn't been in a fight since he was fourteen, yet the

adrenaline fizzing through his veins feels familiar, comforting even. Sam thumps the guy against the wall again for good measure. Skull and tiles meet with a muted thud. Then he lets his fingers uncurl, watches the boy bound for the door, pushing past the gathering crowd.

'You good?' Sam says to Efe, hoping she hears all the other questions wrapped up in those two words.

'Yeah, I'm fine.'

Sam takes a step closer, holds a hand out. 'You wanna get out of here?'

His eyes meet hers, wary and unfocused, her lips bunched together; then she slides her hand into his and clambers out of the tub. They stay like that, fingers interlaced, as they push back through the party. To Sam, the music sounds far away, the whole party muffled, like he is underwater. The lights are still out in the living room and they glide through a strobing, pulsing world.

They pause on the driveway. Sam feels the cold, biting wind on his face and tries to remember the way home. He is shaking. The street around them is quiet. All he can hear is the dance music and the loud blood scuttling between his ears.

'I don't have my coat,' Efe murmurs. Sam turns, notices for the first time that blood is spattering her cheeks, that a few sequins have come loose on her dress, that there's an expanse of bare skin between the dress and her silver strappy shoes.

'Erm, here.' Sam tugs his jumper over his head and waits for her to pull it on. They walk through twisting back streets, Sam scanning for anything recognisable, Efe's movements slow and wobbly. He slows his stride to match hers. At the top of the road, Efe gropes for the railing. She doubles over, sighing as she tugs one heel off, then the other. They clunk down on the pavement.

Sam takes one look at her shoe-less feet. 'I got you,' he says and lifts her onto his back. Her arms fold over his chest and

Sam finds himself acutely aware of every muscle in his body, his mind emptying as her warm breath skitters past his ear. She's still and silent as they turn a corner, then suddenly cranes her neck skywards. Her body follows and the sudden shift sends Sam stumbling to the right.

'The moon. Look how bright it is.'

Sam recovers and follows her pointing finger. 'I think that's a street lamp,' he says.

Efe twists and peers more intently. 'Oh. I think you're right.'

He smiles. 'I know the way from here,' he says.

AUGUST 1999

Seventeen Years Before

Sam rounds the corner a little after eleven. It's mid-August, late morning and twenty degrees outside. The day is breezeless, the sky overcast. Sam's T-shirt is damp at the armpits and sticking even before he enters the park. Phoebe, his younger sister, is trotting along beside him, her backpack trailing along the path and almost tripping her up with each step.

Sam sighs. He's been on edge all morning and is fighting the urge to snap at her. Taking care of Phoebe has been more his responsibility than his dad's since she was a toddler, pretty much since the day his mum left, and that's exactly what he's been doing all summer while most of his friends have been on holiday. Home. Work. Carting his nine-year-old sister around from place to place. Normally he doesn't mind, but on days like this – important days when Sam wants everything to run smoothly – he finds himself resenting it. Already this morning she's spilled an entire jug of milk on the floor and made Sam late because she spent twenty minutes searching for her shoes. He wouldn't even have to do this if his dad, Ken, wasn't working all the time; or if Mrs Felton, their across-the-road neighbour, wasn't away visiting family in Bristol; or if Sam and Phoebe's mum had never left.

With a stiff shrug, Sam pushes the thought out of his mind. He glares down at Phoebe's bag again. 'Pheebs—' he begins, just as she squeals Efe's name and takes off, running in a diagonal line across the grass.

At the sound of Phoebe's voice, Efe looks in their direction. She manages to put her CD player down and get to her feet just before Phoebe crashes into her, wrapping her up in a hug.

'Good to see you,' Efe says.

Sam catches up, jogging the last few metres. 'Didn't I say you'd be making her wait?'

Phoebe pulls a face at Sam, then turns back to Efe. 'Did you bring me any sweets?'

Sam rolls his eyes. At least a hundred times he's told her to start with 'Hi' or 'How are you?'

'What makes you think . . .?' Efe says, smiling slyly as she reaches into one of the many pockets in her cargo trousers and pulls out a lollipop.

Phoebe, practically bouncing on the spot, claims it eagerly. 'Thank you!' she chirps.

'Okay, go play,' Sam says, tilting his head in the direction of the playground. Efe lets out a small breath and returns to her spot on the picnic table. She scoots over so Sam can climb up beside her. Over the last couple of years, without ever consciously discussing it, this has become their place. When they aren't hanging out at Sam's house or Aunty Dora's flat, they are here, overlooking the rusted swings and creaking merry-go-round. This was the park Sam had chosen for his final photography coursework photos. Somehow he'd convinced Nate, Abbey and Efe to spend an evening posing on the empty football pitch. He had taken one photo right as an ambulance passed, and captured the moment all of their faces had whipped round, off-guard for a second and awash in blue light. That one had been his favourite.

'That was nice – with Pheebs. You didn't have to,' Sam says.

Efe smiles and shrugs, the air easy between them.

'No Serwaa today?'

'Gone swimming with her friends.'

'Ah, cool.' Sam nods.

A moment passes. Sam glances at his watch. 'How did we beat Nate and Abbey? I thought they'd be here by now.'

'Three guesses what's holding them up.'

Sam laughs. He doesn't need three guesses. He only needs one.

When Nate and Abbey eventually arrive, forty minutes later than planned, one of Nate's arms is slung over Abbey's shoulders. They're flushed and dishevelled. Sam's seen Abbey from time to time over the summer break, but this is the first time he's seen Nate in almost two months. Pretty much since the end of exams, when he was whisked away to Spain for a family holiday. Now he's back, taller and tanned so dark the freckles scattered on his cheeks have disappeared.

'You've been back – what – two days and she's already got you wrapped around her little finger,' Sam says, going in for a hug.

'You can hardly talk,' Nate replies. 'My dad and his girl-friend drag me off to Spain for a couple of months and you and Daphne *finally* get together.'

Sam, embarrassed now, shoots a self-conscious look first at Efe, then Phoebe, even though she's too far away to hear and it's not like she'd immediately run home and tell his dad about his girlfriend. His sort-of girlfriend. They talk on the phone most nights, but her parents always seem to be loitering within hearing distance of the landline, so Sam's not entirely sure what they are. He imagines it will be clearer in a few weeks when they're off at university, providing they all get in.

'I'm meeting her in an hour, so let's get on with it.' Sam reaches into his pocket and pulls out a carefully folded piece of paper.

'This is it,' Efe mumbles, smoothing out an identical slip.

Sam waits until all four of them are sitting, exam result slips in hand. 'On the count of three.' Sam inhales. 'One, two, three . . .' For a few moments there's nothing but the sound of papers rustling, cars passing behind the tree line and the laughter of Phoebe and the other kids, playing tag.

Sam peeks up at Efe, then Abbey, trying to decipher their expressions. He looks over at Nate and sees he's grinning. 'Three Bs,' Nate says, pumping a fist into the air.

'Really?' Sam says. He catches himself before he says, 'Nah, I don't believe it.'

'Don't sound so shocked.' Nate laughs. 'That's what I do. Get in. Get the job done. Get out.'

'All you do is coast,' Abbey huffs. 'How did you get three Bs and I come out with B-C-D?'

'You know what,' Sam says. 'That's not bad considering how many of our revision sessions you slept through.'

'Whatever, Urkel. Go on then. What did you get?'

'All As.'

'Ergh.' Abbey rolls her eyes, reaching over to give Sam a playful shove.

'Were you close to a grade boundary? You could get a re-mark.'

'Screw the re-mark. None of this will matter when I'm a star,' Abbey says and splays her hands wide for emphasis. 'All I need is talent. Give it five years. My name will be up in lights and you three will still be sitting exams.'

Nate joins in, adding, 'Sam's trying to be a lawyer. He'll be studying until he's forty.'

'Ha ha ha,' Sam says drily, a small smile on his lips.

He turns to Efe. 'How'd you do?' he asks. Out of all his friends she's the one Sam's been most worried about. He'd seen her the day before exams started, when she'd been overthinking and stressing herself out, and he's hung out with her for what feels like all summer long, Sundays reserved for movie marathons of all the videos Sam brings home from work just to distract themselves from results day.

'I passed,' Efe says, her voice quiet and stunned. 'I didn't think I'd – I got in.'

'Wicked!' Nate says.

'Of course you would,' Sam adds. He peeps at her paper. 'A-B-B. All that worrying for nothing.'

'I just scraped by in Economics. Literally one mark over the boundary.'

'Who cares? You did it.'

Later, after Abbey and Nate leave, it's back to just Sam and Efe again. They say little, watching as an ice-cream truck pulls up by the traffic lights. None of the little kids have noticed yet. Sam pulls out some money for when the jingle begins, and Phoebe comes over to plead for a Screwball or choc ice or something.

'So,' he says, with a sideways look at Efe, 'you sure you're good?'

'Yeah, I mean . . . I did it,' she says carefully.

'Your parents will be happy, right? And your aunt?'

'Yeah, so proud . . .' Efe trails off. She pauses. 'I can't really believe I got in. It's not like I'm actually any good at Economics.'

'You got a B.'

'Only because you helped me. Next year's a step up. At some point they're gonna figure out that I don't . . .'

'Don't what?'

'I dunno. Belong. That I'm rubbish.'

Sam balks. 'You're not rubbish.'

'Sam—'

'I promise you're not rubbish,' he says. 'And I got you.'

Efe smiles then, but to Sam it looks like she's still pretending to be happy. He watches as she reaches into her bag for her Walkman, winds the headphone cable around her palm and unwinds it again. Then she sighs and leans over so her cheek is balanced on Sam's shoulder. Everything in him slows to half speed. He doesn't move. He likes the feel of her cheek across his shoulder, those mid-movie moments when she can't help but react and her whole body leans forward, or she pulls her feet onto the sofa and he feels the weight of her body press

36

into his. He loves catching her scent when she passes him in a hallway, and all he can think to do in those moments is to be still. If he moves, he's afraid he'll ruin it.

She sighs. 'Truth is. It's not that I didn't think I'd get in. It was that and . . . I guess some part of me was hoping I wouldn't. Y'know, miss it by a mark or two.'

'Why?'

'If I didn't get in I could do something else. Teach at a drama school or do something cool like Abbey. In a few weeks she's gonna be at some performing arts school in Paris – Paris! – and I'll be right here. Did she tell you about that girl in her tap class? She's going to work on a cruise ship.'

Sam can't believe what he's hearing. 'Since when do you wanna work on a cruise ship?'

'That's not the point. It's about being spontaneous, doing something unexpected, doing something for me,' Efe says. 'What if I do this and there's no way back? Or what if I suck?'

'You won't suck.'

'I think I only applied because my parents want me to follow in their footsteps. They can be so intense, y'know? Sometimes I feel like becoming a teacher or an accountant are my only options.'

Sam scrunches up a brow. 'I thought your mum was a deputy head.'

'She is.' Efe frowns. 'I just want a second to figure things out.'

Sam considers this. Neither of his parents had been to university. They'd been teenagers in a band when they'd had him, but whenever Sam thinks of university, he imagines a place where anything is possible; a place filled with thousands of people just like him. Another step forward in life. And at the end of it all he'd be doing important work and helping people, maybe with a family of his own one day. He'd make it right. This – he lets his eyes fall on his exam results slip again – is the beginning of the life he's planned.

'You haven't even got to uni yet. Maybe it'll be better than you expect,' Sam suggests.

Efe squirms and places both hands over her face. 'I'm being dumb,' she mumbles. 'They just want me to be happy and settled, have the opportunities they didn't have growing up. This is good. It's great. Ignore me.'

Sam's not sure what to say back. He gets it, or at least he thinks he does. He looks from the stars doodled on Efe's trainers to her hand resting on the slats between them. He could reach out and hold her hand in his, cross the four inches of space. Carefully he stretches out his baby finger. He's one inch closer already.

'You should visit. Cambridge isn't far,' Sam says at last. 'I can show you round the city.'

'Yeah, let's do that.' Efe smiles, nestling closer. Sam can feel her elbow grazing his rib. He lets himself relax, lets his eyes close. Above their heads, the sun finally breaks free of the clouds. Sam can hear the voices of Phoebe and the other kids volleying back and forth, hear the rhythmic squeak of the rusted seesaw bolts.

Sam and Efe stay just like this, seconds flitting past and building into minutes. He doesn't immediately notice that someone is watching them. When he squints one eye open, he does so reluctantly, then practically jumps out of his seat when he spots Daphne a few steps away.

'Daph—' Sam begins.

'I've been waiting by those other picnic benches for twenty minutes.' Daphne frowns. She's tiny, tinier still standing next to Sam. He angles his whole head down to look at her and mostly focuses on the layer of glittery brown powder on her eyelids and the matching line edging her lips.

'I meant these benches,' Sam says. 'By the playground.'

Behind him, Efe shifts. Sam watches as Daphne's gaze slides from him to Efe, her eyes watchful and narrowed. He risks a glance over his shoulder and sees that Efe's stuffing her things back into her bag, gruffly drawing it closed and swinging it across her shoulder.

Sam takes a half step towards her. 'You're not staying?' Even as he says this, Sam feels the air go sour; Daphne simmers; even the sun ducks behind a cloud.

'I gotta go.' Efe shrugs. 'My parents have probably been trying to reach me and Aunty Dora's shift will be done at two.'

'Oh, okay,' Sam says, feeling a bit dazed. 'Are we still on for a film this Sunday? We just got a copy of *The Mummy*.'

'Maybe,' Efe says, hands clasping her bag straps tight, already walking away.

APRIL 2000

Sixteen Years Before

When Efe and Serwaa step out of Kotoka International Airport it is early evening. Almost three years have passed since they were last in Ghana. They drag their bags into the warm, sticky dusk, push through the groups milling around, so tightly packed they melt into one throng, move as one body. The girls pause at the other end of the forecourt, toes jutting into the car park. To their right, taxi drivers round up new arrivals, herd tourists into vehicles of questionable roadworthiness and zip off towards the city.

Serwaa is the one who spots Maame in the crowd. She gasps. Her drawstring bag falls from her fingers and hits Efe's leg; she reaches down to rub the spot. When she looks up, Serwaa is running towards their mum. Their arms fasten around each other. Maame smiles widely, then she takes a step back and holds Serwaa's face in her hands, takes in every new detail. Afterwards, it is Efe's turn. The fit is awkward at first: Efe is taller now, her eyes level with the top of Maame's forehead, and the weight of Maame's arms bears down on her shoulders, forces her to stoop. She smells the same. Efe breathes in Maame's sweet scent and feels a warm tide spread across her chest. Even after Maame pulls away, her hand stays on Efe's shoulder.

'Ey, the two of you. Such fine young women you are becoming,' she says.

'They're certainly not small children any more.' Paa's husky voice sounds beside them.

40

'Dad!' the girls squeal, pushing forward to embrace him.

As they drive away from the airport, Efe notices all the subtle ways the city is changing. New buildings are springing up. A spattering of cranes looms over the beige-orange-green skyline. The pace is still slower than London, but it has been dialled up a notch. The cars surge forward with greater conviction. Roadside hawkers move with purpose, materialising at each traffic light, surrounding the cars in an instant. The billboards come one after another, packed together like too many playing cards crammed in a deck, advertising everything from hair products to tinned tomatoes, premium cement to all-night church services and Easter revivals. The sun is glistening off every surface. Roadside stalls and signs are painted red, gold and green everywhere she looks.

For the whole journey from the airport to the house, Maame does not leave one moment of silence. She talks with jittery, excited energy, keeps turning around in her seat as if worried her daughters could disappear.

'What food did they give you on the plane? Here,' Maame says, and passes a meat pie to each of them. 'Or should we stop? You want something else?'

'We're fine,' Efe answers.

'Everyone is looking forward to seeing you girls,' Maame says. 'Efe, did I tell you I saw Nanadwoa on Sunday? Just after church. She was so happy when I said you were coming. I wouldn't be surprised if she was waiting at the house already.'

'So this your friend won't even let you rest small-small?' Paa chuckles as he pulls onto the motorway. He speeds up and the city transforms into a blur of colours that loop and fall into each other.

Maame lays a hand on Efe's leg and grins. 'You and Nanadwoa used to be inseparable. Do you remember that?' Maame asks as if it had been thirty years ago, not three.

'I remember,' Efe says.

The car slows, its bonnet just shy of the gate. Paa beeps twice. Inside, there are shouts, a few moments of frenzied footsteps. Then the gates part, revealing the tall peach house, with its creamy white archways, the double garage and the balcony that stretches across the entire second floor, over-flowing with lush, green crawling plants. It's exactly as Efe remembers. The house boys wait for the car to pass, hurry to close the gate and run up the driveway as the engine clicks off. They don't wait for the instructions. They begin unloading the bags, stand them in a neat line to be carried up to Efe and Serwaa's rooms.

Efe throws the door open, the noise of the neighbourhood rises up in greeting and she fills her lungs with the taste of home.

Efe wakes early. She's grown unused to the birdsong at first light, the golden rays shimmering through paper-thin curtains, the endless whirr of the overhead fan. She dresses, the air around her humid, and slumps down to breakfast. Downstairs, the tiles are cool beneath her feet, dust motes float through the air and she finds her parents in the dining room, two early risers huddled at one end of the table, the drone of BBC radio in the background.

'You're up early,' Paa says, his eyes flitting towards her, voice hitching upwards as if he'd forgotten she was visiting.

Maame glances up from her newspaper. 'Good morning, sweetheart.'

'Good morning,' Efe echoes. She's nervous, eyes lowered to the table as she slides into an empty seat. She thumbs the piece of paper tucked in her pocket and takes a steadying breath, but when she opens her mouth to speak, the blare of a car horn smothers her voice.

'Ɛdeɛn?' Paa mutters. Efe moves to the windows. The sound continues, one long blast as if the driver has collapsed on the wheel. Through the gates, she can just about make out a sleek silver car, see the house boys drawing apart the gates.

Behind her, Maame tuts. 'That must be Nanadwoa at last.' And Maame is right.

Efe makes a dash for the front door, throwing it open as Nanadwoa's car pulls into the driveway. The windows are wound down, Joy FM is blasting loud enough for the whole neighbourhood to hear. The driver's side door flies open and, for the first time in years, Efe finds herself just metres away from her oldest friend. It's a dramatic reunion, the two of them locked together, squealing and swaying and hollering, Efe not certain where one of them ends and the other begins.

'*Atuu*,' she croons.

They separate. 'I don't believe it,' Nanadwoa says, her hands gripping Efe's forearms.

Up close, Efe can see a faint scar bisecting Nanadwoa's brow. Her whole face has lengthened and taken on a new fullness. It makes her look like Aunty Yaa, her mother, the resemblance stronger than it's ever been before.

'It is *so* good to see you!' Efe says.

'Wait.' Nanadwoa crosses her arms, one eyebrow raised. 'I'm not letting you off the hook. Didn't you promise to write?' She's trying to look mad, but Efe can tell she's fake mad, a smile tugging the corner of her lip.

'I know. I know. I'm sorry,' Efe says.

Nanadwoa's mouth lifts up into a half smile. She's already looping her arm through Efe's. 'I can't stay mad. You have to tell me everything – and I mean everything.'

Efe nods eagerly. After all, she has so much to share. She's changed while she's been away – become cooler and braver – mostly thanks to Abbey treating her like a real-life Barbie doll, dressing her up and constructing a world around her. Three years ago, Efe had been terrified she wouldn't make friends, or worse yet, she'd have to endure years studying alongside people who had already decided to hate her. Instead, she's made friends with pretty much everyone she's met, partied all night, made out with boys who had been strangers just hours before. She's tried *things*. And now she's stepped back into her old life and found everything waiting for her, like a favourite movie that she'd simply left paused.

Nanadwoa insists on taking Efe out, showing off her newly acquired driving skills. Efe barely has time to reach for her seatbelt when Nanadwoa stamps down on the accelerator, swoops out of the driveway and drives east, bolting towards the dazzling sun. She drives like a madwoman, commits to the inner lane and hurtles at least fifteen miles over the speed limit at all times, as if she's racing someone only she can see. The wind pummels past the open windows, snuffs out the music.

They arrive at the chop bar windswept and frazzled. It is small, just a cramped cooking area far back from the road-side, large coolers packed with fried rice, a dizzying array of brightly coloured soft drinks. They've managed to squeeze in three small tables between the kitchen area and the parked cars. Efe and Nanadwoa choose one, and Efe hears her stomach rumble, feels her heartbeat finally steadying. The waiter – a lean, dark-skinned boy – tells them two out of four items on the menu are unavailable, so they order quickly, Efe's mind fizzing away, eagerly imagining tasting all the food she's missed.

'So, Miss London,' Nanadwoa asks, leaning forward over the table. 'Tell me. How's UK? What have you been doing all this time?'

'Let's start with you,' Efe says. 'I want to hear what's been going on here.'

Nanadwoa takes a moment to think, then begins listing off recent news. 'Eunice came first in class.' Nanadwoa does an impression of her, hands clasped over an invisible prize.

'Mr Gyasi still hates me.'

Efe gasps. 'Is he still teaching?'

'Yes, but he comes to the market every week to lecture me. If I see him coming, you know I have to hide.'

Efe laughs. 'Wasn't he always like, "Nanadwoa, you have come to talk in my class again? Shame on you. Shame."'

Nanadwoa laughs hard. Her body curls over the table. 'Did I tell you about Kweku?'

Efe glances at Nanadwoa. 'Who's that?'

'The one who works at Ice Bar near Spintex. We started going last year before we graduated, but he was always telling us to turn and face our books.'

'They let you into Ice Bar?'

'Yeah, Winnie's cousin works on the door.'

'Winnie?' Efe pauses. 'Since when did we start spending time with Winnie?'

'Since her senior brother completed his national youth service and came back looking so very fine,' Nanadwoa says. 'She's not so bad if you ignore all the nonsense she talks.'

'I guess a lot has changed since I left,' Efe says. She looks in the direction of the kitchen, her hunger evaporated.

'*Kafra*, Efe. Never mind.'

Nanadwoa places a hand on top of Efe's. 'It's so good to have you back. It hasn't been the same without you.'

'Thank you,' Efe says, but realises Nanadwoa has already stopped paying attention. She's staring past Efe, exchanging flirty smiles with the chef.

'Nanadwoa!' Efe exclaims.

Nanadwoa's head snaps back. '*Gyae me!*' She smiles mischievously, finger-combs her weave and pushes her breasts together. 'Why shouldn't I look? Actually, I'm going to do more than look.' She slides out of her seat and walks over, swishing her hips from side to side.

Over the next few days Efe notices more and more of the things that have changed in her absence. Twice she reaches for a word in Twi and finds it is no longer there. New stores have been built, corrugated roofs balanced over bare concrete slabs; families she doesn't recognise have moved into the houses close by. There's a fresh batch of house girls too. Efe has long been accustomed to the company of the teenage girls whose school fees Maame paid in exchange for help running the house. As a child Efe had been friendly with them all, thinking of them as live-in babysitters who she could always rely on to sneak her sweets or biscuits after Maame had said no. She'd even learned to distinguish their soft footsteps, but either Efe's ears have dulled or the new girls move in near silence. More than once she is startled to see a young girl quietly waiting for her to look up. Only forty-eight hours back and home feels like a pair of jeans two sizes too small.

Efe only feels better on the third morning as she slips her trainers on. She props her feet up on the sun-warmed tiles and laces them up tightly. From her perch at the top of the stairs, she can hear the house girls chatting, the steady growl of the generator and the early morning rhythms she remembers. She looks down at her trainers: a charity shop purchase, scuffed but comfortable, now moulded to the shape of her feet. Something close to happy anticipation simmers inside of her. She bounds down the steps, pulls her arms over her chest to stretch out stiff shoulders. She packs her hair into a bun and runs a hand over the fluffy new growth, makes a mental note to take out her braids later; then cracks the front door open and slips through the gap. She has barely touched a toe down on the driveway when she hears Maame somewhere behind her.

'You're going out?' Maame calls.

Efe casts her gaze towards the gate, but Maame has already swung the door wide and is standing in the doorway, eyes ballooning as she takes in Efe's shorts and fluorescent T-shirt.

'Yes,' Efe replies.

'Where?' Maame asks as if it isn't obvious.

'On a run.'

Maame looks at Efe as if she has announced that she'll be

walking to Japan. 'Run?' She swirls the word in her mouth until her expression lands on distaste. 'Why? Only a fool runs if no one is chasing them.'

'It's for exercise.'

'You? You want more exercise? Aren't you already skin and bone?'

Efe balks. Maame hadn't mentioned the weight loss yet. For three days, they've tiptoed around it, Efe shrinking away each time Maame eyed the small portions on her plate and frowned at her thinner limbs.

And Efe knew she wasn't eating much. She couldn't. It had been a struggle from that very first day when she'd ventured onto campus and the feeling had returned with a vengeance, leaving Efe more overwhelmed than she had been for a while, all her worries solidifying like a lead balloon in her stomach.

It wasn't just the more challenging classes or meeting new tutors that scared her. It was the lecture halls filled with hundreds of students instead of classes with twenty to thirty peers. It was having to make new friends for the first time without Abbey at her side. It was the weekly phone calls from her parents and all the expectations they heaped upon her shoulders. It was all of that and more. But running helps. It takes Efe's mind off things. For up to an hour a few nights a week, her mind is clear. And after a run, when her muscles are depleted and loose, she is so ravenous she could eat anything at all.

Efe knows whatever she says won't hold water with her mum. Maame is still waiting for Efe's response, tapping her foot impatiently.

'I like running,' Efe replies weakly, an answer which isn't entirely untrue. Somewhere between feeling like her lungs are on fire and coming into her stride, she does start to enjoy the familiar strength of her limbs carrying her onwards and the sense that she is travelling faster than the world beneath her feet.

'Where are you running to?' Maame asks.

'Not far, I'll be back in forty minutes, maybe more.'

'Forty?' Maame's hand comes up to her chest. 'Your Aunty Dora has been letting you run on the streets of London for forty minutes?'

'Yes . . .'

'I'm going to talk to her.'

'Mum, please—'

Both pairs of eyes turn to the gate. The heavy iron lets out a groan and Maame's newest house girl, a girl Serwaa's age, slips through the gap.

'Dorothy!' Maame stretches out her hand to wave her over.

'Yes, Maa.' The girl curtsies and scuttles towards them. 'I'm sorry, Maa. My dad asked me to fetch something this morning and the seller was slow opening the shop.'

'Oh, don't worry yourself. Have you met Efe, my oldest?'

'From London?' The girl stops a few paces from Efe.

'Yes. Just the one.' Maame smiles. 'She's going to exercise. Go with her and keep her company.'

'Adɛn?' Efe's tone is harsh and the girl's alarmed eyes drop to the ground. She stands an arm's length away, wriggles uncomfortably in a dress and slippers. Her eyes slowly come up to meet Maame's.

'I don't have clothes for exercising,' she murmurs.

'Don't worry about that. It won't be long.' Maame smiles and steps back into the house as if the matter is sealed.

'Mum? Mum?' Efe calls. Maame does not reappear, but when Efe huffs and stomps off, the girl follows timidly a few paces behind. Efe looks both ways, weighs up her options and catches the eye of a young man on the porch opposite, both he and the squat, one-storey house visible through the wide-open gates. He lifts an arm over his head to wave, displays a tuft of dark hair at his armpit. She remembers Joseph vaguely from the few months before she and Serwaa left for London. She waves back, slides on headphones to

48

drown out Dorothy's chirping questions and hits play on her Walkman. Efe shakes out her legs takes a few deep breaths and begins running down the road away from the house.

For a full minute, even over her music, she can hear the sound of Dorothy's slippers slapping the ground, hear her frantic calls, until she falls behind and fades away. Efe gets into her stride, treading the line where orange sand spills over grey road. Two miles in she veers off the road and cuts through grass that reaches her knees, climbs higher and higher as her lungs cry for more oxygen and the ground curves up to the sky.

She reaches the crest of the hill, panting and out of breath in a way that feels like someone has sucked all the moisture from her mouth, like she has never known water. A thick film of sweat sticks her clothes to her body. But from this vantage point, she can see the main road that wraps around Taifa, the miles and miles of orange-roofed houses sprouting with greenery. Somewhere far below are the markers of her childhood, Nkrumah Junior High School for Girls, which she'd attended on foot, picking up Nanadwoa on the way, joining the tide of girls in brown and yellow uniforms. Below her are the stalls the girls would visit after school, where they'd chat and pretend to ignore the boys as they sucked on FanDangos, the sticky ice dripping down their hands. Years later, behind those stalls, one of those boys had taught Efe how to kiss. It all seems so close now. Efe feels she can stretch out her fingers and touch that time, take hold of the life she had known before England.

Efe takes her time on the way back. She jogs on the spot to dislodge the lactic acid settling under her skin. In the distance, she can see more people on the road; boxes, bags and serving platters balanced on top of their heads; mothers with babies strapped to their backs; weaving motorbikes. The run downhill is easier and she gathers speed, taking in deep lungfuls of fresh air, the birds around her singing. When she hits grass she keeps running, presses on further even when the ache in her thighs begins and her lungs resist. She keeps on until a lightness creeps back into her strides. She reminds her body what it feels like to be alive. Efe moves closer to the tarmac, caught in the propulsion of passing cars until one car veers off the road and comes to a screeching halt in front of her. Thoughts of kidnappings flood her mind and panic bubbles up in her, but instead a dishevelled and sweaty Dorothy falls out of the car, her hands clasped together as if in prayer. Efe almost laughs.

'Madam, please get in the car.'

'I'm on a run.'

'Please. Your mum . . . she asked me to . . .' The girl doubles over, hands clutching her knees. Beads of sweat gather at her temples, and a few people passing by slow to listen. Efe glances past her to the beaten-up Peugeot. The door hangs open. The motor rumbles quietly. She returns her gaze to Dorothy, thinks of the miles that stretch out between here and home. She sighs and climbs into the car. Her eyes meet Joseph's in the rearview mirror and, when Dorothy has buckled herself in, he pulls the car off into the road. Efe cranks down the window, thrusts the handle in frantic circles until she can rest her chin on the metal.

Maame and Serwaa are in the dining room when Efe gets back. She can hear their voices: Maame's voice is loudest, but Serwaa's is rising to meet her. Nothing good can come from joining them, so Efe makes a break for the stairs. She's only on the fourth step when Maame calls her name. Efe skulks back down.

She hovers in the doorway, one hand on the doorframe to steady herself. The other reaches for her ankle, draws her foot towards her bum to stretch the stiff muscle. The sand inside her trainers shifts.

'Yes?' Efe says.

'Go on, Serwaa,' Maame says sternly. 'Tell your sister what you said.'

Serwaa exhales and draws her gaze up from her bowl of *koko* to meet Efe's. 'She asked about my A-level options and all I said—'

'Textiles!' Maame cries. 'This girl wants to study sewing and cutting fabric.'

'I just said I was considering it as an option. My teacher—'

'Ey!' Maame claps her hands. 'What teacher would tell you to be a common seamstress, heh? Am I not a *deputy headteacher*? Do you think me and your dad worked all these years just so you can throw away your education to sit down and do sewing?'

'Akua,' Paa says from his seat at the head of the table, still half-hidden behind a newspaper. All heads swivel in his direction.

Maame rounds on him. 'Paa,' she says just as firmly. 'If I don't say it who will? God forbid I sit back for this to continue.'

Efe looks at her sister. She's seen the hours Serwaa spends folded into a corner of the living room, bent over her sewing machine. She's seen the careful details Serwaa's obsessed over; the hand-stitched hems and delicate beading; again and again, Efe's seen Serwaa's nimble fingers transform a few yards of cotton and velvet into something marvellous. Efe moves her weight and stretches the other leg, the wound-tight feeling in her hamstring lessening.

'*Tena ase*. We all need to approach this calmly,' Paa says, finally folding the newspaper in half and sliding his glasses off.

'I am calm.' Maame huffs, knotting her arms across her chest.

'Then let her speak.'

'Is she not speaking?'

'She's being interrogated.'

'Fine. You talk to your daughter.'

Paa chuckles. 'So when there's a problem she's my daughter, not your own too?'

Maame's nostrils flare, but she pinches her lips together and refuses to reply. Paa reaches over and gives her arm a playful squeeze. Then he turns to Serwaa and, softly, he asks, 'Serwaa, why do you want to study sewing?'

'I want to study *Textiles* because I enjoy it,' she says, then adds, 'And my teacher thinks I'm gifted and talented. I'm already working far above a GCSE level. My final project is better than some of the girls in the A-level class and they're all eighteen.'

Efe stares at her sister's straight back, squared shoulders and, not for the first time, wonders where this fearless streak emanates from. She admires it.

Paa considers this. 'Hmph. No one is saying you aren't gifted, but you're not even sixteen. You need to think about how your choices now will lead to something good in the future. Chemistry, Biology, Mathematics, these are all good subjects. After all this your studies, what job will you get from sewing?'

Serwaa grumbles a reply, eyes on the bowl of cold, congealing *koko*.

'What about Economics? Look at your senior sister. Don't you want to be like Efe?'

This comment catches Efe off-guard. She thinks of her note. For days she's rehearsed how she'd casually bring up the classes she's failing, how she'd explain that it wasn't the right fit, wasn't the right time, how she needs a few months to gather herself, anything to make them understand. The words 'leave of absence' would set off alarm bells for her parents. She planned to couch it in gentle, ambiguous language. She'd call it a break. On the phone, the night before her flight, Sam had wished her luck and reminded her that plenty of nineteen-year-olds took breaks from university. Efe wouldn't be the first and she certainly wouldn't be the last. She imagined him loitering on the landing in his university house, the only one left over Easter break, which meant they could talk on the landline for hours without worrying about who else might be waiting for a call. Efe reminds herself how right he is.

Efe catches a glimpse of her parents' expressions and tries to recall the careful sentences she crafted on the plane. Her eyes flick upwards, as if by some miracle she'd find her words scrawled on the ceiling. 'Actually . . .' Efe doesn't realise she's spoken aloud until Maame whips round on her.

'You? Do you have something to say?'

Efe lets her leg fall to the floor. She shrinks back from the sheer force of Maame's will and gives her head a small shake.

'Good.' Maame claps her hands together. 'Mark it on the wall. No one is reading useless subjects.'

Later, as morning creeps into late afternoon and the compound is freckled with long shadows, Efe steps out of the bathroom. At this time of year, when the temperature soars into the thirties, she showers often, washing the sweat from her skin, soaking her hair, letting the water cleanse her. Efe walks with a towel wrapped around her, stands on her tiptoes to peer out of the window, to a world where red earth meets grass and stone. The house girls laugh as they head home for the day. The gate wheezes shut behind them and, just beyond it, she can make out Serwaa sitting on the low wall by Joseph's house. She's been out there for hours. Efe can't even imagine what they could possibly be talking about, but they sit like old friends, sipping malt, the sky around them darkening.

Efe moves along the corridor, water streaking from her hair down her back. She pauses in the space before her parents' room. Her toes inch into a patch of sunlight. Through the crack between the door and its frame she can see her parents standing at either side of their sitting area as she watches the versions of them reflected in the mirror. She leans in close to hear what they have to say.

'Serwaa was never like this. She was never the type to throw her future away.' Maame sighs. 'Maybe we should bring them back and keep a closer eye on them.'

'And remove them from school now? Serwaa hasn't even completed her GCSEs.'

'But look at the things she is saying. This risk—'

'Is worth it,' Paa says firmly.

'Efe—'

'Is safe. Both of them are, and they're getting a good education,' Paa says. 'It's better for them to study there than come here and wait five, six years to complete one bachelor's degree because UTAG go on strike every two minutes. And even then, what job is waiting for them? Haven't you seen the way people who come with UK and US degrees walk into companies like they own the place? This small boy I work with; he's just two years older than Efe and doesn't even have one speck of common sense but is working at my level all because he has degree from US. One slip of paper makes any job he wants his for the taking. Let the same be true for our girls.'

Maame says nothing in response.

And Paa lets out a low sigh. 'Aside from this small thing with the sewing they are both doing well.'

Maame speaks up now, her voice troubled. 'Something is wrong. I can feel it.'

'Akua . . .' Paa pauses. 'Efe, I can see you.'

Slowly, Efe pushes the door open and mumbles an apology, her eyes trained on the floor.

'It's fine,' her dad replies, yawns widely and places both hands on his stomach. 'I'm tired of talking about this. Let me go eat.' He gives Efe's shoulder a squeeze as he passes. Maame lowers herself into an armchair, reaches a hand towards the dressing table and picks up a comb.

'Want me to do your hair?'

Efe smiles and sits in the space between Maame's knees. It has been years since Efe sat like this, Maame's legs pillars at either side of her while her fingers move in long strokes, parting the hair, smoothing cream onto her scalp. The sweet scent of Pink Oil fills the air. A coolness spreads across Efe's scalp and Maame's fingers get to work.

'All this stuff with Serwaa. It's hard, you know?'

Efe doesn't reply. When it comes to her parents, Efe is prone to giving in, shrinking back, conforming. All her life she's let them tell her who to be friends with and dictate all her wants. Serwaa has always been bolder, so sure of herself, never doubting what she has to say, while Efe has spent a lifetime biting back words, feeling like she's holding her breath. She envies that in her sister and at the same time it leaves her speechless.

'It came as a shock,' Maame continues. 'Maybe I didn't react the best, but that's all I want, the best for both of you. I want you to study well, have good jobs and a comfortable life so you can stand on your own two feet.'

Efe's head sinks into a nod. The minutes stretch out and she watches her legs slowly dry and ash. Maame hums as she combs Efe's hair out, soft repeated motions as darkness falls all around them. It is late when Efe returns to her room. She digs out the letter hidden under a stack of clothes at the back of a drawer. She opens it slowly, reads her clear, articulate sentences, the words she so desperately wanted to be understood. Then she tears it into four pieces, then again and again until shreds litter the floor. She will return to university without saying these words, weighed down by all the things they want for her.

JANUARY 2001

Fifteen Years Before

In the end, Efe has no choice. She is only days into the second term when the lecturer quietly welcomes her into his office and suggests maybe the course isn't right for her. For a few desperate moments, with the other students hovering just beyond the door, Efe promises to redouble her efforts, attend every study group session and stop sleeping if she has to. But she has already done most of these things. The hours she has spent going over her lecture notes, attempting to memorise concepts that twist and flail the harder she tries to grasp them, and sitting in tutoring sessions, her mind so dense and clouded, would add up to weeks if not months.

The man says nothing. He listens to her beg for five minutes straight, too embarrassed to meet her gaze, then gives a curt headshake that ends Efe's degree. Efe doesn't go straight back to the flat. She knows Serwaa and Aunty Dora will be there, full of questions the moment they see the look on her face. What she wants is a few hours somewhere quiet to collect her thoughts. She walks, weaving a route that takes her through the city, wandering from gallery to gallery to gallery until she's finally ready to head home.

In the weeks that follow, Efe's mattress moulds to the shape of her. Aunty Dora peeks in before she leaves for work. In the evenings, she delivers cups of Milo and steaming plates of jollof that Efe leaves untouched. Serwaa tries too. Every morning, before leaving for school, she throws open the curtains and tries to coax Efe out of bed, suggests they walk over to the library or rewatch their favourite episodes of *Top of the Pops* recorded on VHS.

After two weeks of this, Efe wakes to Serwaa standing in the doorway. 'Mum's on the phone,' she says, and Efe's heavy eyelids resist opening.

'Oh and Sam called,' she adds. 'He's home for the weekend and wants to come round.'

He's called again, Efe thinks. She's been meaning to return his calls, but she barely has the energy needed to get up and collect the phone, let alone hold a conversation. And now she has to deal with whatever Maame has to say. It is the first of many phone calls Maame will make to persuade, plead and barter, and Efe can feel a weight settling as she slides her feet into threadbare slippers and pushes her arms into the sleeves of her dressing gown. She wonders how many minutes she has to dawdle before the money on Maame's calling card finally runs out.

'Hello.'

'You're asleep? What time is it there?'

Efe lifts her head to check the kitchen clock, just visible above the netted window dressing and floral curtains. 'It's one twenty.'

'In the afternoon?'

Efe rolls her eyes. There is no time difference and Maame knows this. She is making a point. Maame waits a few moments, then continues when Efe's response doesn't come. 'What's going on? I've been calling and calling.'

'What do you mean?'

'You know what Gifty's daughter is saying? She's telling the whole world that the university is coming to un-enroll you.'

'Josephine doesn't go to my university.'

'Apparently her *obroni* boyfriend does and he says Efe Owusu is no longer in his class.'

Maame's voice is rising and Efe can feel the beginning of a headache brewing at her temples. She sits back on a pile of Yellow Pages and twirls the phone cable around her finger. The flesh turns white, then blue before she releases. Maame has not stopped talking.

'That wicked woman, heh. How can she come into *my own* house, talking-talking about how the mighty have fallen.' Maame finally inhales. 'Now, tell me it isn't true.'

Efe can feel her airway constricting; when she finally manages to force the words out they sound small and hollow. 'I'm not going back, Mum.'

'God forbid! What stupidness—'

'They asked me to leave.'

'Heh?'

'I was failing Economic Theory and there was no way I was going to pass Stats.'

'I don't believe it. My Efe's never failed anything in her life. Ey! The enemy will not prosper. You will take the exams again. You will pass.'

'Mum—' Efe hears another voice in the background, a brief scuffle then Paa's voice comes across the line.

'Efe, it's your dad here.'

She smiles, letting her eyes close and the grey-tinged flat disappear. 'Hi.'

'How are you today? Your aunt said you're not well. She's worried about you. We all are.'

'I'm okay.'

'Are you sure? You need to take care of yourself.'

In the background Maame's tirade continues, evoking the King of Kings to restore Efe's future, demanding he brings back what the locusts have taken.

'So what's going on with your schooling? If something's happened,' he begins, stops. 'You know you can tell me.'

Efe exhales. 'I failed my resit. I was already on academic probation so . . . .'

Paa sighs a deep sigh – the sound of thunder rumbling – and for a moment it drowns out Maame's declarations. When he begins to speak again his voice is slow and soft. 'There are other universities. You're still in the race, Efe. It will all be okay.'

'Sure,' Efe says, but her dad's reassurances do nothing to cool what is already simmering. She is off course, the life she was supposed to live evaporating the moment she entered that lecturer's office. And Efe can't see a way out.

The doubts collecting in the quiet spaces of her mind are multiplying. Soon she will not be able to move under the weight of them. When Efe slinks back into bed almost an hour later, she has a to-do list scribbled around an advert for an affordable plumber. The first item on the list is to go back to university and speak to her tutors. It's followed by over a dozen tasks just like it – a thirteen-step programme to get her life back on track, strung together with parental wisdoms. But as she lets the paper fall from her fingers and welcomes the familiar weight of the duvet, she knows she won't do any of these things they've asked of her.

Aunty Dora waits one more day before she decides she too has had enough. It is barely 6 a.m. when she throws the curtains open and rips the duvet from Efe's body. There is no time to brace herself against the surge of frigid air and the pile of books that is dropped onto her legs.

Efe blinks slowly and extracts herself from the mound. She looks down at the pile of textbooks, prospectuses and newspapers with job listings circled in red pen, then cranes her neck to look up at her aunt, who is standing with her arms folded firmly across her chest. Efe can't summon the energy to deal with this. She runs her tongue over the thick, sticky layer lining her mouth and knows she has at least one task to do today.

'Aren't you going to take a look?' Aunty Dora chides.

'What am I looking at?'

'Options. Your parents have made it very clear that they want you to go back to school.'

'What do you think?'

'I think you should do something. You have to keep going.'
Aunty Dora sinks into the space beside Efe, drawing her close.
The books slope into the gap between them. 'Find something
you want to do then go after it.'

'But what if I—'

'No,' Aunty Dora says, cutting her off. 'Whatever excuse
you're thinking isn't good enough. There's no reason why it
shouldn't be you.'

Efe waits for the mid-morning quiet to settle on the flat.
When she emerges from the shower, the room is thick with
steam, her skin singed. She runs a hand across the glass and
examines the new shadows under her eyes, the narrowing
of her jaw. She traces a finger over unruly eyebrows, grazes
the thick hairs sprouting in every direction, then searches for
the razor, paper-wrapped at the back of the cupboard.

She can still hear the loudness of it all, feel a panicky fluttering
in her chest. Her brain is full and surging with the doubts and
wisdoms her parents have peppered over her for years. This is
what they need from her, all the people who have created opportunities and made sacrifices, all the ones watching.

Efe cuts close to the root, calling forth neat arches. She
winces. A drop of blood blooms, bright red, a perfect circle,
that grows until it spreads itself out over the crease in her
eyelid. She tears off a jagged piece of tissue, holds it to the
cut until it sticks. She's mad at herself, mad in discovering
yet another thing she can no longer do.

Back when Efe was a child, rarely speaking and sometimes
overwhelmed by too many emotions, she developed this habit
of holding her breath until she felt faint. No matter how
badly she wanted to breathe in, she wouldn't, knowing a
little bit of discomfort forced her mind to focus. She needs
something like that now.

Efe exhales, squeezing the blade tighter between her
fingers. She watches the delicate way it shimmers in the light,

then brings it down below her palm. The pain is sharp, startling. To her, this is the exhale of a long-held breath. The flesh yawns open and gives way to white, then a vivid, welling red. There will be later cuts – scores and scores of them – each one attributed to coming disappointments, comments that will leave her reeling. But for now, Efe just watches the blood blossom and wrap itself around her wrist like a bracelet. A small sliver of tissue flutters from her eyebrow to the ground; and, for the first time in weeks, Efe's mind is clear.

It has been days since Efe last left the flat, and when she does there's a dull ache in her wrist and she wedges her hands deeper into her pockets. She feels lighter out here and walks aimlessly as the sky begins to drizzle, the cold pricking like thorns against her skin. She veers off the familiar route as she nears the high street and, when she looks up next, she is by the railway track, staring at the shops tucked beneath the arches.

She lets her feet carry her across the road, past the mini-market and internet cafe, into the store with the hand-painted 'Julia's New and Second-Hand Books' sign. A bell announces her arrival and the smell is the first thing that hits her. The shop is saturated with the scent of aged paper, tinged with earthy coffee. Efe pauses in the doorway and marvels at the walls and walls of books, jammed into tight nooks, spread out on every available surface.

When she steps up to the till, forty minutes later, she's clutching a curling-cornered copy of *Changes*, the same edition she's seen on a high-up shelf in Paa's office. A woman sits behind the till in a neon-pink jumper, a stray loc dangling behind her ear, the rest of her locs hidden beneath a many-coloured headscarf, a kaleidoscope of pinks, blues and purples.

'Find everything you were looking for?' she asks, forming the words around a pen pressed between her teeth. Efe nods, rifling through her purse. 'That'll be £3.99.' The woman punches the numbers into the till. 'Ama Ata Aidoo. Have you read any of her other books? *Changes* is magic, but my personal favourite is *Our Sister Killjoy*. Gosh, this thing—' she winces. Efe watches, shifting her weight on the creaky floorboards, as the woman punches numbers in again and again. She huffs. 'My son made me buy this hopeless thing. What's wrong with a money box and a notebook?'

Efe feels the corners of her mouth lift. Something about her steady tide of words and the overly familiar chat reminds her of Aunty Dora. Maybe that is why she leans over the counter and says, 'Try that one,' pointing to the red button.

The drawer slides open smoothly. Satisfied, the woman hands Efe her change. 'Can you come back every day?' she says with a laugh in her voice then stops short, her face suddenly serious. 'Actually, could you? I was just pulling together an advert for the vacancy. I could really do with the help.'

Efe takes a moment to make sense of this. She glances down at the book still held in the woman's outstretched hands. 'You want me to work here?'

'If you're interested we can start with a trial shift. I just need you to put your contact details down here,' she says, tearing out a piece of paper from a yellow legal pad.

'Why me?' Efe asks, still unsure.

'You can work the till. Clearly, you have good taste in books. And like I said, I could use the help.' She stands and is taller than Efe expected, her hand outstretched and waiting. 'Do we have a deal . . .?'

'Efe.'

'Nice to meet you, Efe.' The woman smiles, revealing a row of even, white teeth. 'I'm Julia.'

Efe glances at the book clasped in her fingers. For weeks she's felt cut loose from the world, without the strength or desire to tug herself back to the ground. Now, just like that, one foot brushes against the earth.

FEBRUARY 2002

Fourteen Years Before

Efe spent months learning the rhythms of the bookshop. Now, a little over a year in, it feels like second nature. On weekdays she walks the two miles from Aunty Dora's flat to the store, jiggles a key in the ancient padlock until it clicks into place and the shutters open with a whine. On cold days, like today, she turns on the heating first, drags rickety wooden tables out to the pavement to the soundtrack of water hiccuping through the pipes. She lines them up right below the front window, where they wait to display crates of bargain books, to tempt passing foot traffic. She moves quickly; her coat stays on until the shop warms up and she can settle down and go through the list of tasks left over from the previous day. Most days she welcomes this unhurried ordering of the space, the unpacking of deliveries and laying out new releases on the circular table in the middle of the shop floor. She is just sinking into her seat when the bell dings.

Ten to nine. Technically the store isn't open yet. Rising, she plans to say just that, but what comes out her lips is the rehearsed 'Is there anything I can help you with?' that Julia insists she greets every customer with.

'I'm looking for a book,' the customer says, unspooling a scarf. 'Where are the new books?'

'New fiction is on that table to your left. New non-fiction would be on those shelves,' she answers, pointing.

He nods, looks briefly at the table but doesn't move. Efe

waits a few moments, watching him hover by the table. 'Do you need something else?'

He gives his head a quick shake. 'I was trying to come up with a suave line, but everything that's coming to mind sounds cheesy.'

'You what?'

'I'm trying to ask you out.'

'Oh.' Efe takes an unconscious step back, bumping into a rack of holiday-themed bookmarks. Valentine's Day, Diwali and Hanukkah wobble on their perch. Efe thinks back to a conversation she had with Julia a week ago, on a slow Wednesday afternoon, and that Julia had mentioned a man who had come into the shop and asked after her. Julia had described him as 'a white guy, late twenties maybe, mousy brown hair, kind eyes'.

Efe isn't sure about the guy, but it seems Julia was right about his eyes.

'What's your name?' he asks, nervously rolling and unrolling the newspaper in his hands.

'Efe.'

'That's a beautiful name,' he says. 'I'm Brian. Can I take you out for lunch?'

Even as she locks up the shop at five to one, the out for lunch sign Blu-tacked to the window and her scarf knotted around her neck, Efe tries to talk herself out of it. Three times she fights the urge to turn back and eat the lunch she has tucked away in the mini fridge. Even as the yellow-fronted cafe comes into view, she toys with the idea of a quick escape. She's just a few feet away when Brian looks up, surprised but grinning, as if he's both shocked and grateful that she made it.

It's the middle of the lunch rush and the only available table is by the window, plagued by a wintry chill every time the door swings open. Efe watches as Brian slides off his coat and drapes it over the back of his chair. She feels nervous, pulls her coat tighter around herself and turns her gaze towards the windows.

Efe has barely dated in London. Back in Ghana, she'd had a crush on a total of three boys, all a year or two older. The year before she'd left for London, she'd started spending time with the last boy. At sixteen, he'd already made a name for himself as a flirt and was known to sneak girls into the boys' quarter when his parents were away. Efe heard the rumours, but was still secretly delighted when she became the latest girl on the list. Days later, she and the boy were kissing on a limp mattress, running their hands over each other's clothes. It happened twice more, but to Efe the memory feels like someone else's entirely. Like it couldn't possibly have been her.

She turns her gaze back to Brian, noting the prominent jawline, the shadow of stubble several shades darker than his hair. There's a certainty in the way he speaks and carries himself. *There's something so grown-up about him, so sure*, Efe thinks.

The waiter appears and Brian orders a sandwich and a cappuccino. 'A double shot,' he adds, then mumbles something about an afternoon pick-me-up and closes the menu with a snap. Efe hesitates. Her thumb rests beside the elegant scroll of a luxury hot chocolate; even now she smells cocoa in the air and can practically taste the rich melty chocolate, like Milo but far more extravagant. But then she glances up at Brian's greying temples and doesn't want to seem childish. She orders tea. 'And apple cake,' she adds.

The table wobbles beneath them. Months from now they'll refer to it warmly as 'their table', remembering the rough grain beneath their fingertips, the first date squeezed into a space so small their knees brushed against each other.

But for now, Efe hugs her elbows and asks, 'So . . . Brian . . . what do you do?'

He clears his throat and says, 'I work in finance.'

'Did you always want to do that?'

'It's what my dad did,' he says. 'What about you? Do you work in the bookshop full-time?'

'I'm the assistant manager,' Efe replies proudly. She doesn't mention that the only other members of staff are a rotation of surly teenagers, each lasting a few weeks because they only show up when they feel like it.

'And before that?' Brian asks.

'Before that I was at uni, studying Economics.'

His eyebrows jut upwards, a flicker of a smile on his lips. 'I wouldn't have taken you for an economist.'

'I'm not. I didn't complete the course.'

'But you want to go back,' he says. It's a statement, not a question. The waiter reappears at their table and for a few moments Efe busies herself, arranging the plates and saucers in the tiny space. She pours too much milk and drops two cubes of sugar in her tea, stirs slowly, keeping her gaze low as she tries to regain her composure. She hadn't known her emotions flashed across her face so obviously and wonders all the things the world knows that she thought she'd hidden from view.

'Maybe,' Efe says, trying to sound causal. 'I might do a course or something. But not Economics, that was enough of a disaster the first time around. Something different.'

Brian nods and takes a bite out of his sandwich, leaves behind a splotch of mayonnaise on his cheek. 'What subject?'

'Mmm,' Efe says, though she already knows the answer. For months, she's spent the quiet hours in the back room of the store, listening out for the ding of the bell, scrolling through webpages on the office computer. First she'd looked at Sociology classes at the local college; then she'd toyed with the idea of an Introduction to Politics course, thinking it might appease her parents, and finally settled on a part-time Art History programme. She was charmed by the notion

66

that beauty could not be extracted from its culture, history. She's read course descriptions and module outlines, calculated how many hours she needs to work to pay for it, imagined breezing through the three-month placement at the end, and the longer Efe researches it, the more her confidence in the idea grows.

She says, 'Maybe Art History' like it is a secret, her voice low, hunched forward over her cake, fork outstretched in the air.

Brian nods thoughtfully. 'Would you want to study locally?' he asks. 'My cousin works in the History department at UCL. I'm sure she knows someone in the Art History programme. Maybe she could help you find some classes to audit. She might even be able to pull some strings when you do want to apply.'

Efe stills. Her gaze drops to the icing sugar dusting her wedge of cake and she tries to imagine a world where strings slope down from the sky, waiting to pull life into a more favourable shape.

'Why would you do that?' she asks. 'You don't even know me.'

He smiles, lifting his cappuccino to his lips. 'But I'd like to.'

It's nearing 2 p.m. when they leave. They fall in step, wordlessly agree to take the scenic route back to the store. He walks so close Efe catches the scent of some expensive cologne on him. It smells fresh and woodsy, like Boti Falls after a summer rainstorm. There are comfortable lulls in the conversation. The buildings watch as they pass, identical grey-brick facades with glossy white windows, everything calm.

Outside the shop, Efe turns the keys over in her hands. The wind rises, making her eyes water and she blinks back the moisture that surfaces.

'Brian,' she asks. 'How old are you?'

'You go first.'

'Twenty-one.'

'Twenty-eighhhtt,' he replies.

She raises her eyebrows. 'Why did you say it like that?'

'Because I'm lying. I'm thirty-two. Is . . . erm. Is thirty-two okay?'

'Thirty-two is good.'

It could be the cold, but Efe thinks he's blushing, the colour spreading from his cheeks right up to the tops of his ears, which are peeking out from beneath his hat. Efe decides then that she'll see him again. There are more lunches. Over the next few months they meet most days at the yellow-fronted cafe, slip into the table that's always ready and waiting for them. And in the afternoons Efe glides back into the shop, thinking about him.

The moment they step into Brian's apartment, Efe regrets coming over. Fuming, she paces to the window and back again, heels hammering the smooth marble floors. The whole place is decadent, full of clean lines and expensive furniture, sharp edges and dark wood. The floor-to-ceiling windows had enthralled Efe the first time she'd visited, but now she marches past them, again and again, seething, while outside a bright strip of London skyline glitters over the Thames, the trees heavy with spring cherry blossoms.

Behind her she can hear Brian fumbling around with yet another bottle of wine even though, thanks to their waitress's prompt service, they split two bottles at the restaurant and there's a neon-pink flush to his cheeks.

Ergh, that woman, Efe thinks. She was already mad that the food was tasteless, and now at thinking of the casual way Brian flirted with the waitress, her mood sours further. Efe too is wine-drunk, tottering as she walks, trying to sort through the slow slurry of her thoughts.

'Okay,' he says, fiddling with a corkscrew. 'Did something happen? You seem like you're mad.'

'I am mad,' Efe says. Three months they've been together and they keep running into the same wall. A little bit of attention from a pretty woman and he can't help himself. 'That waitress was all over you.'

'What?' There's a laugh in his voice. 'Is that what this is about?'

Efe shoots him a look, snatches up her bag and is a few steps from the front door when his fingers hook around her forearm.

'Okay. Okay,' he says. 'It's nothing. It's not like it meant anything.'

'I was sitting right there, like an idiot, and you two were flirting—'

'We were not flirt—'

'Don't.'

'Friendly,' Brian says, slowly as if he's speaking to a child. 'She's paid to be friendly. All she was after was a good tip.'

'She left you her number,' Efe yells.

'She did?' Brian says, actually confused now.

Efe lets out a sound, halfway between a screech and a growl. 'Every time. You make me feel so . . . so . . .'

He works his fingers in between hers, draws her closer until his breath whispers past her ear. 'It was nothing,' he mumbles. Efe bites down on her tongue, her mind clogging, her thoughts on the razor stashed in her purse, but she lets him pull her into his arms. This close she can breathe in his crisp, fresh scent, the delicate woodsy smell just below the surface, like a forest at daybreak. She breathes deeply, quiets as he runs a thumb over her cheek. 'You have nothing to worry about.'

Efe exhales. She takes a moment to remind herself how safe she feels with him. How steady she's been for weeks now. Happier. He makes her happier. She nods and relaxes into him. He's lean and strong beneath her. All muscles pushing against skin. Narrowed hips from years of running, pummelling through the world stride by stride, far further than any distance Efe's ever managed. She presses her head into the gap beside his neck, feet throbbing in her heels. She kisses him. A hand reaches up and grasps a fistful of his hair. She feels his mouth fill with a thin moan, quakes as his hands run up the backs of her legs. She feels bolder, lets her bag fall to the floor. Normally she shies away when his hand drifts beneath her dress, but this time she spreads her fingers wide and pulls him nearer. Encouraged, his fingers slide under her dress. Her insides roil.

'You're shaking,' he whispers. 'We don't have to . . . If you're not . . . '

In response she kisses him harder now, bites down until she can taste blood and leads him to the bedroom. They feel their way through the darkness, undress each other eagerly and slip beneath the featherweight duvet.

She lies on her back, hands clasped at her chest. She feels shy suddenly, equally stunned to see Brian fully naked and awed because he seems to glow in the half-light. When he resumes kissing her, Efe is certain her heart is beating faster than it's ever done in her life.

'You're beautiful. You don't need to hide from me,' he says, his lips at her ear, so close Efe imagines his words slithering right into her mind. She feels his hand clamp around her wrists, pin her arms above her head. Her heart flutters beneath her skin. Then there is paper-thin latex and slight resistance as he enters. Quick bursts. Shallow breaths. Even the air around them quivers, until they curl into each other, exhausted.

Afterwards, Efe rises slowly from the warm ocean of him. Beside her Brian sleeps with lips parted, cheeks rosy and warm. His hair is sweat-slicked to his forehead. She climbs out of his bed carefully, pulling a thin sheet up over her shoulders like a cape. She bundles up her clothes and tiptoes through the dark flat to the bathroom. She doesn't turn on the light. Instead she peers at her reflection in the murky grey half-light, trying to see if she looks any different.

Efe is fully dressed when she nudges Brian awake, her handbag slung over a shoulder, heels clasped in her fist. He opens one eye, squinting, a sleepy smile on his face. He reaches a hand out and drums his fingers on her wrist.

'Where you going?'

'Home,' she says softly.

'You don't have to . . .'

Efe lets out a short laugh. 'I definitely do. If I stay my aunt will find out and start asking questions. And then she'll tell my parents and they'll make it into such a *thing*. Thanks but no thanks.' Efe checks her watch. It's 3 a.m.

'Okay,' Brian says, pulling himself upright. 'I'll drop you off.'

They drive across the city. The roads are mostly empty and it's a mild night, spring tipping into summer all around them. But over the last few months Brian has learned that Efe is often cold. He's wrapped her in scarves, cradled her freezing hands. Without needing to check, he turns up the heat and lets it blast warm air onto their feet. Above them, the traffic lights shine and the street lamps flicker.

Efe sneaks back into the flat and pauses when she sees the strip of light under the bedroom door. 'You're up?' she says, peeking round the doorway, suddenly conscious of the dress, the heels, the smell of sex on her skin. Serwaa looks up, yawns, her arms grazing the ceiling.

'I wanted to make sure you made it home safely.'

'Why? Did Aunty Dora ask where I was?' She feels a panic blooming in her. Too many times to count Aunty Dora has reminded the girls that as long as they live under her roof they're her responsibility, and while Efe's salary is just £1 over minimum wage, under Aunty Dora's roof is exactly where she'll be staying.

'She called from work around eleven but I told her you were in the shower.'

'Thank you.' Efe sinks onto the bottom bunk, slides out of her shoes, lets her dress gather at her feet. She's pulling on pyjamas when she hears creaking slats as Serwaa flops over in the top bunk, her voice saying, 'If I'm covering for you, don't I need to know where you keep sneaking off to? I like that you're happy now, but what do I tell people if you end up in a ditch?'

'A ditch? You're not serious?' Efe rolls her eyes and reaches for the words. Her brain is still foggy and steeped in alcohol. Carefully, she says, 'I'm seeing someone.'

'I knew it.' The slats creak and Serwaa exhales a dreamy sigh. 'Me too.'

'Who, Joseph?' Efe says, thinking back to Easter break, two years earlier in Ghana. Efe had known they'd stayed in touch, but now she thinks back to all the times when Serwaa hurried to hide a letter as Efe entered the room, all overheard conversations and phone cards out of credit. She thought they were just friends, but realises now there was so much more to it.

'He's going to ask permission,' Serwaa says dreamily.

Efe shoots to her feet, spins too quickly and steadies herself against the wardrobe. 'Wait, what?'

Serwaa nods.

'You're marrying him? But you're seventeen. You're still in school.'

'I'm almost eighteen. And I finish my exams in two months.'

'Why don't you take your time? Get your degree or a good job?' Efe lets out a low breath, thinking back to her own disastrous university experience. She pauses. 'Do you think they'll let you?'

Serwaa shrugs. 'Maybe not at first. But they'll come round. Gosh.' She laughs. 'Have you not heard all the not-so-subtle hints they've been dropping about us not visiting them enough? I'm sure they'll be ecstatic to have me back.' Efe chuckles, thinking back to the weekly phone calls with their parents. Serwaa continues, sounding even more sure of herself, 'And I'll still go to university next September. We'll be married but that won't change anything.'

'Wow. Soon to be a married woman.' Efe looks at her sister, stares hard for the first time in a while, and sees that behind the baby face she's no longer a child. Soon she'll be someone's wife. Thinking of the years to come, Efe hasn't imagined anything too different from what they have now. All the while, Serwaa's been imagining something else, planning to leave.

As if reading her mind, Serwaa says, 'It's not like you'll be alone. Aunty Dora's still here. And Abbey's tour ends in a few weeks, so she'll be back, plus Sam graduates next year, so he'll probably move home too. You have friends. And I'll come back and visit all the time.'

Efe nods. They had been a team. She places a hand on the ladder, concentrates on each rung as she climbs and squeezes in. The bed groans. The space is tight, but Efe feels this is where she should be, sliding her hand into her sister's, their shoulders bumping, heads inches from the ceiling.

'Doesn't it scare you?' Efe says whisper-quiet, staring at their legs stretched out beneath the covers. 'How do you know?'

Serwaa says nothing for a long while. Eventually she rests her head on Efe's shoulder and says, 'Instinct.'

Thirteen Years Before

Efe snakes her way through the crowd. The air is thick and teeming with the sticky-sweet scent of wedded bliss. There are hundreds of guests present, everyone from close family members to friends of her parents and people Efe has never even met. A wedding in Ghana is a community affair and Efe can safely assume a third of the guests have never met Serwaa or Joseph.

She feels the press of warm bodies and catches snippets of conversations as she passes. The guests are admiring the brides-maids' dresses, talking about how lovely the ceremony was, speculating just how much money Efe's parents have spent. Others gather around the ever-replenishing buffet, gleaming chafing dishes still overflowing with *waakye*, *red-red*, meat stew and Ghana salad, though they are several hours into the festivities. The ones who have had their fill linger on the patio and spill out down the wide concrete stairs and into the garden. They sway in small groups as the band plays something rich, slow and resonant. The sound fills the night air and expands past the rows of tables, right to the furthest edges of the grounds, where long strings of lights twinkle on the high compound walls and make the house look like a constellation dazzling in the night.

Everything about tonight is celebratory. Serwaa is delighted to be back in Ghana, and Efe feels satiated as she slows beside the fountain, feeling the wisps of its spray dance over her skin. A black-shirted waiter stops close by, lowering the tray of food for Efe to examine.

She frowns. 'Is the kebab finished?'

'Please no. We don't have,' he replies, and Efe nods, reaching past the *chin-chin* and aiming for a small bowl of *kelewele*, just as a hand closes around her wrist.

'*Akwaaba, Efe. Ete sɛn?*'

She turns to see Gifty at her side, beside her two other women from Maame's bible study all dressed in matching kente cloth.

'Thank you, Aunty. I'm well. How are you?' Efe replies in English, draws a small smile from cheek to cheek and steels herself for the barrage of hurtful comments.

Gifty smacks her lips together and begins to speak. 'Oh, I am well. Thanks be to God.' She smiles too brightly. 'And look at you, Miss Chief Bridesmaid.'

Efe's smile tightens. She slips her arm out of Gifty's grasp as the woman steps back to examine her. Efe still feels awkward in the turquoise bridesmaid's dress with its slim bodice exploding into ruffles galore from the knees down.

'What a beautiful dress,' Gifty simpers, plucking a kebab from a passing waiter. 'Of course it should be you out there.'

'Me?'

'Of course you. Are you not the older sister?' She twists a piece of meat off the skewer and pops it in her mouth; still gnawing on the charred meat, she continues. 'Anyway tell me, how is UK? You know my Josephine just completed her third year at Queen Mary and we praise God for lavishing his good gifts on her. So if she's doing that you must be –' she drums her fingers together '– graduating?'

Efe feels her skin crawl under three pairs of expectant eyes. There's not a world in which Gifty, with her ear to the ground and squadron of spies on every continent, has not already heard. In fact, Efe distinctly remembers that Gifty and her daughter were the first ones to break the news and are presumably the main reason why most of Accra had heard. Yet she waits for Efe's response with bated breath, crunching on another cube of tough meat.

'I'm not at school any more,' Efe says, choosing her words carefully.

'And what are you doing now?' An eyebrow inches upwards.

'I'm working.' Efe pauses. 'In a bookshop.'

'Oh!' Gifty lets the smug syllable hang in the air. Behind her, her followers exchange confused looks.

'A shopkeeper?' one of them asks. 'All this your learning to be a shopkeeper?'

'No, I don't own the shop.'

'*Eh-hen*, so even here, our women have their own shops and you, yourself, you work for somebody else. All the way to UK to be a – what – a . . . a . . .'

'Assistant manager.'

'If I was you—' the lecture begins. Efe isn't sure which one of them speaks. She keeps her eyes on the skewer twirling slowly in Gifty's fingers and knows her part is to stand with her shoulders appropriately slumped in remorse and to nod occasionally, imitating someone politely listening to the wise counsel of elders. Efe says nothing as they deconstruct her failings and present them back to her piece by piece. She lets her gaze drift across the garden and sweep across the guests. She can just about see Abbey, Nanadwoa and a few more of her age-mates standing beside what was the party favours table, filled edge to edge with mugs, pens, notebooks and gifts bearing Joseph and Serwaa's grinning faces, but after its early afternoon ransacking, is now topped with empty Guinness bottles and plates yet to be collected. Abbey looks tall and elegant in her turquoise bridesmaid's dress. She's ignoring the conversation right in front of her and shooting sultry looks at the guys hovering on the edge of the group, their chests puffed, sunglasses shining in the twinkling light.

Efe thinks of Sam. She searches for several moments then spots him at the nearby table, sipping from a frosty Supermalt, chatting easily with one of her cousins. She's been meaning to talk to Sam all night and takes an unconscious step towards him, muttering an excuse, but only makes it to the top of the stairs before Maame materialises in front of her.

She's regal in her mother-of-the-bride outfit, head topped in an elaborate gold *duku,* face aglow with more make-up than Efe's ever seen her wear. 'What did Gifty want?'

'Nothing really, just—'

Maame wordlessly steers Efe away from listening ears. A sweaty stickiness forms in the spot where Maame's hand presses to the small of Efe's back, and when she turns to face Efe her face is pinched and smile stiff. She hisses the words out, her mouth in a frozen grin for watching eyes.

'Are you sure?' Maame says.

'Yes.'

Maame stares for a moment, eyes boring into Efe before she relaxes, satisfied.

'Good. You should stay away from her. That woman is a—' Efe doesn't get to hear precisely what type of woman Gifty is because Pastor Eric and his wife come within hearing distance. The man's large frame is only emphasised by the slightness of his wife, the sweet-smiling woman tucked into his side.

'Maame, you've outdone yourself. What a splendid wedding.' He beams and Efe catches a glimpse of two gold canines. 'And let me congratulate you on your promotion again, headmistress. I hope together the wedding and your new responsibilities at school are not proving too much. Are you well?'

'By the grace of God, the whole family is doing well.' Maame places a modest hand on her chest. 'And it is through him alone that I have the strength to wake up each day and do something small.'

'Small? But it's a big job, is it not?'

'Just one hundred and fifty girls, Pastor. In some years we'll see more.'

'Amen.' Pastor nods. 'We will send our Akos to you next year.'

'Akos? Is she eleven already?'

'In October. We wouldn't want to send her anywhere else.'

'Thanks be to God,' Maame coos.

Pastor smiles, folding his hands together. 'You must be so happy to have your girls home.' He turns to Efe. 'Remind me what you do in UK?'

Efe draws her gaze back from the *chin-chin*-carrying waiter, realising the question was addressed to her at the exact same moment she notices Maame stiffen beside her. 'Efe is working for now and returning to university in September.'

Pastor's eyes brighten. 'And what will you read?'

'Actually it's a part-time course,' Efe says, then turns back to Pastor. 'Art History.'

Maame chuckles. 'Children these days, coming with all these modern ideas. Just yesterday I was encouraging her in Pharmacy or Engineering.'

'Engineering is good-o,' Pastor exhales, nodding at Efe with new admiration.

'Even as a small girl, Efe came first in her class. Art is the course she likes today, but there's no need to rush these things. I keep telling her, You don't need to make a decision right now. We can take our time and decide as a family.'

Almost an hour later Efe finds Sam at the far end of the garden, where the plants spill over each other and the air is heady with the fragrance of jasmine. She's watched him taking photos all day, catching the gift-giving, the bridal procession, the candid bursts of laughter as well as the stern-faced family members, but now he takes a swig of water, rests a hand on the tulip tree.

'Hey, Mr Photographer,' she calls as she nears. Efe makes her way slowly, her dress rustling and her heels sinking into the soft grass with every step. 'What are you doing all the way over here? Don't tell me you're still moping because Doris broke up with you?'

'Her name was Daphne. You met her a bunch of times.'

Efe shrugs, places a hand on Sam's shoulder for balance and kicks off her heels. 'I never liked her anyway.'

'The feeling was mutual.'

Efe laughs a full joyous laugh, not the hushed cautious laughter she's used all week, surrounded by her parents' guests.

'And for the record I've been introduced to more girls than I could count.'

'And I'm guessing my cousin played a part in that.' Efe pauses, knowing that the next words will sound like something her parents would say. 'Be careful around Nakwesi. He's bad news . . . and people talk.'

'He's a wealth of information.'

'I'm sure he is,' Efe says, smirking.

'How come you never told me you lived in London?'

The night trembles. Efe is all too aware of the emotions that flash across her face, and is trying too hard to look unfazed. Sam is watching her closely, waiting for an answer that comes several seconds too late. She feels afraid, irrationally so, but tries to laugh it off. 'You know I live in London. We both—'

'No, not now. I'm talking about when you were little. You always made it sound like you just came over for sixth form.'

Efe frowns. She feels her eyes filling with tears despite herself. 'Was it Nakwesi? Is he the one who told you?'

'Why are you this upset? It was one of your aunts. Your dad was there and started acting all weird. And now you're acting weird.'

'I don't have to tell you every detail of my life, Sam.'

'Why are you being like that?' Sam steps closer, but Efe angles her head away from him, looks over her shoulder and back to the party. She can hear the band playing vigorously, see Maame and Paa in the middle of the dance floor, their arms waving overhead, two-stepping in front of a swell of cheering guests. Even Serwaa and Joseph, who have spent the whole day in each other's arms, loved-up newlyweds oblivious to the hundreds of guests flowing around them, have stepped back to watch.

Sam's voice is quiet. 'Efe?'

'Fine,' she sighs, plopping onto the ground as turquoise ruffles poof all around her. She lies flat on the grass. Sam waits a few moments then joins her. It's easier to tell it this way, with their faces staring up at the scorched-earth-coloured tulips and the dark slice of sky, the damp grass seeping into their clothes.

'I don't even remember most of it,' she begins, grimacing. 'Me and Serwaa were born there, but we moved back to Accra when I was six. All the memories I do have – well – they're not exactly good memories.'

'What do you remember?'

'Being afraid,' she says. 'We moved to this really tiny town and couldn't go for a walk or go to the shops without people making comments or giving us strange looks. Sometimes people would shout or point when we'd walk down the street. Sometimes people followed us home. There was this one night, I must've been about five at the time, it was just this normal evening and then a brick came in through the window. After that we stopped opening the curtains. It was fine for a while. We were keeping our heads down, trying to make it work, but one night we woke up to this really loud popping in the corridor.'

'What happened?'

'Fireworks. Some guy stuffed a lit firework through the letterbox. The curtains caught fire and there was this awful chemical smell for ages. We moved back to Ghana about a month later.'

Efe exhales into the quiet that nestles between them. The distant chime of highlife continues.

'I'm sorry, Efe. I shouldn't have brought it up. I had no idea.'

'It was a different time,' she says flatly. 'We were out in the middle of nowhere. People weren't used to different. They didn't want different.'

Efe lets her eyes slowly close. The minutes tick by as she watches the memories on loop on the backs of her eyelids, clearer now with the retelling, and the child in her wants to cry.

'I've never told you about my mum, have I?' Sam shifts, lets out a quiet breath. 'She left when I was twelve. She picked me up from school, made sure me and Phoebe were good, then she left. Didn't even wait for my dad to get home from work.'

'Where'd she go?'

'Dunno. When my dad got home he drove us down to the jazz bar where she performed. It wasn't one of her regular nights, but I guess he figured that was where she'd be. But she was gone.' He exhales.

'What did your dad say?'

'That they'd been arguing, but they'd work it out. He told us to tell people she went to stay with Grandma. After a few weeks, I got tired of that and started making up stories. One week she was a spy, the next she was learning how to be a shark tamer. I think I even told this lady at the bank that she was an astronaut and on a top-secret mission on the dark side of the moon.'

He laughs. When Sam speaks again, his voice is so low that Efe has to strain to hear it, so quiet she doesn't dare move. Shallow breaths flutter in her throat. Sam is showing her a part of him she's never seen before. Something between them delicately slides away. He continues, 'I still think about that. I doubt anyone but Phoebe believed me. She would've been three, maybe. I think I convinced myself. I guess I just didn't want to imagine her – I dunno – working in a shop in Birmingham or teaching in a school somewhere in Brighton. If she was leaving us it had to be for something special, y'know. If she left us for something mundane . . . that I couldn't live with.'

Efe keeps her eyes on the sky, traces invisible lines between the handfuls of scattered stars.

'I've never told anyone that,' he says.

And because she doesn't know how to respond, she stretches out her fingers to find his. Eventually she drops her cheek to the damp grass, watches the rhythmic brush of thick eyelashes against soft dark skin, traces her gaze over his gently parted lips and the dark shadow of hair along his jawline. Sam drops his head towards her too, his breath rippling through the blades of grass that separate them. He gives her hand a firm squeeze and Efe worries he can hear her heart reverberating in her chest. Something in her is loosening. It's there in each rattling breath, deep in her chest. She readies herself for the firm press of lips, the meeting of tongues, the hot sensation surging in her stomach.

She is edging forward when a bottle smashes, impossibly loud in the quiet moment, so both Efe and Sam whip round at the sound. Nakwesi stares through thick sunglasses, looking from his empty hand to the broken bottle on the grass, then shrugs and leans forward, his round stomach slipping through the opening in his pink silk shirt, his arm is around the waist of a girl Efe doesn't recognise, who giggles drunkenly.

'Sorry,' he says in a loud whisper and all that has been fizzing in the air evaporates.

MARCH 2004

Twelve Years Before

By the following spring, Efe is settling into her course and working part-time as a trainee curator thanks to Brian's unceasing connections. She rents a cheap boxroom halfway between her college and the Launi Gallery, but she spends most nights at Brian's place and has practically moved in.

Certain he won't be back until late, Efe lets herself into the apartment and helps herself to leftovers. She sits on the sofa with a plate balanced on her lap and calls Serwaa.

'Hey, it's me,' Efe says. There's a crackle, then Serwaa's voice comes through.

'Calling from your *obroni*'s house, I see.'

Efe lets out a little laugh and tucks the phone between her shoulder and ear. 'Don't mind me. How are you?'

'Not too bad.'

'Were you on campus today?' Efe asks.

'No.' Serwaa yawns. 'They approved my request, so I can go back and complete the year after the baby's born.'

'That's great,' Efe says. 'And how's my favourite nephew?' To Efe, the words sound forced, but Serwaa doesn't seem to notice.

'Heavy,' Serwaa moans. 'I feel like someone's strapped ten kilos of rice to me.'

'How much longer?'

'Three months.'

'Wow, so he'll only be getting bigger over the next few months?' Efe shudders at the thought. 'Better you than me.'

After the call, Efe spends an hour flicking through TV channels and catches the second half of a movie on Sky. It's almost midnight and Brian isn't back when she crawls into bed, but sometime during the night he returns and curls his body around hers.

In the morning, Efe steps out of the shower, the heated floor gently warming her feet. Pale light fills the en suite. She plucks her tub of moisturiser from the shelf, the sugary scent of cocoa butter slicing through the air as she heads back into the bedroom. Beside her Brian stirs, his sleep-soft face scrunching, then relaxing as he flops over to the cool side. There's a buzzing sound. He's still mostly unconscious when his hand gropes along the bedside table and flips the phone open.

'Hello,' he murmurs. A moment later his voice jumps an octave. 'Good morning, Mrs Owusu.'

Efe spins. Every muscle contracts. A glob of body cream slips from her fingers to the bed and an oily stain seeps into the satin. 'Give me the phone,' she whispers.

'Brian. You're speaking to Brian.' He ignores Efe's outstretched hand and wrestles out of the sheets, stumbles away from her. They tussle: her scrambling, him holding the phone high out of her reach. Maame's voice continues to murmur on the other end.

'Yes, I'm well. Erm . . . *E ti si-en?*' he says.

The pronunciation is butchered and Efe regrets teaching him that. 'Phone,' she mouths and glowers until Brian mumbles, 'Yeah, she's right here' and finally hands it over.

Efe takes a deep breath, clutching the phone so tight her fingers are straining. 'Fine morning, Mum,' she says, keeping her voice even and light.

'*Maakye*, Efe,' Maame replies. To Efe, Maame's voice sounds unsettlingly calm. She waits for the inevitable lecture or interrogation, her mind branching off, trying to anticipate every direction Maame could take this conversation.

On the other end of the line Maame clears her throat softly. 'It's still early where you are, isn't it?'

'Not too early,' Efe says with a quick look at the clock. 'Buses and trains start at five a.m. so you can get anywhere early these days.'

'Mmm,' Maame responds.

'It's amazing really,' Efe adds, practically squirming in her skin. 'So reliable.' A pause.

'That boy – Brian – he sounds nice.' Her tone is unchanged, but twenty-three years listening to Maame speak has left Efe's ears attuned to the hidden agenda simmering beneath her words. To her surprise, Efe's detecting a hint of glee. *They've barely exchanged five words and she's already wedding planning*, Efe thinks to herself. And she may be right because whenever Maame calls over the next few months she will always make a point to ask, 'How is Brian?' or say, 'Greet Brian for me' at the end of each call or 'Make sure you prepare *fufu* for Brian', always cooing, her voice silky and sweet. This first time Efe says nothing in response. She has the strange sense that a trap is dangling just above her head and lets the line fill with static and silence, while the minutes Maame has paid for steadily deplete.

After a few seconds Maame chimes in again. 'Well I just called to see how you are. Have you eaten?'

Efe takes her time getting dressed. She blots the cream out of the bedsheet and heads into the living room. Brian, still dressed in boxers and a T-shirt, looks up and pushes a mug of steaming hot chocolate across the breakfast bar – the tea charade from their early days long since abandoned. Efe says nothing as she sits heavily on the nearest bar stool, deliberately pulling her grumpiest face. She glares into the mug, watching the creamy dollop of whipped cream star-fishing out.

'What is it?'

'Really, my mum?' Efe says, hearing the whine in her voice.

'It's not like I knew it would be her,' he says, letting out a small laugh. 'Anyway, we've been together two years. I can't be a secret forever.'

Not a secret, just separate. Just until I'm certain, Efe thinks.

'I've told you what she's like. She'd just tell my dad, Aunty Yaa and Aunty Esther—'

'Those are her best friends, right?'

'Yes,' Efe says. 'And they'll tell their friends. And before you know it the whole church will be talking about us, and by the end of the week every distant relative and anyone who's ever met me will be barging in with their opinions. We won't have any breathing room,' she adds.

'It can't be that bad,' Brian says, a small smile on his lips. 'You've met my friends and all my colleagues. My parents love you.'

Efe sighs, remembering her sweaty, aching feet at Brian's work Christmas party, trying to keep track of names while being paraded around a room full of tipsy bankers. She thinks back to Brian's thirty-fourth birthday dinner, hosted in a restaurant where the bill for twelve came to double Efe's monthly rent. She distinctly remembers biting her tongue and playing the role of the good girlfriend, while Brian's university friends constantly made comments about how 'quaint' and 'well-spoken' she was, remarks that could only be rivalled by the ones where they called her 'exotic'. Maybe it was the shock of it, but Efe found herself laughing along in spite of how uneasy she felt, how much their words had left her wishing the ground would swallow her up. The only ones she'd liked had been his parents. They'd been kind and welcoming on every occasion Efe had seen them, reminding her of the kind-hearted, ever-patient characters in stories she'd read growing up.

Brian turns to the fridge, pulls out a loaf of bread for her and a yoghurt for him. He pops the bread in the toaster then turns back to Efe. 'And who have you introduced me to?'

'You speak to my sister,' Efe says. 'And Nanadwoa.'

'Because none of them live here.'

'You've met Aunty Dora.'

'That only happened because she wanted to know where you were spending all your time.'

And because I've sworn them all to secrecy, Efe thinks.

'I should at least meet a couple of your UK friends,' Brian says. 'What about Sam, the one you're always sneaking off to see?'

Efe rolls her eyes. 'We don't sneak off. You always work late and his office is, like, one tube ride away from the gallery. It's just easier for us to meet after work.'

'Maybe I won't work late one of these days,' Brian grumbles.

'Do you really want to crash a thirty-minute catch-up before he has to head back to the office?'

'Probably not,' Brian says, 'as long as I don't have anything to worry about.'

'With me and Sam?' Efe scoffs. 'It's entirely platonic. He's one of my oldest UK friends.'

Efe knows something big has happened the moment Sam texts. An hour later, when he comes bounding up the stairs at Piccadilly Circus, grinning from ear to ear, the nervous knot in her stomach begins to loosen. *It's something good*, she thinks, noting Sam's excited energy. He can't keep still. He's fizzing with it as he pulls Efe into a secluded side street, the two of them charging past quick-footed commuters.

'Are you sure?' Efe says for the third time.

'Yeah. It was her,' Sam says, a disbelieving smile filling half his face. 'She knew who I was and she – she hugged me.'

Breathless, Sam tells the whole story, first how he explained to the receptionist that he'd been sent from Barnard, Brand & Associates, how he'd been making his way through the office, trying to balance three large box files, when he'd seen his mother answering calls outside the managing partner's office.

She didn't recognise him at first, then their eyes locked, her mouth fell open, she sprung out of her chair and pulled him into her arms, both of them crying and shrieking and laughing, taking no notice of the lawyers giving them wary looks.

'Wow.' Efe breathes out the word. She's heard almost nothing about his mum over the years, but has always nursed a quiet curiosity for this one part Sam refused to speak about. Suddenly, she has a million questions.

'Are you going to see her again?'

'She wants to see me tonight. We're having dinner at this Portuguese restaurant.'

'What about your family?'

'Well.' Sam pauses. 'My dad's working and Pheebs is on her Year 10 school trip. It's probably best I scope her out first, right? It's been years.'

'Right,' Efe says. 'Wow, Sam. I can't believe it was her.'

She looks at Sam again, seeing things almost no one else would notice. All of it is right there on his face, like a map only she can read: how desperately he wants this, how afraid he is this chance could slip away. A misty rain is beginning. In a single moment, many faces lift to the sky and a flock of dark umbrellas take flight.

When her gaze returns to Sam, he is looking at her seriously and she knows what he is about to ask before he says a thing.

'Could you come with me?' Sam asks.

It's late by the time they get back to Efe's flat-share. Sam hasn't said a word the whole journey here. He's oscillating, trying to make sense of the three hours they've waited, both of them silently willing his mum to walk through the restaurant's doors. The scale tips moment by moment, and by the time Efe unlocks the front door, he's sinking into despair.

'Give me a second,' she says.

She leaves him in the darkened hallway and rushes to her

room to make sure it's presentable. She hasn't spent a single night here in almost a month and isn't sure what state she left it in. There are crumpled sheets on the flimsy single bed; the poorly assembled canvas wardrobe leans drunkenly to the left; the circle of mould above the window has grown and a sharp, stale smell emanates from the walls. She scrambles to tidy up the CDs and books, dumps a pile of clothes on a chair and pushes it under her desk. She heaves the window open an inch.

'Sam?' she says.

He takes four halting steps forward and catches himself on the doorframe. His legs are trembling. Without thinking, she settles him on her bed. Her brain goes to Brian, to Nya – Sam's current girlfriend and the first one Efe genuinely likes – wondering for a moment what their respective partners would think. Quickly, she pushes those thoughts out of her mind.

She watches as Sam curves forward and buries his head under tented hands. Efe stills. She has never seen him cry and instinctively turns to the door. Her fingers close around the door handle and there she stops. She isn't sure if she hears it or senses it – this breaking – before the sobs burst through. She can't bring herself to leave.

'It'll be okay,' she says as she gathers him close, feels his breath hot against her stomach, his body slack as if her hands are the only things keeping him from crumbling.

For a moment this is everything, then time collapses. Efe feels it rearranging itself, throwing her back to the long string of almost kisses. To the rainy bus stop on their very first meeting. To Ghana, lying in the grass. To years of Sunday night films pressed shoulder to shoulder on the sofa, turning towards Sam and seeing his face bathed in the blue glow of the TV screen. The long string leading to right now.

She presses her lips to his crown, right where the hair spirals outwards – cut short recently but just beginning to curl. She lets her eyes close, lets his familiar scent fill her nostrils, lets her heart's drums quicken as the seconds pull tight like an elastic band. She isn't sure she's breathing until he kisses her back. She feels his splayed fingers edge beneath her top. The room fills with the musty scent of wanting. She leans into it, breathes deeply as she tugs his shirt over his head, then stretches for the light switch, submerging them in darkness.

His arms wrap around her as they topple, still kissing, onto the bed. A low rumble rises up in Efe's throat and she sheds the rest of her clothes. His lips meet the soft dip of her neck and he kisses greedily, hands flitting across her shoulders, pulling her towards him.

'What's that?' he murmurs, pulling away.

'Shhh, nothing. It's fine,' Efe whispers. It takes her a moment to realise that Sam's hands have lifted off her body entirely. She's still hooking her fingers around his belt buckle when the bedside lamp flicks on.

'Sam!' she gasps, recoiling and hiking up the blanket in one swift move. But it's too late. He has seen.

She can tell by the way he looks past her, into the wardrobe mirror, his eyes wide and mouth slack. Reflected back, in the seconds before blanket meets skin, he catches a glimpse of the long ribbons of black-gold scars criss-crossing Efe's back. Each one thin and jagged. Lightning trails that disappear into the puckered flesh at her shoulder blades.

'What happened to your back?'

Efe feels an uneasiness settle over her. She focuses on a spot on the floor. The blanket feels heavy at her shoulders.

'Efe?' Sam says her name softly this time.

'It's nothing,' she mumbles, then slides into the space beside him, feels the cool bite of the metal of the headboard.

'That's assault. Who did that to you?'

'It's old. And it looks worse than it is. I don't even remember—'

'You don't remember who assaulted you?'

'Not really. I was a kid,' she says, pushing back the tears

that are beginning to fall. 'I don't even know why I'm crying.'

'Efe—'

She sniffs. 'Can we talk about something else please?'

Outside a train pummels past. They both jump. The room quakes. The single-glazed windows rattle. Something gives way. Sam sighs and buries his face into hers. She feels his breath breeze across her cheek, then nose, just before he tilts her head upwards so their lips meet, softly this time. Gently.

Years from now, he will hear the whole story from Paa, whose voice will be low and gravelly as he recounts those final months in the UK. Maame will be unspeaking a few feet away, her hands gripping her knees, teeth cinched around her bottom lip. Sam will hear all about the months of bullying, the kids singing as they tied Efe to the chainlink fence in the playground, pulled a skipping rope tight around her neck first, then brought it down on her back, over and over again, the plastic whistling as it snaked through the air. At night, his brain will conjure up the sounds of her screams – unheard or ignored by the teachers – until break-time ended – and know that when they finally thought to look for her she was already unconscious. And he'll know all about what came after: the sirens wailing, the hospital stay and the hurried move back to Ghana that same week, Efe's months of silence and the skin grafts her body rejected, before the doctors gave up and her parents swore never to set foot on British soil again.

When Efe wakes, the room is stuffy. The mini heater pulses from its spot under the desk. Sweat forms at her armpits, underneath her breasts and along the back of her calf where Sam's leg loops around hers. She eases away from him and palms the mattress in search of her underwear. She slips out of bed and the door closes with a soft click behind her.

In the shower, she lets the water scorch his touches from her skin, clean his taste from her tongue. When she returns Sam is awake, propped up in her bed, his scent seeping into her sheets. He yawns, stretching his arms up. A hand brushes the corkboard covered in theatre-show programmes, cinema-ticket stubs, a photo of her and Brian at a roller rink, taken the year before on their anniversary. She forces herself to look away.

Sam smiles at her. 'Hey,' he says. The duvet falls to his belly button and Efe makes a conscious effort to pull her eyes away from the dark curls on his chest. She looks out at the train tracks and tugs her bulky dressing gown tighter.

'Hi,' she says.

Sam shifts. 'Do you want to – I mean – we should probably talk—'

'No need,' she says, not quite able to meet his eyes. 'But we can talk about the other thing – if you want to.'

He shrugs. 'I dunno why she'd act like she wants to meet me and not show.'

'You know where she works. You could ask her.'

'So she can lie to me or disappear again?'

'No. I just meant—'

Sam gives his head a quick shake. 'It's better this way. Now I can pretend none of this happened.'

'What about your dad and Phoebe?'

'It was a chance encounter. It's not like she meant to find me.' He's trying to sound chill but his voice betrays him and wobbles slightly. 'Now no one's disappointed.'

Efe lets out a quiet sigh. 'It's okay if you still want to give her a chance. Maybe she freaked out—'

'You don't get it. Your parents are still together. My family's lived on the same street since I was seven. She could come back any time she wants to and doesn't. I can't force her.'

Efe nods. She says nothing because she can think of plenty of people who've spent their whole lives doing things they don't want to do.

AUGUST 2005

Eleven Years Before

Sam wakes when Efe moves. She slips a leg out first, then withdraws herself from their entangled limbs. He grumbles. Through the narrow slit of a half-opened eye, he watches as she uncoils like a length of rope, draws herself up until she is sitting. Moonlight slices her in half and the thin sheet drapes across her lap.

'You're leaving?' he murmurs.

'Go back to sleep,' she whispers.

Sam doesn't resist. He closes his eyes and focuses his mind on her movements: the soft pad of footsteps, the chink of a glass against the counter, the gurgle of water at the sink, then she is back and he feels the weight of her gaze on him.

There have been months full of nights just like this: long summer nights with the bedroom window cracked open, through to mid-autumn evenings, the trees heavy with golden leaves, and winter nights with the sun blotted out by grey. And now, after almost eighteen months of mostly unplanned meetings, piece by piece, they have built a world where nothing else matters. There are no Nyas here, no Brians, just a delicate balance, the two of them suspended with the whole world at their feet.

'What are you doing?' Sam asks drowsily, eyes still closed.

'Nothing. Go back to sleep.'

'I can't sleep when you're watching me.'

She laughs, a full glorious sound. 'You're not sleeping yet. It doesn't count.'

When Sam opens his eyes again the light is different. Bright morning rays stream in through the window and Efe is at the foot of his bed, wriggling into yesterday's jeans. Playfully, he stretches out a toe and nudges her. 'Come back to bed.'

'I have work today.'

Sam turns onto his side so he can look at her properly, props his head up in his hand. 'Go in later.'

'Can't. I'm helping set up a new exhibit. I told Marilyn I'd be in at ten,' she says. 'Anyway, aren't you meeting Nya today?'

Sam is just dozing off again when he hears a furious banging at the front door. He lifts his head from the pillow thick with Efe's scent and squints towards the hallway. The knocking doesn't stop. Sighing, he digs through crumpled clothes and pulls on tracksuit bottoms and a semi-clean T-shirt. One arm is halfway into the sleeve, elbow near chin, when he reaches for the latch and Efe barges in. He has just enough time to stagger out of the way. Already, she's yelling.

'You broke up with Nya?' Efe fumes. 'Why would you do that?'

Sam's sleep-soft brain needs a second to catch up. 'Who told you?'

'Who told me?' Efe whirls round on him. 'She told me. She's waiting outside your house like a stalker.'

'Wait – what?' Sam moves towards the window.

'Don't look!' Efe throws her hands in the air, and Sam stops, unsure of his next move. She paces furiously in the small space.

In the weeks since the break-up Sam's imagined just how he'd explain it to Efe. He pictured himself striding into the gallery, pulling her aside while she was leading a tour or about to step into a meeting, and he'd kiss her, in full view of everyone, not caring what her colleagues thought, waiting for the onlookers to erupt in cheers, just like in the movies. He wanted to tell her that he thought about her all the time, that he was all in and so sure they could make it work. But reading those sentences back felt like stepping off a cliff.

'I thought you'd be happy.'

'Happy?' She stops pacing and stares at him now, a hard look in her eyes. 'Happy that you did the exact opposite of what I asked you to do?'

'It's not like that.'

'Go on,' she says, bringing her hands to her hips, 'tell me. What is it like? When did you make this decision you were so sure would make me happy?'

Sam bites the corner of his lip. 'A few weeks ago.'

'Weeks?' She huffs.

Sam thinks back to an evening three weeks ago, right at the start of August. He'd spent all day with Efe, not having sex, just watching old movies, cooking and making out a little, like teenagers. Secretly, these are the days he wants to last forever. And on that day, as the credits had rolled, he'd looked at his watch and realised he was late to meet Nya.

'You should go,' Efe had said, already reaching for the almost-empty bowl of popcorn. And in a moment of clarity, Sam answered, 'I could break up with her,' then squirmed in the prickly silence that followed. Efe froze, cradling the bowl in her lap like an infant, so Sam kept speaking, nervousness working its way into his voice. 'Actually, I've been thinking about it for a while,' he said. 'With work and everything she's got going on, we barely see each other as is. Did I tell you she's got this summer job? Crazy hours. She won't even notice. I'd have more time for us.'

The 'us' hung in the space between them. Eventually Efe had reached a hand out and interlocked her fingers in his. 'Don't do that,' she'd said at last. 'What we have is enough.'

But Sam had done just that. And back in the entryway, Efe is seething. He shakes the memory loose and tries to focus on the present. He watches her hands come up to her temples.

'Weeks,' she repeats. 'How could you—? I can't believe you did this, Sam.'

'I just needed to break up with her,' Sam says. 'I'm done sneaking around.'

'We had a deal,' she says. 'When we're together we're together. Out there –' she points to the door '– nothing changes.'

Sam's head tilts back. An involuntary groan escapes his lips. *This is ridiculous*, he thinks. *I did the right thing*. What comes out is: 'You're not being serious.'

'Of course I am. Why—'

He takes a step forward, closing up the space between them so they are toe to toe, his breath coursing across her forehead. He is so close he can smell her. 'You want to know why?' he says, louder than he intended. 'Because this isn't just screwing around any more.'

'Don't say that,' Efe says, shrinking back. Her voice is smaller now. She pulls her elbows up and hugs them close.

But now that Sam has started, he finds he can't stop. Something in him is unravelling. The words come up of their own accord. 'Come on! It's you, Efe. It's always been you. We could give this a real go and all you want is a couple of hours with me before you run back to your bigshot boyfriend.'

'Brian—'

'Why are you with him anyway?' Sam is yelling now. 'You're not you when you're with him.'

Efe's mouth snaps shut. Her face pinches tight and Sam is certain he's said the wrong thing.

'You don't get to break up with your girlfriend and *claim* me. I'm not some trophy or prize. And you certainly don't know everything about me or *my* relationship. I can be someone with him and someone else when I'm with you. I'm still me.'

'Decide. Which version of you do you want to be?'

Efe scowls. 'Are you seriously forcing my hand?'

'You know what – do whatever you want. You know where I stand.'

Efe's still thinking about that conversation days later, on Sunday afternoon, as she rides the lift up to Aunty Dora's flat. Every time she visits she notices new touches and details: freshly painted walls, a new community noticeboard in the foyer. Even the lift's rumbling behind the living room wall seems quieter.

'You got rid of the sofa bed,' Efe says, sinking into an almost-new sofa.

'What do you think?' Aunty asks.

'It's nice,' Efe says as she runs her fingers over the chocolate-coloured suede. A small tray of drinks sits between them.

'How's work?'

'Good.'

'And how's Brian?'

Efe takes a breath, rises from her seat to take a closer look at the ornaments in a neat line above the electric fireplace. She moves slowly, traces a finger over the smooth ceramic skirts and bonnets, feels Aunty's eyes on her back.

'He wants to marry me.'

This is the first time Efe's said it out loud, the first time she's mentioned it since she discovered the small box hidden inside his underwear drawer two weeks ago. In the silent flat, with the Thames glittering past the window, her hands had trembled as she lifted the box from its hiding place, brushed her fingers over the crushed burgundy velvet, and found the large creamy stone set in a thin gold band winking up at her.

Aunty Dora stays perfectly still, nothing more than the arch of an eyebrow in Efe's peripheral vision. 'You don't sound excited,' she says.

'He's a great guy,' Efe begins. 'He's stable. He works hard. He's dependable. He loves me.' She pauses. 'And I love him.'

'Really?'

'Of course I do,' Efe says, but after three and a half years, she knows she still isn't sure. If she'd carried on the list Efe would have to mention the things that annoy her too, and lately that list was growing exponentially. First there was the way he'd started speaking over her, ordering for her in restaurants, treating her like a child even though she's almost twenty-five. She wasn't sure if he'd always slurped his coffee or if this was a new development. All she knows now is that he breathes clumsily, fumbles through the same moves during sex then grunts as he climbs off her and does a heavy-footed plod into the kitchen to slurp his coffee some more. If she carried on, she'd have to mention how much she thinks of Sam still. Even since they've stopped speaking, he's still the first person she thinks to call when something good happens. She wonders if she's really sure what she wants, if she can ever be certain, if she might just miss the thing she's needed all along.

'Hmm,' Aunty Dora considers this. 'Are you trying to convince me or yourself?'

Efe sighs dramatically, lowers her head to the cool wall.

'I like him. Your parents like him. But you're the one whose opinion really matters.' She pauses. 'Maybe you don't want to hear this, but I always thought you'd end up with Sam . . . All that time you spent at his house when you were little, doing that film thing. What did you two call it?'

'Sunday movie marathons,' Efe says, chuckling to herself.

'And all those phone calls. The two of you spent hours on the landline so the internet wouldn't work and no one else could get through. Gosh, I used to think to myself, what on earth do these kids have to talk about every night? And after he found out you dropped out, the way that boy left everything and came down to see you. I thought to myself, huh? Isn't that something.'

Efe feels herself thawing, remembering it all. She lets out a soft groan and says, 'We're not even speaking right now.'

'That can be fixed with one phone call. Or better yet, are you going to his dad's birthday party?'

Two weeks later, Efe climbs out of a taxi still wondering if this is a good idea. She walks up to the front door, her heartbeat blaring in her ears, a large bottle of rum clenched in her sweaty palms. She knocks and waits, willing herself to stay, focusing all her attention on the 'Happy Birthday' banner sparkling behind the windowpane. A woman Efe doesn't recognise opens the door. Glancing at Efe's tight smile and gift in her hand, she says, 'Everyone's in the garden,' and steps to the side.

Efe has spent years in this house, slotting neatly in beside Sam's dad, Ken, his sister, Phoebe, and – Efe feels her breath catch – Sam. She treads through the near empty living room, past the armchair covered in coats. In the kitchen, she finds large coolers of fried rice and rice and beans on the table, all the counters crowded with aluminium trays of food, bowls heaped high with salad, coleslaw and fresh fruit. She nods approvingly at it. A few kids – Ken's friends' kids, Efe assumes – are loading up paper plates with golden spring rolls and kebabs. They scurry away, in fits of laughter, when the woman standing by the microwave shakes a plastic spoon in their direction. 'Richard, Michaela, if you don't—' but Efe doesn't hear the threat because she steps into the garden, where guests are hovering in small groups, a pillar of smoke wafting up from the barbecue, a half-dozen older women chatting in a small circle of wooden chairs.

Phoebe is the first one to notice Efe hovering, one hand still on the back door.

'Efe!' she shrieks, her voice high above the music. She tears herself away from a group of girls, fifteen-year-olds in matching shorts and spaghetti-strap tops, each a different colour of the rainbow. Just as Phoebe pulls Efe into a bear-hug, Efe spots Sam. His head spins towards her and there's the breaking of a hopeful smile that dramatically curves downwards when Brian steps down into the garden behind her.

'Hey, I'm Phoebe,' Phoebe waves and introduces herself.

'Brian,' Brian replies, extending a hand outwards.

For two hours Efe and Sam tactfully avoid each other. They spin in different orbits around the tiny garden.

'This is Brian.' Efe finds herself repeating the words to each new face. She says this to people she doesn't yet know. To the circle of aunties who wave her over, delighted and curious at the one white face in the crowd, plaguing him with a hundred questions. They welcome him in, grinning as he points to unfamiliar foods and asks, 'And what's this made of?' and 'Is that one spicy? Just a bit please.' And as the time passes, Efe's nerves dissipate. Somewhere along the way they find Ken and present him with his bottle of birthday rum.

There's the sound of a commotion nearby. At the far end of the garden, children hyped up on fizzy drinks are bouncing in an excited circle around Sam, who is pretending to spar with pint-sized fists. Soon enough it's five against one. The youngest ones, three- or four-year-old twins by Efe's estimation, hang around a leg each. And more kids race across the garden, ignoring their parents' half-hearted calls to leave Sam alone. It takes eight of them to bring him to his knees. Sam falls slowly, his cries exaggerated, one arm stretched towards the sky before he's lost beneath the bundle. An older boy drops heavily to the floor beside him, slapping a palm against the grass. 'Three, two, one . . . ding, ding, ding!' Most guests have stopped to watch. In the end one of the mums interrupts. 'Okay, that's enough,' she says, laughing. 'Let him go.' Reluctantly, the kids get back to their feet.

Efe, too, catches herself chuckling. Embarrassed, she shoots a subtle glance in Brian's direction and tucks a braid behind her ear.

'That's Sam, ri—' Brian begins, still watching the spectacle peter out, but something sparks in Efe and she cuts him off, makes a hurried excuse and dashes inside to the bathroom. Upstairs, perched on the edge of the tub, she waits for the spark to die down. On her way back downstairs, Efe hovers at the window. From here she can hear the tinny sound of Black Eyed Peas through the speakers and see Brian chatting happily to one of Ken's old bandmates.

Sam materialises at the top of the stairs, holding an ice pack to his brow, apparently just as embarrassed to see her as she is to see him. Their eyes dart away.

She's the first one to look back. 'Wow, they really got you.'

'Someone jabbed me in the eye.'

'Want me to find out which one?' Efe offers, but Sam isn't laughing. His face hardens.

'What are you doing here?'

'Your dad invited me.'

'But—' Sam sighs. 'Why'd you bring him?'

'He had the day off. I couldn't exactly say he wasn't welcome.'

'Whatever,' Sam says and turns towards the bathroom.

A desperate spark rises up in Efe and she steps into his path, raising a palm to the centre of his chest so his heart is thrumming against her fingertips. 'I actually . . . The only reason I came here . . .'

'What?'

'I wanted to talk to you.'

Sam's face doesn't change but something wary forms behind his eyes.

Efe's mouth is dry in an instant, but she pushes on, trying to grapple her thoughts while they swing on a pendulum.

'I—' she stammers. Exhales. *Oh God, why is this so hard?* she thinks. The words are clogging in her throat. She feels them choking her while the moment – their chance – is slipping away. She needs to say something to fix this, to bring them back to what they were. No, she needs to make them better than they were before. None of the games and mess this time. Just the two of them. Together. Everything good and right.

'I—' she begins again, as Sam's nostrils flare. She sees him shutting down and pounces, but not with the words she has planned. Instead she says: 'I don't know what I want.' She pauses, just as surprised as Sam is.

A muscle twitches in his jaw. He drags a palm across his face. 'I've had enough of this,' he says, pushing past and slamming the bathroom door behind him. Efe stands in the silence that follows. She has convinced herself that there is some invisible force drawing the two of them together, that they'd always snap back together – a two-piece puzzle – but now she can see he's cut himself loose and whatever it was hangs slack around her middle.

Efe can't find Brian in the garden. She backtracks through the house until she spots a flash of his T-shirt in the porch.

'There you are.' He smiles, slotting his phone into his pocket. 'I've got to go. Work.'

'You're leaving?' Efe repeats dumbly. 'It's a Saturday.'

'I know. I hate to leave.'

'But you're doing it anyway.'

Brian sighs. His gaze meets hers. 'This doesn't have to be an argument.'

'It's fine,' Efe says. A beep sounds outside. 'You already called a taxi?'

'I looked all over for you.' Brian taps his pockets, mumbles to himself as he checks off wallet, phone, keys. 'Stay with your friends. Have fun. I'll see you tonight,' he says.

'Sure.'

Sunken, Efe steps back into the garden. Above the heads of partying guests the last rays of sunshine radiate. She reaches for her bag and swings it over her shoulder right when Ken looks her way, a shot glass raised high in the air. 'Efe, your boyfriend asked me to tell you he had to leave.'

'Yeah, I know – I think I'll just—' Efe says, turning towards the house.

'Hey, not so fast.' Ken laughs. 'We just cracked open the rum.'

Efe wakes where they put her. As the alcohol thrums through her veins, the evening comes back to her in vague snatches: drinking games; dancing barefoot in the soft grass to Missy Elliott; flickering candles on an extravagant chocolate cake, so rich and sweet it made her eyes water; later a botched attempt at sobering up, huddled up on the kitchen counter, wolfing down lukewarm burgers with a side of mac 'n' cheese, her fingers smeared and sticky with ketchup. At some point in the night, Ken had to be helped up to his room, a friend under each of his arms, jolly, slurring, singing at the top of his lungs, snoring the moment his head touched the pillow. Then as they drifted into the early hours, the guests began to peel off.

Efe opens her eyes. Through the alcohol haze the room slowly comes into focus: Sam's room. Rather, his old room. It has been two years since he lived here, but lying here, sprawled out on top of the covers, a thin blanket draped over her, it still feels like his. She imagines his life has seeped into the walls, his presence felt in more than the light patches where posters were left too long on the walls, a ghostly feel to them in the interplay of light and dark. Efe searches for her phone. She palms the mattress, draws herself up and shakes out the blanket.

'Sam?' she whispers into the silence. It comes back to her then: their dismal conversation and her mouth refusing to say the things she'd planned on saying. It was like she was there, watching herself, watching the whole interaction – a train falling off its rails – and afterwards, all she was left with was the lax feeling at her middle that made her feel utterly alone.

'Sam?' she says again.

She's sure now. Sure as she listens to the dead-of-night house stirrings. Sure as the stairs creak under her bare feet. Sure as she prods the sofa with her big toe, whispers, 'Are you asleep?' until he wakes. She waits as the sleep washes away and he peers into the darkness and squints at her.

Through the doorway, in the kitchen, the neon-green numbers on the microwave turn from 3:59 to 4:00. A sound-less night.

'Efe?' He rubs his eyes and sits upright. The blanket rests on his shoulders. 'Are you still drunk?'

In response, Efe lowers herself onto his lap, places her knees on either side of him and hooks her fingers under his shirt.

'You are drunk.' It's not a question this time. There's a frustrated edge to his voice. 'We can't do this. You're out of it.'

'Shhhh,' she says, pressing her lips into his neck, his chest. 'I'm not drunk. I know what I want. I know who I want.'

Sam stills, then draws his head back to look her in the eye. 'You're sure?'

She nods, then kisses him fiercely. She moves along the right side of his face, feels the beginnings of stubble on her lips as her hands dip lower. In the kitchen, her phone flashes an alert, but the missed calls from Brian will have to wait. For now, Sam's lips are on hers and she's tasting a hint of mint on his tongue. Finally, Sam starts to move. His hands curl around her waist, lips press along her chest, little bursts that send shocks racing through her. She's gulping air, her back arched, face turned towards the ceiling.

'Shh,' he whispers as he lowers her down to the couch.

She reaches down, unhooks her knickers and wraps her knees around him, draws him close, lets out a low sigh as his fingers slip inside of her. A warm breath licks across the smooth, soft skin of her belly. There's no time for the clothes to come off fully. They kiss hungrily, a blanket draped over them. The world recedes as they come together, stifling moans in the quiet house.

Efe wakes before six with a dead arm, her head swimming in alcohol, Sam wrapped around her. She gets up, smooths out her crumpled dress and collects her things slowly: her bag from the garden, shoes from the hallway, phone from the kitchen.

At Brian's flat, she uses her key and is surprised by how quickly she's stopped thinking of it as home. He'll be on a run, she knows, thankful for an hour or so alone as she wanders from room to room, stuffs her things into a duffle bag. She wants to rid the place of any trace of her existence, disappear into the morning without explanation.

In the bathroom, she plucks her toothbrush from the holder, brushes her teeth and pops it into the bag still damp. Outside the windowless bathroom, storm clouds gather; thumb-sized people open umbrellas, unfold newspapers over their heads and hurry to shelter. The rain falls thick and hard and carries Brian home early.

Efe is almost done emptying her drawers. There are two drawers to go when she hears the front door open.

'Efe?' Brian's voice calls out, his footsteps a squeaky plod over the polished marble.

She looks at the clock. A snare closes around her. She cannot bring herself to respond, worries that her voice will give her away before she has the chance to order her spiralling thoughts. She glances up and sees he's at the bedroom door, flushed pink, wet hair hangs limp over his eyes.

'Hey, you,' he says. 'I waited up last night. Where were you?'

Efe holds completely still, summons her voice at an even keel. 'Nowhere. I drank too much and stayed over.'

'How was the rest of the party?'

She stays completely still, a small pile of pyjamas wilting in her hands as Brian kicks off his shoes, stretches into a lunge. His gaze flicks back to her. She hasn't answered.

'Good,' she says.

'What's with the bag?'

Efe tries to answer but the words are out of reach. Brian speaks again, his voice lower now. 'Why are you packing?'

'I thought you'd be on your run.'

'The rain . . . I cut it short.' He moves towards her, stops at the other side of the bed. 'Are you packing *all* of your things?'

'I have more things,' she says, 'at my place.'

'Your place?' He looks shocked for a second, then wounded. Through her eyelashes she watches as his head dips. 'How long are you gonna be at your place?'

'Bri—'

'Are you seriously doing this?' he asks.

'What do you want me to say,' she says, a whisper barely audible under the rain needling the glass.

'Don't go. Or at least tell me how the heck we got here. What's going on?'

'I'm sorry,' she exhales, hurrying to wipe away tears brimming.

'Sorry. That's it? Efe . . .' He reaches for her. 'I love you.'

She flinches. Her fingers contract around the bag handles. She'll have to come back for the rest.

'Did you hear me? I said I love you,' he says, frenzied now. She feels his cool, damp palm on her cheek, keeps her gaze level as he searches her face. 'Say something,' he says.

'I haven't been happy—'

'And I can help you through—'

'With you. I thought we could make it, but I'm not happy. I haven't been—'

'So what? It's all been a lie? Is that what you're saying?'

'I'm saying I want something else,' she says. 'I'm really sorry.'

He crumples. The path forward is empty. She allows herself
one last look to take it all in: the shape of his face, full mousy
brown hair, silvering at the temples. Five seconds. She counts
them under her breath. Then she makes her way past. Her
fingers close around the door handle and she steps out into
the world someone new.

MAY 2006

Ten Years Before

Abbey's first big show in London opens on a mild May evening. She's invited pretty much everyone she knows, so Sam and Efe have had this date pencilled in the diary for months. Sam is nearing the theatre, still thirty metres away when he spots Efe. She is on the phone, twirling a braid around her finger and pacing back and forth over a small section of pavement just outside the main doors. She looks up and smiles when she sees him approach, pausing so he can lean forward and kiss her.

'Sam's here, I gotta go,' she says, the phone still to her ear.

'Serwaa?' Sam mouths.

'Nanadwoa,' she mouths back.

'Tell her I said hi,' Sam whispers.

Efe nods, turning her attention back to the call. 'Yeah, definitely. Tell me how it goes. Bye.' She snaps the phone shut and slips her free hand into Sam's. 'I already did,' she says.

'And what's new with her?'

Efe considers this for a second. 'That army guy she's seeing wants to fly her out to the Ivory Coast. Just for a long weekend. She was walking me through her outfit choices.'

'Oh.' Sam raises an eyebrow. 'So, it's serious?'

Efe smiles. 'It might be. It looks like she really likes this one.'

They move towards the entryway, joining the short queue of people waiting for their tickets to be checked. 'Oh,' Efe adds, remembering, 'she wants to know if we're going to be in Ghana for Christmas. That's still the plan, right?'

'Yeah, let's do it,' Sam says, biting down on a smile. They've officially been together for eight and a half months. Things are going well – really well. On his morning commute, when Sam isn't poring through case files, trying to get ahead of the day's work, he finds himself circling adverts for flats in the newspaper; he spends his Sunday mornings scrolling through listings online and calling friends and friends of friends to ask for any recommendations. Sure, they'd be renting for now, but they'd be living under the same roof. Beyond that, Sam imagines buying a place with Efe. Then one day, not too far into the future, raising a family with her. He wants all of it – eventually – just like the movies. But for now, he's excited to meet Efe's family again, not just as another fragment of her and Serwaa's lives in London – but as Efe's boyfriend this time.

'How was your day?' Efe asks as they step into the auditorium.

'Good, nothing new to report,' he says, even though a more accurate description would be 'busy' or 'relentless'. In the almost three years since Sam joined Barnard, Brand & Associates, he's spent every day trying to set himself apart from the other junior members of the team. At work he's assertive and focused, speaking up until false confidence solidified into something real and his boss, Walter Barnard himself, had gone from nodding approvingly in meetings to seeking out Sam's opinion and asking Sam to take the new intern, who happened to be Walter's stepson, under his wing and show him the ropes.

'How's the Jameson case?'

'Walt's given me two more people, so we'll definitely be ready in time for the hearing.'

'Awesome.'

'Yours?'

'I got to sit in on a workshop today, we – I mean – Marilyn's started this whole programme, trying to bring in local artists to

109

work with kids in the community. Get them to see that working in a creative field is a viable option, y'know, whether that's art, music, drama. It might even help get our name out there.'

'And how was the workshop?' Sam asks.

'Good,' Efe says. 'I felt a bit silly at first. I haven't done anything like that since I was a kid, but it was fun. Amazing – actually.' She glances down, self-consciously tucking a braid behind her ear.

'You should do more of that,' Sam says, and he means it. For years he's seen her doodling on napkins, coffee cups, on pretty much every available surface. He knows that she can whittle away a whole afternoon absentmindedly sketching, just like she can spend a whole weekend gallery-hopping.

More often than not, Efe stays over at Sam's place and wakes up before him. Twice now Sam has awoken and caught her in the act of drawing something, creating something out of nothing as Sam likes to think of it, and the sight of her, bent over a piece of paper, awash with lilac morning light, makes him stop short and still.

Inside, the foyer is full of people and abuzz with murmured chatter. There are at least three hundred people, by Sam's estimation, the venue just a ten-minute walk from Piccadilly Circus and the main West End. *It's impressive*, he thinks to himself, *how Abbey has ended up here, doing exactly what she said she'd do all those years ago.*

'Remind me again what the play's about?' he asks.

'In Abbey's words it's all about "clashing cultures and generational friction". Her character's the daughter of immigrants who are freaking out because she moves in with her much older, very much-married boyfriend and his wife.'

'It sounds complex.'

'I think the word she used was "dynamic".'

Sam laughs.

'Tickets please,' an usher says, then leads the way to their seats. They stop in the stalls, the usher gesturing to two empty seats in the middle of the row. On both sides they are hemmed in by families with young kids. Sam glances at Efe, sensing her uneasiness.

He decides to be confident. 'Can we get past?' Sam says, leading the way into the row. The people rearrange themselves to let him past. He hesitates, practically standing over a woman with three kids under four; one on her lap; another, a girl, whining and pulling at her mother's skirt; the oldest, a boy, yanking down the fold-down chair and squealing with delight each time it snaps shut.

The woman looks up, flustered. Sam supposes she's in her thirties, older than they are, but she has large, wide-set eyes that make her look young and startled. She reminds him of his little sister.

Sam glances at the chair and clears his throat. 'E8 and 9?'

'Oh right,' the woman mutters and hurriedly yanks her son away from Sam's seat. She's overflowing with apologies; her son is wailing at the top of his lungs. Sam looks over his shoulder to where Efe is still hovering in the aisle, casting desperate looks around the rapidly filling auditorium. They both know there won't be any other available seats. The show is sold out. Efe meets Sam's eye, sighs and shuffles in beside him, sitting on the edge of her seat so she is as far as she can be from the bellowing child. She eyes them all with caution, as if she's been forced to sit beside a wild animal.

A minute passes. Instead of settling down, the kid is only getting louder, his face reddening by the second.

'Look, Tyler! This chair does the exact same thing,' the woman murmurs, pulling down the chair on her other side to demonstrate. Indignant, her son shakes his head and points at Sam's seat.

'That one!' he whines.

The woman glances at Sam nervously. 'Sorry about this. The babysitter cancelled at the last minute but he should calm down soon,' she says, then leans forward to rummage around in a bag. 'He's just overtired.'

She offers her son a bag of apple slices which he promptly dumps on the floor. In the end she manages to placate him with a bag of Wotsits. He's sniffling, stuffing handfuls of crisps into his mouth, but at least he isn't crying. Relieved, the woman slumps slightly and lets out a long breath, then turns to Sam. 'So how did you hear about the show?' she asks.

'We know one of the actresses. Abbey. She's my girlfriend's cousin and I've known her since secondary school.'

The woman beams. 'Abbey's wonderful, a rare find from what I hear. My husband, David, is the director. He's talked so much about her.'

'And you are?'

'Tara.'

'I'm Sam.' He extends a hand out for Tara to shake. 'And this is my girlfriend, Efe.'

At the sound of her name, Efe's gaze shifts towards them. She smiles a brief, tight smile, then looks back at the stage.

Behind Tara's back, her son is smearing orange dust into his clothes. Sam opens his mouth to say something, just as Tara's daughter squeezes into the space between them and deposits a toy in Sam's lap.

'And who are these little ones?'

'This,' Tara begins, gesturing towards her daughter, 'is Taylor. And that one's Tyler. Say hi, Ty. And our youngest is Teresa.'

Sam leans forward to get a closer look. A small, round face nuzzles out from between the folds of a blanket. 'She's tiny,' Sam coos.

Tara smiles again and bounces the baby in her arms. 'Fourteen weeks.'

*　*　*

By the time the show ends, Efe is even more agitated. They are standing in a tiny, brick-walled bar, deep in the basement of the theatre. A faint smell is emanating from the walls that reminds Sam of the Central Line in summer. He watches as Efe dabs at the orangey stain on her blouse with a damp tissue. It's the result of one of Tara's kids – it was dark, so Sam isn't definite which one – squeezing a carton of Capri-Sun too tight, the liquid arching in a neat rainbow, right over Sam's lap and landing on Efe. They haven't seen Tara or her kids since the lights went up.

'I don't understand why she didn't step out of the theatre earlier,' Efe fumes. 'Abbey's going to come with her inquisition to ask what we thought of the show, and I won't be able to say anything because I couldn't hear a damn thing.'

Sam doesn't understand her anger. He wants to laugh. 'They're kids. Kids cry. They can't help it.'

'I know that,' Efe mumbles. 'But if your kids can't sit through a two-hour play, don't bring them.'

'She probably only came to support her husband.'

'Fine. Support him, but leave the kids at home. How do you not see that they ruin everything?'

You can't be serious, Sam thinks, but a small worried bead begins knocking around in his mind. The comment unsettles him. He wonders if he should push it, but a bigger part of him is afraid of where the conversation might lead.

Instead, Sam says, 'I'll get some drinks,' and makes his way over to the bar. There are just two bartenders. The queue is five-people deep. For a while, Sam gets stuck making small talk with the tall, bearded actor who played Abbey's character's dad, who's getting progressively drunker the longer they wait. Almost fifteen minutes have passed by the time Sam makes his way back to Efe. He moves carefully, trying to keep the glasses steady as he elbows his way back through the crowd.

'There you are,' Efe says when she sees him. She's more relaxed now. Sam spies an empty glass in her hand, which she puts down and accepts the red wine Sam holds out for her. With her free hand, she gestures towards Abbey. 'Look who it is.'

'Abbey,' Sam grins, stepping in for a hug. She has changed out of her costume and is wearing all black now. Her hair, which has been dark brown for as long as Sam has known her, is bone-straight, a jet black so dark and shiny it moves like a shimmering river after dark. She looks poised, elegant.

'I'm so glad you made it,' Abbey says. 'What did you think?'

Sam is quick to give praise, rattling off a response about her stage presence and amazing performance in the final act. By the end, Abbey is practically bouncing on the balls of her feet, giddy.

'Loved it. I couldn't look away,' Efe echoes.

'This one's gonna be a star,' a man adds, stepping into the space beside Abbey. It takes Sam a moment to recognise David, the director, mostly because he's aged at least ten years since the headshot in the programme. There are flecks of grey in his beard and his hairline has begun to drift backwards.

Abbey giggles. 'If I do make it, I'll have you to thank.'

'It will be all you. You were born to be on the stage.' To Efe and Sam, he adds, 'I tell you, the moment I set my eyes on her I knew.'

Abbey laughs again, placing a hand on his, teasing. 'But you still made me audition?'

'Only so everyone else could see it too.'

They're both a little drunk, speaking louder than necessary and flirting recklessly in full view of the cast and audience. David's hand moves to Abbey's lower back. Sam and Efe exchange a wordless look. He takes a sip of his lemonade.

David turns his attention to Efe. 'And what do you do?' he asks.

'I'm a junior curator at the Launi Gallery.'

'Ah,' David says with a smile, 'I can always sense a fellow creative.'

'I wouldn't say that. I do bits and pieces. We're a small team, just three of us.'

'I'd love to come by some day.' Sam feels his jaw tighten, watching as David's gaze strays up and down Efe's body. Abbey sees it too and her smile falters, but David is still lingering, his eyes fixed on Efe.

'Can I count on you to show me around?'

'Err—' Efe begins, but Sam has already taken an unconscious step forward. A split second later he feels Efe's fingers hook around his arm. His gaze flits towards her. Something silent passes between them.

Sam takes a moment to steady himself. 'We met your wife and kids,' Sam says, a little pointedly.

'You did?' David says, his hand slipping from Abbey's lower back, throwing a frantic look over his shoulder. 'I thought they headed home.'

'I think they did,' Sam says. 'Cute kids. The youngest is just a few weeks old, right?'

David nods.

'How long's the run?' Efe asks, directing her question at Abbey.

'Six weeks here, then we'll go on tour over the summer. We'll be in fifteen different cities up and down the country. Next year, maybe New York. Broadway. David's got connections.'

'New York?' Efe says, a wistful look settling on her face. 'That's incredible. I've always wanted to go.'

DECEMBER 2006

Ten Years Before

It is mid-morning and Sam is still asleep. Twice this morning Efe has checked in on him, walking through the shared living room and peeking into the bedroom that was Serwaa's before she got married, each time surprised to find him still curled up under a thin sheet. She is too warm to sleep under anything. It is December so the harmattan haze has come low to kiss the earth and it feels like the whole Sahara is wafting through the air. Even under normal circumstances, Efe has never been able to sleep past 7 a.m. when she is in Ghana, something about the light and the sound of the house girls going about their tasks rouses her in a way traffic passing through the high street never does. On her third trip, Efe climbs in beside him, wraps an arm over his chest and slips a leg between his until they are interlocked like a pretzel.

She misses this. Her parents refuse to let them sleep in the same room; both of them insist on keeping up appearances even though Efe and Sam now live together in a studio flat in London.

'Morning,' Sam says, eyes still closed, a sleepy smile spreading across his lips.

'When are you getting up?'

'What time is it?'

'Almost eleven.' She burrows closer, their faces just centimetres apart when his eyes blink open. He reaches a hand back towards his shoulder blades.

'My back's so stiff,' he says.

'What did you expect?' she says, thinking about the day before, the four hours Sam spent playing on his hands and knees with two-year-old Kobby, while Serwaa, Joseph and Efe watched on, chatting and catching up. 'You're getting old,' she adds, teasing.

'Hey!'

'Oh my gosh! Your breath.' And at this both of them are laughing, jostling, Efe wriggling away and Sam pulling her closer.

Half an hour later, Efe is making her way down the corridor when she glimpses her mum lingering on the landing, wearing a white T-shirt and retying the long green skirt at her waist. Efe considers turning back before Maame sees her, but she thinks of that a second too late, right after Maame's face has lit up at the sight of her.

'Efe,' she says brightly, looping her arm through her daughter's. 'Come. Let's talk.'

Efe sits awkwardly on one of the armchairs in Maame and Paa's bedroom, watching as Maame settles into the one opposite. She feels a vague sense of unease, waiting for her mum to begin.

'I'm glad you brought Samson here. He's a very nice boy. Very polite. Good home-training.'

'I know,' Efe says slowly, trying to work where her mum is going with this.

'But you shouldn't let this thing go on for too long without making it all official.'

Efe opens her mouth to speak, but Maame isn't done yet. 'Even nice boys need to be serious. They need some encouragement. Me, I want a grandchild but you shouldn't think of bringing one into this house before Samson has made his intentions known.'

Efe balks. 'You have a grandchild. Kobby isn't even three.'

'You shouldn't let him be the only one.'

117

Efe looks to the door, silently hoping that Paa will make an appearance or one of the house girls will burst in screaming about a fire. She prays for any interruption. Anything.

A few tense seconds pass. Efe takes a deep breath and rises from her seat. 'I should get back to Sam.' She is across the threshold, Maame a few steps behind her when they bump into Sam on the landing. He is showered and dressed now, skin over-moisturised and gleaming. As Efe draws nearer, she catches the scent of his cologne and grows heady with it, desire instantly thrumming through her. She loves that he still makes her feel like that.

'Samson.' Maame's voice is high and bright again.

'Good morning, Mrs Owusu,' Sam says.

'What are your plans for this evening?'

'Nanadwoa's having a party,' Efe cuts in. 'I told you about it yesterday.'

'Oh.' Maame frowns. 'I was hoping the two of you would join me tonight at church.'

She gestures to her T-shirt, which Efe only now realises has 'Holy Ghost Revival 2006' emblazoned in green above Maame's breast. Efe can think of nothing worse than a forty-eight-hour event, praying and worshipping in a sweaty amphitheatre alongside six hundred other people.

'Nanadwoa's expecting us,' Sam says, slotting his hand into Efe's, their fingers intertwined.

'What time will you be back? I'll make sure there's food for you.'

'It's a party, Mum. We'll eat—' Efe says, but Maame cuts her off.

'Has Efe ever made *ampesi* for you?'

Sam looks at Efe for confirmation. 'Was that the one with boiled plantain?'

'Yeah,' Efe says, and turns back to Maame. 'We've only made it a couple of times.'

At this Maame's lips tighten in displeasure. 'You cook *together*?'

118

'I taught Sam how to make a few things. His *kontomire* might even be better than mine.'

'I see,' Maame says, and Efe feels the corners of her mouth curl up in response. She's confident that Paa hasn't cooked a single meal since her parents got married in the late 1970s, and imagines anything beyond lighting the stove to reheat stew is beyond him.

Maame clears her throat. 'She learned it from me, so I'll make some today and you can see how the master does it.'

'Sounds great.' Sam nods.

'Anyway, we should go,' Efe says, tugging Sam's hand and pulling him in the direction of the stairs.

That evening, they take a cab to Aunty Yaa's house. The last time Efe was in Ghana in December was years ago, and she stares through the windshield at the lingering harmattan haze, her eyes dry and aching. She remembers it from her childhood: weeks a year when she couldn't see further than her fingertips; dust that settled on her eyelashes; how her lips would permanently be cracked and bleeding. All around them cars are crawling forward, red lights shining for as far as she can see.

When they get to the party, Efe recounts the day's events to Nanadwoa. She is nursing her second drink, feeling happy and tipsy, while Nanadwoa is at the stove piling plates high with food. The sharp smell of kerosene lingers in the air.

'My mum is too much,' Efe says, laughing. 'She flashed my phone at least five times this afternoon. My credit is nearly finished.'

'What does she want now?' Nanadwoa asks.

'To know what Sam wants to eat on Christmas Day.'

'Ey.' Nanadwoa turns, her brows hunched together. 'Didn't she ask you to smuggle turkey all the way from UK?'

'And it took up half the space in my hand luggage,' Efe complains, 'but Sam doesn't like turkey so now she wants to know what else he will eat.'

Nanadwoa laughs. 'What about your dad?'

'He loves Sam too. They've been playing chess and *oware* every afternoon since we landed.' She pauses, thinking back to the hours Sam spent practising until he could finally beat the computer. 'Actually, I think he only learned because he wanted to impress my dad.'

'You better not let that man go hungry. I can't have your mum calling to say I didn't feed him,' Nanadwoa jokes and hands Efe two plates topped with *waakye*, spaghetti, meat stew and a single boiled egg on the side.

Efe rolls her eyes but takes a plate through to the other room. Sam is standing near the centre of the room, surrounded by some of Nanadwoa's guy friends, talking animatedly about football. Somehow Sam, who only pays attention to football when it's the World Cup, has won over four guys he met just an hour ago. Secretly Efe loves it. She loves how Nanadwoa's friends have thrown their arms open wide to welcome him; loves how easy it was hanging out with Sam, Serwaa and Joseph; loves that Sam has started to think of her family as his. She presses a hand to his side lightly and passes him the plate.

'Thanks,' he mouths.

Back in the kitchen, Nanadwoa picks up the conversation where they left off. 'You should just get married,' she says, looking up from her plate. 'No matter what you do he's already their son.'

Efe forces herself to laugh. She wants to make light of Nanadwoa's comment but, in truth, she's started to think about forever. There are mornings when Sam brings her breakfast in bed just because he knows she's had a hard week at work. A handful of times they've stayed up talking all night, reminding Efe of the late-night calls during their university years that continued long after Efe dropped out. She likes being with him. She likes loving him. And it surprises her how different it was with Brian, how she could wave goodbye in the morning and barely give him a second thought until she walked into the flat late at night. Then, she'd told herself she was just busy, that if she had two minutes to think she'd find herself thinking of him, but it isn't like that with Sam. Thoughts of him crowd her mind whatever she's doing, whatever time of day.

'Okay,' Nanadwoa says, wiping her hands at last, 'let me see to my guests.'

Efe stays, finishing off her food and hurriedly washing the plates in the sink before Nanadwoa returns. She is rinsing the last one when she hears a voice behind her.

'Ten years later and you're in the same place I last saw you.'

Efe doesn't need to turn around to know who it is. She knows the moment something shifts in the atmosphere, as if all the air around her is thinning to nothing. She recognises that deep, resonant voice.

'Daniel,' Efe says, reaching for a napkin to wipe her hands. 'I don't think it's been that long. Maybe nine years.'

'It feels longer,' he says, nodding slowly. 'How are you?'

'Well,' she says.

His gaze drifts across her body. 'I can see that.'

A ripple of energy passes between them. Daniel is taller than Efe remembers. Back when Efe was fifteen and Daniel sixteen, they'd been the same height, but now he is at least five inches taller and stocky. There are other, more subtle changes. A more defined jaw. A small, jagged scar just below his right eye. He still has the same broad nose, the same full lips, the bottom one a warm pink. Efe remembers spending hours kissing those lips, years ago, back when she discovered she was one of many girls Daniel invited round when his parents were at church conferences and gone for eight or nine hours at a time. Still, every time he opens his mouth to speak, Efe feels her heartbeat quickening, her body fizzing like tiny electric shocks are pulsing under her skin.

He is smiling into his drink, eyes lingering. Efe gives her head a small shake and reminds herself to speak.

'Did you make it to the US?' she asks.

'Chicago. I'll be going back in September for medical school.'

Efe beams. 'I knew you'd do well.'

'But you didn't stick around to see it for yourself.'

At this, she laughs. 'Do you really need an audience?'

'Not just any audience.'

Efe falls silent and lets her gaze drop to the floor. Desperately she wishes her face would stay still, even though she can feel a thousand emotions rushing through her all at once.

'What about you?' Daniel asks. 'What do you do now?'

'I'm a junior curator at a gallery.'

Efe meets his eyes again, noticing how his eyebrows rise as a smile moves across his face.

'Good for you,' he says, then pauses. 'You should know my mum still asks after you.'

'And what about you?' Efe asks, surprised by her own boldness.

'Why do you think I'm here? It's not like we ever got to explore this thing between us.'

She swallows. Her eyes flick to the open door. *This is how rumours start*, Efe thinks. *He's always been a flirt.*

'I should go,' she says firmly. 'My boyfriend is in the other room.'

'*Eh-hen*, so you're not married? That means I still have a chance.'

'That's a big assumption.'

'Just stating facts,' he says, moving so close Efe can feel his body heat radiating. For a second, she thinks he'll lean in and kiss her, but he stays like that. Neither of them move closer. Efe's gaze drifts to the door again. She steels herself and walks on without looking back.

Sam is at the far end of the living room, fishing a bottle of Supermalt out of a bucket of ice water. Efe makes her way over, wrapping both arms around his waist and resting her cheek between his shoulder blades.

'Hey,' he says, turning, pulling her closer. He has a curious look on his face. 'Everything okay?' he asks.

She nods. 'Everything's great.'

Nine Years Before

The night before her wedding, Efe doesn't sleep. She is awake for hours, back in her childhood bed in Ghana, her nerves ripening into jittery anticipation, as the day begins to dawn. Compared to the two years that have hurtled past at break-neck speed, this last night creeps on slowly, Efe listening to the steady rhythm of aunties pounding yam in the garden, the crunch of tyres on the driveway, and Maame's clear and level voice, directing the caterers and decorators.

She knew her parents would be thrilled the moment they'd heard the news. After all, Maame had been eager to plan another wedding since Serwaa's, and her not-so-subtle hints about 'making it all official' had been getting more insistent for a year now, ever since she'd heard that Sam and Efe had moved in together. And, true to form, the day they'd announced the engagement, over a blurry Skype call that kept freezing and glitching, Maame had erupted into a flurry of happy tears and promised to take care of everything.

The guests begin arriving at 7 a.m. Within an hour the garden is swollen with people eager to take their seats in the newly erected tent. The truncated version of the guest list that Sam imagined, but Efe never believed was possible, has long since been abandoned; almost three hundred people are downstairs and more will arrive to celebrate after the official knocking ceremony.

Efe expected her friends to be here, helping her get ready, Serwaa at the very least, everyone laughing and joking like kids at a sleepover. She hasn't seen them in hours and suspects Maame has roped them into helping unload chairs or forced them to line the hallways with flowers. Instead of them, Efe only has her make-up artist for company. The girl is young. She's probably a year or two out of senior high school, but her face is set in stern concentration and she speaks in a firm, clipped way that means Efe is quick to follow her instructions and says nothing about the noise of her heeled sandals hammering on the tiles.

'Look down,' the girl directs and applies a dense layer of setting spray. After it dries, she holds up a mirror for Efe to see the final look.

'Oh wow,' Efe murmurs. She'd asked for a natural look, but barely recognises the face looking back at her. Her features seem sharp, her heart-shaped face angled and flawless, her wrists and crown adorned gold, her dark skin radiant with a shea-butter afterglow. Above her eyes, gold halos of eyeshadow melt into green, her eyelashes extend for miles. She wonders if this is too much while pressing a finger to the tight cornrow. Beneath the glossy, black weave, her scalp is faintly throbbing. She'd planned to wear micro-braids that would last the honeymoon and a few months after the wedding, but Maame had peeked out from under the hooded dryer and convinced Efe to go with a weave styled in a complicated updo.

'That's the way all the young people are wearing it now,' she'd insisted.

Similarly, two months before the wedding, Maame had called and declared she'd found the perfect cloth and presented it to the grainy webcam like an offering. All fifteen yards of kente were a deep emerald woven together with wisps of gold and amethyst thread. Together, they'd pored through magazines and pieced together elements until they had the design just right. And that week, Maame had dedicated every evening to standing over the seamstress's shoulder and over-seeing its creation. Now, swivelling towards the full-length mirror, Efe stands enraptured, taking in the intricate beading along the neckline, the high back to cover her scars, the figure-hugging material suddenly expanding into an elaborate trumpeting skirt, forming a full circle almost two metres behind her. She had always imagined a classic look, but this version of her is poised and stylish. She is more grateful than she could put into words.

'*Medaase paa,*' Efe says as the girl packs her things into a bag and slips out of the room with a brief smile. A moment later there's a knock at the door.

'Come in,' Efe calls and looks over her shoulder as Serwaa enters the room, dressed in white bridesmaids' cloth, Kobby on her hip, a neat rainbow of emerald kente at her waist.

'Aww, you look beautiful,' Serwaa gushes, holding out a small bowl of still-warm fried plantain. 'This is for you.'

Efe accepts the food gratefully and watches as Serwaa settles the squirming toddler on the bed. She leans over to wipe snot leaking from her son's nose. Efe wants to spring forward, save her powder-blue sheets from grubby hands, but decides to restrain herself and keep an eye on his every move.

'All this heat and he has a cold,' Serwaa says even though Efe doesn't ask.

'How's Sam?' Efe says. All morning she's wanted to text Sam, despite the fact that his UK phone doesn't work here and they're rarely apart for long enough to need separate SIM cards.

'Alive,' Serwaa says.

Efe huffs. 'I'm gonna kill Nakwesi. I *told him* Sam's not a big drinker.'

'Nakwesi takes his duties very seriously, but it sounds like he took it easy on Sam – just Guinness and a couple of shots of bitters,' she says, with a shrug and an expression that says, what did you expect?

'Is everything else set up?'

'The people Maame hired brought too much *wahala* – common schoolboys –' she hesitates as Efe's expression grows nervous – 'but it's fine, we finished it ourselves. It's wonderful. The guests are happy. The peacocks are calm—'

'Peacocks?'

'Don't ask. Someone Dad works with keeps them as pets.'

Efe gives her head a small shake. 'Don't you think it's too much?'

'For *our* parents?' Serwaa raises an eyebrow. 'Have you forgotten that there were three ice sculptures at my wedding – in the middle of July?' She throws her head back and laughs. 'You know they always do too much and Mum loves to put on a show. You might have avoided all of this if you married the *obroni*.'

Efe chuckles. 'And you don't think it's too soon for Sam and me—'

'You've known each other ten years, since you were – what – sixteen?'

Efe nods, wringing her hands. 'I know. I just worry. We're not always on the same page. Sometimes I think I'm going to let him down or screw things up. He wants us to be a family with kids and all of that, and I want him, I do, but not the rest of it. He says it's fine, right now, but he'll just keep pushing and—' Efe's voice cracks. Tears gather in her eyes.

'Hey, hey, stop that. You're going to ruin your make-up,' Serwaa says, reaching for a tissue and dabbing Efe's eyes, carefully, catching every tear before it falls. Afterwards, she holds Efe and it feels like they are young again, pressed together on a bunk bed, the ceiling just above their heads.

'Talk to him,' Serwaa says softly. 'I don't know everything, but I do know you should keep the lines of communication open.'

Efe nods, letting Serwaa take her hands in hers. She squeezes, and Efe feels her worries lifting.

'You can make it work,' Serwaa says. 'People have made it through far worse. Take me and Joseph. We don't always agree. I thought I'd be collecting my degree by now, but Kobby came along so quickly and Joseph still needs time for his business to get off the ground. But we've talked about it. The world won't end if I wait for Kobby to get a bit older before I continue my studies.' She gives Efe's hands an encouraging squeeze back. 'You and Sam will be just fine. Never in my life have I seen two people better for each other.'

'Thank you,' Efe says and they hug again, Serwaa's calm energy seeping into her sister. When they release, Serwaa's eyes have filled with tears.

'What?'

'It's just so sweet,' Serwaa says. 'One more thing.' She dips a hand into the plastic bag dangling from her wrist. 'Sam stopped by last night and asked me to give this to you.'

Efe unclasps the palm-sized box. She slips the delicate, gold necklace out and, in her hands, the diamonds catch the light. She traces a manicured finger over the graceful infinity loop. 'It's gorgeous,' Efe murmurs, and Serwaa reaches out a hand and helps her with the needle-thin clasp.

When the knocking ceremony begins, Efe goes to stand by the window, trying to squint through the billowing swathes of creamy white chiffon. She has to hand it to her mum, it's quite amazing what they have done with the place. What is usually a sparse, barren corner of their garden is now an architectural feat, draped in flowers shipped in from Kenya the night before. Everywhere she looks her parents' lavish love is on full display.

She watches as the Mensahs arrive, Sam first, followed by Ken and Phoebe, trailed by a delegation of thirty people bearing gifts. The music is loud and jubilant, the guests who are able to stand are up on their feet, clapping and craning their necks to watch the procession. Once inside the tent, the music dips and, though Efe can hear the drawl of voices coming through the speakers, she can't quite make out the words. She imagines the families are greeting each other, gifts being presented to Efe's proud parents. It's only when the sound of laughter rises up from the garden that she knows the formal proceedings are over and it'll soon be time for her to make an appearance.

Efe is hot beneath the cloth. Without the blasting air conditioner, there is a languorous heat in the air, the morning still and breezeless. Aunty Dora's arm is clasped around Efe's bicep to stabilise her, and she whispers encouragements as they take wobbly, shuffling steps to the far end of the garden. Efe walks slowly, navigating the heavy weight of the train behind her, kicking out the trumpeting skirt with each step. Grass gives way to wooden slats. Chairs scrape and her skin prickles as she passes, her dress a punctuation of colour amongst a tide of guests in white. A ripple of approval spreads across the garden.

For the fourth time that morning, Pastor Eric, who is acting as emcee and the spokesperson for Efe's family, raises the mic to his lips and asks Sam, 'Is this the beautiful flower you have come all the way from UK to pick?'

A taut hush falls across the room. She's holding her breath as Sam's fingers pinch the corners of the cloth. Suddenly, he is right in front of her, their faces are only inches apart; his eyes light up, an adorable grin stretched from cheek to cheek. Out of the corner of her eye, she can see the guests watching them intently, waiting for Sam's answer. But she doesn't think about them; she thinks about Sam and how much she wants to lean forward and kiss him.

'Is this the flower?' Pastor Eric repeats.

'Yes,' Sam says, beaming. Close by there is the frantic clicking of a camera shutter. When the clapping dies down and they emerge from beneath the cloth, Efe blinks at the harsh daylight and tent sparkling with colour. She lets her eyes sweep the room, returns Phoebe's subtle thumbs up. Beside her, Ken smiles happily, half focused on the festivities, the other half focused on Nakwesi, who's leaning into the gap between Ken and Phoebe, explaining a play by play of the proceedings. The families sit facing each other, so Efe has to turn and look over her shoulder to see Paa dabbing reddened eyes and Maame pressed as close to him as possible without climbing into his lap. Bottles of schnapps and cellophane-wrapped hampers are nestled at their feet. Just off to the side, by Serwaa and Joseph, are suitcases stuffed to the brim with luxury toiletries, clothes and other gifts. All of the guests are clutching dark green gift bags and fanning themselves with large souvenir fans, a stretched and over-saturated photo of Sam and Efe printed on the pleated fabric, a photo Efe has never seen before. She has no idea where Maame found it.

'Very well,' Pastor says, addressing the crowd. 'We have a saying here in Ghana, *Woforo dua pa a na yepia wo*, which means it is when you climb a good tree that we push you. As a community we will not support the poor decisions, but –' he gestures first to the front row where the rail-thin elders sit in pride of place, then to Efe and Sam – 'we can all agree this match is a very good choice indeed.'

In her peripheral vision, Efe sees Maame's head bob in agreement. She says a hearty amen.

Pastor continues, 'All the charms of abroad life and our dear daughter has found one of our own. Praise be to God.' One of the photographers nears and Efe feels the corners of her mouth lift in response. A second later, Sam's hand slips into hers. They're both nervous, overly aware of the roomful of eyes sizing them up.

Efe thinks about everything that led to this moment; the easy conversations: Sam joining in with phone calls back home, Efe's open invitation to hang out with Sam's family; the afternoons teaching him to cook her favourite meals;

breakfasts catching up about colleagues and meetings; their days bookended with each other; the gradual enmeshing of their lives and all the things they do for each other without it being asked; all the things they don't have to explain. Sometimes they're happy just to sit together in silence; the roots of their lives deepening and growing ever more entwined, seeing each other in ways that are closed off to the rest of the world, realising slowly and all at once, this is the beginning of forever. In truth, Efe can't picture anyone else standing up here with her. There's no one else she could imagine choosing to be with again and again. No one else who calms her like he does, makes her feel like anything she could possibly worry about is already taken care of – like nothing could take them by surprise.

Pastor Eric continues, gesticulating to Sam's family for the guests who haven't been paying attention. 'Everything is in order. Samson has come with the support of his family, brought good gifts and made his intentions known. So for the last question, I will hand over to our dear brother Paa.'

Paa gets up to speak in careful, considered words. 'Efe, Sam,' he begins, 'as a father all you can hope for is the best for your children. This world is not easy-o, but we are very happy you have decided on this course and hope that you love each other well and grow together in all the years to come.'

'Amen,' a voice in the crowd calls.

He pauses, lets out a breath like a low whistle. 'Efe, you have our blessing, but this choice is your own. What do you say to this proposal?'

Efe's gaze flits across her parents, Sam's family and all the watching guests. A protracted silence follows in which the world falls silent and all Efe can feel is Sam's hand in hers.

'Yes,' she says and the guests clap, cheer and holler.

JULY 2008

Eight Years Before

Sam steps out of the cafe and into the street. The bell rings out behind him and the hum of industrial fridges, the calm lull of Italian chatter over the radio and the scent of baking pastry is replaced by the smoggy London smell. All around him the high street is waking. Dog-walkers, Sunday morning joggers and other early risers scuttle down the pavement under the watch of a dozen storefront windows. A bus peels away from the bus stop and Sam makes a quick dash across the road, the coffee cups teetering in their Styrofoam tray. An Americano for him. A vanilla latte for his wife. He smiles to himself, still loving the sound of that word.

In his other hand, he keeps the freshly made cannoli upright. The warmth seeps into his palm and the honeyed aroma floats up from the box, a smell that takes him back to their engagement. One glorious week off before his official start date as an associate lawyer, five of those days in Italy, where they'd picked up coffee and cannoli every morning, napped in the afternoons and strolled through Como's cobbled streets at dusk; and on the last night, out on a boat, the city reduced to lights glinting on dark waters, he'd proposed, and Efe had said yes. Then she'd thrown her head back and laughed, remarking that it was *so like Sam* to make a simple holiday into something monumental. He'd secretly hoped that would be the beginning of a tradition. Something theirs alone to take home.

To the right of the nail salon, Sam rearranges the things he's carrying, slides a key into the front door and climbs the narrow stairway up to the studio flat. All winter they've slept squashed together, wearing jumpers and jogging bottoms on top of pyjamas, saving scrupulously, watching the puffs of condensation spill from their mouths, the flat wheezing and shifting in the small hours.

And now they've made it to summer. Efe lies facedown, a thin sheet covering her middle and one leg, the other leg sticking out over the edge of the mattress. Through sheer pyjamas, Sam can make out the outline of her back, the hourglass dip at her waist and the decades-old scars.

'I'm back,' he says, nudging the front door closed with his foot.

Efe stirs and lifts her head from the pillows. She yawns and flops over. 'What time did you get in last night?'

'Two thirty,' Sam says and holds the pastries aloft. 'I got coffee and cannoli.'

'Awww, happy anniversary, babe.'

Sam smiles and edges past the foldaway bed. Unfolded it takes up most of the floorspace; the rest of the space taken over by a tiny kitchen, a rickety table with two chairs, and the bathroom, which is more of an offshoot from the main room than a room in its own right. He kicks off his shoes and climbs back into bed fully dressed.

They sit shoulder to shoulder, biting into buttery puffs of pastry and taking small sips of coffee, now decanted into gilded teacups, part of a wedding present from Efe's parents and probably the most expensive thing in the studio.

'Ready?' Sam says and reaches into the bedside drawer for the gifts he's stashed there. A paper anniversary. Three hundred and sixty-five days.

'This is for you,' Efe says, placing a gift bag on Sam's lap. He peeks inside, pulls out framed prints from the wedding. Frozen-in-time versions of them stare up from beneath the glass.

In the first photo they're in matching kente cloth, flanked by Efe's parents on one side, Ken and Phoebe on the other, Ghana lush and shining all around them. In the second photo the party is in full swing, both Sam and Efe dancing, Efe sweating off her make-up, uncaring, beaming, the unsmiling elders just visible in the background.

'What do you think?'

'I love it, thank you.'

He waits, watching as she unwraps her gift. It's an elegant leather five-year diary with thick, creamy pages, the type of practical gift Sam would've chosen for himself. He watches her face intently, searching for a reaction. She runs her fingers over the deep purple leather, her married name Efe Owusu-Mensah engraved in golden flourishes on the front.

'Open it,' Sam hears himself say. On the inside he's jotted down things like: *Efe's promotion to Senior Curator, Sam makes Junior Partner, buy a house, visit Ghana.* In May 2010 Sam's written down *Baby?* in neat slim letters.

At this, he notices a tightening of her lips. Her finger hovers over the word, then comes down on the page until the characters are blocked out completely. For several long moments there's nothing but the sound of pigeons cooing on the window ledge and voices rising up from the street.

She clears her throat. 'Seems like you've got it all figured out.'

Sam's eyes flick to her face. He's nervous now and wraps an arm around her waist, kisses the spot where her baby hairs spill onto her forehead.

'Don't get mad.'

'I'm not mad,' she says. 'I just hate the pressure. I'd rather focus on work. I'm good at it – really good. I think I could really make something of myself.'

'We don't have to have a kid. I'll take any future as long as you're in it.'

She relaxes then, rests her cheek on his shoulder, snuggles deeper into the sheets. 'I don't wanna get up,' she murmurs.

'We can stay here . . . start making babies.' He lifts her hand to his face, presses his lips to her yellowy palm.

'You're gonna need your other wife for that.'

'She's all booked up until 2020.'

'What a shame.' Sam feels Efe's arms loop around his neck and shifts until he's hovering above her. He leans forward and kisses her nose. 'Just picture it: a baby with your nose,' he says. Another kiss. 'And your eyes.' Another kiss. 'And your lips.'

'What does it have of you?'

'My brain—'

'What's wrong with my brain?'

'Fine.' He laughs. 'Your brain. All of you. Every single cell.'

'Eh, I'm not convinced. When Serwaa was born it took me at least two years to get used to her being around.'

Sam laughs. Through the tugging of clothes and tangling of bedsheets that follows, the diary flops to the floor and lands with a muted thud. But it's all there – a neat little life down on paper. They don't know yet how easily an unplanned life can surface and settle, like waking up to a snow-covered world where everything recognisable is buried.

Sam checks his watch again and picks up the pace as he steps off the train, slipping through the gaps between the slow-moving evening commuters and breezing through the barriers. Just this morning he promised Efe he'd be at the gallery an hour early to help set up, but consistently underestimates the time needed to cross the city and didn't account for signal failures on the Underground.

Only at two other points in her career has she been this excited about an artist; the first was a Pakistani painter, who she'd managed to secure two pieces from. The second was a Kenyan MA student. And now Nico. Nico, the inimitable photographer who Efe has been speaking about for weeks, enthused with almost giddy excitement.

Phoebe is waiting under a deep auburn awning when Sam arrives.

'They started about twenty minutes ago,' she says, leading the way into the gallery.

'And how's Efe?' Sam asks.

'She's doing great up there, but she's pissed at you.'

He groans inwardly and follows his sister down a narrow stairway that opens up into a dimly lit basement. Black-framed photographs are spotlit on crisp, white walls. The space feels intimate, the audience huddled close together on wooden benches.

'Hey, Dad,' Sam whispers, taking a moment to settle onto the bench beside his sister. Ken smiles and reaches over to pat Sam's shoulder. The audience are focused on the front of the room, where Efe is perched on a high bar stool beside a petite woman, tilting a microphone back and forth. Nico has an accent Sam can't place.

'And how would you describe the collection?' Efe asks.

Nico considers her answer for a moment before speaking. 'To me, HomeHalves is all about the mixing of cultures. Growing up, after my parents separated, I moved back and forth between Ife and Osaka. As you can imagine, travelling between Nigeria and Japan could be a bit of a culture shock.'

A laugh rises and ebbs from the audience.

Nico continues, 'But this collection is my attempt to reconcile those two disparate experiences and find a way to create something harmonious.'

People begin to move around when the lights come up. The room crackles with murmured conversations, the chink of wine glasses, soft footsteps as journalists move from piece to piece. By the weekend the crowds will begin arriving, lured in by the reviews of the 'unmissable' exhibition that focuses on the 'haunting exuberance' of Nico's photographs. The now four-person team behind the Launi Gallery will be lauded as visionaries, and Sam will keep every clipping he can find and feel a surge of pride each time he sees Efe's name in print.

After Ken and Phoebe leave, Sam mills around on his own, sipping a ginger beer from the open bar. He knew the pieces would be extraordinary. In the first photo a group of delighted children ride a rickety, steel-framed bicycle. And in the background there is a shot of a busy road, the pavement outside clogged with dark-suited office workers. Ife overlaid on Osaka. The mismatched images aligned perfectly and the effect is arresting.

The one that really catches Sam's eye is at the far end. On the other side of the glass, a family crowd onto a sagging, brown sofa – four generations, if Sam counts correctly – and at the centre a young mother embraces her son, both grinning at something out of shot. And in the background, just a peek of a built-up skyline is visible through the window. This is the family Sam had always dreamed of in the years when mealtimes were just him, his dad and Phoebe around a table.

'Sam, right?' Nico is beside him, a hand extended. 'Efe talks about you all the time. She's incredible.'

'Right,' Sam says, shaking her hand. He glances across the room and spots Efe encircled by journalists, feels a warm bubble spread across his chest before his focus returns to Nico. 'Yeah, she is. Shouldn't you be doing the rounds?'

'Needed a break.'

Sam gestures to the nearest photograph. 'These are amazing,' he says, and her face lights up.

'This one's actually my favourite. I know I'm supposed to love all my children equally, but I won't tell if you don't.'

Sam laughs and takes a half step closer to the photograph. 'How did you manage to diffuse the light like this? And what aperture did you use to get this level of depth? It's impressive for such a small room.'

He turns and Nico's expression has changed into something curious. 'Are you a photographer?'

'No.' Sam laughs. 'I did it as an A level, kept it up for a few years in uni. Not seriously.'

'I see. Now you're a –' she takes a step back to examine the well-tailored suit and T.M. Lewin shirt, the official wardrobe of all the male associates at Barnard, Brand & Associates – 'a banker? No. Some other corporate bot?'

'A lawyer,' Sam corrects. 'Housing and property.'

'Quite a change.' Nico nods. 'If you ever want to get back into photography, give me a call.'

During the taxi ride home, Sam makes a quick assessment of how bad it is. They sit with the middle seat empty between them, Efe's face turned to the window, the car jostling, the air silent and stale. By the time Efe is ready to speak they are going to bed. Sam is pulling on pyjamas when she begins.

'I thought your client meeting ended at four. What was it this time?' she calls from the bathroom, her voice raised over the running tap.

'Signal failures.'

'Signal failures?' Efe repeats. She rounds the corner with two dabs of toothpaste on her cheek where spots are forming. 'An hour and a half late because of signal failures?'

Sam pauses. He could mention that it was an hour and twenty minutes; instead, he runs a nervous hand along the nape of his neck. 'I got held up after the meeting. Langfield kept talking.'

'There's always something. Why say you'll do something you have no intention of doing?'

'Of course I wanted to be there, but work—'

'We all work. There's a life outside of work.' She sighs. 'You're the one who wants a kid so badly but you're never here for the family you do have. Remember Friday night dinners with your dad and Phoebe? They were your idea and you haven't made it to a single one in months.'

'Things will calm down in a few weeks. Two months max.'

'I'll believe it when I see it.'

Sam wants to defuse the tension and apologise. He opens his mouth to say something, but Efe gets there first.

'Oh,' she adds. 'Phoebe's thinking of applying to study Sociology at uni.'

Sam's gaze narrows. 'Wait, what? What happened to Law?'

'I don't know,' Efe says. 'Maybe she's changed her mind watching you work eighty-hour weeks.'

'I was with her today. She didn't say anything.' He reaches for his phone, wonders if it's too late to call.

'She asked me to tell you. She thinks you'll be annoyed.'

Sam considers this. He remembers being her age, how hard he was trying to stick to his plan and get everything right. But Phoebe's different. She's steady, deliberate. Maybe she'll be just fine. 'What did you tell her?' he asks.

'That she has time to decide and she doesn't even need a degree to be successful.'

'Ah, so you want her to be like you and Abbey in sixth form? Weren't you two out there committing grand theft larceny?' he says, teasing. A smile tugs at the corner of Efe's lips.

'Ha ha ha,' she says drily. 'Shoplifting a few times is hardly a life of crime. I never should've told you.'

Sam laughs, reaches across the space and pulls her into his lap. The mood sweetens.

'Seriously, she's not you, not everyone has their whole life figured out at seventeen. Give her time.'

'All right, Bonnie,' Sam says.

'That makes you Clyde.'

Seven Years Before

Efe slides into the middle seat. Just twenty-one steps from the house to the car and already she can feel the muggy Accra heat, a breezeless, suffocating day, the sweat slick between her thighs. Sam squeezes in beside her. At her other side crates of soft drinks dig into her hip.

'Okay, everybody ready?' Paa asks, looking over his shoulder, first at Efe, then at Sam, checking on them as if they are children.

'Ready,' Efe replies, giving Sam's leg a reassuring squeeze and leaning into his side as the car backs out of the driveway.

The flat in Aburi is tucked into the lush, green hillside in a bright yellow building with large balconies that look out over the complex's manicured lawns and the communal pool, lined with palm trees. Climbing out of the car, Efe can hear the birds singing, hiding somewhere within the trees. The air is calm. The tall grass is still. And the dust rises and swirls around her ankles.

They climb three flights up, Paa leading the way, Maame at the back.

'*Akwaaba!*' Serwaa beams, throwing the door open. She greets them in pyjamas and house slippers. The room behind her is empty except for the banner slung across the sofa, the dining chairs pushed against the walls and a DJ assembling speakers on a small raised stage.

'Sorry, we're late. I'm sure you can imagine what happened.' Efe grins. And she steps forward and hugs Serwaa.

'Let me guess. Mum made everyone late and still needed to stop somewhere on the way?' she whispers back, their heads pressed together. Efe nods and they laugh, separating and, for the first time in two years, Efe stops to properly take her sister in. At twenty-four, Serwaa has grown rounder. Her baby face remains, but her soft edges are even plumper now, cheeks fuller than after Kobby's birth. The first baby cast a perpetual tiredness over Serwaa, but left her body virtually unchanged. This second child has made her something else entirely. It's thickened her neck, stomach and hips, and christened her with a wider-than-wide smile.

'Where's Abena?' Maame asks.

'I let her sleep so she'll be awake for the service,' Serwaa replies. 'Let me fetch you some drinks quickly, then I have to bath before people arrive.'

'Go bath. Let Efe collect the drinks,' Maame instructs, adjusting her blouse and sinking into the sofa. She sits just as Joseph rounds the corner in a vest and trousers. He is rounder too than the last time Efe saw him, the white cotton vest stretched tight, a damp slug trail sloping from the neckline to his stomach.

'Ey, I didn't know my own had arrived.' He casts his arms wide to greet them.

'So,' Sam says after everyone is settled. 'The naming ceremony was supposed to start twenty minutes ago and neither of you are ready?'

Maame shrugs. Both Joseph and Paa chuckle. Paa slides his glasses off his nose to wipe them. Joseph is the one who answers. 'Ghana time, we say eight, people come at ten.' He leans forward, slaps Sam hard on the shoulder. 'You'll see. Two hours from now the whole place will be full.'

And Joseph is right. By ten o'clock, when Joseph and Serwaa are making their grand entrance, every seat is filled.

They saunter in, the whole family matching in a luxurious red and yellow ankara print. Serwaa's eyebrows are pencilled into dark shapely arches, her lips shimmering and gold-hued. Joseph grins widely, one hand on Kobby's shoulder, steering him through the crowd, the other raised to shake hands with everyone he passes. Now the flat is full of familiar faces, every three paces they stop to say hello, Serwaa beaming, showing off the slow-waking baby bundled up against her chest. Everyone fawns over her, pressing to get nearer, holding their arms out expectantly, hoping for a snuggle with the month-old girl child. Kobby has managed to slink away and is running around somewhere nearby, already hyped up on sugary soft drinks, zipping between adults' legs, crashing into anything fragile with the reckless spirit of a child determined to bring destruction.

The music begins, a low murmur of highlife beneath the milieu. And with it Maame reappears, having made a quick escape earlier in the morning muttering, 'If I come to Aburi and don't see Esther, she will kill me-o,' and disappearing into the flat downstairs just as it was time to set up the decorations and carry the drinks up from the car. Refreshed from not lifting a finger, Maame strides in now, swishing in her heels, her best friend close behind.

'Ey, is this Maame?' and 'Maa Akua!' The voices follow Maame as she passes, waving, greeting guests like an adored politician. She stops beside Efe and Sam. They stand against the bare walls, having relinquished their seats to two of Joseph's elderly aunties. Esther's mouth drops open as she sees Efe, her face drawing itself into a suitably exaggerated expression. 'This cannot be Efe.'

'Hi, Aunty Esther.' Efe smiles, stepping forward for a hug.

'This cannot be the same girl who would sit in my house all day and not open her mouth to say a single word. Is this you?' she says playfully.

142

'That was a long time ago,' Efe replies. She places a hand on Sam's arm to draw him into the conversation. 'This is Sam.'

'My son,' Maame nods proudly, a hand resting on Sam's shoulder. 'Efe's husband. The one she met in London.'

Esther nods. 'Yes, your wedding was some years ago now. I remember. I was supposed to come but I was staying with my daughter in US at the time.'

'It was two years in July,' Sam says.

'It wasn't the same without you,' Efe adds. She looks up just as Nanadwoa enters the living room and rushes over.

'Welcome back,' Nanadwoa says. Efe is amazed at her flawless make-up, the lip liner accentuating her heart-shaped mouth, the dress that wraps around her curves.

'Ey, is that not too tight? You want everyone to be looking at you?' Maame steps back to get a good view.

Nanadwoa only grins. 'Aunty, please. That's the point.'

Maame's lecture is quelled by the two fingers tapping on a mic. Eyes turn to the stage as Joseph and Serwaa clamber up, Abena tucked into Serwaa's arms, Kobby by his parents' side and clawing at Joseph's trouser leg.

Pastor Eric holds the mic up to his lips, addressing the crowd. 'Testing,' he says. 'God is good.'

'All the time,' the crowd chants back.

'All the time.'

'God is good.'

'Okay, we are here today to join with Mr and Mrs Addo as they celebrate the birth of their dear daughter. In our culture the child brings one name into the world and any other names the father must choose for the child. Joseph, what is her name and what is the name you have chosen?'

Joseph raises a square of white cloth to his brow. He clears his throat, lowers his lips to the microphone. 'The name she brings is Abena and her full name is Abena Efe Christine Addo.'

Efe feels her hands come to her chest, Nanadwoa's elbow at her ribs, Sam's arm squeeze at her waist.

'What a fantastic name.' Pastor nods approvingly. 'Someone bring the drinks.'

The audience wait as he drops a finger into a cup, places it on Abena's tongue and repeats the gesture with the second cup.

'One is water. One is alcohol. In the same way, this child should always speak the truth and not confuse one thing with another.' He looks up and over the audience crammed into the small space. His gaze lands on Nanadwoa and the words dry up in his throat. 'Eh – erm – eh,' Pastor mumbles. A low titter rises up in the back corner. Pastor gives his head a quick shake and comes to his senses.

'Let us pray,' he says. The prayer lasts for almost ten minutes, circling round and round, praying a blessing over each of Abena's names, over her life, her brother, her parents, her family home, her future health, her future happiness, education and prosperity, rebuking attacks of the enemy, countering anyone who speaks ill of her and finally praying for misfortune for anyone who intends her harm. Pastor stamps his foot down to finish, then stiffly lowers his upright arms and the music begins.

'Want me to get you a plate?' Sam asks.

'Please,' Efe replies.

He gives her a quick kiss and joins the tide of people already shuffling towards the kitchen. Just as Efe loses sight of him amongst the bodies, Serwaa appears at her shoulder. 'I need to use the bathroom. Come on, hold your namesake.'

Abena's dewy skin is warm beneath Efe's fingers, her large eyes blink and dark eyelashes flutter. She looks sleepy and calm. She doesn't make a sound yet Efe has never been so uncomfortable. She is graceless holding the baby. Her arms are outstretched, bent at awkward angles so when Abena twists, her head lolls to the right like a ball on a string. From the sofa, one of Joseph's aunts cackles, loud enough to be heard over the music, and nudges the woman beside her. The second woman frowns and motions for Efe to pull the baby close. She glances down at Abena, but her arms won't move. The room heaves like a heartbeat. The music thumps. Above their heads, fans spin frantically, circulating nothing but heat and body odour. The few people who aren't queuing for food try to dance in the confined space. Efe feels the weight of multiple eyes on her.

'Do you want to hold her?' Efe asks, turning to Nanadwoa, a desperate plea in her voice.

'No, I'm enjoying this,' Nanadwoa laughs. 'You look so awkward. She's a baby, not a bomb. Is this what you'll be like when you have your own?'

'My own what?'

'Baby.'

'Baby?' Efe shakes her head. 'No, not me.'

Someone speaks behind them. Efe turns, swinging the baby in a neat arc.

'So, Nanadwoa, you don't know how to wait for your own mother?' Aunty Yaa says.

'Look at the time you're now arriving. You want us both to miss the naming?'

Aunty Yaa rolls her eyes at Nanadwoa, then notices Efe standing beside her. 'Ey! Efe, is that you? My old eyes cannot see.'

'Hi, Aunty. It is me.'

'So you're back in Accra and didn't come to greet me in my own house?'

'*Kafra*, Mummy,' Nanadwoa says. 'They only landed last night.'

'Of course we're coming,' Efe insists.

'We?'

'Me and Sam. He's just gone up for food.'

'Ey!' Aunty Yaa claps her hands eagerly, turning to her daughter. 'See, Nanadwoa, Efe is Mrs Owusu-Mensah now. She came with her *husband*. This your age-mate has a husband and what of you – heh?'

Nanadwoa's lips purse. Efe senses this is part of an ongoing conversation.

Aunty Yaa turns back to Efe. 'You know she broke up with Joshua. Very nice Fante boy. He was – erm . . .'

'A captain,' Nanadwoa fills in.

'A captain in the military.' Aunty nods proudly. 'Good home. Good job. Good family. And she breaks up with him. What for?'

Efe speaks with Nanadwoa at least twice a month, yet she had not heard about the break-up. On the most recent call they'd discussed work, a week-long trip Nanadwoa was planning to Nairobi, all the things they'd do when Efe was back in Ghana, but not this. Efe had been distracted, her attention split between the call and whatever else she'd been doing. She can't remember if she'd even asked and wonders if Nanadwoa hadn't mentioned it deliberately.

Aunty Yaa continues. 'Your friend comes with her husband and what are you doing all day – heh? Sitting in my house and not even lifting one finger to clean.'

'Maybe I have someone else in mind,' Nanadwoa responds.

'Aunty, there's no need—' Efe begins but Nanadwoa's voice carries louder.

'Mummy, stop. I'm having my fun for now. All this marriage talk – it's too much.'

'You, this girl, you think when you finish playing your games a husband will come and find you? Husband from where?' Aunty Yaa tsks loudly. 'And you too, Efe, you shouldn't let your junior sister be too far ahead of you. It is you who should be setting the example. Look at Serwaa, she already has two. Your own soon come.' She pauses. 'Why are you holding the baby like that? You should bring her close to you.'

Nanadwoa smirks and takes a half step away, out of the firing line. Abena feels heavier in Efe's arms. She draws her closer, but there's a feverish heat as soon as she touches Efe's chest.

'Actually,' Efe clears her throat, 'I'm not doing that.'

'Doing what?' Aunty asks.

'Having children.'

Aunty Yaa gasps. Someone on the sofa cries, '*Adjei!*' Efe is suddenly aware of the listening ears, the knotting in her stomach. Her throat dries and she casts a desperate glance over her shoulder, searching for Sam or Serwaa or anyone.

'God forbid,' Aunty Yaa says in a hushed voice. The living room suddenly feels fuller than it was a few moments ago. Efe feels bodies jostling as people make their way in and out of the kitchen. More guests are drifting through the front door. The crowd presses in around her. Efe doesn't recognise most of the people who stop to chime in, but they mutter fiercely, throwing out phrases like 'what foolish talk', 'so selfish' and 'sacrifice'. One of Joseph's aunts calls out, 'Don't tempt the devil.' The other, siding with Efe, shrugs and says, '*Nsateaa nyinaa nnye pe*' and the proverb only aggravates the others. The circle tightens. Finally, Aunty Yaa, the voice of the people, raises a hand to quell the others.

'Efe, there's no need to be scared, *wa te?*' She speaks slowly, her palms cupped together. 'Motherhood is a joy. A blessing.'

The encircling heads nod in agreement.

'It is hard too. No one is saying otherwise. We all know there is lots of sacrifice. But when your time comes, you'll see that it's also your job as a woman to be miserable so your child can be happy.' She ends with a decisive nod. The crowd disperses.

Stunned, Efe looks down at Abena. She's wide awake now, looking up at Efe and her gaze is suffocating. All around her people are shuffling back to their seats, satisfied that they've said their piece, and Efe feels suddenly grateful that she and Sam only make the trip out to Ghana for special occasions. Nanadwoa directs a terse whisper at Aunty Yaa, 'Mummy, if Efe does not want to have children, is it your business?'

'Don't mind her. She'll change her mind,' Aunty Yaa says, shouldering her way towards the kitchen. 'When the baby comes, will we not be here celebrating?'

Nanadwoa casts Efe a sympathetic look. 'I bet you don't miss that.'

Serwaa returns. 'Thank you,' she says, plucking the baby from her sister's arms. 'Why are you pulling that face?'

'My mum just lectured her.'

'Welcome home,' Serwaa chuckles. 'How bad was it?'

'Bad,' Nanadwoa confirms. 'Efe and Sam will be on the next flight back to London.'

In typical fashion, Nakwesi arrives at the naming hours late. He rolls in at that particular sweet spot: late enough for the party to be in full swing, the guests merry, and early enough for food still to be available, even though the most brazen guests have already stashed plastic-wrapped take-home plates in inconspicuous hiding places. Sam watches Nakwesi's slow procession of enthusiastic greetings, hearty backslapping and vigorous shaking of hands. When he gets to Sam, they greet like brothers reunited. A wide smile breaks across Nakwesi's face and his open palm comes down so hard that the skin between Sam's shoulder blades stings and the bottle of malt clinks against his teeth.

'Ey, Mr London,' Nakwesi says, still grinning.

'Long time,' Sam replies.

'You're just the man I was looking for.'

'I am?'

'Of course.' He rubs his hands together. 'Let me pick my plate and we go talk.'

While Nakwesi edges towards the kitchen, Sam searches for Efe in the crowd. He spots her perched on the edge of the sofa, flanked by Nanadwoa and Serwaa, the sagging banner right above their heads. Sam mumbles his 'Excuse-me's as he moves towards them. Efe's eyes flick up as he approaches.

'Nakwesi wants to talk. I'm gonna be outside.'

'Okay. We'll be here,' she says, sending him on his way with a parting kiss.

Outside, in the mild evening, Sam leans on the balcony's metal railing and looks down at the communal garden. The palm trees stand to attention, evenly spaced along the tall white wall, their branches held skywards as if awaiting a blessing. He swishes the dregs of his malt. To his left a circle of older men slump in plastic chairs and throw back small bottles of bitters. Sam watches them, a small smile on his face.

A few moments later, Nakwesi steps out onto the balcony. 'All right,' he says and looks from the huddle of uncles to Sam, then juts his head in the direction of the garden. They walk the three flights down, stroll onto the lawn. The music from the party fades. Sam sinks into the grass. He kicks off his sandals, rolls up his cuffs and slides his feet into the pool, his gaze resting on the rippling blue water.

Nakwesi settles himself on a nearby sunlounger, careful not to spill his food. The scent of fried fish wafts. Deep red stew seeps into the paper plate.

Around a mouthful of yam, Nakwesi begins. 'So what's going on?'

'With me?' Sam says.

'Yeah, when's it going to be you and Efe up there?'

Sam thinks about this for a moment, a low laugh rising. 'Soon, if I have my way.'

'Ah.' Nakwesi's eyes lift from the plate. He nods knowingly. 'So she's the one keeping you waiting? Not the other way round?'

Sam thinks back to the conversation he overheard earlier. If he's honest with himself – there have been other comments too. Dozens of off-handed remarks over the years that always seemed to say the same thing in one way or the other. Usually he shrugs them off. But now, the thoughts percolate.

For years, since the early months of their relationship, all Sam's envisioned is their future together and their future children: gorgeous dark-skinned babies, with tight coils and Efe's large eyes, full lips and pert nose. Even before they were officially a thing, he had names picked out – one for a boy, another for a girl. And in his brave moments he would've shared them with Efe too, had she ever asked. An uneasy feeling stirs. When he looks up Nakwesi is still looking at him, waiting for an answer.

'Something like that,' Sam mutters. He knows Efe has a habit of blowing things out of proportion. Overthinking. Examining and re-examining her options, ruminating over things she perceives as mistakes. It's a big deal now, but Sam thinks that maybe when they're older she'll warm to the idea, that some biological alarm will go off and this big thing between them will simply cease to exist. He tries not to expect too much. He simply hopes.

Six Years Before

When Efe gets home, Sam is sitting on the end of the bed, shoulders slumped, too shocked and drained to remove his coat or shoes. He doesn't know how long he's been sitting in the dark flat like this, only that he resurfaces when he hears the front door opening, Efe humming out in the hallway, the rustle of coats, the clunk of her shoes as they meet the ground.

'You home?' she calls out. No need for names or context. And Sam listens to the soft tread of bare feet as she approaches. He dredges up his voice.

'In here,' Sam croaks.

'Have you been here all evening? Marilyn's birthday drinks were today. I texted. We went to a karaoke bar. You could've joined us.' She pauses on the threshold, heels dangling from her fingertips. 'Why are you sitting in the dark, you weirdo?' she says, a light laugh in her voice. Sam stirs but doesn't respond.

Efe hesitates, reaches for the light switch. 'Did something happen?'

'What?' Sam tries to shake himself out of it but his thoughts are slow and muggy.

She kneels in the space before him, clasping his hands, her eyes fixed on his. 'Did everything go okay with the Hollingbrooke case? The settlement meeting was today, right?'

'Yeah.' He pauses. 'They settled.'

'Oh.' She smiles, relieved. 'That's great. Is there something else?'

'I quit my job today.'

Sam feels the moment Efe stiffens. Her brow furrows, lips slightly parted like the moments before she wakes. 'You . . . quit?' she echoes.

Sam shifts. He wants to say something – to explain – but he's still trying to process the day's events himself. For weeks, a new unsettled feeling had been tunnelling through Sam's mind, small but growing. A flare bursting through a dark, still night. For years he's been surrounded by the ambitious and self-assured. Sixth form. University. The trainee pool at Barnard, Brand & Associates. Caught in the riptide, Sam thinks about how fiercely he wanted every promotion, how he'd angled to be involved in all the prestigious cases, how unwavering he'd been, treading the path he'd set for himself as a teenager as if that alone would guarantee happiness. And now that desire to chase every opportunity is gone. He imagines it floating away, a small speck of a balloon in a clear blue sky.

'I quit.'

Sam sees Efe caught in the bright, sharp shock of it, like headlights that suddenly appear in the darkness or the rapid burst of panic after taking a step and only finding air. She lets out a long breath, presses a thumb and finger over closed eyes. 'Give me a moment,' she says.

'We're not the good guys,' he says weakly, thinking about the office that afternoon, the celebratory air fizzing through the twelfth floor, the staff gathered for a mid-afternoon drinks reception. From the front of the room, Sam took in details he never normally notices. He remembers the pink spot of blush on Wilson's white shirt, Aster's windswept curls, Barret still harrying around the office just outside the glass conference room, the clammy tightness of his boss's hand on Sam's shoulder and the damp sheen on his face as he'd passed Sam the mic.

'I —' Sam began as the flare rocketed skywards. He'd still been looking at Walt, his boss, when Sam had said, 'I think I need to resign.' Sam had paused and cast his gaze across a roomful of bemused colleagues, waiting for a punchline. Even Langfield, Sam's closest competition since starting at the firm, had fumbled, his smug smile waned. To Sam's left, Walt chuckled nervously. 'Consider this my notice,' Sam had said, firmly this time, and stepped off stage.

The crowd had parted as Sam made his way to the door, Walt hot on his heels, voice low and urgent, muttering about how Sam should take some time. 'You've worked so hard on the Hollingbrooke case, burning the candle at both ends. We can all see that. Take a few days. A week. I'll set up a call with Brand and the other partners. We'll talk, whenever you're ready,' was the last thing Walt had said before the lift doors dinged open and Sam let it carry him to the ground floor. Already the news was spreading across the office like wildfire. And out in the lobby, Sam loosened his tie and headed out into all that was ahead. Hours later, sitting here and explaining it to his wife, Sam waits for her response. The only one that really matters.

'Okay,' she says, whisper-soft. 'You'll have to finish your notice period, but you can find something better. We'll figure it out. There's still time.'

'Okay,' Sam says and feels a pang of affection stretch towards her.

She turns and slips open the dresser, pulls out a small, battered shoebox. 'I found this.'

Sam reaches for it hesitantly. He hasn't seen this box in years and moves slowly, the bed squeaking beneath his shifting weight. He slips the lid off. A musty aroma wafts upwards. Sam remembers it as if from a past life. Carefully he lifts the camera out of the box. It's small, like a toy in his hands. He runs a thumb over the strap, remembers the trail of raised bumps it always left along the back of his neck. He touches that same spot now.

'Why don't you go for it?' Efe says.

'Being a photographer? As in working for myself?'

'Chasing your dreams.'

'I don't know.'

'What's stopping you? We have an emergency fund and I'm working. At least dip your toe in and try it out for a couple of months, or try it part-time alongside something else? Do you really want to wake up a year from now, or five, or fifty, and know you didn't even try?'

Sam exhales, turns the camera over in his hands. He feels himself collapsing inwards. It seems to take all his energy to push the box to the side and reach for her. He feels a surge of gratitude when they fall back, stretching out on the tiny burgundy leaves of the bedspread. Her fingers slot into his. She is the only thing that feels real. Never before has he felt so close to her, the length of her body against his, navigating this shift in life together. She leans in and kisses the bald patch in his beard where the soft brown skin peeks through. They stay like this for a long time, in the delicate moment on the edge of something new.

'I love you,' he says.

'I love you too.'

Sam has no more words and for a while neither of them speak. Not yet. Efe breathes steadily, twirls his curls between her fingers. They lie like that, until her laugh rumbles the silence.

'What's so funny?' he says, lifting his head.

'This situation,' she says. 'Mr Five-Year Plan did something spontaneous.'

'I can be spontaneous.'

'You're level-headed, optimistic, the absolute love of my life, but spontaneous you are not.' She laughs again, rolls her eyes. 'Is that who you really are? Surely, you can't be the same man I married.'

He breaks into a laugh too, draws a hand over his face. 'You're right. I don't know who I am any more.'

MAY 2011

Five Years Before

Efe rouses from sleep simply. One moment her eyes are closed, the next they are open, and for a few seconds she lies as still as she can, letting the wisps of last night's dream scurry into the corners of her mind. Her eyes glaze over the needle-thin cracks in the ceiling. She isn't sure why she is awake – just aware of Sam stretched out beside her, the alarm that is yet to go off and the slight queasiness lining the back of her throat. When the feeling refuses to subside, she drains the glass of water at her bedside and rises and walks to the bathroom, feeling hotter and more nauseated with each step. There she rests her forehead on the cool mirror.

'You don't look good,' Sam says a few moments later. Efe jumps. Not for the first time, she wonders how he's managed to sneak up on her, but before she can speak, he's pulling her close, placing an upturned palm on her brow.

'I feel awful,' Efe moans, catching the scent of something that makes her stomach flip.

'Back to bed,' Sam says and leads her back to their bedroom. She sinks into the pillows, lets him lift her legs into the bed. The familiar weight of the duvet settles back on her.

'Where's your phone? I'll call Marilyn and let her know you're not coming in.'

'Just give me a minute,' she says, her mind tallying up all the things she has to do, realising she doesn't have the time to be sick today. She can hear Sam moving around the kitchen, the kettle boiling, cupboard doors banging shut. And when he returns bearing crackers and peppermint tea, Efe places a cracker in her mouth and sucks, gratefully, waiting for the nausea to subside. She reaches for her phone, silences the alarm before it rings, scrolls through a high stack of notifications silenced the night before.

'I'm late.' Efe forms the words around a soggy cracker. Mild panic settles over her.

'What?' Sam says, pausing halfway out the door with a towel slung over his shoulder, fingers curled on the doorframe.

'I didn't get my period.'

At this, his eyes brighten. Something eager and excited puffs up in his face. 'Do you think you could be . . .?' Sam lets the question trail off.

'No,' Efe says. She is certain. They are careful – always – precisely to avoid predicaments like this. Predicaments. She thinks of teenagers: horny, careless teenagers screwing in the backs of cars or while their parents are at work, quick-they'll-be-back-in-an-hour-sexed teenagers. She and Sam have been married almost four years. That is not who they are.

'We should get a test, right? Just to rule it out.'

Efe doesn't remember falling asleep. When she wakes, the smudges of colour slowly coming into focus, there is a blue plastic bag on the bedside table, and through the thin plastic she can see a smooth white-boxed pregnancy test. *Just in case*, the Post-it note says. Another note wedged between the crackers and tepid tea reads: *Eat these.*

She sits up, calls Sam's name into the empty flat and heads for the bathroom. The minutes slow down as she watches, waiting, perched on the edge of the bathtub. She raises her palms to her breasts and wonders nervously if they're more tender or heavier than they normally are, and wonders where Sam got the test. Only the Londis on Station Road is open at this time in the morning and she imagines the test tucked between off-brand baked beans and two-ply toilet roll. It's probably out of date – if that's possible.

When the plus symbol appears, Efe cannot speak, cannot swallow, cannot breathe. All she can do is let her feet carry her out into the hallway just as the front door swings open. Her first instinct is to hide the test in the waistband of her pyjamas. She feels her grip tighten and tries to sound calm.

'You're back,' she says.

'Forgot my wallet.' Sam shuffles into the kitchen, mumbles as he scans the counters. 'Got it!' When he steps back out he's holding the wallet high, like a victor's trophy. He pauses. His eyes move to the thin plastic tube, clutched in Efe's hand so tight the tips of her fingers have gone pale. Something in his face stills.

'You took the test?'

'Yeah.'

'And?'

'It's positive.'

'Positive? Really?'

'Yeah.'

Sam leaps forward, taking Efe in his arms, hugging her, laughing, spinning her round in the narrow hallway. 'This is amazing! You're amazing. I love you. A baby! We're having a baby.'

Efe lands back on the floor breathless and dizzy. Already she's lapsing into fear, feels it lodged in her throat, like a marble nestling deep in her airway. Sam's watching her, expecting her to speak, but she can't yet. Suddenly uncertain, he second-guesses himself. 'You're not happy?'

She balks. 'Why would I be happy? We can't keep it.'

'But that was before.'

'Nothing's changed, Sam.'

'Everything has. We have our own place, stable jobs. I get it. I know you're worried but—'

She shakes her head firmly. 'I still don't want to be a mother.'

'It's not about you being a mum. It's about *us* being parents. This is our kid.' Desperately, he glances over his shoulder, remembers the time.

'You're gonna miss your train,' Efe says.

'I know. I have a meeting first thing. Can we talk about it when I get back tonight? Please.' Sam backs towards the door, stumbling over his own feet.

Efe stays there for a long while, firm and resolute, before climbing back into bed. She glances at the test again and again. Nervous. Already, she is coming undone as the morning rushes ahead without her. Her plans are splintering into fragments too small to put back together and this is just the beginning.

That night when Sam comes home, Efe is in the living room preparing. All day she's been moving around the flat as if chasing a thought. And now, she hears the door open and lifts her head towards the sound.

'Sam?' she says and steps out to meet him in the corridor.

'Hey, how're you feeling?' he asks.

'Better,' she says. She forces her voice to sound light and casual as if she hasn't been thinking about this for the last twelve hours. 'I think we should consider all of our options.'

'Okay,' he says, 'I've been thinking too. Just tell me what you need.'

Efe pauses. 'What?'

'I really think we can make this work. We have good jobs. I can go full-time at the legal aid office—'

'The whole point of you leaving Barnard & Brand was to have more time for photography.'

'But this is a baby. *Our* baby. And we already have a spare bedroom. We can unpack the boxes and finally make use of the space.'

Efe turns her head to the right. Through the open doorway she can see the boxes stacked up against the wall, the lumpy sofa bed and the semi-unpacked prints turned to face the wall. She's been imagining a home office or a library stacked floor to ceiling with books. In place of the old sofa bed, she's pictured a velvety chaise tucked right up under the window, where the evening light streams in, reading with her feet tucked beneath her throughout the cool winter months. That was the deal two years ago when Efe reluctantly agreed to go with this property instead of the ground-floor flat with the garden she loved the moment she walked in. That's what Sam had promised.

She steels herself and brings to mind all she's planned to say. 'We're not negotiating. We can't have a baby.'

'Why not? Tell me what you need.'

Efe pauses, suspicious, crinkling her brows together. 'I'm not ready.'

'Let's get ready. We can read all the books and go to those – what do they call them – those classes to prepare.'

'I can't take a year off work.'

'That's fine. You could take nine months off. Six?'

'Sam, I'm not going to sit here on my own for six months while you're at work.'

'I don't have to be. I crunched the numbers both ways. We'll have to make some changes, but if you want me at home I can go down to three days a week. I might not even have to go into the office every day.'

'I need my family. After Kobby and Abena were born, my parents helped Serwaa out a lot.'

'Great, they can come and stay,' Sam offers. 'Any time. And I'll be here every step of the way.'

And on it goes. They talk well into the night, moving from the hallway to the sofa as night rolls closer and closer to daybreak. Through the windows, the sky is a deep, endless black. The street lights blink on. It bothers Efe how convincing he sounds, so certain he's planned and accounted for every problem she throws his way. He rebuffs her every fear, makes it all sound so simple. Something fractures. Deep inside, Efe's resolve is weakening. She knows she will do it then. Maybe a part of her has known since the hug in the hallway, moments after the words were out of her mouth, as if he'd spun her round and deposited her in a new reality, already untethered from who she was seconds before. When it is over, Sam opens up his arms and Efe allows herself to be held. A hand circles her back. He kisses her softly where her baby hairs spill onto her forehead. She closes her eyes and tries to believe.

JANUARY 2012

Four Years Before

Efe wakes just after dozing off. Outside the sun is rising, a streak of gold breaking through a bleak, dark morning. She stretches one leg out into the cool strip of mattress. For a brief moment she feels settled, waking slowly like she does every few hours, sometimes several times an hour, never getting used to the strange feeling of the baby stirring inside of her. But today, there is pain. Even from the beginning it is a sharp pain at her back, like a jolt of electricity zipping under her skin.

'Efe?' a voice calls. Her head snaps up to the sight of Maame hovering at the foot of the bed, nightgown wrinkled, hands clasped as if in prayer. Since her parents' arrival a week ago, Efe's awoken to the same sight each night, has started to envisage her mother staying up all night, loitering just outside the bedroom door, waiting.

'Is it time?' Maame asks. When Efe nods, Maame goes to the nursery to wake Sam, who rushes in a minute later, eyes wide and alert, hair flat on one side and sleep still wrapped around him.

He takes in the scene: Efe on the edge of their bed, a tense hand cradling the underside of her stomach, the warm, musty liquid soaking into the mattress. 'Contractions? How far apart are they?'

'I don't know,' Efe replies as another surge rocks through her. Somewhere beyond the pain she can hear her parents' low voices drifting in from elsewhere in the flat, Sam dashing around, stuffing extra things into the hospital bag, shrugging off his pyjamas. When she can focus again, he's hopping on one foot, trying to cram a leg into his jeans.

They hobble-walk down the stairwell, moving slowly, the only sound the hushed creaking of Efe's worn-thin hips. Finally, they emerge in the pre-dawn world. They arrange themselves in the car: Efe's parents in the back, Sam behind the wheel, Maame reaching through the gap to hold Efe's hand in hers. Despite the blasting heat, all four of them shiver, staring silently at the defrosting windshield and the empty road stretching out ahead of them.

At the hospital, Sam fills out Efe's admission paperwork. He knows just as much as she does, has been at her side for every appointment, every scan and test, meticulously jotting down notes in a small black notebook, which he flicks open frequently. As the pregnancy has progressed, he's taken to planning with the same military precision in which he handles his cases. He has been the one to read countless parenting books, research NCT classes, mother and baby groups; he is the sole reason they have a month's supply of lunches and dinners crammed into their freezer so they have meals prepared for after the baby's born.

'That's great,' the midwife says, skimming through the paperwork. 'I'll show you to your room.' She gives Efe an encouraging nod. 'Ready?'

Efe gulps. Thirty-nine weeks leading to this moment. She is as ready as she'll ever be.

After the initial examination, Efe is sent to walk up and down the corridors.

'Four centimetres,' she fumes, dressed now in a pale green papery gown that stretches wide like a tent, a hand positioned below her heavy stomach. For an hour, while her parents are eating breakfast in the hospital cafeteria downstairs, she meanders the halls of the maternity ward, Sam at her side, squeezing his hand each time another contraction hits until they are both whimpering in pain. A small huddle of midwives chat casually at the reception, nibble on digestive biscuits and sip from mugs of coffee, a sight that simultaneously makes Efe's stomach rumble and leaves her feeling nauseated. She tries to remember the breathing techniques from the NCT classes and focus on the bubblegum-pink walls. Instead her breath comes out in ragged wheezes and her mind seizes each time a contraction builds.

'Could you get me some ice?' she asks. The gown is already sticking to her.

'Do you want me to wait until your parents come back?'

'It's fine,' Efe says, and Sam turns and retraces his steps down the loop of the corridor back to the ice dispenser near the lifts. Efe settles herself into a chair, watches a couple amble in: the man lost within a cloud of barely contained panic, the woman in the wheelchair, face pinched tight, curled around a bump. Efe flashes a solidarity smile as the midwives jump into action and the couple are whisked into the depths of the ward. Twenty minutes later, as she and Sam make their slow journey back to her room, she hears the baby's cries and slaps a hand on the wall. 'I was here first!' she wants to yell, but the words are tucked behind another wave.

'Forty-five seconds, eleven minutes apart.' Efe stiffens as the midwife slips long fingers between her legs, 'aaaand . . . four centimetres dilated.'

'Still four?' Efe gasps, struggling as she props herself up on her elbows to peer over the bump.

'Just six more.' The midwife pulls off blue latex gloves with a snap, then pats Efe on the knee. 'Baby's taking its time. Try and breathe through it. These things aren't always a straight line.'

'Ergh!' Efe lands back on the bed with a thump. 'Please. I need this to be over.'

Maame, who has been silently observing the scene from her perch on the armrest of Paa's chair, leans over to place a hand on Efe's forearm, her palm covering the faint scars. 'Ey, it's not so painful now. Back home, you'd be lucky to get this gas and air.'

The midwife smiles politely. 'First grandchild?'

'No.' Maame shakes her head. 'Her junior sister has two already, but this one will be another delight in our life.'

With her face to the tiled ceiling, Efe blinks and watches the world blur behind tears. Sam tilts a cup of melting ice chips towards her, and Efe grabs one and chews hard, ignoring the sharp sting in her teeth.

'You're doing great,' Sam says, giving her shoulder a quick squeeze that seems to say: 'Thank you for doing this. I know this hasn't been easy and you've had your doubts.'

Efe drops her face to the right and looks to him. He talks softly, a crackle of nerves under each syllable and a wearied but encouraging lift to his lips. Already – just four hours in – she's too tired to smile back. She pictures all the ways this will worsen: the hours of ever-increasing pain, grunting, groaning, pushing, tearing. Sam's fingers interlock with hers. *Thank you*, Efe thinks, but when he leans close to press his lips to hers, she can taste coffee and hears the crinkle of a paper-wrapped croissant in his pocket. At the sound and smell, she thinks she might cry.

By nightfall, everything speeds up. The pain is at its worst and Efe feels her fear taking over. Two invisible hands wring her muscles out; tight and furious pains scorch through her. In the too-brief seconds between them, Efe lies back, fumbles desperately for gas and air. In the back of her throat, she feels tangy bile rising. Her head is hazy now. The world moves at half speed and voices drift past her like bubbles floating through air, not quite registering even when they say, 'It's time, Efe. You're fully dilated.' She bears down and pushes, hands clamped around her knees, panting in the murky minutes when Friday night rolls into Saturday morning.

'That's it. Keep breathing, Efe,' she hears. Sam's hand is circling her back, his expression encouraging.

'I can't do this,' she wheezes.

'It's almost over. You're doing so well,' he murmurs. Beneath her skin the baby shifts. She grits her teeth and pushes long and hard, until there's a final tug and a judder deep within her.

'A little girl!' the midwife exclaims.

Exhausted, Efe uncurls. Her head comes down on limp hospital pillows and a streak of warm blood is oozing down her leg. She lets her leaden arms sink to her sides and peers down at the wrinkled, shivering person, reddened and slick with bodily fluids. More than anything, all Efe wants to do is close her eyes and sleep. She cannot summon the energy to wrap her arms around the infant.

'Hi,' Efe exhales, whisper-quiet, watching a small nose nuzzle into her chest, the trembling of a lip before a mighty wail breaks through. The flinch is involuntary. 'Hi, you,' Efe says again, more nervous this time. She casts a fretful look around the roomful of watching faces, feels the expectation radiating like a wall of heat. *This is too much*, she wants to say, but already, it is over. They lift the baby from Efe's chest, measure, weigh, wipe and swaddle the wriggling child in a crisp, white blanket.

'Dad, do you want to hold her?' someone asks.

Sam's eyes are wet with tears when they place the baby in his outstretched arms. He beams, counts ten glorious fingers and ten toes, presses each to his lips. The baby's nose wrinkles. His broad smile widens. Her eyes flutter open and fix on Sam. The bellow drops back down to a sniffle. All around them the room stills.

In those first minutes of parenthood Sam's world recedes, the moment charmed, soft-edged and glittery. He barely allows himself to blink, as he tries to hold tight to every detail

– the feel of her skin under his fingertips, the tight coils of hair, still damp and shining under the fluorescent lights. Carefully, he extends a finger and places it in the soft dip where forearm meets bicep. Here a dark birthmark is forming, a perfect fit for his fingertip. He coos down at her, exhales an even, 'Welcome to the world Olivia Amma,' and in response Olivia lets out a sound that's partway between a gurgle and a laugh. In that instant, Sam imagines a whole future. He imagines nights rocking her to sleep; filming her first bumbling steps into Efe's outstretched arms; jogging beside her while she learns to ride a bike; he sees a bubbly four-year-old skipping towards school gates. As if all those moments are out there waiting for them, he sees it all.

Our joy is complete, the text message reads: a blast message sent to the majority of the contacts in Maame's phone, followed by a photo of Olivia – red-faced and blotchy, mid-cry – and the details of her arrival. Even Efe receives it. It is buried deep beneath the congratulatory text messages, which she finally pans through on Sunday morning in the minutes before they take Olivia home. Sam is busy filling out the discharge paperwork. Maame and Paa are back at the flat, preparing for Liv's arrival. And for Efe, it feels like her life is barrelling at great speed into something unimaginable, with who-knows-what up ahead.

There is a new rhythm in the flat. For the first five weeks, when Efe's parents are staying, they are the ones who dote on the baby. It is Paa who takes her out in the pushchair and circles block after block until she falls asleep, Maame who bounces, burps and changes. They are the ones who host the parade of visitors, serve drinks and bring out plate after plate of freshly made *bofrot*, *chin-chin* and *nkatie* cake. Aunty Dora and Sam's family are the first to call in, then extended family members, friends, colleagues, neighbours and people who are practically strangers – all of them in awe of Olivia, delighting in every gurgle and new facial expression. From the sofa, Sam and Efe watch as the baby is passed from arm to arm; they accept every offer of help, and bask in the gentle ease of those weeks.

They joke about it, late at night, in the evenings that first week Sam is back at work.

'I practically had to wrestle Liv out of your dad's arms,' Sam says, sitting so the mattress sinks under his weight. At this Efe laughs. To her, having time for just the two of them makes it feel like they've travelled back in time, back to when they were newly married in the studio flat, so sure of all they'd planned.

'I know,' she says. 'I was here all day and only had to hold her for feeds.'

'Do you think I should say something?'

'They're only here for one more week,' Efe says. 'Leave them be.'

After Efe's parents leave, she is certain the baby becomes more difficult, like a silent alarm bell is ringing in a place that cannot be reached.

She cries ceaselessly. For hours Efe circles the coffee table, cradling the writhing bundle to her chest, until her patience is frayed and both of them are exhausted. She finds herself staring at the clock at ten thirty, eleven, twelve, willing Sam to come home. She learns to shower with the bathroom door open, listens intently for the first hint of a cry, and when it comes, leaps out of the tub and into the hall towel-wrapped, dripping wet, soap suds streaking down her calves. Eight minutes. Just eight minutes alone until the piercing wail choruses, and when she stumbles in Olivia's crumpled face looks up at her and pauses mid-wail, as if making an accusation.

Day by day, Efe's life is consumed by unpredictable cycles of waking, feeding, changing and sleeping. She misses her commute, the packed train carriage and days deliberating over funding applications and the heart-in-her-throat moments examining each newly arrived painting for damages in transit. Without sleep, the circles under her eyes darken to a deep mauve. Her unwashed braids dangle on two inches of new growth. The hair at her temples is already falling away in clumps. She can't remember the last time she had twenty minutes to herself, and the thought of a thirty-minute lunch break or eating a Pret sandwich over her computer brings tears to her eyes.

With Sam at work, taking care of the baby leaves Efe almost no time to get a drink of water, let alone eat a full meal. She doesn't know how other mothers manage it and can tell the weight is falling off her, see it in the suspicious looks Aunty Dora throws her way and how she takes it upon herself to start visiting three times a week, each time dropping off more food than Sam and Efe have space for. Efe imagines she's thinking back to Efe's university days when her weight last plummeted and doing what she can to avoid a repeat of that time. But Efe's body has been unfamiliar for almost ten months now. All of her energy is focused on getting through each hour with Olivia, and Efe is discovering new things to agonise over with every day.

The health visitor airily dismisses Efe's concerns, barely looking up from her checklist. On phone calls home, Maame puts it bluntly. 'Calm down and let her cry,' she says. 'You can't carry her up and down like this.' But Efe cannot stay calm when every rash looks like meningitis. Each cry could be a sign of a virus or infection. Efe is certain something is very wrong with her daughter.

At the GP, Efe mentions the rash, excessive spit-up after feeding, complains that Olivia never sleeps for more than ninety minutes at a time, and is aware of the slightly delirious speed of her words, the smell of baby sick on her skin, the clothes she hasn't changed in three days; but Dr Varma, a warm, grandfatherly man, nods sympathetically and lets Efe complain for as long as she wants. A framed photo of three thirty-something women, surrounded by dark-haired and brown-skinned children, sits beside his keyboard, and he glances over at the photo, his face moment-arily lit up, before he prescribes Gaviscon for Infants and an arsenal of creams for the rash. Efe accepts the prescription with a murmured thanks, feeling close to tears. In the line at the pharmacy, with the crinkly green paper in her hand, she feels both glad to have her worries validated and a sharp sting of dread now her fears have been confirmed. She is certain more will go wrong. She's waiting for it.

Though the days feel insurmountable, it's the nights that hit Efe hardest, nights when Olivia is inconsolable. Every night, Efe hovers just above Olivia's cot, hands trembling and quashing the urge to cry. Naively, she hopes Olivia will soothe herself and go back to sleep, but she always gets louder, nearing the volume Efe thinks of as siren-pitch, a level that conjures up the feeling of a knife serrating skull from scalp. Miraculously Sam never wakes. She is secretly suspicious he's pretending and wants to elbow him or take the binder open on his chest and fling it across the room. On a few occasions when he's happened to wake up in the middle of the night, whatever conversation they have always devolves into an argument that she replays on a loop in her mind, fearful of all the ways Liv has changed them – the gap between them widening.

Now, Efe settles back into bed, the baby propped up on a pillow at her breast. She gropes for her phone and the screen reads 2.33 a.m., only thirty-seven minutes since her last feed. With a heavy sigh, Efe's head flops back. She can see a dark slit of sky between the curtains. From where she sits it is as dark and glossy as an oil spill. She can hear, but not see, a group of girls making their way down the road, laughing loudly, barking out a drunken chorus of 'Call Me Maybe' into the night.

By 4.12 a.m., when Efe is pacing up and down the hallway in a fruitless effort to get Olivia to fall back asleep, her only consolation is that they'll probably both sleep through the torturous mother and baby group. For two nightmarish hours a week, a dozen women gather to gush about their infants, compare milestones as if preparing for the Baby Olympics – *did you hear James is sleeping through the night; Eloise is practically holding her head up; Anna's advanced for her age, rolling over already – at fifteen weeks!* And Efe nods dumbly, saying nothing. Somehow she's found herself in a group full of superwomen who delight in motherhood in all of its facets, their children immaculate and high-achieving even as infants, and beside them Efe feels the disparity most acutely, like an anchor pulling her down below the waterline.

Four Years Before

Most days Sam is eager to get home from the legal aid office. He spends his work hours half-focused on his ever-increasing caseload, half-thinking of Liv; trying to recall her sleeping face from that morning; the way her chubby, baby-soft legs look when she's sitting on his lap; the way she breaks into a gummy smile whenever he walks into the room. He is in awe of her. A whole person. A family.

When Sam finishes up for the day, he heads to a crowded train platform and squeezes into a carriage packed so full with commuters he can feel a stranger's breath at his ear, but he would endure the journey a dozen times over just to spend an evening with his family. He walks home from the station briskly, head lowered. A lazy drizzle falls from a bleak, late April sky and he dips into the nearest supermarket to pick up nappies. Standing in the hallway, fifteen minutes later, he pulls off his coat, lets a sprinkling of raindrops fall to the floorboards. He plans to take over from Efe so she can have an hour or so to herself, and hopes he's not too late for bath-time. He'd like him and Liv to have matching beards made of candyfloss-scented bubbles, to swaddle her in the yellow hooded towel that makes her look like a duckling. He doesn't make it home in time most nights. He means to, but often finds himself stuck in client meetings or filing urgent injunctions, returning home long after Efe and Olivia have gone to sleep.

'Efe?' he calls.

'In here,' she replies.

Even before Sam rounds the corner and sees his wife tapping away at her laptop, her face lit up in blue light, he knows something is different. Her slightly frazzled air that usually follows all day at home with Olivia has evaporated. Today Efe is all smiles and lightness, far cheerier than Sam's seen her in weeks.

'Hey,' she says, momentarily glancing up from the screen, her fingers still typing.

'Hey.' Sam's gaze moves from Efe on the sofa, a toe outstretched to gently rock Olivia in her bouncer, to the heap of muslins smeared with baby vomit, to Bear-Bear facedown on the rug, to the bottle tipped sideways on the coffee table, a puddle of drying milk on the dark wood, the teat still drib-bling steadily. From the floor Sam picks up the soft-cornered guide for first-time parents, its pages bent and crumpled. In the months before Olivia's birth Sam pawed through it and read it from cover to cover – twice. Large sections are blotted in yellow highlighter, his tiny notes penned into the margins. This too smells like baby sick. He sighs heavily. Tension crin-kles at his shoulders. His mouth struggles to form the words: 'How was your day?'

'Great,' Efe replies, still typing furiously.

'Really?' Sam says as he plucks the leaking bottle from the pool of creamy milk. 'Anything I should know about?' He tries to make the words sound casual.

'Actually,' Efe begins. Her fingers slow. 'What're you doing on Friday?'

Sam walks to the kitchen, empties the bottle and places it in the steriliser, reaches for a sponge to clean up the spill. 'Friday . . .' he calls. 'Friday's my photography day. I've got to finish editing the photos from that birthday party.'

'Do you think you can do that and take care of Olivia? I'm needed at the gallery.'

Sam stops in the doorway. 'But you're on maternity leave. Isn't Marilyn covering your projects?'

'She is.' Efe rises and reaches for the muslins. 'But she broke her leg skiing in Italy and can't fly back until next week at the earliest. The grant review meeting is this Friday and they need someone to step in.'

'Can't someone else do it?'

'That someone is me. I'm the project lead. I wrote *the entire* application.'

Bent in front of the washing machine, Efe doesn't see that Sam's head is shaking.

'What happens if the funding's approved? Will they want you back in now, full-time?'

'Maybe. Probably just to get the project rolling. I don't know.'

'We need to know that,' Sam says.

'And we'll cross that bridge when we get to it.'

Sam can't make sense of what's happening. 'We haven't even crunched the numbers. With childcare these days, it might not even make sense for you to go back—'

'Let's just get through Friday, okay?' Efe snaps in a way that makes it clear this is anything but okay. She slams the washing machine door shut.

Sam forces himself to take a breath. 'Efe—' he says, the very moment Olivia's cry begins in the other room. Sam's head flicks towards the sound. He exhales and turns back to his wife. Neither of them move.

That night, Sam calls Maame. He knows he needs to broach the topic with Efe again but he can't bring himself to. Instead, he waits until she's in the shower and sneaks out to the furthest corner of the living room.

'Hello?' Maame's voice sounds bright and relaxed on the other end.

'Good evening, Maa. *Wo ho te sɛn?*'

'Samson! By the grace of God, me and my own are very well.' She laughs. *'Wo ho yε?'*

'Aane, me ho yε.'

'What about Efe and Amma?'

Sam's eyes move in the direction of the door. He speaks quietly. 'They're both well. Olivia is getting bigger every day and Efe, she's good, busy with work.'

A silent moment passes. 'Work?' Maame says, her voice creeping upwards.

'Yeah.' Sam feigns innocence. 'She's preparing for a big meeting at the end of the week.'

'This week?' Her voice raises an octave. She kisses her teeth. 'Heh! So these people won't let her rest? She should go to work and leave Amma?'

Sam shrugs. 'She's pretty set on it.'

'Hmph,' Maame grunts. 'Don't worry, let me talk to her.'

In the morning, Sam overhears another conversation – half of a conversation really. He listens from the nursery, Olivia bundled in his arms suckling softly on a bottle. Efe's voice drifts in through the open door and as soon as Sam hears the Twi he sits up straighter. Right from the beginning her words are terse, her voice wrapped in thick reams of frustration.

'It's not a waste of time. I like my job,' she says, then exasperated she adds, 'She'll still be young when I get back.'

Quietly, Sam moves to the doorway, resettles Olivia in his arms. Closer, he can hear Maame's firm tone, the annoyance in her voice. Efe rubs the heel of her hand over reddened eyes. Her just-waking smell – sweet and muggy with a hint of lemony-fresh bedsheets – hangs in the air in front of Sam. From where he hovers he can glimpse her, the cordless phone to her ear, her thumb and index finger pressed to her forehead. He can only imagine the cutting words and the empty threats Maame's making.

'I don't have to do something just because you say so,' Efe says. 'I want to use my brain again. I'm cooped up in here all day changing nappies, feeding and tidying spit-up. And I'm not saying I *need* time away from her, but if I did, would it be such a bad thing?'

The phone call ends abruptly. Sam moves a half-second too late, finds himself still bent into the corridor when Efe's eyes land on him. Wordlessly, he steps back into the nursery as Efe passes. She doesn't look his way.

That Friday, Efe leads Sam and Olivia to a coffee shop near the gallery. 'Okay, how do I look?' she says, nervous energy radiating. Sam pauses. She's wearing a short-sleeved blouse and skirt he's seen her in countless times and, aside from her slowly shrinking bump and fuller chest, Sam realises that Efe is thinner than she's been in years, almost as thin as she'd been back at university. As if noticing his hesitation, she tugs at her blouse and runs her hand over the buttons strained against her chest.

Sam swallows, his mind snagging on other things from that time. He thinks back to the summer of 2006, her breathless whisper when she'd told him of the three years spent hiding razor blades deep in the pockets of her handbag and the choking feeling that only eased with the sharp shock of a cut. He'd run his fingers over old scars and listened as she'd told him it had been years since she'd last needed to do that, reassured him. But still Sam wonders, wonders how he could've been there all those years and never known, wonders if she's found her way back there.

Efe looks at Sam, waiting for his answer.

'You look fantastic,' he says, his throat thick. 'I believe in you.'

Only after Efe leaves, does Sam realise he needs the bathroom. Two tables away a waitress is clearing tables.

'I'm so sorry. I need the bathroom, could you—' Sam gestures to Olivia nestled in the buggy.

'Oh yeah, sure.'

Sam rushes in and out, comes back to the waitress playing peek-a-boo with wide-eyed Liv.

'She's adorable,' the waitress smiles. 'How old?'

'Fifteen weeks,' Sam replies, settling back into his seat.

Another woman chimes in, leaning over her cappuccino and squinting into the buggy. 'You're doing *such* a great job.'

Sam chuckles and flushes with pride. 'Thanks. She's an angel – makes it easy.'

'I bet.'

Sam gets on with his work. He doesn't realise almost two hours have passed until he looks up and Efe is standing in front of him, her arms scissored across her chest, her braids soaked and dripping onto his laptop. He didn't even notice it was raining.

'You got her to fall asleep?' The question sounds like an accusation. Sam follows her gaze to Olivia sound asleep in the buggy.

'Yeah. It wasn't too hard.' He yawns. 'I just rocked her, gave her some milk. She was out like a light.'

Efe's lips press together. 'Fan-fucking-tastic.'

Cappuccino woman's eyes dart up. Her mouth falls open. She recovers quickly and pulls her gaze back to her mug. Sam shifts uncomfortably. 'Did the meeting not go well?'

'No, it didn't,' she says. 'Can we go now?'

'Do you wanna talk about it?'

'No, Sam. I want to leave.' All around the quiet cafe conversations end, eyes peek up from behind oversized ceramic mugs and people try to look like they aren't staring.

'Yeah, okay. Let's go,' Sam replies and begins sliding his things back into his bag. By the time he releases the brake on Olivia's buggy, Efe is already out the door. She charges on ahead, her face forward, braids whipping in the sideways winds. Sam loses her in the swish of black coats and dark umbrellas. He wrangles the buggy, trails a dozen steps behind.

When he gets to the car, there's still forty-one minutes left on the parking meter and she's leaning against the passenger's-side door, mouth set in a frown.

Sam tries to work out what to say. *If this is her reaction after one bad meeting it must be too soon*, he thinks to himself, but in a situation like this there are no right answers. He's still mulling over what to say as he folds the buggy down and climbs into the car. Beside him, Efe kicks her shoes off.

'Maybe it's for the best,' Sam says. 'I know how much you've put into that project, but there's really no rush to go back. Liv's only going to be this age once, isn't that what all the parenting books say? Don't you wanna be here for it?'

Efe stills, one hand frozen on her top button, her coat slumped across her knees. In her lap, Olivia whines quietly, twists her face towards the damp circles on Efe's chest. Through the wet patches, the shadow of a dark nursing bra is visible. In those seconds, Efe forces herself not to react to those words. She turns her face to the window and tries to concentrate on feeding Olivia, feeling deep within her the muted sensation of a crack streaking across a windowpane.

MAY 2012

Four Years Before

Sam's last client of the day is late. According to the log book, he's expecting a Mrs Gabrielle Jallow, a fifty-two-year-old woman fighting an unlawful eviction. Sam leans back in his chair and waits, runs a finger over the initials scratched into the dark, varnished wood. Through the dust-covered blinds, he can see the slow-moving high street just beyond the legal aid office, the same limited view he's stared at since he started helping out here a little over a year ago.

He thinks of it as penance. He'd like to phase into full-time photography at some point, but for now he spends four days a week here to atone for all his years at Barnard, Brand & Associates, finally helping bring justice to people he'd spent his career fighting. Back then most of his work had been for mega-corporations and developers, clients so flagrantly entitled they made politicians look like saints. Now Sam is proud to be helping the people who really need it.

George, the part-time law professor who owns the clinic, is the person who won Sam over in the first place. George has a teenage daughter and a son eleven months older than Liv and often reminds Sam, 'Best time's the baby years. After that they start walking, talking and catchin' an attitude.'

Sam takes a sip of his lukewarm flat white and checks his messages. One from Efe reads: Can you grab toilet roll? Another message flashes up right as the office door swings open and a nervous-looking woman steps into the room. 'Mrs Jallow?'

Sam says, extending a hand. Throughout the meeting, Sam ignores his buzzing phone. It goes off seven more times. Only after he shows Mrs Jallow to the door, almost two hours later, does Sam pull it out from his pocket. His brow furrows at the missed calls. A new message reads: Call me back and when he does, the sound of Efe's voice, breathless and shaking, tells him everything he needs to know.

Sam doesn't think to knock on his boss's door or explain where he's going. The moment he steps out of the office, he begins to run through the criss-crossing pedestrians, mentally calculating the quickest route to the hospital. The whole journey, heading south of the river, his mind races at full speed, thoughts churning and spiralling. He thinks of all the questions he should've asked Efe but, when he tries to call again, he has no signal. The landscape hurtling past the window is a blur. Above it the sky is tinted teal and a halo of light is slowly disappearing behind the horizon.

Thirty-five minutes later, Sam barrels into A&E. Before the automatic doors swish open, he catches sight of himself in the glass: the sheen of sweat on his forehead, tie loose around his neck and top button undone. It's a dozen steps from the doors to the reception desk, and when he gets there, Sam finds he is clinging to the counter, his voice louder than it needs to be.

'I'm looking for my dad, Kenneth Mensah,' Sam says. 'M-E-N-S-A-H—'

The nurse blinks at him. She uncrosses her arms and slowly types the letters out using just her pointer fingers. Sam swallows and digs his fingers further into the counter.

She gives a small shake of the head. 'I can't see anyone by the name—'

'He's here.'

'Who called you? Did a doctor ask you to come to A&E, sir?' she asks flatly.

'My wife called. Could you look it up again?'

While she types it out a second time, Sam glances around the room. The A&E is buzzing. There are clusters of people in every available space. Blue-scrubbed medics burst in and out of double doors, cradling clipboards, checklists. Names are volleyed across the room. Heads turn. Patients quietly rise from their seats and follow. Sam takes in the scuffed magnolia walls. Besides the sad NHS posters that sag in their frames, the only piece of decoration is a plastic sunflower on the reception desk.

'Sam?'

His head turns at the sound of Efe's voice and he immediately feels relieved. She rises from her seat and moves towards him, shifting a wriggling Olivia in her arms, almost tripping over the blanket trailing on the floor.

'Hey,' he says. Up close, she looks frazzled, her eyes red and puffy, a dark ketchup stain on her hoodie. Something about seeing her like this reminds him of his mother and the thought surprises him. He shakes it loose. 'What did they say?'

'Not much. The paramedics brought him in a couple of hours ago. One of the neighbours found him unconscious behind the wheel and called 999.'

Behind her Phoebe appears, clutching a paper cup of water. The corners of her lips drift upwards. Sam pulls her into a hug, then notices her chewing nervously on her bottom lip – a new habit that will become permanent in the weeks and months ahead.

'I missed the call.' Her voice breaks as she says this. 'I'm his emergency contact. I should've been there. He never should've been out there—'

'Hey, don't do that,' Sam says firmly. 'No one is to blame. We need to find out more information.' He places a comforting hand on her shoulder. They wait.

Sam thumps into the seat beside Efe and focuses on each breath. Seeing him near, Olivia reaches small, chubby hands towards him and whines until he scoops her up. Phoebe sits in the chair opposite. After a few minutes a sour-faced man, cradling his wrist, is summoned by a doctor, and the row is entirely empty but for her, a lonely island in a sea of mint-green wipe-clean seats.

Almost an hour passes. A steady stream of people come and go through the double doors. The waiting room grows quieter. Sam catches himself glancing up expectantly each time someone in scrubs looks in their direction. In his lap Olivia resists sleep. Her hands pad against his face, claw at the sky. She turns one way then the other, getting tangled in the blanket.

'It's the light,' Efe says. 'She won't go back to sleep if it's this bright.'

Sam can think of many times when she's fallen asleep in the bright glare of daylight, but he says nothing as Efe takes Liv and bounces her, begins laps of the bleak waiting room. Without Liv on his lap, Sam's foot taps incessantly on the grey speckled linoleum. The *tap tap tap* is just getting to him when someone appears. 'Mensah?'

'Yes.' Both Sam and Phoebe spring to their feet. Efe closes up the circle a second later. The doctor's eyes are barely visible under a blunt bob. From what Sam can see, she has one of those faces that could place her anywhere between twenty and almost forty.

'Can we see him?' Sam asks, pushing the words past the phantom hands tightening around his throat.

'Yes, but you can't take infants on the ward.'

'Right,' Sam nods. He feels Efe's eyes dart to him.

She drops her voice to a whisper. 'Sam, I want to be there too.'

'I know you do. Phoebe and I will go in first, then come out and find you.'

On the other side of the double doors, a noxious clinical smell hits sharp against the nostrils, and deeper into the ward, silhouettes of people are visible behind paper-thin curtains.

Phoebe gasps when she sees him. The doctor pulls back a curtain and there he is: perfectly still and frail-looking in green cotton, half of his face dragged down by an invisible force. She rushes over, cradles his hand in hers. Sam takes in the sight and looks away quickly, tries to focus on the dirt beneath his fingernails. Behind him, the doctor clears her throat. When she begins to speak a rosy pink spreads across her cheeks, but her voice is level, as if she is reading off a teleprompter.

'When paramedics arrived on the scene, your father was slumped over the wheel of his car, breathing, no visible signs of injury. He was semi-conscious but incoherent and kept asking for a . . .' The doctor pauses to check her notes. 'A Rebecca.'

Sam practically flinches. 'That's our mum,' Phoebe says.

'Should we wait—?'

'No,' Sam says, aware of how brusque he sounds. 'They're separated. Can you get back to my dad?'

The doctor moves her attention back to her notes. 'He was experiencing dizziness and numbness predominantly on his right side. The CT scan didn't show a bleed, but the team will book him in for an MRI in due course.' The doctor takes a moment to adjust a name badge that reads 'Dr Ng', pauses, then adds, 'We can't confirm yet, but all signs point to a stroke.'

'Oh my gosh.' A wound-tight feeling coils tighter around Sam. His arms hang heavy at his sides. 'How bad is it?'

'We won't know the extent of the damage yet. We'll transfer him to the stroke unit in the morning.'

'Is he going to be okay?' Phoebe asks. 'What's the best- and worst-case scenario?'

The doctor shifts uncomfortably. 'We should know more after the MRI.'

'Okay.' Sam nods, wanting Efe here the moment before he sees the curtain ripple, a flash of her orange hoodie slicing through the grey-green world. Efe. He feels relief for a second, then anger.

'Where's Liv?' Sam moves towards her, stepping through the gaping curtains.

Efe takes an unconscious step back. Her voice, when it comes, is small. 'She's with one of the nurses.'

'You left her with a stranger?'

Efe's hands splay uselessly in the air. Her head shakes. 'No, she's . . . she's a nurse.'

Sam is fuming. It doesn't cross his mind that he did the same thing a month ago, dashing to the bathroom while a woman at a nearby table kept an eye on Liv. Things are different now. His dad is sick. Sam's world has been upended.

He charges past, forgetting that his whole life he's had to tread carefully, be intentionally kind, likeable and smiley, so everyday actions aren't misconstrued as hostile or intimidating. Now, he doesn't care what they think of him. He is sprinting.

Efe is somewhere behind him. She catches up just as Sam explodes into reception and rips a sleeping Olivia out of a blonde nurse's arms.

'Oh my God!' she yelps. A hand comes up to her heart. Her eyes dart from Sam, shoulders shaking, gripping Olivia to his chest, to Efe, breathless, doubled-over, hands on her knees.

'She was no problem at all,' the nurse says. She looks like she might be sick.

SEPTEMBER 2012

Four Years Before

Efe has memories in this kitchen. Even after all these years, the walls are still sunflower yellow and the cabinets the same walnut-brown colour; the stove still takes at least two tries to light; and when Efe closes her eyes and focuses, she can smell popcorn in the air, as if years of movie nights have soaked the scent into the walls. It's all the same, only Efe's older now, Sam is nowhere to be seen, their daughter is napping in the living room and Efe's father-in-law is sleeping upstairs. *This isn't so bad*, she tells herself, just as a wail lets her know Olivia is no longer dozing. Efe abandons the vegetables she's chopping. Cautiously, she nudges open the door and peers in through the gap, but Liv, still rubbing her tired eyes, spots her immediately and cries louder until Efe gives in and plucks her from the travel cot.

Each time she tries to place Liv on the floor she cries, her pudgy fists clutching handfuls of Efe's clothes.

'Liv,' she says, reaching for Liv's teddy bear and waving it in front of her face, but her daughter, whimpering now, turns away. 'Really? You don't want Bear-Bear?' Efe places her hand to Liv's forehead.

'You don't feel warm,' she murmurs, but Liv's been fussy all day so Efe pulls her close and makes her way back to the kitchen. The whimpering quiets.

'I really don't have time for this,' Efe mutters to herself. The countertop is cluttered with vegetables for Ken's soup.

She has to organise his pills, make sure he does his daily exercise as they've skipped it twice this week. She's waiting on a call back from the pharmacy and would like at least five minutes for herself today.

When the soup is simmering, Efe settles down on the sofa with Liv pressed to her chest and her laptop beside her. She pulls up one of the usual Mummy blogs she rotates through, searching for advice. In the comments section, strangers fight about the right age to introduce sugar, proclaim the benefits of all-organic breakfast options and baby-led weaning. Before having Liv, she didn't know there was so much to argue about. After a few minutes of trawling through snarky and cutting comments, Efe switches to the Launi Gallery's Facebook page. She scrolls through photo after photo of her colleagues at the launch of the Art After Dark event, an event she spearheaded.

She snaps the computer shut, shifts Liv to her hip and makes her way upstairs carrying Ken's lunch.

'Are you awake?' Efe asks, the tray with Ken's lunch and pills wobbling.

'Rebecca?'

Most of Ken's speech is hard to decipher, his left side still weak and partially paralysed, but Efe can make out Sam's mum's name and hear the hopeful rise in Ken's voice as he says it.

'No, it's me, Ken.' She places the tray on the bedside table and opens the curtains so he can see her clearly. 'Efe,' she adds.

The functioning side of Ken's mouth curves down. He stirs deeper into his sheets. Fingers grip the thin blanket, then a spark of clarity emerges.

'Efe,' he says slowly. Then he repeats it, remembering.

Efe still struggles to see him like this. She's known him since she was a teenager and the whole time he's always been the biggest personality in the room, always so capable and sure of himself. And now he's different. Thinner. Tired all the time. Just as inclined to snap about something that had never bothered him before as he is to break down and cry over the smallest inconvenience, every emotion swollen and bloated like a strong wave, powerful enough to knock Efe off her feet.

Efe settles into her chair by the bed and rests the bowl in her lap. 'You have to eat your food, take your meds with no complaints and we have to get back to your exercises too. Don't think you got off lightly.'

After each mouthful, Efe reaches over to blot soup dribbling down to his chin. Liv is playing on the rug, making gurgling sounds. Efe looks over to see two fingers shoved into her daughter's mouth, her cheeks are coated in a thick layer of drool. She rises without thinking, planning to roll up Liv's damp sleeve, and is still looking the other way when the bowl lurches and hot soup sloshes into Ken's lap. He howls, uses his good hand to smack the bowl away. Soup splatters the walls and ceiling.

'Oh my God. I'm so—' Efe begins, but his good arm is careening towards her. She hears the crack before the pain explodes across her jaw. Her tongue crunches between her teeth.

'You did that on purpose!' he yells.

There's a sharp ringing in her ears. The baby is crying. Ken is still swinging wildly. She backs out of the way of a second punch and, flailing, Ken thumps onto the floor, tangled up in the duvet and thrashing, hand still reaching for Efe's feet. Olivia's cries intensify until Efe stumbles over, scoops her up and runs from the bedroom. Halfway down the stairs she trips, clutches Olivia tighter as her feet fly high into the air and she slams back into the sharp edge of a step, tailbone first. A screeched breath escapes her. She hobbles the rest of the way to the front door with Olivia in tow and calls Sam.

* * *

Efe is huddled on the front steps, her chin resting on Liv's head, biting back tears she won't let fall, when Sam pulls up at the house. Almost an hour has passed. Efe holds a bag of frozen carrots to her throbbing jaw. The ache in her back has spread itself thin and wide, crackling down her nerve endings so the pain stretches from her lower back down to her thighs. She's relieved to see him. She doesn't notice the firm set in his jaw until he starts speaking.

'Efe, we've talked about this.' He's circling two fingers at his temple, the vein thick and pressing out from the skin. Quick little breaths.

Efe stops short. They're close enough to touch, but have unknowingly positioned themselves on either side of the concrete paving stones. Opposing sides of a battle line. Efe braces, unsure what comes next.

'What is it this time?'

'He's freaking out.'

'This is the fourth time in two weeks,' he grumbles. 'I can't rescue you every time something goes wrong.'

Sam's words hang in the air between them. As if hearing them for the first time, he looks panicked, like he wants to pluck them from Efe's memory and swallow them whole. Several emotions chorus through Efe in a moment: shocked disbelief, sadness, indignation, fury.

Sam brings his hands to his temples, elbows spread wide. 'Wait, I—' he begins, but Efe cuts him off.

'You ungrateful dick,' she yells. 'He punched me.'

'He what—'

'You have no idea what I've been through today.' She spits the words out, then follows up with actual spit, a creamy glob that lands in the yellowing grass. Her chest heaves. 'He's your dad. You go in there and deal with him.'

She strides past, gets in the car and slams the door as hard as she can. Liv is crying again. Efe gropes around in the footwell. She pulls out a toy Olivia dropped there days ago.

It lights up. A chirpy American woman sings the same three nursery rhymes on rotation, so Efe deeply hates whoever bought it. But right this very second, she's almost relieved that it interrupts all logical thoughts.

Sam goes inside. Efe watches his silhouette move from room to room. The sky turns purple. Phoebe gets back from work and Sam returns to the car, silent and tight-lipped as he climbs into the driver's seat. Efe is pretending to sleep, her body angled away from him, her arms hugging herself.

They're halfway home when Efe says in a terse whisper, 'This isn't working. I think you need to accept that he needs more help than we can give him.'

'We can't afford more help.'

'Then we need to find the money because I can't keep doing this. I'm with him four days a week and it isn't getting any easier.' Waiting in the car, Efe has convinced herself that Ken's small signs of improvement were all in her imagination. There could be months or years of this. 'You didn't even ask me if I wanted to do this. You just assumed I had all this free time because I'm at home with Liv all day.'

Sam looks ready to shoot back an answer, but something wavers and he pulls into a side street, turns off the engine.

'Between the two of them . . .' Efe's crying now, her voice breathy, wiping a palm across her cheeks.

Sam undoes his seatbelt and stretches over the gap, pulling her into a hug. 'You're right. I'm sorry,' he says, breathing the words into her hair. 'We'll come up with something else. Give me a week. Please.'

Four Years Before

'Sorry we're late,' Efe says, wrangling the too-wide buggy into the hallway of Aunty Dora's flat. She is flustered, sweaty, acutely aware of the moist patches spreading outwards from her armpits.

'Did Sam drop you off?' Aunty Dora asks, glancing over Efe's shoulder mid-hug and into the empty hallway.

'No, we took the bus.'

'I could've come to you.'

Efe shakes her head. 'I had to pick up Ken's prescription, and really needed to get out of the house. We've been stuck inside all week,' she says. She's trying to sound breezy, but her routine with Liv revolves around the weekly mummy and baby group, sensory play and irregular GP appointments, all within walking distance of the flat. She knows how fussy Liv can be and rarely risks taking her on long journeys without the car, so the thirty-five-minute bus ride has left her feeling on edge. She takes a minute to compose herself, winces as she lowers the baby bag to the floor and runs her fingers over her sore shoulder. Even without seeing it, she knows, beneath her top, the skin is tender with a purpling bruise. She shrugs off her coat and shoots a nervous glance at the buggy. Mercifully, after thirty minutes of intermittent wailing, Liv finally fell asleep on the final stretch of their journey, the walk from the bus stop to Aunty Dora's estate, and Efe's relieved to see she's still asleep.

'Let me give you this now before I forget,' Aunty Dora says, and Efe gratefully accepts the plastic bag, the jars of millet flour knocking against each other.

'Are you sure she'll eat *koko*?' Aunty Dora says, leading the way into the living room.

'I'm gonna give it a go,' Efe says. 'She's regressing and Mum suggested it.'

'Regressing?'

'She's being an absolute nightmare. Seven wake-ups last night and anything I feed her, she spits right back out. They say it's normal. Some babies are like this at the nine-month mark.' She thinks back to earlier that morning, two hours of coaxing and pleading, feeding, pacing so much she bored a hole through her socks and the yellowy soles of her feet were visible through the fraying cotton.

Until all her days were confined to the flat, Efe had never known how small a place could become, how suffocating. It was just after 6 a.m. when Efe gave up; by then there'd been crying on both their parts and an attempt at breakfast that left Liv's cheeks smeared with soft peaches and orange goo coating both of their hands.

'Oh, it shouldn't be like this.' Aunty Dora shakes her head. 'What did Sam say?'

'I barely see him. He's either working or one of us is taking care of Ken. I can't even remember the last time we had an actual conversation that wasn't about childcare or his dad's recovery. It's awful. I was meant to be back at work months ago, but that didn't happen and now we have to wait until January for a space to open up at the nursery.' Efe's complaints are snowballing now, her eyes welling up with tears. 'I just wish I knew this is what it would be like. I'm trying to keep a handle on this one part and she's driving me crazy.'

'Efe,' Aunty Dora says softly, 'you should talk to Sam. Listen. That boy loves you. All these years he's been here.

190

That year you dropped out of university, wasn't he coming by this house every weekend?'

Efe nods, holding back tears. These days she is always on the brink of tears, surprised by how breakable she feels.

'And you need to get some rest. Go lie down.'

She casts a nervous glance towards the hallway. 'What if she wakes up?'

'You think I don't know how to take care of a baby?'

In the quiet of Aunty Dora's bedroom, Efe slips her shoes off and stretches out on the bed. Most days she feels like she could keel over, and today, as soon as her head hits the pillow, sleep is rising up to meet her.

When Efe wakes up, hours later, she catches the scent of something baking, a warm, buttery aroma hanging in the air. Sleep has made her slightly less jittery. Her walk is a little lighter as she drifts down the hall, stops to peer in at the living room, where a Nollywood movie is paused on screen, and carries on to the kitchen. Aunty Dora is sliding a tray of meat pies out of the oven when Efe enters, Liv tied to her back, sucking contentedly on two fingers, taking in the world from this new vantage point.

'You didn't wake me?'

Aunty Dora looks round and sees Efe. 'You were sleeping. And Amma wanted to spend quality time with Grandma Dora.'

Efe slides into a chair, draws her hands to her elbows. 'Has she been okay?'

'She's fine. She's had some milk and we changed her nappy,' Aunty Dora says. 'Feeling better?'

A small smile tugs the corners of Efe's lips. 'I think so.'

'Good.' Aunty Dora sets two pies down on the table, and for a few moments they pick at the still-warm pies, the pastry buckling beneath their fingers.

'What are your plans for today?'

Efe's eyes flick to the clock. She thinks for a moment. 'Not much. I have to stop by Westfield and return some clothes.'

Aunty Dora nods. 'Don't be so hard on yourself. There are so many people here to support you, *wa te?*'

'Thank you.'

'And promise me you'll talk to Sam.'

'I will.'

Efe starts to feel courageous as she walks down the road, the warm autumn sun on her face, the air cool and refreshing. *I can do this. It's not that bad,* she thinks, glancing down at her sleepy daughter. With every step Efe's confidence grows. She strides past the high street that's no more than a handful of independent shops, quirky cafes and Londis on the brink of closure. Weeks from now it will reopen as a shiny, bustling Co-op. Efe's resolve carries her right out to the train station and she feels the whole world unfurling at her feet.

She hesitates at the entrance. The smooth ramp had filled her with a sense of ease, but now, looking at the yellow and black tape slung across the only accessible barrier, she can feel second thoughts rising. She holds her Oyster card limply and glances down at the baby gazing up at her and all the bags hanging precariously off the buggy – too many things. She scans the empty station, purses her lips at the gate, just as she hears footsteps behind her.

'Could you—?' she asks, gesturing to the bags.

'Oh, sure,' the man replies, already lifting the baby bag onto his shoulder, taking the buggy in both hands and breezing through the small space before the barriers whizz shut again.

On the platform it is a very different story. Olivia is stirring, whining, staring at Efe with growing suspicion. The yellow letters glare at them announcing that the train is delayed by eight minutes. Efe draws her gaze along the track. She's lost sight of the man from earlier and is distracted by a crowd of teenagers that pass, skiving school, laughter spilling, music blasting through their loudspeakers. Before she has a chance to look the other way a train speeds past like a bullet. There's an unnatural billow that leaves Olivia looking shocked and frightened. Then the wailing begins.

Efe rifles through the bag. It is stuffed to the brim with spare nappies, a change of clothes, bottles of tepid water, warm milk, cold snacks, toys and books to keep Olivia entertained. Right at the bottom Efe finds the dummy. Olivia nibbles on the gummy plastic then spits it out, crying louder. The teenagers shoot her looks and move away just as their train rattles in. By the time Efe has wrestled the buggy into a cramped row and squashed herself into the outer seat, she can feel the tears gathering. The train begins to move and Efe is fraying. She pulls Olivia into her lap and bounces her around for a few minutes. She tries the bottle and when Olivia spits it out again, Efe glimpses an angry red gum, just splitting to reveal a sliver of white tooth. Without thinking, she reaches a finger out to examine it. The wailing intensifies. It's shrill, the sound of an alarm invigorated with brand new batteries, and saliva puddles around Olivia's cheeks, mixing with fresh, furious tears.

Efe can hear the exasperated tutting and exaggerated sighs of the nearest passengers. They shift around her, eventually rise and move away or further down the train. She keeps her eyes low as the stops hurtle past and the carriage slowly empties; Olivia's scream finally quiets to a soft whine and she stills in Efe's arms. Efe exhales, lowering her back into the buggy.

With Liv finally soothed, tiredness swoops low. Efe folds her arms across her handbag and curls her body away from the buggy. She struggles to keep her heavy eyelids open and does not have the energy to lift her face from the worn seat fabric, rough beneath her cheek. Instead, she stares across the aisle, past the empty seats and out the windows as the train rolls into the city and more and more buildings spring up.

Efe's eyes blink open. She catches a glimpse of the Clapham Junction sign behind the bobbing heads and her eyes are just beginning to close again when the panic flares. She leaps out of her seat, feet touching down on the platform just as the doors beep and swish closed behind her. She's already eight steps away, the train engine growling beside her, when she remembers the baby.

'Oh God, no!' She's back, jamming a finger into the button, slapping a frantic palm on the metal. 'Open the doors! My baby! Open the doors!' she yells. The words trip over each other, knock against her teeth. The passengers look her way just as the train begins to move.

'Ma'am, you need to stand behind the yellow line.'

Efe keeps banging, trying to prise open the doors while stumbling along beside the train.

'Ma'am! There'll be another train in ten minutes.' The voice is closer now. 'Miss!' A hand yanks her from the doors and Efe crumbles. She smacks into the ground, eyes fixed on the disappearing train. She can hear herself screaming, senses the pack of frozen commuters, silently gawking at her. Then she hears the impatient huff of the station attendant right above her, his breath hot on her scalp.

'Ma'am, please could you just calm down. Did you leave something on board?'

Efe looks up at the spotty teenager, concentrates on a patch of uneven stubble half-hidden behind a knitted navy collar.

'My baby.' She pushes the words past the boulder in her throat and watches as the teenager's mouth drops open, his eyes widen a fraction. 'Shit.'

He takes her to an office. Through the gap in the door, Efe can see the crowd dispersing. Life carries on. 'I'm radioing my supervisor,' he says. 'Is there anyone you need to call?' Efe digs around in her pockets, empties her bag and turns the entire thing inside out. Her mind goes back to Aunty Dora's bedside table, her phone charging by the lamp.

'I don't – I don't have my phone. I need to call my husband.' Her voice quivers. The world begins to spin.

'Okay, what's his number?'

Efe blinks. Once. Twice. She lifts the number from her brain like a long thread of pulled sugar, and watches as it appears in smudged blue ink on a bright yellow Post-it note.

'Cool – I mean – not cool, erm, sorry. Do you want some water?' the boy asks, stuffing the Post-it into his pocket, already reaching for a plastic cup. A garbled voice comes over the radio. Efe can't work out the words buried in the static.

'One minute,' he says. He hands the cup to Efe and steps out onto the platform. Water ripples in her trembling hands. For several moments she teeters on the edge of the hard plastic seat. Her mouth hangs open, her body sways and she can taste sharp acrid bile at the base of her throat. She puts the cup down on a grubby surface and curls her quaking hands around her thighs. She wonders if the tunnelling of her vision is what it feels like to die.

She catches snippets of a conversation over a crackling radio. 'I can't put her on the next train, it's not calling at Victoria . . .' he pauses. 'Oh, I dunno. I'd have to check the timetable.' Another pause. 'Of course I radioed the driver,' he sighs. 'No, that won't work. It's cancelled.'

Efe finally cries. Large, heavy tears fall into her lap. She grapples with the feelings rising up in her. She's on her own. Angry and relieved all at once. For the first time in forever, the ringing in her ears has stopped; between her muddled thoughts there's space for silence. She closes her eyes and imagines a life filled with pockets of quiet. She imagines that everything is different, that she has time for morning runs and after-work drinks. She dreams of the life she had, her memories taking on a rose-coloured hue: work; commuting, squashed between strangers; having a purpose outside of nappy changes and bedtime routines. She imagines a world glittering with possibility, more colourful and rich for it, that the dark stretch marks that carve up her body simply disappear, fall away like melted crayon, leaving nothing in their wake and taking her back to before. A small smile spreads across her lips. The tears stop falling and she opens her eyes to see a whole world through the slit in the door, so she rises, knots together her frayed edges and steps out into the warm, bright day.

Sam is at a photoshoot when he gets the call. 'I'll be one sec,' he says, apologising and stepping away from the smiling couple. 'Yes.' Sam cups the phone between his ear and shoulder. 'You're calling from where?' he asks.

'The office at Clapham Junction,' a voice repeats. 'Am I speaking to Samson Mensah?'

'Yes,' Sam says.

'This is the station manager at Clapham Junction train station.' A pause. 'This is highly unusual but I'm calling about your wife . . . . and your baby. A daughter, I believe.'

Sam's hands stop adjusting the focus; he straightens up. 'Are they okay? What's happened?'

'Yes, they're both fine, as far as we're aware, but they've become separated. Your daughter, she was left on a train. Staff pulled her off at Victoria so she's safe.'

Sam feels his legs weaken. 'Oh my God,' he drags a hand over his face. Blinks. 'How did this . . . Can you put my wife on the line?'

Sam hears an announcement in the background, a voice calling out trains to Richmond, Twickenham. The person at the other end takes a levelling breath. 'I'm afraid your wife's not here. She was. But now she's – erm – gone.'

Sam drives home hastily, his stomach churning like a cement mixer, his brain zipping through a hundred eventualities. He imagines Efe lying at the bottom of a ditch. Turning into an alleyway, a shadowy figure lurking. He pictures her clambering drunkenly on train tracks, headlights growing large behind her. He calls her again and again, redials the moment it goes to voicemail. At the flat, he parks haphazardly with only three wheels on the pavement. Something on the car's underside scrapes loudly.

Two policemen are waiting on the doorstep. It could be a scene from a movie: Officers 1 and 2 arrive on scene, pivot as Sam approaches.

'Hi, thanks for coming,' Sam says, trying to ignore the bunching of his shoulders whenever police are near. He overcompensates, puts on his extra-friendly voice and holds out a hand.

One of the officers – dark-haired, mid-forties, utterly forget-table facial features – dips his head, begins speaking with a light Cockney accent. 'Mr Mensah, we're here about your wife and daughter. Station staff notified us that there's been an incident.'

Sam hears *accident* and swallows, draws his unshaken hand back to his side. 'Yeah, they said my daughter was left on a train. None of this makes any sense. She's a baby. My wife is with her. There's no way she's not.'

'We've got an officer en route to Clapham, should know more soon,' the officer says flatly.

'Right.' Sam nods. He hates being in such close proximity to police officers. He's spent a lifetime avoiding them. He guesses the other officer is a few years younger, only vaguely interested in the case. Sam concentrates on keeping his gaze level, his stance open and voice polite. His phone dings.

'That her?' the officer in charge asks.

'No. I've been calling. She hasn't answered. It's my sister. I'm just gonna reply to this message.'

Once they're upstairs in the flat, Sam wishes he'd got here first. The police nose around without asking. Sam feels one of them trailing him as he moves from room to empty room, phone to one ear, listening out for the dim vibrations in case Efe's left her phone at home.

Sam is about to leave a voicemail when Aunty Dora's voice comes over the line. They talk, and after he clicks off the call, he turns back to the officers.

'That was her aunt. My wife went there this morning and forgot her phone,' Sam says.

'That's unfortunate.' The officer clucks his tongue, pulls a thin notebook off his belt. 'Don't suppose I could ask you a few questions.'

Sam glances towards the door. 'What about my daughter? I thought we—'

'Questions won't take long.'

They move to the sofa. Sam presses himself right back as if he is trying to flatten it. It's harder than it should be to sit still. Sensing the nervous energy winding its way through his body, Sam concentrates on keeping his leg from bouncing and wipes his sweaty palms along his jeans. His hands bunch tight and he grits his teeth as the officer tracks mud across the cream rug, hikes up his trousers and takes a seat on the coffee table.

'What do you want to know?' Sam reels off all the basics, only pausing when the officer says, 'Could you tell us about your wife's mindset this morning and over the last few days?'

Sam hesitates. 'Her mindset?' he echoes. Months of concerning comments and interactions come to mind. Sam knows not to mention a single one of them; instead he pushes them to the side, moves to the defensive. 'What does that have to do with anything?'

The officer glances down at his notes. 'Witnesses said she seemed . . . distressed.'

'Oh.' Sam brings a hand to his mouth. 'This morning she was fine, maybe a little stressed.'

He jots this down. 'Any idea why?'

'Just the usual stuff. Bad night's sleep. Baby driving her up the wall.'

'And does that happen much – the baby driving her up the wall?'

'No.' Sam lies, watching as the other officer shuffles into the kitchen, waits for his squeaking shoes to quiet. 'No more than normal.'

'And how much is normal?'

Sam's had enough of this. 'How many more questions?'

The officer purses his lips and shrugs. An overly casual gesture that wouldn't be out of place on a TV show. 'We're just trying to understand what happened.'

'But how is this helping? Why is no one looking for her? And when can I see my daughter?' Sam asks.

'We've got a unit out looking for your wife and station staff have been informed.' The dark-haired officer rearranges himself. The table creaks. 'And as for your daughter, you should be able to see her soon. Medics always do a once-over in cases like this and social services will need to be involved.'

'Social services? Is that really necessary?'

The officer sighs heavily as if he already regrets what he has to say. 'You do understand that child abandonment is a criminal offence?'

Sam's gaze shifts to the younger officer as he steps back into the room. Sam's voice sounds desperate now. His head shakes. 'It's not that. She made a mistake. She'd never intentionally—'

The officer clears his throat, looks at Sam sadly then back to his superior. 'Jim says she reported it then walked right up out of there.'

'Left without Liv? Nope, that's impossible,' Sam says. He looks down at his empty palms as if he'd find answers etched into the curve of his life line.

'CCTV doesn't lie. Our guy spoke to the CSAs, the station manager and a half-dozen witnesses. They all said the same thing.'

'No,' Sam mutters. He can't get the pieces to fit. He wants them to leave so he can get out there and look for her, get his daughter back. He wants everything to stop moving so quickly so he can catch his breath. Then he hears the door open. Hope surges and Sam's on his feet, pushing past before either of the officers move.

Efe stands alone in the doorway, her coat sagging over her shoulders, her expression sombre, her eyes pink and swollen.

'Thank God,' Sam says. He wants to reach out and hug her. *They've got it all wrong*, he thinks, then steps forward and sees the papery shopping bags dangling from her fingertips. He stops short. 'Please tell me Liv's with you.'

Her bottom lip creeps into her mouth. Tears are glistening in her eyes. Sam can't believe it. He pushes past, flings the door open on an empty stairwell, staggers forward and cranes his neck to peer down three flights of stairs. His pulse quickens. He feels his stomach turn over and over again. Cracks are appearing in the story he's told himself.

'Where is she?' Sam says. 'She's meant to be with you.'

He turns back as Efe lowers her bags to the floor, silent tears falling now. She pushes them into the space beneath the coat rack. They crinkle. As she stands, two braids fall loose. Sam can't think. All around him the air is receding into a vacuum. He moves towards her, calls her name but she won't look at him.

'Efe, where the hell is Olivia?' he says.

A notebook snaps shut. A small strangled sound escapes Efe's lips and she shrivels at the sight of the police officers. Sam is only vaguely aware of the snap and the stern voice whistling through the air when it speaks. 'Mrs Owusu-Mensah, we need to have a word with you.'

They ride in the back of the police car. A thick silence looms over them. Neither of the officers speak. The police radio continues at a hushed murmur. Sam can barely see the officers through the metal grate, can barely see the entire front of the car so he concentrates on taking deep breaths as an unfamiliar world rushes past his window. At the police station they're separated. Sam isn't sure where Efe goes, but he's led to a bleak waiting room with drooping grey blinds and a roofless Barbie doll house in the corner. An hour ticks by, Sam fidgets, still feeling like he could vomit, and dabs at a dark smudge on his shoe. He wants to do something, to know what's happening. They tell him nothing. Outside the room, the police station milieu continues. Sam listens to the rise and wane of voices, tries to spot the officers that brought him in.

'I just want to see my daughter,' Sam says again and again to anyone who will listen. A receptionist. A passing police officer. They tell him to sit down and Sam wills himself to be calm. It's late afternoon when Olivia is returned to him, her face blotchy with tears, eating fruit snacks by the fistful, carried in the arms of a thin, bespectacled woman, dressed from head to toe in beige and brown. Dizzy relief washes over Sam. He stumbles towards them, breath hitching in his throat, sputtering partial sentences. 'Liv. Thank God. Is she okay?'

'She's all checked out. Completely fine,' the beige-brown woman says, lips set in a straight line. She extends a hand. 'I'm Miss Warner, the social worker reviewing your case. And the family liaison officer will be in any minute.'

Sam nods, gaze still fixed on Olivia. 'Can I hold her?'

'Absolutely.'

Sam buries his face in Olivia's baby-soft curls, breathes in her sweet, familiar scent. She paws at his face. Her hand comes away damp with tears. Sam swallows hard and makes a silent promise never to take his eyes off her again.

It's almost 1 a.m. by the time Sam puts Olivia to bed. She's whinging and clingy so he holds her for a few minutes after her breathing evens. The day has dragged on and Sam feels he could fall asleep right where he stands. Instead, he tugs off his rain-damp coat and propels himself into their bedroom. Efe is still in her jacket, the blue bedspread sunken around her and dark with rain. She sits with her back to the door, staring blankly into the middle distance. He stands there and watches her. Just a moment or two.

'The social worker will be over first thing tomorrow morning. Did they tell you that?' These are the first words Sam has said to her since they marched her out of the flat, questioned and evaluated her for three hours, until they were confused but satisfied. Now, the whole bedroom feels weighed down by the events of the day, as if a sinkhole opened up at its centre.

'Efe?' he says. 'Did you hear me?'

She nods. Sam inhales, presses his feet into the ground and concentrates on staying upright. He can hear the distant drip, drip, drip of water droplets plinking in the kitchen sink and the space between them seems infinite.

He lets out a long, low breath, chooses his words carefully. 'Why did you take her on the train in the first place?'

'I needed to go out. I thought we could manage . . . I didn't think anything would happen.'

'And now we see how that worked out.' He balls up his coat and throws it on the bed.

Slowly, Efe curls her body around to face him. She stands. 'I wasn't thinking straight. I couldn't hear myself think.' She drops her head into her hands, crying noiselessly. Normally, he'd do something to comfort her, but Sam forces himself to stay where he is. He still needs space.

'So you thought it would be a good idea to leave and go shopping? Why didn't you go get her, or wait for them to bring her back?'

'I don't know. I wasn't thinking. I just –' she hesitates, voice breaking. 'No one tells you it's gonna be this difficult. Every day is so hard. I can't explain—'

'Help me understand. What do you need me to do? Tell me. What is it? You need more mum friends? You want to go back to work? Want me to take the night shift with Liv more often?'

'That's not—'

'What am I missing?' Sam asks, a desperate edge to his voice. 'I can't read your mind.'

He sees it then. It's there in the way Efe's hands come up to her elbows protectively, teeth gnawing on the bottom corner of her lip. A flash of his mum the last time Sam saw her before she left. He's startled into silence, remembering the sight of her crouched behind a three-year-old Phoebe, stroking her hair as she opened and closed one of her nursery rhyme books, the chorus of 'Mary Had a Little Lamb' playing a few bars before Phoebe, giggling to herself, snapped it shut again. And then his mum had turned, pulled Sam into a hug and stood there, her hands around her elbows, teeth on her bottom lip. She had reminded him of a deer caught in bright headlights a second before it bolts. Not meeting his eye, she'd muttered something about heading to the jazz bar, which Sam had thought odd because she normally waited for his dad to get home first, but he'd nodded and watched her leave and, after that, it had been just him and Phoebe for hours. Sam rarely lets his mind go there, but the thought presses against his skull and suddenly, urgently, he needs to convince Efe to stay. Sam feels like he hasn't looked at her – really looked at her – for months, hasn't noticed how depleted she is, how battle-weary. How hard the days with Liv have been on her.

In order to keep the roof over their heads and his father cared for, he's slipped back into something resembling his old Barnard, Brand & Associates work schedule, only now he's drifting in and out of tribunals, court hearings and endless appeals. Losing more than he wins. And he hasn't been here for Efe at all. The long workdays, the short temper. Little by little he let her down.

'I'm not good at this,' she says at last. Her voice is faint, breaking.

'Maybe it's me too,' Sam says. 'Maybe we need more help.'

Four Years Before

Sam can tell Maame is mad by the set of her jaw, the way she refuses to look at him directly. When he greets her, she flicks on the blender to drown him out. Onions, tomato, scotch bonnet and peppers whiz into a tangerine-coloured tornado. Barely four hours after they touch down on UK soil, jollof simmers on the stove. Chicken marinates on the counter. Suitcases are tucked under the coat rack. In the living room, Paa has managed to pull out the sofa bed and is wrestling the mattress into a fitted sheet. Olivia is down for a nap, sleeping peacefully through it all, and Efe, after initial hellos, is staying far out of the way, cooped up in their bedroom, under the covers.

Sam had hoped Efe's parents' presence here would make things easier. Instead, he doesn't know what to do with himself. He stands awkwardly by the door, feeling like a child waiting to be called on, watching Maame flutter around, pinging from task to task. She abandons the blender and moves on to vigorously cleaning the dry foods cupboard, a bowl of soapy water at her feet.

'Let me do that,' Sam offers.

'No,' she says, her tone clipped. 'And why can't I find a single sharp knife,' she says, waving a hand in the direction of the empty knife block.

'They're here,' Sam says, reaching for an ice-cream tub, hidden at the back of the Tupperware cabinet. He slips it open, presenting Maame with all the knives and razor blades Sam could find. He's hidden all the pills he could find too. It's just a precaution. But a necessary one. He thinks of all the changes he's noticed in Efe since social services got involved: her renewed hesitancy around Liv, how she returns to bed at every opportunity, sleeping for hours and ignoring the plates of food Sam leaves by her bedside. It reminds him of what she was like after she dropped out of university. Sam still remembers how frequently he came back to the city to check on her, but each time she'd be thinner, her skin sallow, and afterwards he and Serwaa would exchange curt whispers on the stairwell, trying to work out what to do. How to help her stay above the waterline. This time, Sam is alone.

Maame looks up from the tub of knives and gives him a sharp look. 'Samson,' she begins then stops. 'Call Efe and Paa in here.'

Obediently, Sam returns the knives to their hiding place and does as he's been asked. He wants to suggest they sit in the living room. Sam's dad had never been one for formality but, in the TV shows Sam watched growing up, family discussions were always held in the living room, everyone huddled together on overstuffed sofas in various states of ease and anxiety. But he doesn't mention this. It may be Sam and Efe's flat, and Maame and Paa may be here at their invitation, but it's clear his in-laws are in charge and he and Efe are the ones being sat down.

'Look,' Maame begins. 'We have something we want to say.'

'These things are better said in person,' Paa adds. He hooks one arm over Maame's shoulders. They seem solid now, bolstered.

'We didn't want to say too much on the phone. But even before you called, Sam, I knew that something was wrong. I could feel it in my spirit. All last week, I could not close my eyes and sleep. Not one night.' She sighs dramatically.

'Which is why we really appreciate you coming here at such short notice,' Sam says.

Maame continues. 'The two of you are trying. We can see that.'

Sam nods gratefully. Five days ago, over the phone he'd reassured them that everything is fine – everything will be fine – they just need a little help to get back on their feet. He glances over at Efe and notices she looks like an anxious bird, cautious, uneasy, eyes flitting in every direction for a trap.

'But we cannot sit back for this to continue.'

Sam's gaze snaps back to Maame.

'I don't know the battles Efe's facing, but for her to leave Amma like this, there must be something seriously wrong. We've decided to take the girls home,' Maame declares.

Sam balks. 'What are you talking about? Which girls—?'

'Olivia,' Maame says. 'And Efe too if she will come –' she corrects herself – 'if she has any sense, she will collect the passports now and we'll go before something worse happens.'

Stunned, Sam's gaze moves back to Efe. Maame's talking like she isn't here, and Efe hasn't moved an inch since Maame began speaking. Sam is staring at her, desperately looking for some sort of reaction to understand what she's thinking.

'It takes a village to raise a child. This country doesn't have the proper support system you need.' Maame draws her attention back to Sam. 'Do you even know your neighbours?'

Sam swallows. He thinks of the elderly woman downstairs, who sometimes collects their parcels, and the American man across the hall, who's no more than the opening and closing of doors, shuffling feet on floorboards, the murmur of a voice on the other side of a wall. 'What does that matter?'

'Be reasonable. Here small children are hard work. Back home there's always someone who can help.' *Back home,* Sam echoes. When they'd decided to go through with the pregnancy they'd agreed on regular trips to Ghana, twice a year at least, not just making the trip out for special occasions. And when he's honest with himself and when things are tough, Sam agrees it would be nice for Liv to not just visit, but grow up surrounded by family: cousins and grandparents, a bigger family than Sam could ever offer her. When she's old enough she could attend Maame's school. Paa would dote on her and teach her how to play *oware* and chess so well she could beat fully grown adults. But he's just registered this thought when a second feeling emerges. A tight-fisted panic. This is the family he's always wanted. Him, Efe and Liv. And this is their home. If Efe's parents want to take his family away from him, they'll have to prise it from his fingers.

'It's only until Amma's a little older – just four years.'

'Four years!'

Sam looks at them, slack-jawed. He wants to laugh but can't drag the sound up past the hollow spaces inside of him. The whole idea is illogical. And at that moment a breeze blows in through the open window and whips around them, and it feels like they're balanced on an edge of a cliff, in the stomach-clenching seconds before they fall.

'Look, Efe is not well,' Maame says, her voice deliberately calmer now. 'These things don't happen where we're from. She needs to be at home with her family and Amma is young; she needs to be with her mum.'

'This –' Sam gestures to the room around them – 'this is a family. *My* family. We wanted your help—'

'And this is the help we're offering. This country ruins people. We should've never – never—'

'No,' Efe says. The word grates out of her mouth and it's as if a spell is breaking.

Maame sputters. Paa chimes in, voice soothing. 'Efe, take time. You don't have to decide too quickly.'

'It's not an option. Our lives are here,' she says, and her voice is clear and steady. Sam is surprised. A weight lifts. He doesn't know when she decided to stay but, in his mind, he's making a plan. He'll do better. She can have any life she wants. He'll do anything to make this work.

Maame draws a deep breath. 'We've come all this way to help and all you two want to do is stop us.'

Paa exhales and squeezes the bridge of his nose. 'Maybe we should give it more time. Is it by force?'

Maame is frantic now, watching her ally falter. 'No, Paa. We agreed. What if something else happens to the child? There is no time.'

'*Me dɔ*, please.'

Efe exits. Maame rushes after her, her voice straining upwards, her outstretched fingers grasping nothing but air. She stumbles over the washing-up bowl, still resting on the floor next to the emptied cupboard. Soapy water spills out in every direction. In the same moment she splits open. She groans, draws her hands around her stomach, collapses inwards as the feelings she'd hidden begin to break through. Maame reaches out and slaps an open palm on the nearest counter. Paa is there in an instant, catching her before she falls. Slowly Maame pulls herself upright, unbuckling, tears thick in her eyes. Her voice, when it comes again, is stern but quiet, her gaze trained on Sam. 'Whatever happens next is on you.'

Sam forces his lungs to expand and contract long after they leave. He feels adrift in the sudden quiet. He looks at the simmering pot. He isn't hungry, and knows Maame has barely cooked in almost two decades so the rice will be soggy and the chicken will have too much Maggi. He moves slowly, lifts a hand to turn the stove off, the oven, then sighs and traipses soapy water down the hall. He takes a still sleeping Olivia from the playpen to her cot, then stands in the rectangle of light outside their bedroom door. Efe's long body is curled up in a knot, her breathing steady. Sensing him there, her head moves an inch, just enough for Sam to see her eyes flutter open, expectant. He kicks off his shoes and slips in beside her fully dressed.

He's too close now to take all of her in, but he runs his hand in small circles along her back, looks from the dip of her shoulders to the slope of her neck, the rise of her chest as she whispers, 'Have they gone?'

'Yeah, they probably went to Aunty Dora's or found a hotel,' he replies. 'And I'm sorry. About everything. We can figure it out. Let's not go back to how it was. I'm here. You're not alone.'

Efe falls quiet, her voice small. 'You said that before she was born. Remember? You said that but I've been alone this whole time. You promised.'

'I know. I'm sorry. Let's change that,' he says softly as he reaches across the space and threads his fingers through hers. For the first time in what feels like a lifetime, she doesn't pull away. Sam has questions. They gather in his mind like birds on a ledge, but the moment feels too tender. Fragile. He doesn't ask. Instead, they lie there, breathing in time, watching the evening light slant. The ceiling inches higher. They rest in a decision made, not yet knowing all the ways a decision alone will never be enough.

PART TWO

JANUARY 2015

Two Years Before

Olivia's third birthday comes round in the blink of an eye. Efe is certain that just yesterday her daughter was a baby, stuffing toes into her mouth and never sleeping through the night, and now she is a walking, talking toddler. At three, she is sweet and kind; she takes after Sam and Efe in many ways, but somehow Liv has also inherited Serwaa's joyous smile, Paa's sense of humour and Maame's immovable spirit. She is a collection of all of the people Efe loves. To Efe, getting through the last few years is a miracle in itself, one that needs to be marked and celebrated.

Three hours before the party begins, Efe wipes a hand across her brow. Despite the January chill outside, she is sweating. The kitchen is warm, the windows misted with condensation. The two largest pots are simmering on the stove.

She reaches for her phone to check her to-do list for the umpteenth time that morning, but it begins ringing the moment it's in her hand. She sighs. Maame has called twice this week already, and Efe is certain this conversation will be another reiteration of ones they've already had.

'Hi, Mum,' Efe says, keeping her voice bright and peeking at the stew simmering in one of the pots.

'Efe,' Maame says. 'How's the party-planning?'

'Good.' Efe glances up at the clock. 'We're making good time.'

'What are you cooking?'

'Jollof, fried rice and stew. I'll make the coleslaw next.'

Maame makes an approving sound. 'And the birthday girl? How's Amma?'

'Yeah, she's great,' Efe says, glancing over her shoulder to where Liv is playing in the living room, rummaging through the pile of blue and yellow balloons spread across the rug. 'The dresses you sent her are way too big but she likes them.'

'Don't worry. Let her grow into it.'

'Yeah, I know.' Efe gives the stew a quick stir, pops the lid back on and waits. 'Are you not going to ask about Sam?'

On the other end of the line, Maame makes a sound between a grunt and a tut. 'I'm sure he's fine,' she says stiffly.

Efe wants to laugh but rolls her eyes instead. Paa took a week to thaw, but Efe is consistently surprised by how long Maame is able to hold a grudge. Her infamous rivalry with Gifty has been going on for three decades now, neither woman able to say exactly why it began but, after all these years, it shows no signs of slowing. Even though Efe is steadier now and it was her choice to stay in London, Sam still bears the brunt of Maame's anger.

'I know you're still mad at him—'

'I'm not mad,' Maame interrupts, her voice firm. 'All I'm saying is that if Samson had been supporting you when you were unwell nothing bad would've happened. Look at Serwaa and Joseph . . .' And on Maame goes, rehashing the same conversation they've had a hundred times over the last two years.

Efe leaves it at that, only speaking when Maame finally finishes what she has to say. 'You could still ask how he is,' Efe says.

Ten minutes later, Sam returns from the shops. At the sound of his keys in the lock, Olivia is at the door and on Sam's hip by the time the two of them shuffle into the kitchen, her arm draped around Sam's neck, her face nestled into his chest.

'Find everything?' Efe asks, reaching for the bags.

'I think I bought every pack of sausage rolls and party food I could get my hands on,' he says, drawing down the zipper on his winter coat and unwinding the scarf at his neck. Efe spreads the packages on the counter. It will be too much food for the twenty-five guests invited. Efe is sure of it. Yet, she couldn't help but send Sam out into the sleeting rain to buy extra provisions. Everything has to be perfect. When Olivia's first birthday had wheeled round, Efe still felt like she was drowning, flipping back and forth on an hourly basis, locking herself away in the bathroom whenever Liv had a meltdown, still questioning if she'd made the right decision in choosing to stay. By Liv's second birthday things were improving. A small get-together had been hastily planned and just as hastily cancelled when Liv brought home a bug and all three of them spent the next forty-eight hours puking. So this birthday, the first Efe and Sam planned together, has to go off without a hitch.

'If I put everything out on the table can you get her dressed?' Efe says. 'I tried earlier but she wanted you.'

'I got it,' Sam says. He pulls Efe close, places a kiss on her forehead and breathes her in deeply. 'Say bye to Mummy. Let's get your costume on.'

Efe's nerves finally begin to settle when the table is laid out and most of the decorations are up. The kids will be plied with crisps, sandwiches and sausage rolls; everything brown and beige, covered with breadcrumbs and stuffed with preservatives. She moves to the window and Blu-tacks blue film to the glass. Light comes in through the cutouts and transforms the room into a glorious underwater scene.

'Fishes,' Olivia says, the word a slithery hiss.

Efe turns, watching her daughter toddle in wearing one of the outfits Maame sent over, a sage-green dress with a giant, frilly underskirt. The dress had been Efe's then Serwaa's back when they were little girls. Though they have made it to Ghana just once since Liv was born, Efe is pretty sure the photo of her in that dress still lives on the desk in her dad's office.

She looks at Sam. 'What happened to her starfish costume?'

He gives his head a small shake, then crouches down so he's closer to Liv's height. 'Remember how you said you wanted fishes at your birthday party, so Mummy and Daddy bought that starfish costume you really wanted? Don't you wanna put that on?'

Olivia considers this for a second, bottom lip jutted out, brow creased in thought, then gives her head a shake and makes her way across the room to keep playing with the balloons.

'It's not worth it,' Efe says with a sigh.

'Green still works,' Sam agrees.

Later, when the guests begin to arrive, none of them mention Liv's outfit, not even Phoebe and Ken who had been full of compliments when Sam sent photos to the family WhatsApp group.

By early afternoon, there are almost a dozen kids running around, plus parents from the mum and baby group; Miss Bea, Liv's childminder, is leading a game while Aunty Dora and Sam's family watch on. The living room feels cramped. Efe is used to gallery openings, exhibitions, networking events where she talks for hours about how brilliant her clients are. But she is beginning to feel content. *There are similarities*, she thinks, watching the guests chatting amongst themselves, sipping cups of neon-blue hot chocolate that Sam presents to each guest on arrival, a starfish-shaped marshmallow floating in each mug. She catches Sam's eyes and then they are both beaming; and suddenly Efe is immensely happy they made it through the hard years, and that she's still here.

Later, when the kids are running amok, spilling or dropping something on the floor every few minutes, Efe steps into the kitchen to catch her breath. She pulls out her phone, hoping for just a few moments away from the chaos. She scrolls through the first few messages. Then Sam arrives, hot on her heels.

216

'Abbey and David can't make it,' she says aloud, eyes still skimming the text message.

'Aren't they on honeymoon?'

'They got back on Thursday but they're pretty exhausted apparently. Liv's gift should arrive on Monday.' Efe sends off a quick reply, not mentioning that the party started almost two hours ago. She looks at the empty platter in Sam's hands. 'What's that?'

'Sandwiches, but I've got it,' he says. 'Why don't you relax?'

At this, Efe folds her arms around Sam and kisses him, the platter wobbling in his hands. She steps back, finally exhaling after hours of hurrying around, finishing party preparations and cleaning up spills caused by the dozen children ambling around the flat. She's been trying to manage the whole day as Maame would, constantly roving the room, filling up empty glasses, making sure guests have eaten more than enough, overseeing everything. She's survived this test of parenthood, and the end of the party is in sight.

'Actually,' Efe says. 'It's probably a good time for cake. Can you get Liv near the table and cue up "Happy Birthday"?'

'Sure.'

The cake is extravagant, three tiers of funfetti, ordered from a specialist bakery six weeks in advance. To go with the theme, the cake is a golden sandcastle surrounded by pink seashells and blue-green waves made of perfectly piped buttercream. Efe has it settled on the counter and is sliding three candles out of their packaging when she hears the door creak and Phoebe's voice close by.

'Efe,' she says, sounding relieved. 'I've been trying to catch you.'

'You have?' Efe looks up. Bustling around the party, Efe has barely been aware of Phoebe shooting her looks, edging closer as she refilled bowls of Smarties and popcorn.

Efe watches as Phoebe glances over her shoulder furtively, then pushes the door so it creaks closed. Something about the sound unsettles Efe. Her stomach is clenched a moment before Phoebe takes a steadying breath and speaks.

'I found her.'

Efe already knows who Phoebe is referring to. Since that evening eighteen months ago, staring at the little yellow house on Phoebe's laptop screen, there have been updates about the search for Sam and Phoebe's mum every few months. For eighteen months Efe has been sworn to secrecy, both of them agreeing it was better this way, that there was no point mentioning it to Sam until they had something concrete, something real. The first few weeks of searching threw up almost nothing: just a letter from the new owner of the house, apologising and saying they had no record of a Rebecca Mensah. A month later they'd received a message from an old bandmate of hers, saying she hadn't heard from Rebecca in almost fifteen years but sending over a contact for someone who might know where she was. And then two more updates before news dried up and Phoebe began toying with the idea of hiring a PI. But somehow all of this has landed them here, with Phoebe beaming and close to tears, her face alight, talking too quickly about forwarding addresses and water bills and saying she has an email address.

'You have her email address?' Efe repeats, her muddled brain still trying to keep hold of all the moving pieces.

'I'm saying she emailed me back.'

Efe thinks of Sam. She's had endless opportunities to tell him what Phoebe was doing. She's kept silent all this time, had never imagined it getting to this point. Secretly she'd hoped she'd never have to say anything at all. Efe needs a moment to collect herself. She turns her back to Phoebe and begins rifling through the drawer in search of matches. Her heartbeat is quickening. The kitchen suddenly feels warmer. Sweat is gathering on her forehead. Her words, when they come, are gruff and clipped, sounding like the words of a stranger.

'Don't tell Sam,' she says. 'You have no idea how much work he's put into this party. Just give us today.' She thinks of Sam back in early November, Liv's birthday still months away, but he'd taken Liv's idea for an under the sea themed party and run with it. She thinks back to how he'd researched bakeries, trawled through reviews of party decorations, curated a playlist and traipsed from shop to shop in search of the perfect gift bags. He'd made a spreadsheet for goodness' sake.

'Don't you think he'll want to know?' Phoebe says, her voice soft.

Efe isn't sure what he'll want, but she is certain Sam won't appreciate finding out in the middle of a party with twenty-five guests in his house. She plans to pull him aside after everyone's gone home and tell him gently. He deserves that much. She is too focused on the conversation at hand to notice that the music in the living room is fading.

'I know you're excited, Pheebs, but don't tell Sam. Not today. Please.'

'Don't tell me what?'

Efe hadn't even heard the creak of the door opening, but Sam is standing there, his brow furrowed, eyes on her. She tenses. The box of matches crumples in her fist.

'What's happening?' Sam says, the laugh in his voice lilting when neither Efe nor Phoebe begin to answer. He turns to Phoebe. 'What shouldn't you tell me?'

At this, Phoebe shoots Efe a panicked look. In a split second, a silent conversation passes between them and, before Efe can stop her, she says, 'I found Mum.'

Sam's expression changes. He looks flustered, disbelieving. 'You're not serious,' he says. Then his gaze moves to Efe and the doubtful smile flickers.

'I hired a private investigator and I found her. I got in touch with her and she emailed back. Yesterday.'

Sam gives his head a small shake and raises a palm to his forehead, struggling to process. 'What about Dad?'

'He knows,' Phoebe says. 'He's known from the start.'

Efe can hear the tinkle of Liv's laughter above the other kids', the murmur of conversations, the first notes of 'Happy Birthday' thrumming through the sound system.

Sam swallows. His Adam's apple bobs. Efe takes a step forward the same moment Miss Bea slips in through the door.

'I've got all the kids in a neat line, so I'd say we're about ready,' she says, then falls silent, her lip curling with an unasked question. She looks from Sam, to Efe and Phoebe and back again.

Sam is the first to shake it off. 'Great, thanks,' he says, then turns to Efe. 'Cake?'

Efe recovers, lights the candles. She pulls out a knife, tears off a piece of foil and hurriedly wraps the foil around the handle, trying to salvage their perfect day. She strides into the living room a minute later, the cake held aloft. The guests begin singing. People are getting out their phones.

'I'll take it,' one of the mums offers, holding Sam's camera unsteadily. Efe squeezes in behind the table and holds the cake up in front of Liv, and for a second it's just her, Liv and Sam illuminated in the soft yellow light. Efe looks down at the swirls of blue-green buttercream shaped like waves. Just before the party, Sam had run his finger along the back of the cake, insisted she try some, and when he brought his finger up to her mouth, the icing was so sweet her eyes watered.

'Say cheese,' she hears Ken say. She's still thinking of that moment as Sam's arm wraps around her waist. He squeezes. Their eyes meet. An unspoken conversation happens, both of them remembering they're still in this together. They're good. Then, Efe and Sam turn to the crowd of waiting guests and smile.

MARCH 2016

Seven Months Before

Efe's hopeful that the hardest years are behind her. Things are easier now Liv is older and her needs aren't so all-encompassing. Efe tries to find fun things for them to do together. Outings. Baking. Games. Today Efe and Olivia are making pancakes, the air scented with cinnamon and vanilla. Olivia is at Efe's elbow, swaddled in an apron but still dusted in flour.

'Oops,' she mumbles, eyes moving from Efe to a broken fragment of egg shell floating in the batter.

'Here, let's try this,' Efe says, reaching for a spoon. She wiggles the piece to the edge of the bowl. Right as Efe fishes it out, she feels the weight of a gaze on her. They both look up. A smile crests the very moment the shutter clicks.

'Perfect,' Sam whispers and lifts his eye from the viewfinder.

'How long have you been standing there?' Efe says, feeling a smile at her lips.

'About a minute,' Sam says as he comes close and folds his arms around Efe, presses his lips to her neck. 'Good morning.'

She taps him playfully with the spoon. 'Great. Now you're up, you can set the table.'

They move to the dining table. When the pancakes are done, Sam and Liv take the first two plates through and Efe brings up the rear. She settles into an empty chair, glancing at a Facebook message on her phone screen.

'Abbey's messaged,' she says. 'She's doing a show in London this summer, some off-West End Shakespearean thing.'

'Cool. How is she?' Sam asks, reaching for Liv's plastic cup and topping it up with juice.

'Fine,' Efe says, then corrects herself. 'Not fine. I told you she and David are in a rough patch, right? Maybe we should go and see it to support her.'

Sam nods, reaching over to slice Liv's breakfast. 'Yeah, why not?'

'Okay, I'll book tickets and see if Aunty Dora can babysit.'

They've only seen Abbey a handful of times since her wedding. In Efe's memory, David had spent the entire day desperately trying and failing to placate both Abbey and his pre-teen children – all of them glaring and simmering with anger by the end of the reception.

Efe and Sam chat easily over breakfast. She raises a mug to her lips, taking small sips of tea.

'What are your plans for today?' Sam asks.

'I'll probably head over to the studio and see how Nico's getting on. She's not answering again and I've got some news to deliver.'

Sam's eyebrows rise, interest piqued. 'That *Guardian* profile you mentioned?'

'And the *New Statesman*. They both want full features and interviews, but you know what she gets like when she's deep into a project. It might not work out.' Efe repeats this to herself regularly. A self-imposed bottleneck on her growing excitement. 'What about you?'

There's a puckering of lips. Sam tilts his head to the side. 'Liv and I are heading to the childminder's. And I have an hour or two of editing before I prep for a shoot this afternoon.'

Efe nods. 'Any word from Phoebe about –' she hesitates, sneaking a look at Olivia to make sure she's preoccupied – 'your mum?'

Instantly Sam's face hardens. He takes a moment to reply and when he speaks his voice is flat and blunt, the way it always gets when he speaks of his mum.

'I know they've met up a few times. Maybe two or three.'

'So it's going well?'

'Dunno.' Sam shrugs. He clears his throat and puts down his mug of coffee. 'It's got nothing to do with me.'

Efe nods even though it's just as much to do with Sam as it is with Phoebe. It was one thing helping Phoebe find her mum, searching for answers to a lifetime of questions. But even Efe is astounded by just how easily Phoebe's let her back in – Ken too – as if twenty-three years of absence could be wiped away overnight.

Efe wants to keep talking about it, but she can already see Sam's walls coming down. She changes the topic. 'Don't forget to pay Miss Bea,' she says. 'The childminder's fees are due tomorrow.'

'Remind me how much it is this month.'

'Four hundred and eighty.'

'Got it.'

When Sam and Olivia disappear into Liv's bedroom to get ready, Efe settles down with her laptop to work. She's still skimming emails when Olivia returns, teeth cleaned, face washed and dressed for the day ahead. Quietly, she slides into Efe's lap, legs swinging high above the floor as Efe brushes her hair, slicks it back into two neat afro puffs.

'Okay, time to go,' Sam says, leaning through the doorway. Olivia skips over to him. Efe rises, her knees stiff. She walks towards Sam and folds her arms around him, pressing her body up the length of his. She lets her eyes close, feels his tender kiss on her forehead. Then she raises her face and brings her lips to his, tasting honey and coffee.

'Don't forget to pick her up at three,' Sam says.

'I won't.'

'Love you.'

'Love you too.'

'Bye, Mummy,' Olivia says, peering up from under her raincoat, a pair of frog ears on top of her head.

'Bye, sweetie,' Efe replies. 'Have fun with Miss Bea.'

Efe gets off the train at Whitechapel. Above her head, the sun perches high above the taller buildings, watching the city, releasing its hold on the morning. She walks like her feet barely graze the floor, angles her head higher. It's a short walk to Nico's studio, a former Turkish takeaway with rugs and blankets tacked to the shopfront windows to muffle the noise from the road outside and stop people peering in. She leans on the buzzer, waits a few moments and leans on it again.

'Oh, I thought you were the postman,' Nico says, stepping aside to let Efe in.

'You let the postman in?'

From the headphones hanging round her neck to the tart tang of acrylic paint lingering in the air, Efe can tell she's been hard at work. In the back room, most of the industrial kitchen has been torn out in favour of a small steel sink and a wide-open workspace. The windows are flung wide, the space bright and airy, the walls a pale blue so light it looks white until you look closely. At the far end of the room, a canvas is draped in cloth. Efe knows Nico well enough not to ask, but to wait until she offers. 'The art tells me when it's ready,' is her favourite phrase, fine on most occasions but infuriating when their backs are up against the walls and Nico is weeks past a delivery date.

Efe loves the space. She had been the one to find it, nestled a bus ride away from most of her other city-dwelling clients and walking distance from the Launi Gallery, where she still helps out as a consultant. Years ago, she and Nico had reconnected for coffee again and again, month after month, until an ad-hoc business relationship formed, one that works around Efe's family life. Thankfully, Efe has made it to every one of Nico's openings, including solo shows in Paris and Stockholm, and was the one to put her forward as the Swainson Gallery's artist in residence. She's taken on new clients, earns a generous commission. Her career has found its feet.

'Do you have news? Is that why you're here?'

'I'm here because you're not answering your phone,' Efe says. 'And yes, I have news.'

Nico nods expectantly, shakes her hair loose. The locs are new, freeform, black dipped into gold. A month ago, over the phone, she'd told Efe with a laugh that both of her parents despise them, the one topic they've agreed on in almost three decades. And Efe had laughed knowingly. 'If it's not this it's something else,' she'd said.

'So . . .' Nico leads.

'The *Guardian* and *New Statesman*.'

'You're kidding, a feature?' Nico gasps, a hand over her mouth.

'A whole profile on you and the new collection.'

'Wow, oh my gosh! Thank you.' Nico grins and pulls Efe into a tight hug. 'We need to celebrate.'

'We'll celebrate when it's all done and dusted,' Efe says.

'Fine, fine,' Nico says, still enthused. 'Either way we're going to toast,' she says and offers Efe water from a cracked mug.

'Cheers,' Efe says, 'to continued success.' They clink mugs.

Afterwards, Nico pulls off the cover and both of them take in the pencil silhouette sketched onto canvas. Efe cocks her head to the side. Nico has always been one of Efe's most innovative clients, but something about this new medium has invigorated her; the scales so expansive, one piece could fill a whole wall. Efe prattles on about details and timings while Nico adjusts the pencil sketch, rubs out a wisp of a calf, so a thigh trails off into nothing.

Forty minutes later, thoroughly caught up, Efe says her goodbyes and pauses at the front door. 'Oh, and your mum's texting me again. Please return her calls.'

'I will,' Nico says, chin pinched between her thumb and pointer finger. 'I just need to focus for a few more days. I'll call her at the weekend.'

'That's the day after tomorrow,' Efe says.

'Oh.' Nico pauses. 'Next weekend.'

As Efe lets herself back into the flat, Serwaa rings. Her face flashes up on screen, the Skype bubble floating just above her eyebrow. 'Thank God, someone who can calm me down,' she howls, the moment the video call connects.

'Why? What's wrong?'

Serwaa launches in. 'Let me tell you the way Joseph is getting on my nerves. That man will walk past the same rubbish on the floor ten times and not stop to pick it up. Sometimes it's like he doesn't have a brain. You know what he said to me yesterday? He said that next time I go out I should wake Afia and take her with me. Does that make sense? She's asleep and he's just sitting at home anyhow. He's talking about what should he do if she wakes up. The girl is almost two – acting like he doesn't know how to hold or feed a child. Did he not feed the other two? Is that my job alone? Did I impregnate myself? If he stays home with her he's not doing me any favour.' Serwaa kisses her teeth. Like a slowly deflating balloon, she lets the rest of her anger seep out. 'Okay. I've got it out of my system. How are you?'

'Me?' Efe chuckles. 'I'm fine.'

Off screen there's a brief scuffle. 'Kobby, Abena, say hello to your aunty.' Efe watches as two heads bob into view; they say hello in unison.

'I can't believe how big they are,' Efe says.

'They grow every day. You should come and see for yourself.' Serwaa leans closer to the screen, peers in just as the crackling starts and her movements disconnect from her voice. 'Where are you coming from? Did I interrupt something?'

'I went down to the studio to see Nico.'

'With good news?'

'Well,' Efe says. 'She's being profiled in a few big newspapers. It'll really help to elevate her.'

'Oh, congratulations, Efe.' Over the static, Serwaa's voice ebbs high and low. 'So work is the reason why your skin is glowing like this? I thought you were going to say you were pregnant again.'

'God no,' Efe says before she can stop herself.

'So, you still don't want to give Olivia a sibling?'

'She is more than enough for us,' Efe says.

Serwaa laughs. 'Well keep doing what you're doing. Success suits you.'

Efe smiles. 'What else is going on?'

'Have you heard from Nanadwoa?' Serwaa asks.

'Not in the last few weeks. I've been meaning to call her. Why?'

'She got pregnant by Pastor Eric.'

Efe's jaw falls open. 'Are you serious?'

Serwaa nods. 'Everyone's talking about it. Apparently the affair has been going on for years. He's the one that moved her to that flat in Cantonments. His wife came into bible study yesterday and accused him in front of everyone. You should've seen the way she was drunk, crying and screaming in the middle of his message. The deacons didn't even try to hold her back and in the end it was *him* who had to leave the building.'

'Oh my goodness.' Efe cannot think of anything else to say. She cannot begin to imagine how Nanadwoa is feeling.

Serwaa nods. 'Anyway, you should speak to your friend.'

Efe returns to her work half dazed and unfocused. Later, in the bathroom, she gazes at her reflection in the soft white lighting, Serwaa's comment still circling in her head. She doesn't feel any different. She isn't glowing and can't make out anything other than a small red spot forming on her cheek – no brilliant glimmer or radiant flush – so she pushes down the fear nibbling at her and goes to pick up Olivia. The pre-school rush-hour traffic begins early today. Efe outpaces the slow-moving parade of buses and cars that edge forward, dashes across the road and arrives at the childminder's at 2.56.

'Oh great, you're early,' Miss Bea says and disappears back inside to get Olivia. Efe waits in the entryway, pulls out her diary and works backwards. She searches for the little 'P' scrawled in the top corner beside the date. She does the maths twice. Twelve days late. Efe's stomach clenches just before Liv zips out of the house and crashes into her thighs. *It could be a mistake*, she thinks, *stress or something*. Momentarily calmed by that thought, she turns her attention back to her daughter, the chubby brown face peeking out from below a lime-green hood.

They dawdle. It takes double the time to get back to the flat because Olivia stops to hop over every crack in the pavement, examine every twig, peer at the daisies pushing up between sparse patches of grass, tightrope-walks across the sections where tree trunks buckle the pavement. Efe's brain oscillates between work and this new worry – the one she won't let herself fully think about. Just to be certain, she buys a test, slips it into her bag before they head home. And at home she is too afraid. It's taken years of small adjustments, learning to share the weight of parenthood, and now she and Sam have finally established a rhythm that works for them. Sam does mornings. Efe does evenings. Liv is at a childminder's three days a week, and they split the other days between them, both fitting in work around her.

Feeling the tightness in her chest, Efe knows she doesn't want another child undoing the progress they've made, another baby shackling her to home. She spends all evening trying not to think about it, though as evening wears on, the fear rolls in like a low fog, bleeding out across the floorboards, spreading quietly until it's impossible to see past it. She busies herself, hopes that at any moment she'll feel her period arrive and know there's no need at all.

That night, Efe lies in bed. The worry settles into something solid and heavy on her chest. Outside, the sky darkens. Sam is oblivious and fast asleep beside her, breathing evenly, one foot poking out of the duvet, half of his hair pillow-flat, his face marred in sleepy creases. Efe cannot sleep. Her thoughts go to the insomniac end months of her first pregnancy, weeks twenty-eight through to thirty-nine when she caught sleep in snatches: on the sofa, in front of a movie, twice in the shower and had to catch herself before falling, while a restless Olivia tossed and turned in Efe's uterus, wriggling for weeks on end. This time what keeps her awake is the dread she feels at the possibility of another baby. The fear nestles in the forefront of her mind – this solid immovable thing – while she gazes up at the lightening ceiling, stares at the swirling patterns she can't quite make out.

She finally gets out of bed sometime in the early hours, feeling weary. She checked her phone at midnight, 1.16, 2.21 and 3.58. She doesn't check it now. Instead, she turns her dry eyes to the pale sky and guesses that it's nearing five. Quietly, she rummages in her bag for the crinkly paper and heads, shoeless, into the bathroom. She perches on the edge of the toilet and tries to muster up some confidence. She thinks about how careful she is. How, in the weeks leading up to Liv's first birthday, the GP had walked Efe through all her contraceptive options and how diligently she has been popping small white pills daily since then. She knows she did not miss a single one. *It must be a mistake. A blip*, she thinks, then watches as two red lines bleed into the small window, so vibrant they glow. 'Ninety-nine point ninety-eight percent effective,' the GP had said. 'As good as one hundred,' and he'd smirked, tapping away on his computer. In Efe's memory his head had wobbled like a human-sized bobble-head. She wants to go back and smack him.

'This isn't happening,' she whispers. She won't let it.

She can hear the doors closing, her future shuttering like an abandoned mall, boarded up, empty and echoey. The bathroom walls creep towards her. The flat is too small. She needs to clear her head and stuffs her feet into shoes waiting by the front door, tugs a coat over pyjamas and steps out into the cool morning air.

She walks aimlessly, her head low, and concentrates on each ragged breath filling her lungs and the stale unbrushed-teeth taste lining the inside of her mouth. Few people are out at this hour – an hour reserved for dog walkers and serial killers. She passes a small park, the hedges and tended grass barely concealing benches that normally house a huddle of smoking teenagers at night. A half-mile from the flat, Efe feels the patter of light rain against her face. She digs her hands into her pockets and finds the pregnancy test there, the box crumpled, the red lines luminous under a blanched sky. She almost drops it, feels her fingers spasm before she stops herself. The wind curls around her bare neck.

She imagines Sam taking the bins out on Tuesday morning. All it would take is a small rip through the thin black plastic and the test could come tumbling out. *He'll want this baby too*, she thinks to herself and she shakes her head, shoves the test, packaging and all, into the nearest bin. She waits twenty minutes before she sees the orange lights flashing, a slow hunkering procession as the vehicle makes its way towards her. The rain picks up. When they near, she realises they're all men, hollering back and forth, moving efficiently in hi-vis, heads bent away from the rain. Efe waits and watches while they collect the rubbish, holds her breath as piles of black plastic drop into the unseen depths. One of the men looks in her direction. His eyes meet hers and he crinkles his brow at the pyjamaed black woman standing at the roadside. Efe feels uneasy. The clouds dip. Then he nods, curls the corners of his mouth upwards and moves on.

Only then does Efe turn back to the flat. She arrives speckled with spring rain, a fresh scent lingering on her skin. Sam stirs as she climbs back into bed, loops an arm over her waist and murmurs something that sounds like, 'You good?'

'Yes,' Efe whispers and closes her eyes at long last.

Six Months Before

For weeks, Efe makes no mention of the pregnancy. She returns to her nausea-less, headache-less life and carries on like usual, hoping it goes away on its own. A single word pricks in her mind: *baby* when she makes a cup of tea each morning and *baby* when she and Sam settle in for a movie one Friday night, her legs draped across his lap, and she takes that first halting sip of wine; *baby* in those brief step-out-of-the-shower seconds when she catches sight of herself in the glass doors and stops to examine her body. Soon this becomes a daily ritual. She searches for the smallest changes, tries to remember when she first noticed the ballooning of fingers or the low, rolling ache in her heavy breasts when she was pregnant with Olivia.

Two and a half weeks after Efe takes the test, she wakes up exhausted. She is half-buried in the pile of plump pillows. All throughout the bedroom, the morning light shines like a phone with the screen turned up too bright. She winces, drags her limbs over each other until she can squint at the clock: 9.02 a.m. She stays there, listening to Sam and Olivia's voices drifting through the thin walls, catches the smell of toast and honey in the air. She opens her eyes again an hour later as Olivia, sticky-fingered and peanut-butter-and-honey-smeared, clambers in beside her, scrambling under the covers. Efe can hear Sam's voice projecting from the corridor, the loud counting coasting up to twenty.

'Good morning.' Efe yawns.

'Shh, I'm hiding, Mummy.' Olivia giggles as Efe pulls the duvet over her head, keeps giggling when Sam appears at the door. He grins at the jiggling lump, then his eyes flick over to Efe.

'You're awake,' he says.

'I'll be up in a minute.'

His head tilts to the side. 'Feeling okay? How was your meeting with the ICA?'

'Exhausting week. Excellent meeting. They're taking two of Simon's pieces.'

Efe gets up just before eleven, lugs her leaden limbs out of bed and shimmies out of her pyjamas. She takes up her spot in front of the mirror. *Baby* floats up to the surface of her mind. She examines her reflection, a palm just below her belly button on the pouch of soft skin. She's been looking into her options and supposes she'll have to make an appointment soon, but can't imagine doing so without Serwaa at her side.

'What are you doing?' Sam says, his voice cutting through Efe's train of thought.

She spins towards him, feeling like a kid caught with her hand in a cookie jar. She drops his gaze, hurriedly tugs on an old T-shirt and leggings.

Sam's playful smile wilts. 'Efe,' he says, sounding nervous now. 'What's going on?'

A hot prickle bites the back of her neck. She cannot speak and presses her face into her hands. She feels faint. Dizzy. Through the slits between her fingers, she watches Sam blur behind the rising tide of tears she cannot push down.

'Efe?' Sam calls her name again, then there's the whine of crossed floorboards and she feels her body tense a moment before his arms close around her shoulders. She thinks she's going to be sick, but what comes out is the truth, a breathless flurry of words, and when she lifts her head he's smiling.

Not a regular smile. A shellshocked, ecstatic smile, stretching so far his eyes bunch up into thin creases. He looks exactly how she'd imagined.

'You're excited,' she says. It is more of an accusation than an observation.

'Of course I am. This is amazing. We're having another baby!'

'We already have one,' Efe says flatly.

'Yeah.' He chuckles. 'And now Liv can have a little brother or—'

'No. We already talked about this.'

'But that was hypotheticals. You really can't be considering—'

'Nothing's changed. I just got my life back and we're barely getting by—'

Sam's smile falters. He lets out a sound halfway between a sigh and a gasp. 'Don't worst-case scenario this. I know it was tough when Liv was little,' he says, 'but it could be better this time.'

'And it could be so much worse,' Efe says, throwing her hands into the air. 'Were you not there when I hadn't slept in weeks and left Liv on that train? What about when my parents showed up and tried to take her away from us? Doesn't that scare you?'

'Of course it's scary, but they left and we figured it out. We have a rhythm now.'

'A rhythm—' She laughs, a hard, blunt laugh.

'Just hear me out. Liv starts school in September. And it's not a huge shifting going from one kid to two.'

'Except I'll have to completely reassess how I do my job and—'

'We can make it work. We did it once. We can do it again.' His arms wrap around her. He breathes the words into her hair, holds her until she begins to soften. 'Just wait, okay? Let's not rush into anything,' he says and slips his hand into hers. They lower themselves onto the unmade bed, sit shoulder to shoulder.

'Don't tell anyone,' she says. 'I need to think this through and—'

'Okay. That's fine.' Sam nods, knowing he'd agree to anything in that moment. 'We'll be fine,' he says. Efe's surprised by how calm and confident he sounds, even though he's known for less than five minutes. Efe's known for weeks and still can't move past the doubts balled up in her like a fist.

After that, things start popping up. It's impossible for Efe to pretend that none of this is happening when baby things lurk around every corner. First it's a plain babygro wedged in the side of a drawer reserved for the hairdryer, extension leads and miscellaneous socks. Efe takes the laundry basket off her hip, sees a flash of white amongst the cables, and reaches into the drawer, carefully. It's tiny – infinitely small – so small she can hardly believe babies come in that size, even though the one growing inside her is barely the size of an olive. Days later, a teddy bear appears on a high-up shelf in the living room. A small price tag hangs off its ear and when Olivia asks for it, Sam replies coyly, 'Sorry, Liv, that's for someone even smaller than you,' with a wink. Liv doesn't understand but Efe freezes. *Even now, he can't help himself*, she thinks, inwardly irate. She wants to yell, but could just as easily burst into tears, seeing Sam so puffed up with giddy excitement. Instead, she lowers her fork, pushes the thought down and presses her hand to the smooth spot below her navel, reminds herself she still has options.

It takes a few days, but Efe finally plucks up the courage to bring up the thing that's been hovering in the back of her mind since the day she took the test. Her thoughts keep circling back to the god-awful early months when Olivia was small, the endless crying, smearing food on herself, and Efe was delirious and frayed, bowed down under the laborious effort of mother-hood that began again each morning. She can't do it again. She readies herself as Sam turns out Olivia's light and tiptoes back to their room. He hovers in the doorway and scrolls.

'What do you think of this playmat?' he asks, his phone extended towards her.

Efe's first thought is that it looks tacky; the purples and yellows clash and the butterfly hanging from the cross-section is nightmarishly large. All she's googled in the last few weeks are variations of 'How much does a baby cost?' and 'Likelihood of postpartum depression recurring'.

'Not a fan,' she says. Inhales. 'But now we're on the topic, why are you buying baby things?'

Sam glances up, his face crinkling. 'Errr . . . because we're having a baby.'

'No,' Efe says firmly. 'I'm pregnant but we haven't decided if we're having another baby.'

'Efe—'

She clears her throat. 'I'm telling you I don't want another child. You're my husband and I love you, but I can't go through with this,' Efe says, not thinking about what that means. The specifics can stay hazy and out of reach. All she knows is that she won't be revisiting the months following Olivia's birth if her life depends on it. And it does.

'Please,' Sam murmurs, reaching for her, but Efe pulls away.

'I don't have the energy to keep arguing with you,' she says, lowering her head into her palms. She can't look at Sam right now. She hates that after all these years and all these conversations, he still can't see it from her point of view. When it comes to this they have always been on opposing sides and always will be. She hates that he can want someone he has never met more than he wants her, the person standing right beside him. Efe realises now that she should've done something sooner, found a clinic and booked an appointment the day she found out. She never should have let it go on this long and certainly never should have let Sam find out. *How could I be so dumb*, she thinks to herself. *I'll be smarter this time around.*

* * *

Later, when she steps into the bathroom, Efe is still thinking about the babygro and the teddy bear. There'll be more baby things just like them. Each one a pebble placed in front of a door. Soon there will be so many of them Efe won't have the strength to open it. She draws the shower curtain open and feels herself breaking. Everything in her is saying run. Run away from this life. From the baby. Get as far away as she can because it's already out of hand.

By the time Efe clambers into the tub she is crying and shaking. She raises her face to the spray and lets the water beat hard against her chest. She stays there for ages until she loses track of time entirely. The water is tepid by the time she climbs out. She has one foot on the bathmat when a bus charges past the window. A startling sound. Her nerves already wound tight enough to snap. She still feels more agitated than she's been in who knows how long. Dizziness hits and she presses a hand to the quivering wall. Her stomach roils. Her vision goes spotty. She closes her eyes and tries to concentrate on each deep breath, her head resting against the bathroom door. She can hear Sam on the other side, humming along to a song she doesn't recognise. It does nothing to quell the panic rising up in her. When she is finally steady, Efe reaches for the door handle. She raises her lips at the corners, curves her mouth into something that resembles a smile.

MAY 2016

Five Months Before

Efe feels lighter as she steps out into the forecourt. She carries a single efficiently packed suitcase, no larger than a weekend bag, and slips easily between the other just-landeds who droop beneath a half-dozen bags and lumber behind unwieldy trolleys that drift one way or the other of their own accord. She hovers at the edge of the car park, resting her bag by her feet, and pauses to unzip her jacket. Already, the warm air encircles her and the thin material sticks to her skin.

It has been more than two years since Efe last set foot in Ghana. The last time she visited Liv was still a toddler, too young to remember the flying visit to celebrate Afia's birth. Efe feels the urge to jump in a taxi and head to the nearest beach, wade out into the water and leave all her cares shimmering on the surface. She has been gone for eight hours and knows Sam will have picked Liv up from the childminder's by now. He won't be expecting her yet, so she assumes she has another hour or two before he really begins to worry, but she is wrong. The moment she switches her phone on, a flurry of missed calls and messages clog her screen, all of them from Sam.

The phone starts to vibrate in her palm. He's calling again now. Her phone screen flashes up a photo of them taken a year earlier on Christmas morning, both of them wearing the matching pyjamas that had been a gift from Phoebe, Sam's arm slung around her shoulders, her lips pressed to his cheek. She remembers it like it was yesterday, how happy she was, how happy they both were. She stares at it, her heart in her throat, until the call rings out and the screen fades to black. Only now is the realisation of what she's done beginning to dawn.

Thankfully, she hears Serwaa's voice calling her name. Her thoughts move away from Sam, and Efe scans the crowd until she spots Serwaa jogging over, both arms waving high above her head.

'You're here,' Efe says, relieved.

'Eish, I didn't know if I'd find you. My phone battery died,' she says, pulling Efe into a hug. Efe breathes in the warm, familiar scent of her sister's perfume. Serwaa releases Efe, takes her bag and eyes the empty space around her suspiciously. 'Is this all you brought?'

They drive. Serwaa pulls onto the motorway and speeds up, the green-orange world blurring at their windows, the signs above pointing the way to Aburi.

'So,' Serwaa says, 'is there some kind of emergency I don't know about?'

'Not that I know of.'

'Ahh, okay.' Serwaa pauses. 'So what's going on then?'

'Nothing.' Efe laughs, trying to make light of it. 'I just needed to get away, clear my head a bit.'

Serwaa rolls her eyes. 'Clear your head,' she says, her voice full of disbelief. 'If you need to clear your head, you go for a walk or a drive, not whatever this is. You think I don't see you ignoring Sam's calls? I wouldn't be surprised if he's been trying to call me too.'

'Has he?'

'I left him a voicemail after you called me, but I don't—'

'Oh no.' At this, Efe lowers her head into her hands and lets out a long groan. She turns her phone off just as Sam's name flashes up again. 'I can't speak to him right now.'

'Look,' Serwaa says softly. 'You can't stay here and hide forever. Every couple goes through hard times. You just need to—'

'You were right. I'm pregnant,' Efe says, feeling the sting of tears in her eyes. 'And before you congratulate me, I'm not happy about it.'

'Oh,' Serwaa says, then falls silent. She rests a comforting hand on Efe's leg. 'It's not so bad. At least three of my friends have been through this same predicament, but you can't ignore him forever. What are you going to do when the baby comes? You really think he'll be okay with you keeping his child from him?'

'I'm not having the baby.' As soon as Efe says this she knows it is true. Everything about the last few weeks has felt unsettled and erratic. She hadn't even planned the trip to Ghana, just felt herself panicking and paid an extortionate amount for a ticket at the airport, trying to outpace the feeling that her life was crumbling around her, trying to get as far away as fast as she could. A half-day travelling has cleared her mind. A plan is forming.

Serwaa looks at her warily. Her mouth twitches and her hands grip the steering wheel tighter.

'I finally have my life back,' Efe continues, more certain now. 'I can't waste three more years falling apart, just to put myself back together again.' She takes a breath. 'Do you still know that gynaecologist? Joseph's friend, do you have his number?'

'A gyna— Are you out of your mind?' Serwaa gasps.

'Serwaa, please. I'm asking you to help me find a qualified doctor, not a backstreet agent.'

'Go back to your UK. Isn't that where they do this type of thing every day?'

'There are clinics here too, and I need you by my side. I don't think I can go through with it without you.'

Serwaa exhales, veers into the middle lane to overtake a green and yellow taxi belching noxious puffs of grey-black smoke. 'No,' she says. 'I don't know of any clinics. Don't involve me in this.'

They say little else for the rest of the journey, thirty-five more minutes to Aburi; the radio jabbers between them and, to their left, the river courses and snaps at their heels. Late that night, Serwaa comes into the guest room which isn't really a guest room. While Joseph is visiting his sister in Kumasi, Abena is sharing Serwaa's bed so Efe can have a room to herself. She is sitting, still thinking about the baby, puzzling through her options and wondering who else she can turn to, when she hears a light knock at the door.

As if reading her mind, Serwaa announces, 'I'm only giving you this because you're my sister and I want you to be safe,' she grumbles, thumbing a small piece of paper with the doctor's phone number scrawled in black ink. 'And you're lucky, Emmanuel was working in Germany and only moved back last year. He works past Koforidua. It's out of the city. No one will know you there.'

'Thank you.'

Serwaa clutches the paper to her chest and doesn't move when Efe reaches for it.

'Is there more?' Efe says.

'*I* make the phone call,' Serwaa says, eyes glistening in the soft light. 'If I'm going to help, you need to trust me too.'

Days later, Serwaa pulls up outside the government hospital. The building is bigger than Efe expected, three floors high, the fading paint a creamy beige colour, the whole building surrounded by low, green hedges. Long after Serwaa eases the car into a space and turns off the engine, neither sister reaches for the door handle.

Efe can sense that Serwaa wants to say something but she sits, hands in her lap, staring out at the empty courtyard. This pensiveness in her sister is new. Efe waits, tries to steady herself by resting a finger on the space below her belly button. She has the tiniest bump now and tries to think of it as an orange nestled under her skin. The thought doesn't calm her.

Serwaa lifts her eyes towards the hospital, then speaks. 'I didn't want to ask, but the other doctor, she said maybe you're having an affair. Is that the reason for all of this?'

Efe's eyes spring towards her sister; she thinks back to the kind-eyed doctor she'd met two days earlier at the clinic, the same one who'd seemed genuinely disappointed when she said she couldn't terminate because she'd calculated that Efe was twelve weeks and two days into the pregnancy, two days over the limit to be treated at the clinic.

'The doctor thinks that? Of course not,' Efe says. 'How could you even ask me that?'

'What am I supposed to think? You've barely told me anything. You show up with a few hours' notice and ask me to help you do this.'

'Sam is the father. There's no one else it could be.' She swallows. 'But it's not that easy. I'm just getting the hang of it with Liv and we can't bring another child into the mix. And you know what, I don't want to go through it again. I don't. It's hard and miserable and I'd have to take a step back from work, now, when so many of my artists are on the brink of something big.'

'If you need help, come home. You won't have to lift a finger. I'm—'

'I can't be pregnant right now – or ever.' She is firm, thinking back to her pregnancy with Liv: the months fraught with worry, daily growing more and more uncomfortable in her own body, the inexplicable bleeding, all the invasive tests, being petrified the whole way through that something would go horribly wrong and neither of them would make it.

'Efe—'

'No,' Efe says, smacking a hand down on the dashboard. 'I'm not asking you to convince me. I'm asking you to stand by me. Please. Just stand by me.'

Serwaa falls quiet. She raises a hand to teary eyes then lets her gaze move past Efe. She reaches over her, and both sisters hold their breath in that moment her fingers close around the door handle and pull.

Efe is supposed to be the last patient of the day, but two other women are still in the waiting room, both pretending to be immersed in glossy magazines, actively trying not to make eye contact. Serwaa shifts uncomfortably, fiddles with the plastic bag in her hands. Efe has barely left the flat since she arrived. Even now, in a virtually empty waiting room, almost fifty miles from Serwaa's flat, she worries someone will recognise her and put this thing to a stop.

A nurse rounds the corner. She looks in their direction and comes bustling over, bursting out of a uniform at least two sizes too small. 'Yes?' she says.

'We're here to see Dr Emmanuel,' Efe answers.

At this, the nurse nods, a barely perceptible movement, then turns on her heel and leads the sisters down a short hallway and to a door labelled 'Exam Room 4'. They step silently into the room, which is bare except for two plastic chairs, a chunky computer circa early 2000s and a reddish-brown examination bench in the corner. They hover awkwardly, then Serwaa lowers herself into one of the plastic chairs; Efe rests a hip on the examination bench, refuses to sit.

She is nervous suddenly, warmer than she's ever been in her life, and can feel the sweat collecting under her armpits, the droplets of moisture gathering in the crook of her arms, the quickening heartbeat fluttering at the base of her throat. Unspeaking, the nurse hovers at the door, stays with her back to the wood until there is a light knock. All three women jump.

'Dr Emmanuel,' Serwaa smiles, relieved now.

'Sister.' He greets Efe too, and gestures for her to sit back on the table, to pull her top up. He pulls on magnolia gloves and reaches for the gel. Efe focuses on the ceiling, watches the glint of gold on the tiles.

'Do you want to see?' Emmanuel asks. Efe's head snaps towards him. He's probably older than Efe first thought. Mid-forties. At least ten years older than she is. Around his eyes there's a small cluster of wrinkles, more obvious in this light along with the silver curls peppering his scalp.

'No,' Efe says when the tightness in her throat recedes. In her peripheral vision, she sees Serwaa shift, smooth her hands over her skirt.

'Okay,' he says. 'The pregnancy is more advanced, but we will give you some anaesthetic and make sure you're comfortable for the procedure. And we'll monitor you afterwards, but you should be free to go in the next few hours.'

Efe nods, focusing on how simple it all sounds. *It will be okay*, she tells herself. He places the reader down and turns back to the screen. 'Doreen,' he says, turning to the nurse still standing by the door. 'Bring the paperwork. Let me collect the anaesthetic.'

They get started. The hospital around them is eerily quiet. Both Doreen and Emmanuel slip into protective robes and wear solemn expressions behind their masks. Efe lies flat on the table, her feet propped up and finds herself unable to focus on anything but the warmth spreading down from her waist and the rustle of papery tissue beneath her. Efe is only dimly aware of the distant tugs and tension. Serwaa's fingers slip into hers and she feels stronger. Sure. They breathe in time.

In truth, Efe has always known there would be no baby. Right from that first moment when the small kernel of possibility revealed itself. It doesn't cling to life the way Olivia had done – fiercely – refusing to go unnoticed in deep-muscle aches and unparalleled nausea, which caused Efe's head to spin and nostrils cockle in the early weeks, long before the child pressed out and away from her mother's body and showed herself to the world. The new baby is different. Unobtrusive. As if it has already decided to be a fleeting thing. For weeks it has hidden under her skin, cells multiplying in darkness.

After they are finished, Efe grits her teeth, pulls her knees towards her stomach as the cramping sensation begins. The pain is getting stronger now and Emmanuel and Doreen watch her, checking her pulse, exchanging nervous glances from the side of the bed. Serwaa is the one who moves almost constantly, buzzes at her sister's shoulder, murmurs quiet encouragements, wipes Efe's sweat-slick face.

An hour later, Efe is unravelling. She feels faint. She should've been recovered enough to go home, but instead every few moments the examination room recedes into darkness. Even when her eyes are open she sees the world in fragments. She is sweating. Doreen's face in circles above her head. A handbag on a plastic chair. The dimpled cream concrete of the ceiling. Emmanuel's fingers on a limp wrist, which Efe soon realises is her own. Then Serwaa. Serwaa shakes her awake, pulls Efe upright. Efe hovers on the edge of the table, breathes through clenched teeth until she begins to feel better.

On the other side of the room, Emmanuel and Doreen are whispering, terse, short sounds, like a bickering couple. When they separate, only Emmanuel comes over.

'Okay.' He claps his hands. 'Are you ready to go home now?' His voice is too bright, the smile too stiff.

Serwaa turns towards him. 'Go? You're the one who said you wanted to monitor the progression.'

'These things take time and we don't have all the time in the world. She should take some painkillers and rest.'

Serwaa looks away. 'What next?'

'You brought the towels I told you to bring? Put them down in the back of the car. Let her lie down there and sleep. She should be fine in a few days. If not, she can take these.'

He stuffs a small pack of tablets into Serwaa's hand, curls her fingers around it. 'Two every four hours with food. No more than four doses in a day. Keep her at home and wait for the pains to pass.'

Serwaa grumbles as she lifts Efe's arm onto her shoulder, hoists her onto unsteady feet. In this shuffling, sluggish walk they make their way down the deserted corridor and out to the car. Efe pauses whenever the sharp twisting ache hits, carries on when it wanes. She collapses into a back seat, a hand to her spasming, curdling stomach.

Outside, the dusky sky glows red. When the pain is too much she bites down on her fist, hard, until the tang of blood rises up between her knuckles. She can feel the car jostling beneath her, her tightly wound muscles waiting for the pain to pass, but as it lingers, Efe lifts her eyes to the red-gold setting sun slipping past the window and is certain her whole world looks bigger.

The next few days come in snatches. Efe remembers waking and sleeping, pockets of day, slivers of night, a parched throat, the clinginess of a top soaked through with sweat, the welcome relief of a cool flannel brushed across her scalding skin. The pain lessens like a TV with the volume turned down low. And the writhing dreams will come back to her later, weighty nuggets slow to make their way to the surface. Right now, she opens her throbbing eyes and waits for the blobs of colour to take shape, waits as Serwaa's profile slowly crystallises.

Her sister kneels beside her, knees on a thin sleeping mat, elbows propped up on the mattress beside Efe, eyes closed, lips moving silently. Serwaa, who has barely prayed of her own volition in years, lets her quiet sisterly pleas float heavenward. Efe feels a flush of embarrassment. She worries she's interrupting a private moment, drags her heavy head to the left, concentrates on the pink dawn scissoring through the slats.

'You're awake!' Efe feels Serwaa's grasping hands all over her.

'Hey,' she replies. Her voice comes out hoarse. Efe lifts a hand to her raw throat and feels like it is lined with gravel. 'How long have I been asleep?'

'Two days. With a fever, but that started to come down some hours ago.'

'Oh.' Efe lifts her head slightly. She can feel now that her head is throbbing and catches the sharp scent of fever in the air.

'How're you feeling?' Serwaa asks. 'Do you think you can eat something?'

Serwaa moves Efe like a child, props her up against pillows, spoons white rice into her mouth and explains. 'Eish, the way you scared me. I didn't know if you were going to make it. I was this close to taking you back to that nonsense hospital.' Serwaa pauses her spooning and holds up two fingers, a hair's breadth between them.

'Did you call the doctor?'

Serwaa kisses her teeth. 'Dr Emmanuel. Hmph. That man stopped caring the moment we settled the bill. All he said was that it was probably an infection.' She says this part in a voice steeped in disdain, rolls her eyes and scoops up more rice. 'I kept calling anyway. I was desperate. The useless man turned his phone off.'

'I feel much better now. We must be past the worst of it.'

'God I hope so.'

Efe spends the next day on the sofa, dozing through the lessening cramps. Sometime in the early afternoon, her eyes flutter open to the bright afternoon light and the sound of activity in another part of the flat. It's only after the front door closes and Efe hears the sound of Maame's voice close by that she fully wakes. Alert now, Efe pushes herself upright, a hand on her stomach, and consciously quiets her breath, keeps perfectly still. Serwaa is out there too and she can hear the nervousness in her sister's voice. In her own chest, Efe feels something tight and fearful.

'Mum, you didn't have to,' Serwaa calls. She's projecting loud enough for Efe to hear clearly.

'I was passing through the market and decided to pick this one for you and bring something for my grandkids.'

'Ɛyɛ fɛ,' Serwaa says. 'You probably can't stay long. Can I get you something before you go?'

'Bring me water,' Maame says. 'And let me rest my feet a while before—' As soon as Maame walks into the living room the conversation falters. Her jaw drops. Serwaa rushes in a few paces behind, clutching a bottle of water in her hands.

'Ey! Efe, what are you doing here?' Maame is upon her then, pulling Efe into a tight hug and swaying back and forth. 'When did you get here? You didn't tell anyone you were coming,' she says, cradling Efe's face between her hands.

'It was a last-minute decision.' Efe tries to sound cheery.

'Are Sam and Amma with you?'

'No, I came alone,' Efe says. She isn't sure what gives her away, just that Maame takes a step back. Something in her grin slackens.

'What's going on?' she asks, her voice firmer now.

'Nothing.' The question is addressed to Efe but it is Serwaa who speaks. She jumps in quickly, too quickly. Maame's suspicions grow. Her gaze narrows.

'Nothing – heh – then why is she hiding?' Turning back to Efe, she adds, 'Why are you hiding?'

'I'm not hiding, Mum. I just wanted to visit.'

'Ey, so your visiting means your own parents don't even know you're in Ghana. Is that right?'

Serwaa intervenes. 'Mum, she's not hiding. She's just . . . it's a surprise.'

'Stop shielding your sister. You're lying to me. You think I don't know when you're lying? Both of you.' She fans her hands outwards, her voice growing louder.

Despite the breeze drifting in through the open window, Efe feels light-headed. Her body is still battling an infection. This is the longest she's been on her feet for days. Cramps keep coming in waves. Despite the bulky sanitary pad, something warm oozes down Efe's leg. Over Maame's shoulder, Serwaa keeps giving her anxious looks.

'Nothing's wrong, Mum. I just needed some time. A break.'

'From what? London?'

'Just stop it. Please. You don't need to involve yourself in everything.' Efe lowers herself back onto the sofa, pressing her legs together. She can hear the sounds of Serwaa's kids splashing in the pool downstairs. Maame circles her.

'Break from what? Is it London? Is it Sam?' She pauses, latching onto the idea. 'You left him, didn't you? God forbid. I knew something had brought me to this house today. I won't sit by and let you throw away your family. Samson is a good man.'

'You don't even talk to him any more.'

'Because I came there and he wouldn't—'

'Pack my bags and ship me off like you did? Do you know how hard that was? Do you not remember what those kids did to me?'

Maame's mouth falls open. 'I sent you to London for your own good. You were older. You were safe,' she says bitterly.

Efe groans and lowers her head into her hands. Maame is still speaking. Serwaa's pleas are barely audible. 'She should be resting.'

'Exactly. She doesn't look well. Look what this decision has done to her.' She lowers herself to her knees, places her hands on each of Efe's thighs. 'Efe please. I'm begging you. Look at how he's cared for you all these years. How many women want a fraction of what you have?' She casts a desperate look at Serwaa. 'What has he done that's so bad? Whatever happened, you can sort it out.'

'Mum—'

'Efe, I'm begging you. Think of the child.'

At this Efe breaks. She is fuming. 'That's all I'm meant to do, huh? Think about the child. Think about my husband. Do what everyone wants even if it makes my life miserable. You want to know why I'm here?'

Serwaa stumbles forward. 'Efe, don't—'

'I had an abortion, okay? That's the real reason. I got on a plane, came all the way out here because I was pregnant and can't stand the thought of having another baby.'

The full force of Efe's words strike Maame. She recoils. A hand comes up to her chest. For a few seconds she sounds like she's choking on air, then she croaks out a few words. 'You . . . You . . .' She cannot bring herself to say it. 'What about Sam?'

'He doesn't know. This is something I needed to do for me.'

Maame's eyes land on Serwaa, an accusatory finger raised. 'And you . . . you helped her?'

Serwaa's gaze drops to the floor. Instinctively, an arm moves to her stomach, brushes against the first home her children had known.

'Mum—'

'Oh my God.'

The sky is just beginning to lighten when Efe arrives at her parents' house. At this hour, she assumes the gate will still be locked, the heavy gold padlock nestled between the metal bars. She is surprised to find it opens easily. Standing on the driveway, Efe looks up at the house, silhouetted in the lavender morning glow. The houselights shine bright. She moves swiftly past the empty parking space and pauses at the front door.

Efe isn't sure why she feels the need to knock, but in the quiet that follows she strains to hear the patter of footsteps or the muted chorus of the house girls singing as they begin their morning tasks, but she comes up empty. It is Maame herself who comes to the door – a week since Efe had seen her last.

'Mum?' It is not quite a question but surprise still rises up in Efe's voice. Maame too seems surprised, and then the hardness returns to her eyes and the mask goes up.

'You're early,' Maame says.

Efe falters. She wants to remind Maame that she was the one who asked Efe to come over at the crack of dawn, who insisted on it. It is early, but Efe is only fifteen minutes earlier than the time they'd agreed upon. 'I was up anyway,' she says. 'I haven't been sleeping well.'

'Hmph, I wonder why.'

Both Efe and Maame let the words hang in the air. There will be no giving in. Moments pass before Maame lets out a breath and says, 'Help me with the tea,' and Efe follows her through the house. In the kitchen, Efe reaches for the gold-rimmed cups, places them on delicate saucers with gold-filigreed edges. These are the only items Maame brought back from England thirty years ago, each item painstakingly wrapped in tea towels or bundled up in clothes.

Efe places a matching gold teaspoon on each saucer. She runs her thumb over the intricate ridges as she searches for the words to say, but it is Maame who speaks first.

'Ready?' she asks. Efe nods, not sure what she is ready for. She reaches for the tray and follows Maame. In spite of how slowly she walks, the tiny spoons ding with each step. Looking back she will remember that sound as the ringing of an alarm, the final moments before she looked up to see Maame at the front door, ushering in the elders.

Maame had told.

The tray almost slips from Efe's fingers. She stands rooted to the spot, trying to order her thoughts as the men fill the foyer, prepared for battle.

'Elder Kwabena, Elder James and Pastor Eric, you remember my oldest, Efe.' Maame's voice drips with honey as she stretches her smile too wide at each man in turn.

'Efe, nice to see you again.' They nod. Efe takes a cautious step forward, feels her knees tremble. They move into the formal living room and settle on the sofa.

'Won't you offer our guests some tea?' Maame says.

Efe glances down at the tray still in her quaking hands. Tea sloshes. The men thumb at doll-sized cups. She can feel Maame watching her, dissatisfaction coming off her in waves.

Efe sits. She has barely seen these men in the almost-decade since her wedding. She steals a peek at Elder James's pock-marked cheeks, Elder Kwabena's thin wrists – skin stretched over a collection of bones – slow-moving men who have been old and frail for as long as Efe can remember. Affection surges and Efe catches herself. She won't let herself sympathise with the ambushers.

'So,' Pastor flashes a smile. A gold tooth glints. 'Your mum has told us you have left your husband and are refusing to go back to him.'

Efe's racing heart slows. Her gaze drifts to Maame and back, relieved that Maame has not told them the intricacies of the situation. Their threats will just be to send her back to London, not shun her and ruin her reputation. Efe's tongue feels like a brick in her mouth. 'Am I not allowed to travel?'

Pastor looks surprised then. 'So you do plan to go back to him?'

'I haven't decided.'

'And what is your reason for leaving him?' Pastor asks.

Elder James leans forward. 'Did he beat you? Betray your marriage vows?'

'No, nothing like that.'

'But it is you who decided this.'

'Yes,' Maame interjects, leaning so far forward that her chest meets her legs. 'She didn't even stop to discuss with anyone. And this whole time she won't take five minutes to answer his calls. Not one.'

Efe flashes Maame a look, trying to work out how she could possibly have known that.

Pastor Eric's eyebrows rise. A dozen wrinkles crease his forehead. 'And why won't you speak to him, Efe?'

'I . . .' She pauses, swallows. 'That is between me and my husband.' Even as she says the words, Efe feels Maame stiffen beside her.

Pastor clears his throat, then tries a new tactic. 'And where is the child?'

'She's with her father.'

'A child's place is with the mother.'

'And you say that from all your years of child-raising? How is your marriage, Pastor?'

Maame practically leaps out of her chair. 'Ey! Efe, don't be so rude. These men are here to advise you.'

Pastor's eyes dart to the men on either side of him. He titters nervously as if the whole city is not buzzing with the stories, then clears his throat and turns back to Efe. 'Your mother asked us to come here and talk to you. Will you not listen?'

'I am listening. I just won't—'

'See to it that you return to your husband this very week.'

Efe cannot believe what she's hearing. She falls quiet, startled for a moment before she manages to find her voice. 'I won't let someone whose own marriage is in shambles come and dictate what I should and shouldn't do. This is between me and Sam.'

Elder James gasps. A tense silence follows. Maame's foot is tapping vigorously on the ground. Efe holds her gaze steady as the men begin to murmur like vultures on a high-up branch. Elder Kwabena clasps one hand in the other, speaks gently. 'Efe, you have heard the proverb "*Woforo dua pa a na yepia wo*" yes?'

She nods solemnly, remembering it from her wedding day, and knows where this conversation is going.

'Then I have to tell you what you have done is not good. We cannot support this your decision.'

Efe tries to listen to what follows. She gets distracted by Pastor reaching for the plate of biscuits. He chews greedily, still grumbling about Efe's attitude, talking between bites. Efe can see the sludgy crumbs smeared across his tongue, spilling out from the corners of his mouth. She wonders how Nanadwoa can stand it.

When it is over, Elder James sighs, slowly rising from his seat, the others close behind. 'We only came to advise you at this your mother's request. Now we have done so.'

As soon as the front door closes behind them, Maame explodes, rounding on Efe. '*Adɛn?* Why are you behaving like this? They've only come to talk some sense into you and you think you're too big to listen.'

'Do you think any of those men know what it's like to be a mother?'

'You too have forgotten that you are a mother. This is not how you should be behaving.'

'Is that why you've sent everyone away, so I don't embarrass you—?'

'This is going to stay with you,' Maame says, spitting the words out. She wrenches a sigh up from the bottom of her stomach so the sound scrapes along her throat. 'Maybe you feel proud of yourself now, but this will follow you all the days of your life. No matter what you've done, you're still that baby's mother.'

With this said, Maame seems drained, her shoulders slumped forward. 'Go back to your husband, Efe. There's nothing left for you here.' Then she turns her back on Efe and takes slow strides up the stairs; and Efe finds herself anchored to the floor for several seconds, while the house around her echoes.

MAY 2016

Five Months Before

Sam's taxi pulls off the main road and begins its ascent up the foothills. From here on it is an uphill climb into Aburi. On one side of the road, a thicket of lush, verdant trees leans out partially obscuring a bright blue sky. Bro Caleb, the taxi driver Sam hired at the airport, sings poorly remembered song lyrics, hums along to Peace FM and whistles through the gap between his teeth. The rosary hanging inches from Sam's face swings like a metronome from the rearview mirror. The taxi itself, with the hacking cough of its engine and three out of five seatbelts replaced by thick rope, jostles beneath them. Sam keeps his eyes on the cream-coloured apartments that pass by a window smudged with greasy fingerprint marks. He squints at them, looks from the railings to the roofs, counts the orange-brown balconies and points at a faded yellow building he's pretty sure is Serwaa's.

'This one,' he says, with a nod to the driver, just before the taxi veers to the roadside. Both the radio and engine cut out. All Sam hears now are the chirping birds, hidden somewhere out of sight.

'You want I can wait?' the driver offers.

Sam pauses with one hand on the door, the other on the holdall wedged into the footwell. His plan is straightforward: he'll find Efe, get her to talk to him, then fix what's wrong so they can both go home. He's assumed she'd be with her sister, but maybe she isn't; maybe this will be a continuation of the wild goose chase that started two weeks ago. Apart from showing up at Serwaa's apartment, Sam has very few leads.

'Yes, wait,' Sam says. 'I need to check something.'

The man grins smugly, pleased with himself, then lowers his cap over closed eyes as Sam heads for the building. Just beyond the barrier wall, Sam can see a crystal-blue pool and deck chairs. He lets himself in through an unlocked gate. On the third floor, he finds garish plastic toys – no doubt imported from China – on the balcony he thinks belongs to Serwaa. Chalk markings run up the exterior wall and, when he looks closely, he sees that they're maths equations. Confident now, he knocks.

There are light footsteps on the other side, then the door opens and Serwaa looks stunned. 'Sam, what are you doing here?' she asks. Her eyes drop to her slippered feet and when they flick up again Sam recognises something that could be guilt or shame. 'Efe's not here,' she says.

'Where is she?'

'Taifa,' Serwaa says and instantly regrets it. A hand claps over her mouth.

'Your parents' house?' Sam asks, but Serwaa doesn't answer. She won't stop speaking, her voice is pitched higher than normal, words coming out so quickly they bump into each other.

'You should stay and wait for her. She'll be back any minute. She's probably on her way already.' She turns now, wanders into the flat and Sam follows. 'Are you thirsty? Let me send Kobby to the shop for soft drinks. Or do you want something to eat?'

Sam feels irritated responses sitting on his tongue. He's so close to the answers he's wanted for weeks – the answers they've denied him. He imagines himself here, waiting, distracted with plantain and Supermalt, groggy and full, while Efe sneaks off to someplace else. He has no intention of staying here and certainly won't be stage-managed. The holdall on his shoulder has a few changes of clothes, enough clothes for a week, but Sam knows he'll stay as long as it takes to convince Efe to return with him. He hoped it was just miscommunication, but wonders just how bad it is if Efe can't even bring herself to face him.

Serwaa takes a step towards him, backs away again, nervous. 'Won't you sit?'

'I'm not staying,' Sam says firmly. 'I have a taxi waiting.'

Serwaa looks at him pleadingly – a look Sam doesn't understand – but says nothing as he sets his bag down and turns to leave. Back out and down the stairs he goes, to wake his snoozing driver and take another journey, back the way he came. These are the last hours when Sam's life is still within the bounds of what he can imagine. And for years to come, Sam will long to return to these hours of blissful ignorance, will wish he'd stayed.

Sam sees Efe long before she sees him. He hasn't taken his eyes off her parents' gate since the taxi pulled up minutes ago. Bro Caleb is fidgeting and drumming his thumbs on the wheel impatiently as if Sam isn't paying for his time. Sam straightens when the gate creaks open and Efe steps through the gap. He's alert now, watching her, his magnificent wife too preoccupied to notice the heads she is turning as she walks in a long, linen sundress, stark white against dark skin, a brave choice with the rust-coloured dust whipping around. She parts the crowd, crosses the quiet road and moves towards them. Sam scrambles for the door handle and steps out of the taxi when she's just a few metres away.

To Efe, it probably seems like an apparition: Sam here in the blinding sunlight, emerging through an opening where worlds collide. She comes to a stop, lets out a small gasp, a hand held over her mouth; he watches as she squeezes her eyes shut and opens them again slowly, trying to make sense of the illogical thing she's seeing.

'Efe—' Sam says quietly, trying to rein in the emotion rising up in his throat.

'Sam?' Her voice curls upwards, still not sure.

He reaches for her and she lets him. Softly he says, 'I've been calling for weeks. Thank God you're okay. You . . . you are—?'

'I'm fine,' she says, her gaze slinking away from Sam and back again. She clears her throat. 'Where's Liv? Is she with you?'

'Aunty Dora's got her, but she's missed you. We both have.'

Efe nods. She tries to say something, but the words catch in her throat and her eyes are wet and shining.

'I'm sorry,' Sam says. For what he isn't sure. He gathers her close, breathing in the familiar warm cocoa-butter scent of her body lotion and a hint of perfume. He's just so happy to have found her, knows he'll do whatever it takes, say whatever she needs to hear. 'Should we find somewhere to talk?' he asks, exhaling the words into her hair. She is shaking, nodding, slighter than she was the last time he held her. Sam nods too. He holds tight for a minute more, then guides her to the taxi and slides into the back seat beside her. His finger finds the soft skin on the inside of her wrist. He draws neat circles over the ghosts of old scars from another life, another time, and he stays like that as the car eases into motion, as if some part of him is afraid she'll disappear into thin air or throw herself out of the car at the next red light. He won't lose her again.

Not far from Oxford Street, Efe gets antsy. An inexplicable traffic jam traps them on a back road bloated with cars, and she is eyeing the pedestrians passing by the window. Sam watches her reach forward and tap the driver on the shoulder. 'Can we get down here?' she asks. 'If you go straight, you can meet us by the restaurant beside Calbank.'

Sam and Efe walk the rest of the way on foot, pushing through the bustling people and past stalls engulfed in imported goods; they duck into a restaurant tucked between Calbank and Shoprite. On the inside it looks like a dim lounge bar. Sam squints. When his eyes adjust to the darkness, he sees most of the booths are empty. A bartender is hunched over a table in the back, fiddling with the dials on a radio. With the exception of the staff and a man in his sixties, sipping Lite Beer alone in a booth, the place is empty. It has only just passed noon and a bored-looking waitress makes her way over and greets them.

'*Akwaaba*,' she says, then switches to thick, heavily accented English. 'How ah you today?' She beams. 'What can I get you to drink?'

'*Sobolo* please.'

'Ey! Don't come and spill it on this your dress – is very fine.'

Efe smiles at the compliment and scoots her chair forward. The waitress turns to Sam. 'And for yourself?'

'Do you have ginger beer?'

'Please, no. We don't have.'

'Supermalt is fine.'

Efe and the waitress carry on talking with the familiarity of old friends. Sam looks from one woman to the other. It's like he isn't even here. Like he hasn't come all this way. He feels the ache of clenched teeth and the irritation, like a pebble on the back of his tongue, an ever-present threat that could roll back and choke him. When he speaks the words are pointed and tone harsher than even he expected. 'Are we just going to pretend this is normal?'

Efe's mouth drops open. She smiles politely at the stunned waitress and mutters, 'Can you give us a minute?'

Sam lets out a long breath, waits until the woman is out of earshot before speaking. 'Efe.' He pauses. 'What are we doing here?'

'Eating. Do you want to try—?'

'No,' Sam says firmly. 'I mean, why are we here? In Ghana. Why aren't we in *our own* home, in London, with Liv? Why did I have to come all the way out here just to have a conversation with my wife?'

Efe squirms in her seat, wedges her hands between her thighs. 'I'm sorry,' she says, not looking at him. 'I just needed some time.'

'Do you know how hard the last few weeks have been – how worried I've been about you, about the—?'

'Sam,' she says. 'Please.'

He'd been so sure they could make it work and, now they're face to face, still nothing makes sense. 'Look, Efe,' he says. 'Whatever's happened, whatever's going on, we can make it work. We can go home and figure it all out.'

He can hear the fraught edge in his voice, feel a light rapping on the inside of his skull. 'Explain it to me,' he says. 'I – I can fix it.'

The waitress reappears then. 'Oh,' Efe says, drawing back as the deep burgundy drink is placed in front of her, the white straw already tinged purple. Sam's drink meets the table with a light clink. He eyes it, wraps a hand around the cool glass. Mechanically, he raises the glass to his lips and sips, then places it down again.

'Come home with me,' he says softly.

Efe doesn't reply. She hooks one ankle around the other, sits up straighter. Sam stares at her and realises that for the first time in a long time she's closed herself off to him. Her walls are up. Her eyes are reddening again and when she speaks her voice is breaking. 'There's something you need to know.'

Sam sits up straighter too, eager for the conversation to come to some kind of resolution. 'What?'

She takes a deep steadying breath. 'I'm not pregnant any more. I – I ended it. A week ago.'

Sam hears the words but can't put them in an order that makes sense. The whole suggestion is implausible. 'You . . . what? How could you—?'

'You weren't being realistic. Did you not see how messed up I was after Liv?' Efe sighs heavily. 'Another baby would've

260

ruined everything – ruined us. I couldn't tell you . . . because I knew you'd never agree.'

Sam's expression doesn't change, but he feels his muscles getting tauter the longer she speaks, a bowling ball of pressure striking his chest. 'It wasn't your decision to make,' he murmurs. He presses a hand to his head. It's hot, clammy; he feels the blood surging inside his skull. 'We could've managed. I told you I had it covered. I had a plan.'

'The same plan you promised me before Liv was born?'

Sam stops short. 'No, we're a team now.'

'When it comes to Liv, yes, we're a team. But you saw how hard it was for me when she was little – for us – are you really happy putting all that at risk? All we are right now?' Her palms come up to her face. She looks exasperated, exhausted suddenly. 'I get it. I'm the problem. *I* couldn't bring another kid into this world. I felt like I was losing my mind for a year straight and don't have it in me to do it again.' She pauses. The words come out laboured, effortful. 'There were no good options.'

An image comes to Sam. He imagines his wife in a sterile doctor's office, her feet propped up on stirrups, her woozy coming back to the world after the surgery, unsteady on her feet when the cramps begin to rock through her, the baby born dead. His baby.

The next seconds, Sam sees in slow motion, his mind suspended above his body, watching as a version of him rises from the table. He sees Efe's head follow him as he moves. Her eyes are wide and panicky. She is speaking again, faster now, apologising maybe, wiping away snotty childlike tears with the back of her hand. He watches himself jerk an arm away when she reaches for him. The staff are trying to pretend they aren't watching, but they are. Sam cannot hear her. She is receding. He watches himself cross the room and walk right out into the merciless heat.

By the time Sam is back in his body, a bitter taste coats

the inside of his mouth. His shirt is damp with sweat and, beneath the thin cotton, his stomach is convulsing. He doubles over and lets out a wet hacking sound. Releases nothing but air. Only after he takes a deep breath of the stagnant water in the roadside gutter, mixed with debris and sun-warmed rubbish, does the Supermalt make its way back up.

'Ey.' A tough hand thumps heavily on his back. Sam peers up to see Bro Caleb leaning over him, his shirt open, sunglasses lowered, a cigarette clenched between his teeth. 'Drink,' he says, and Sam takes the water he's offered and rakes a hand across his mouth. There's a fizzing in his nostrils. He can feel Efe's presence behind him, but he doesn't have it in him to turn around and face her yet. He crouches, lets his arms hang heavy, his fingertips brush the ground.

Sam takes in the world from this new vantage point. He stares out at the peeling buildings, the people carrying on, unhurried busyness. A bus full of tourists pulls up. One or two look over as they pass. There is something firm digging into his chest. His fumbling fingers make their way to the spot. In his chest pocket, Sam finds his passport. He stares at it, then blinks as the world disappears behind black, opens his eyes again and everything is back in vivid colour.

'Sam?' Efe's voice is small but still manages to cut through everything else.

He splashes some of the water on his face, winces at the sharp shock of it. Seconds stretch tight and tense. He doesn't know how long he stays like that, just that when he finally pushes himself up, his legs unsteady beneath him, her voice comes again.

This time he turns. She looks the same as she always did. Unchanged. From the outside you'd never know. Cautiously, her empty hands stretch out towards him. She sniffs and her eyes are tear-filled again. Sam knows she won't come near him yet, and he suppresses the instinct to go to her, draw her into his arms and rock her until she's emptied of all her tears. Instead, he tries to see her anew, draw a distinct separation between how he's always seen her and who he now knows her to be, whoever that is. *Maybe I never knew you at all*, Sam thinks.

'Take me to the airport,' Sam says.

An uncomfortable look spreads itself over Bro Caleb's face. He looks from Sam to Efe and back again. 'The madam?'

'She's not coming,' Sam says and grimaces.

He slumps in the taxi under the weight of answers he wishes he never knew. He's kept his promise. He hasn't mentioned the baby to anyone but her. No one else knows. No one would ever know. He can feel the truth hanging over him, a storm cloud Sam supposes will follow him wherever he goes, for years to come. He doesn't imagine he'll ever be okay.

When the first tears prick his eyes, Sam wipes them away. He wipes away all the ones that follow. He is already approaching the airport by the time he remembers his bag, the clothes he's left behind. And he knows there's nothing left for him here. None of it matters. A new ticket. A cramped middle seat. A small oval window, through which the view is spliced in half by a smooth, white wing. From where Sam sits, even when he cranes his neck, he can't see the grey tarmac, just a section of the wing and above it bright blue sky, edge to edge. He stares out at it for a long time, and wonders how long he'd been staring at part of a whole, only seeing what he'd wanted to see.

It's late at night when Sam's Uber pulls up outside of Aunt Dora's place. For twelve hours and thousands of miles, he's been impatient to get back here, to hold Liv in his arms. He knocks twice before Aunty Dora answers. Through the narrow gap between the door and its frame, Sam can see her eye peering intently over the chain, a black hairnet and floor-length nightgown, covered in daisies.

'Sam,' she says, and the door closes. On the other side there's the sound of fingers fumbling, the chain dinging against the latch, then the door opens.

'It's late,' she says, stepping aside so Sam can pass.

'I know. I'm just here to get Liv.'

'Is Efe with you?' Sam hears her voice echoing out in the hallway, more concern after the door closes, and she says, 'Where's Efe? I thought you went to get her.'

Sam ignores her. He strides down the hallway into Aunty Dora's room, where Liv is stretched out on one side of the double bed, her back to the wall, Bear-Bear squeezed tight to her chest. Sam lifts her into his arms. Liv is fast asleep, heavier than she is when she is awake. Without waking, she nestles into him and he welcomes her recognisable scent and the hint of bubblegum toothpaste.

Behind Sam, Aunty Dora nears, her voice a firm whisper. 'I'm talking to you.'

Sam exhales, shifting Olivia in his arms as he turns to face Aunty Dora, her expression stern, arms folded across her chest. 'What happened? Where's Efe?'

'Accra.'

'She stayed?'

'She can stay there forever for all I care.'

Sam is expecting the appalled look that follows. What he isn't expecting is the shove. Her face is scrunched up in anger before she softens, lets out a breath.

'Whatever's happened, don't give up on her. She's not thinking straight. You two always work it out.'

'Stop defending her. You don't even know what she's done.' He flounders. 'She's—'

'I know you shouldn't give up on her.'

Sam wants to groan, but Aunty Dora is still speaking. 'No one gets an easy time in this life, but that girl needs you. Efe isn't good at asking for what she needs – she never has been – and that's fine. But whatever is going on, she needs you.'

Sam doesn't want to do this now, not when he's travelled almost ten thousand miles in less than two days, the plane cutting through the pink underbellies of clouds into a burning red sky. Not when he hasn't slept and has been wearing the same clothes for thirty-nine hours straight. Not when he's maxed out their credit card with the visa expenses and last-minute flights. Not when the burden of all he's learned in the last sixteen hours bears down on him, and everything he loves sits in broken shards at his feet. There was a time when Sam would've believed her. Now, he feels like eternities have passed.

There are so many feelings for Sam to wade through. In the following months, he'll begin to sift through them, try to comprehend. But for now, Sam rubs the heel of his hand to his eyes, then lowers a finger to the dark spot on Liv's bicep – the birthmark – still a perfect fit. He knows this is the child he can still protect. He's silently been making this promise since she was a bright bean on an ultrasound image and recommits himself to it again now.

JUNE 2016

Four Months Before

Efe sweats uncomfortably the moment she steps out of the air-conditioned car into the muggy air. All around the car park, people fan themselves with scraps of paper and glossy graduation ceremony pamphlets. A woman one row over pauses to prop her handbag on the hood of her car and digs around for melting packets of FanIce, which she passes to the eager children at her side. Beside Efe, Abena notices this too, stands up straighter and a flash of pink tongue creeps out of her mouth. Kobby, who's too busy kicking up a small cloud of yellow dust, doesn't notice. Neither does Serwaa as she refastens Afia, her youngest, onto her back, or Joseph as he climbs out of the car last and shades his eyes with one hand. For weeks Efe's had nothing to do but mill around Serwaa and Joseph's flat, occasionally cook, spend time with the older children and comment on how intense and unrelenting the heat is. Each morning she wakes early and paws at her scorched throat. And each night she watches the mosquitoes bob lazily through the too-warm air.

Efe draws her gaze away from the woman and looks to the yard sprawling between a trio of tan buildings with sloping brown roofs. The air ripples and the cluster of schoolgirls at the far end seem to wobble in the haze. To the side, Efe can make out a group of younger girls playing *Ampe*, their shorn schoolgirl hair growing out into puffs of tight curls. She smiles

266

to herself as she watches, imagining Liv playing with them. In Efe's mind, she looks exactly the same as she did over a month ago. Still carrying the adorable full cheeks from infancy, her tiny coils just long enough to pull into afro puffs. She wonders how over a month could have passed already; if the patch of dry skin behind Liv's ears has cleared up; if she still hates cauliflower and loves carrots. She wonders who her daughter is without her.

'Ready?' Joseph says, and Efe feels Abena's hand slip into hers just before they begin to walk across the yard. They head towards the rows of chairs and take up seats right behind the graduating class. Paa, standing to the side of girls in royal-blue dresses with cropped black curls, waves them over. They have just a few minutes to settle before the teachers stride to the front to the jangle of a lone tambourine and mistimed clapping. A nearby speaker comes on and lets out a high-pitched squeal. The chattering audience hush themselves.

'Grandma,' Abena says, craning her neck for a better view.

'Yes.' Efe nods, feeling a mild panic bubble up in her. Maame hasn't spoken a word to her in weeks. Efe's certain Maame has been dodging her. Whenever she's called or visited the house, she's found herself confronted by one of the house girls, reciting the same rehearsed answer, '*Kafra*, Aunty. Madame is not here,' even though Efe had felt her presence emanating from somewhere close by, even over the phone. Now the very sight of Maame puts Efe on edge.

She sits up straighter, watching as Maame brings her lips low to the microphone and it squeaks before she says, 'Good morning.'

'Good morning,' the schoolgirls chorus.

'Ey, what a fine day.' She smooths a hand over her skirt. 'I want to start by welcoming everyone who has come today to celebrate our senior girls. They have studied hard and each of them has a bright future ahead of her.'

There are songs, speeches, and eventually, the students are

called up to collect their awards. One by one they walk up to shake Maame's hand and collect their certificates. Applause swells up from different sections of the crowd. When the last girl's name has been called, another teacher appears on stage.

She clears her throat and smiles widely. 'Okay, we have one last gift for our own dear headmistress.' Maame pauses halfway to her seat, her eyebrows screwed together. The teacher smiles wider and continues, 'She is a mother, grand-mother, wife and our mighty headmistress, and on this day we want to honour her too. Twenty years, she has worked at our own dear senior high school, thirteen as headmistress, always battling tirelessly for every single girl who wants to study hard and go on to good things. Mrs Akua Owusu aka Maame, please accept this small-small token from us.'

Someone breaks into a praise song. A clap erupts. Two girls from the graduating class come back on stage staggering under the weight of a large cellophane-wrapped hamper. Bottles of imported soaps and biscuits push against the plastic. Over the cheers and singing, the teacher says, 'Mrs Owusu's family is with us today. Please come for photo.'

Efe feels Paa put an arm around her shoulders as the family stand, a few people clapping as they shuffle past and make their way to the front. Maame and Paa stand in the middle, Serwaa, Joseph and Afia crowd on Paa's right, Kobby and Abena stand to the front, and Efe moves to the space beside Maame. Maame contracts at Efe's touch. There's a barely discernible twist in her lips and a sharp huff through her nostrils. Something in Efe's throat hitches. She adjusts for the photos and smiles stiffly until the photographer is satisfied.

People begin filing out. Efe wants to say something, but Maame already has her back to her and is talking animatedly with the emcee. Efe stays near, waiting for her opportunity, certain Maame cares far too much about what people think to blatantly ignore her here.

'Wasn't that guy in your year at school?' Serwaa asks suddenly.

Efe turns just as a familiar face pushes through the crowd. 'Daniel?' she says, a little shocked.

'You're back,' he says, looking at her with a playful glint in his eyes.

'I am,' she says, stepping away from her family. 'So are you, I take it.'

'Yeah. I just took up a six-month contract at Korle-Bu.'

'The teaching hospital?'

'Yeah,' he grins, a finger coming up to stroke his goatee. The air fizzes.

Efe shifts her weight to the other leg, steadies herself. 'That's amazing.'

He is still smiling, his gaze holding hers. He lets out a small chuckle. 'So I didn't just hear you were back,' he says, pausing to lick his lips. 'I heard you finished things with that lawyer husband of yours.'

Efe falters. She takes a moment to compose herself, remembering how the only thing that travels faster than light in Accra is gossip.

'Anyway,' Daniel continues. 'I'd love to take you out sometime.'

Efe doesn't hear this, she's too busy watching her mother over his shoulder.

'I'm sorry. I have to—' Efe pushes past, taking long strides to catch up with her mum. 'Mum,' she calls out, reaching for her arm.

Maame turns, smiling stiffly. 'What do you want?' she says, her smile looking more like a grimace with each passing second.

'To talk to you,' Efe says.

'Me?' Maame says. 'You want to talk to me – heh? You think I want to talk to you?'

Efe winces, and Maame takes the opportunity to shake her arm free of Efe's grip and scurry off towards the exit. Neither of them notice a small group of the teachers watching. Later there will be whisperings and speculating, more gossip to add fuel to the fire. *Her own mother, heh? What has this one done now?*

Efe is still frozen to the spot when Serwaa finds her. 'Do you still want us to go see Nanadwoa?'

Efe swallows. 'Yeah, that would be great.'

They make their way back over to where Paa and Serwaa's kids are sitting. Kobby and Abena are crouched low, peering into Maame's hamper and claiming items for themselves.

'Dad, will you watch the kids? Efe and I will meet you at the house this evening.'

Paa looks from Kobby to Abena, and finally to Afia in Serwaa's outstretched arms. He laughs. 'You must be joking. Where is your husband?'

'Please, Dad. Joseph had to work and Efe hasn't seen Nanadwoa in ages.'

'And so what?'

'Daddy, please. You know the children love you.' She leans over and kisses him on the cheek.

Leaning out of the stifling car, Efe slips her shoes off and taps them together to shake off the worst of the dust. She glances at the thermostat, sees the temperature is hovering around forty-two and welcomes the biting cold of the air conditioning. Serwaa drives towards the exit and takes a left, easing the car over the unpaved sections of road, manoeuvring carefully to avoid the jutting rocks and sprawling ditches filled with murky water and burnt-orange-coloured earth.

'She's still not speaking to me,' Efe says when they pull onto the main road.

'Who? Mum?'

'Yeah,' Efe says, nervously working her fingers under the seatbelt.

Serwaa shrugs. 'Give her time.'

'And what about Sam?' Efe says.

Serwaa puts her hand on Efe's and gives it a soft squeeze. 'Give him time too.'

Efe feels the sharp prick of tears gathering in her eyes. 'I didn't think things would get this bad,' she says, but what she means is she never wanted it to get to this point. Never wanted any of this.

'And there's nothing to say things won't get better.'

The traffic isn't too bad, so the journey from Maame's school to Nanadwoa's apartment building takes forty minutes. By Accra standards it's a small miracle, and Efe doesn't even realise they've arrived. At some point in the journey she lapsed into silence and began flicking through photos of Sam and Liv as is her habit these days, her own form of self-inflicted punishment. Her favourites of Sam are the ones from when they lived in the studio flat. Every time she comes back to them she's amazed by how happy they look, how young and carefree. She scrolls through a dozen of Liv: her smiling over a bowl of soggy cereal, crouched over a sandcastle at the beach, dancing with Ken in the living room.

She looks up and realises they've stopped at a security checkpoint. The wrought-iron gates are topped with two feet of electric fence, and behind that Efe can see the crisp, ultra-modern apartment building, impossibly white, with row after row of wide, glass balconies. A security guard approaches the driver's door, calls up to Nanadwoa's flat before waving them through.

They take the lift to the fifth floor. The metal doors part and Nanadwoa is standing on the other side, arms flung wide to greet them.

'*Atuu!*' She wraps her arms around Serwaa first. 'Thank God my people have arrived,' she says and Efe steps forward into her arms. 'Ey, Miss UK has returned.'

'It's good to see you too,' Efe says, a lump forming in her throat as her eyes drop to Nanadwoa's bump. 'This place is nice.'

'It's full of wealthy ex-pats and business people from UAE and all those countries,' she says with a wave of her hand. 'This is the type of luxury they expect. Even in Ghana.'

She leads them into the apartment. Aside from the enormous wraparound sofa and the bright, fuchsia bougainvillea growing up the back wall, everywhere Efe looks is white, glass and steel. Efe can't comprehend how Nanadwoa will bring a child into a space like this.

'*This* is your place?' Efe says.

'Eric bought it when we were dating. I was living with my mum and he wanted me to have my own space,' Nanadwoa says, placing a hand beneath her neat bump as she sits. Efe's eyes keep coming back to it no matter how hard she tries to stay focused. She and Serwaa sit too, but the sofa is so large there's enough space for a fully grown adult to lie in the space between them.

'Help yourselves.' Nanadwoa gestures to the drinks laid out on the coffee table. 'If you're hungry I have *omutuo* and peanut soup.' Then she reaches for a packet of toffee sweets and begins unwrapping one after another, popping them into her mouth.

'How was the SHS graduation? That was today, right? I wanted to come but this woman has locked me up in my own house,' The second part of this, Nanadwoa raises her voice to say and seconds later, as if summoned, Aunty Yaa appears in the doorway.

'Ey, I didn't know you girls were here,' she says.

'We just arrived,' Efe says. Both she and Serwaa stand to greet Aunty Yaa properly.

Afterwards, Aunty Yaa steps back and tilts her head in Nanadwoa's direction.

'And what's this one saying about me?'

'That you won't let me go anywhere.'

Aunty Yaa kisses her teeth. 'Heh – you want to be going up and down, all over Accra, in this your condition? You want those women to come back and start climbing the walls?'

Efe gives Nanadwoa a look, and Nanadwoa waves a careless hand in Aunty Yaa's direction. Turning to Efe, she explains.

'That wife of Eric's came last month to make her threats. Talking about how he paid for my apartment with church funds, so if she wants it she can take it from me. It's too much.' Nanadwoa shrugs. 'I want a peaceful life.'

'You? A peaceful life?' Aunty Yaa says, incredulous.

'What's the worst thing that'll happen if I go and live my life? It's not like I'm going to get pregnant again.'

'Hmph.' Aunty Yaa grunts. 'The way people are talking-talking about what you've done to poor Pastor and his family. Never again will you know peace.'

'Me?' Nanadwoa's mouth falls open. 'What I've done to him?'

Aunty Yaa raises a hand. 'Please, Nanadwoa. It's enough. The soup and *omutuo* is prepared.' To Efe and Serwaa she says, 'I'll see you next time,' reaches for her handbag and closes the door gently behind her.

'Did you hear how she speaks to me?' Nanadwoa pipes up the moment her mum is out of earshot. 'It's almost three weeks now that she hasn't let me leave this apartment.'

'Maybe she's worried—'

'About a child? She loves children. How many times has she talked about grandchildren? And now I'm having a child and she's mad.' Nanadwoa kisses her teeth.

Efe and Serwaa exchange a look. Neither of them mention that Aunty Yaa had expressly stipulated marriage first, followed by children, on at least a hundred different occasions.

'How are you coping with everything?' Efe asks. 'Have you heard from Pastor?'

Nanadwoa stiffens. 'That man promised to buy land in my name when the baby was born, now he sends me five hundred cedis here, two hundred there, small-small guilt money. I haven't seen him in almost two months.'

A small part of Efe is amazed that Nanadwoa is taking this in her stride, but then again she has always been resilient in ways Efe could only dream of. And Efe had had Sam. A rare man who'd wanted a baby so badly he'd been the one to talk her into it, who broke down every problem and tackled them with clear, practical solutions when all Efe could do was spiral.

'Men these days aren't serious,' Nanadwoa continues. 'One girl I work with was living with her boyfriend for two years. They have a child together. Only this year she started putting pressure on him, saying they should do traditional marriage because her parents are getting old. You know what he said to her?'

'What?' Serwaa asks.

'He tells her they're just friends.' She claps her hands for emphasis.

'God forbid.'

'Anyway,' Nanadwoa says, leaning back into the sofa. 'The two of you are lucky. This city isn't easy-o.'

For half an hour they chat, Serwaa providing most of the gossip from town, Nanadwoa filling in the gaps with the latest news from society pages and recent gatherings, and Efe saying little.

'See,' Nanadwoa says when Serwaa reels off the last of it, 'I can tell you everything in the latest episodes of *Veera* and *Kumkum Bhagya*, but do I know a single thing happening in my own hometown? No.'

There's silence for a few seconds, and Efe realises they're both looking at her. She hasn't said anything for several minutes and her face is doing that thing again, exposing emotions she didn't mean to share. She is thinking about Sam, who still hasn't answered her calls or replied to her messages. She's starting to think maybe she's pushed him too far. She's not sure there's a way back for them.

Nanadwoa leans forward and stretches a hand out, still too far away to reach.

'Efe,' she says softly. 'Are you okay?'

'Yeah, I'm fine,' Efe says, too quickly, her voice cracking.

'Are you sure? I don't know how you can be in Ghana and be looking this sad.'

'I'm not—'

'I know what you should do,' Nanadwoa says, interrupting.

'What?' Efe says, already feeling defensive, suspicious of whatever Nanadwoa is about to suggest.

'You should talk to my cousin, Lawrence. He's an artist. Go talk about art, draw or whatever. Maybe it'll help and you won't be moping around any more.'

Four Months Before

Three weeks back and already Sam's growing used to the spaces Efe left behind. He's stopped expecting her to walk through the front door at any moment and has started hoping she won't wander in any time soon. He doesn't know if he'd be able to face her. He finds himself thinking of her often, of the baby, his thoughts marred with equal parts love and anger. Each time she comes to mind he has to remind himself of that conversation and the family she took away from him, knowing it's all he's ever wanted.

In the last few days he's stuffed the teddy bear and babygro in a plastic bag and buried them deep in the airing cupboard. And the pain has lessened slightly. In truth, Sam's angrier with her than he's ever been with another person, so sharp the hurt is, so heavy the storm cloud. He doesn't know what it means for them in the long-term, but Sam spends the balmy summer nights relearning how to sleep alone, stretching out little by little, the blankets piled in a heap at the end of the bed.

He notices a new nervousness to Liv. She reminds him of himself after his mum left. But she is much younger than he was, far more breakable. He explains Efe's absence as best he can, pulling Liv into his lap and letting her thin arms loop around his neck, the morning after he returns from Ghana. By the time Sam is done both of them are crying. But it isn't enough; questions will resurface and he'll keep coming back to it, explaining carefully, using soft words that might minimise the blow for a four-year-old. And for the questions Sam cannot answer, he learns to avert these with well-timed offers of ice cream from the van that hovers outside the park. He learns that anything is better than the endless lull of another evening alone, that after he puts Liv to bed his thoughts can run riot and quashed memories snake to the front of his mind. He learns that when thoughts are rioting a drink mellows him. Though he has never been one for drinking, even in his teenage years and twenties, Sam learns to like the fullness of beer, the burn of a spirit making its way down his throat.

As for her family, Sam's done with all of them. Calls go unanswered. He's blocked them all on Facebook, which is why he does a double-take when a reminder pops up on his screen. Abbey's show is tomorrow. The tickets are waiting in his inbox, forwarded on by Efe months ago. *Are you attending?* the notification asks. He hesitates, cursor hovering over the decline button, but something gives him pause. He scrolls through the promotional photos until he gets to the cast shots: the dress rehearsals full of smiling faces, kids frozen in time with their arms splayed wide in the middle of what looks like a dance routine. There's one of Abbey centre stage alongside a single pianist. The starring role she's been chasing for years. And she looks happy, her face raised to the beacon of a single spotlight, grinning so wide her eyes scrunch between cheeks and brows. Sam needs something to take his mind off Efe. He could use a little happy.

Sam feels a little reckless as he gets off the train at Covent Garden. Yet he is bolstered by the feeling as he breezes through the barriers and walks with his head bent over his phone, following the blue dot on a map. The theatre is tucked between a Boots and a pub. He makes his way into a low-ceilinged room, an unmanned bar on the far wall, the pungent smell of damp and beer filling his nostrils. Sam guesses there are forty seats, fifty max, crammed into the small space – a repurposed dance floor – and half of them are empty. He finds a seat in the fourth row, hoping he falls short of the stage lights, and scrunches further down into his seat. The rest of the audience sit in pairs and small groups, mostly friends and family members of the cast. Sam busies himself, feigns interest in the programme he picked up at the entrance and tries to ignore the trio of tourists in the row behind him, all wearing visors and loudly rustling in backpacks. Finally, the lights dim. A hush falls. A single spotlight breaks through the darkness. And there she is. Abbey.

After the show, Sam paces outside the door. The afternoon is warm and breezy. He watches the people stride past in ones and twos, heads down, headphones in, absorbed in their own worlds. The door creaks open. Two of the cast members pass by, bags slung over their shoulders. One of the two, Sam recognises as the woman who played Abbey's best friend, and he wants to ask them if they've seen her, if she'll be out soon, but he chickens out and they pass before he can say anything.

Sam tells himself he'll only wait another minute. Alarm bells are rising in a quiet corner of his mind. He counts down from sixty. He's on twelve when the door creaks open and Abbey exits. She doesn't see him at first, then her eyes flick to him, momentarily widened with shock, then settle on familiarity.

'Sam! What are you doing here?' she gushes and pulls him into a hug. Out of her costume, in dark leggings and a thin cardigan, hair bundled up into a bun, she looks more casual than he's seen her in years.

'I saw your show,' he says.

'Really? I can't see anything with those lights.'

'Yeah, you were amazing.' He smiles and drags a hand over his forehead, forces his mind to string coherent sentences. 'I just thought – as I'm here – what're you doing now?'

'Now?' She considers this. 'I'm probably just gonna buy a sandwich. I'm meeting a friend later but that's not until five.'

'If you're eating anyway, do you wanna join me?' he asks. 'We could find a restaurant.' A pause. 'And catch up about the show. About life.' Sam can hear himself rambling.

Abbey glances down at her phone to check the time. 'Yeah. We can do that.' Then she hoists her bag higher on her shoulder, and they begin walking.

'I'm glad you didn't have other plans,' Sam says. 'I didn't know how I was going to convince you to bunk.'

Abbey laughs. 'Look who's changed his tune. It was always the other way around, Mr Studious.'

They walk away from the theatre, dash across the road, giddy laughter smothered by the wind and the blare of a passing bus. The cobbled square awaits them.

'It's been ages,' Abbey smiles, 'I keep meaning to call you guys, but it's been one thing after another.'

'Yeah, too long.' Sam clears his throat. 'How are you? How's David?'

'I'm great now we're separated. You know what I learned? Some people are trying to figure life out. The rest of the world are just dicks.'

Sam nods in agreement. 'Yeah, you're better off without him.'

Fifteen minutes later they are seated at a nearby restaurant. The smell of fresh pizza wafts through the air, forks clink and diners around them chat easily.

'Who's the friend?' Sam asks.

'It's more of a colleague than a friend. We teach a drama class on Saturday mornings and need to run over a few details in the script.'

'You teach now?' Sam says, eyebrows raised.

'Tap, modern and drama,' Abbey seems to deflate slightly as she says this. 'It pays the bills. Shows like today's are a one-off.' She laughs but the sound comes out stiff and forced, like a line she's said a hundred times. 'No one's knocking down my door to give me a role.'

'Oh,' Sam says, shaking his head. 'But you were incredible – really – and you always have been.'

He thinks back to Abbey, the confident teenager and twenty-something, and how sure she was that she'd end up on West End stages and in leading roles on Broadway. They'd all believed.

A brief smile plays on her lips. 'But the students are great,' she says. 'A couple have two left feet, but there's this one little girl – Yasmin – she's only eight but she's incredible. I've never seen a kid pick up steps like she does.'

Sam grins.

'I'll miss them when I'm away.'

'Oh,' Sam says, disappointed. 'Are you going somewhere?'

'Edinburgh. For the Fringe. An old friend is putting on a play. Five actors, performing in a dingy pub, but I figured I could give it a go.'

Sam nods. The lunch rush is waning. Early diners are beginning to take their seats. A waiter comes by to clear the plates.

'More wine?'

Sam looks to Abbey, then glances at the clock: 4.41. 'What time do you need to go?'

Abbey frowns, leans forward to look at the time too. Sam catches the scent of her perfume, something feminine, fresh and citrusy.

'I don't have to go,' she says, drawing the words out slowly, and Sam brightens. 'I just need to make a quick phone call so we can reschedule.' Abbey excuses herself and slinks past the diners huddled around narrow tables.

Sam pulls out his phone, which has been buzzing intermittently all day. He dips into the family group chat and sees a few new messages from Phoebe, the latest one asking for the name of the Japanese restaurant Sam and Efe went to last year to celebrate their eighth wedding anniversary.

Mum and I are gonna go for lunch next week. Open invite x

Reflexively, Sam's jaw tightens. He's already told Phoebe in no uncertain terms that he doesn't want anything to do with their mum; he doesn't want to hear about her; and he certainly doesn't want her in his or Liv's life. This time he messages his dad and asks him to tell Phoebe to stop.

Sam lets out a breath, trying to bring his focus back to the afternoon he was enjoying up until now. He tries to push all thoughts of his mum from his mind. He doesn't want to think about Efe either because when he does everything comes back to the baby. He thinks of the baby a dozen times a day, all his waking hours. Then in his dreams, his head rests on the swollen curve of Efe's belly; a small dimpled hand curls around his finger; the smell of baby powder lingers in the air.

Sam looks up to see Abbey making her way back towards him. Above her head, hundreds of bottles of vintage wine glisten.

'Everything okay?' Sam asks, putting his phone away.

Abbey nods. 'Did you order?'

'Not yet,' Sam says, raising a hand to flag down the nearest waiter. 'But have whatever you want. This one's on me.'

They keep talking. One drink turns into two, then three; eventually they order dessert. The restaurant orbits around them. The diners change, the lights dim.

A bottle of wine in, Abbey's tongue loosens. 'Did I tell you this is the longest I've been single since I was – what – thirteen?' she says, splitting the last dregs of wine between both of their glasses.

'How long since you and David split?' Sam asks.

'Three months.'

'Three months?'

'Yeah,' Abbey says. 'I'm rubbish at it. It's like my brain drives me crazy sometimes.'

'David doesn't know what he's missing.'

Abbey's head bobs enthusiastically. 'I was a great actor before I met him. I'm starting to think he was holding me back the whole time. He only ever wanted me in his shows. Not that he ever finished them.' She sighs. 'He started writing his "magnum opus"' – she puts this part in quotes '– the year I met him. But did it ever materialise? Ten years with nothing to show for it.' She laughs, sharply, leaning back in her chair. 'And my career goes up in a cloud of smoke right along with his.'

'You still have a career,' Sam says.

'He wouldn't even let me go for *Dreamgirls*.' She sighs. 'I would've been perfect.'

'And you can get there. You just need that breakout role, right?'

She clinks her glass against his. 'Exactly.'

After finishing the bottle and ordering dessert, they hover on the steps outside the restaurant, a cascading floral arrangement brushing the top of Sam's head. In the hours that have passed, the sun has dipped low on the horizon, the sky awash with golds and oranges. Still neither of them are quite ready to leave. They stand so close Sam can see the thin line of eyeliner topping both of Abbey's eyes, a wispy piece of white thread on her eyelashes, and Abbey's wide, dark pupils.

'I need to be honest,' she says. 'I know what's going on with you and Efe. Clearly not all of it, but –' she pauses '– enough.'

'And you're still here.'

She nods slowly, holding her gaze steady on him. 'I am.'

They kiss. Gentle and unsure at first, Sam shutting down the part of his mind telling him to stop. He feels Abbey shift, certain she's about to pull away, but she doesn't and a few seconds later he feels her fingers at the nape of his neck – so light he could be imagining it – then the bloom of salted caramel as her tongue makes its way into his mouth. For a moment he thinks, *This could be enough.* His feelings for Efe are complicated now. There have always been times when they drove each other crazy, but he can't remember being this furious with her, angry enough to do something like this. It still hurts, but with Abbey, the pain is deadened and manageable, something close to forgetting. Imagining. Remaking. Undoing.

When they part, a broad smile spreads across her lips. Already, he wants to do it again. They catch a train out of the city. It is late and they are kissing in the twenty-four-hour Co-op, hesitancy giving way to something akin to passion, pressed up against freezers lined with frozen vegetables. They head back to the flat and stumble up the steps. Sam fumbles with his keys. His head is foggy and the keyhole dances. Wine bottles chink in a plastic bag. They abandon their shoes in the hallway. A trail of clothes is strewn across the landing.

In the morning, when Sam first realises he's naked and the events of the night before come back to him – the shedding of clothes, the knocking headboard, their sweaty bodies slicked together – he'll try not to feel guilty, try not to think at all, but it will be there, twisting in his gut. The story Sam will tell himself is this: she left him. She got rid of the baby – their baby. She destroyed their marriage. But in this moment, Sam doesn't think that far ahead. All he knows is that three weeks have passed since he came back from Ghana, and for the first time in all those weeks, here with Abbey, Sam doesn't think about the baby. He doesn't think about his wife.

Three Months Before

Efe grips her bag tighter and runs for the approaching *trotro*. She hears it before she sees it, her ears alert to the deep-throated cry of the conductor, the high shriek of a metal exhaust against the tarmac. Traffic breaks. It's a quick dash to the middle of the road, a clamber over the metal barrier, and she comes out on the other side. Up ahead, the patched and re-patched minibus sputters to a stop, its wheels yellowed with dust, a cloud settling around it. Efe spots a queue forming and slows her pace, smiles as the conductor – a chubby boy in a green T-shirt – jumps down from his perch, dangling out the window of the vehicle.

He waves the passengers on. Efe is the last one to board. The bus seats sixteen, but already nineteen are crammed on, not including small children on adults' laps and the two stick-thin boys who share a seat in front beside the driver. Efe squeezes in at the back, the grey leather seat ripped so yellow foam presses through the gash. The bus is pulling out again when the conductor comes over, hunched beneath the low ceiling. He shifts his weight with careful expertise as they pick up speed and jostle along the pot-hole-filled roads.

'Where are you going?' he asks in Twi.

'Anumansa Street,' Efe replies.

'Four cedis, *mepaakyɛw*.'

Efe pays the fare and watches as he moves forward row by row to collect fares from the new arrivals. He stops beside the woman who boarded just ahead of Efe, and smiles down at the child in her lap. 'And you?' he asks.

'Kinbu,' the woman says, shifting the child over her shoulder and rooting a hand into her bag.

'Two cedis.'

Efe can see the child properly now, a little boy with even brown skin, round eyes and a halo of midnight-black curls. She guesses the child is almost a year old, watches as he sucks contentedly on a fist, drool caking his mouth and cheeks. He's a cute child, with his full cheeks and large, searching gaze. When Efe lets herself, this is the type of child she thinks the baby would've grown into. He is always a little boy in her imagination. A little boy with Sam's smile and her nose. If she'd gone through with the pregnancy, she would've been five months pregnant now, the baby the size of a grapefruit. Yet another person Efe would inevitably let down. And at this thought, Efe feels something constrict in her, like a coil tightened by invisible hands. For the rest of the journey she keeps her eyes low, watches groundnut shells scattered on the floor rush this way and that.

Twenty minutes later, Efe steps out into the humid air on Anumansa Street. The roadside is thick with people, the air swollen with noise. It's coming from every direction and, for a second, Efe struggles to orientate herself. Then she spots the red-, gold- and green-painted Indomie stall on the corner and walks towards it. The studio is one road over. Efe turns onto the quiet street and bounds over the gutter, moves from pavement to empty road. Just as she nears King of Kings Confectionery and The Lord Most High Reigns Hair Braiders, Boutique and Salon, the scent of ixora rises to greet her.

She turns left and stops outside a bright yellow garage, the shutter hoisted up so she can see the studio space inside. 'Good morning,' Efe calls.

Greetings of 'Fine morning' and *'Maakye'* come in a chorus of voices.

'Is Lawrence here?' Efe asks, and a man stops working on a sculpture at the back of the room and comes outside, still wiping the clay off his hands.

'I'm a friend of Nanadwoa's. She said I should reach out to you.'

'Yes,' he nods. 'You're lucky. A spot has just come up for rent. You can come and practise your art. Any time. Day or night.'

For a second, Efe thinks she has misheard. 'Practise? No, I work with artists. I run a company back in London.'

She feels the nearest artist look her way, feels the ripple of attention, but Lawrence is looking at her, shaking his head slowly.

'We don't talk about that here. The studio is a place for people to practise, experiment, to discover their craft. We have one space available.' He raises an eyebrow. 'Nanadwoa didn't tell you?'

'No,' Efe says, feeling silly that she came all this way. 'I'm not an artist.'

He looks like he could laugh, his face scrunched up.

'What?' Efe says, a little defensively.

'Maybe you haven't practised art recently, but you are an artist. I can always tell.'

Efe huffs. She could never envision herself doing something like this, which is precisely why she leaves it to her clients – artists with years of training and practice – not someone who has barely drawn out more than directions since she was a child. The whole notion seems laughable, like a toddler racing an Olympian, yet she feels her fingers tingling. Unsettled, she looks past Lawrence and takes in the studio's warm yellowy paint, the hibiscus flowers that creep up the outer wall.

Inside, the space is wide open, the concrete walls and floor bare, with the exception of the harsh blue stripes of paint that divide up the space. She watches the way the light moves in the room, how fresh and open it makes the space feel, like anything could come forth, like anything is possible. One of the artists is whittling away at small pieces of wood, the table behind him crowded with masks and palm-sized animal carvings. Efe watches the way his hands move. His face is scrunched in concentration. The wood shavings curl like little ribbons the colour of blanched almond.

At the far end of the room, another artist is a hair's breadth away from a taut piece of canvas so large Efe wouldn't be able to contain it even if she stretched out both arms as far as she can reach. It is still a work-in-progress, but Efe can see a swimmer taking shape. The foamy, white spray of the ocean's breaking waves are pieces of shredded cloth, the water itself plasticky remnants of carrier bags. Even the paint is so gritty and textured Efe swallows the urge to run her fingers over it. And through the centre of the canvas, a black body is cutting through the waves – an almost silhouette – captured mid-stroke, a long arm arched high over a head, broad swimmer's shoulders, a collection of muscles rippling under the skin. There is a brusque quality to the work. Rough lines, a delicate subject. Efe has crossed the room without realising. She stops and feels herself quake.

Lawrence seems to sense the shift in Efe. He wanders over, his stance relaxed and confident. 'The owner lives upstairs. Should I tell her we have someone for the opening?'

Slowly, Efe nods. Lawrence smiles now, moves towards the door and stops. 'You speak Twi, right?'

'Of course,' Efe replies.

'Good. Don't let her charge you Boga price.'

Over the weeks that follow, the space becomes familiar to Efe. Translucent, paint-speckled tarp is a new addition. It hangs from the ceiling to divvy up the space and Efe's learned the boundaries of her station, and slowly picked up the rhythms. She keeps track of who works in the mornings, who works late at night and who does very little work at all. She knows that Hannah builds models of cities with dried-out coconut husks, knows that Lawrence jumps from project to project on a weekly basis and is currently threading political newspapers through a wire frame, a vaguely human shape to it.

Early on, Efe had tried sculpting but found it impossible, her hands never quite conjuring up what her mind had imagined. When she moves on to painting, she pulls up images on her phone and sketches them out as a starting point. She finds herself scrolling through pictures of Sam and Liv. It's been almost eleven weeks since she last saw Liv. Her anniversary with Sam is days away. And even though Efe has spent hundreds of pounds and travelled thousands of miles to shed her past, her thoughts always come back to them.

In the studio, Efe rewrites her story. She can pretend her past is uncomplicated, let the bumps and ridges of her life smooth out. She's started to imagine what it would be like to bring Liv here, to show her around Accra now that she's older. Maybe if Efe can just get Sam to talk to her, they can make progress, maybe even eventually find their way back to who they were before.

She works with a focused, frenzied energy. She chooses a few moments of her life to sketch out, and plans to erase the pencil after she's confident in the watercolours. She works on each painting independently, but later she will see similar colours popping up again and again. Reds. Greens. Blues. Violets. A whole rainbow of memories on canvas. She experiments, adding so much water it looks faint and washed out in places, like it's bleeding out on the page. She moves between light and heavy brushstrokes. Then she sits back and takes the whole work in. A whole morning races by.

She's vaguely aware of the radio playing in the background, the rotating cast of presenters as morning turns to afternoon; she knows that not long after the local news begins, Kojo will walk out to the main road and return with yam and *kontomire*. It's late afternoon when she glances over at the clock and packs down for the day. There's a pleasant ache stretching from her wrists right up to her shoulder blades. She's so absorbed in her work, she doesn't notice Lawrence's presence close by until the tarp beside her rises and he strides into the space.

'What do you think?' she asks, with a glance over her shoulder. A giddy self-consciousness rises up in her the moment the words are said.

Out of the corner of her eye, she sees a crinkling of lips, a slow nod of approval.

'Didn't I say you were an artist?'

Before leaving for the night, Efe decides to stretch her legs. She goes on a quick walk, her phone at her ear, and tries calling Sam again. Even with all that's happened, he's still the first person she wants to call when anything good happens. Sam's spent nine weeks not answering her calls, so she's surprised to hear his gruff voice on the other end of the line. She's only heard him speak like this twice: once when a van had backed into the car on the day they were moving into the studio flat; the second time when talking about a rival at Barnard, Brand & Associates. Even when Efe had been at her worst, in the argument after she'd left Liv on the train, he'd sounded more sympathetic, angry but straining to understand. Now, she barely recognises his voice.

'What is it? What do you want?'

'To talk,' Efe says, realising how stupid she sounds as soon as the words are out of her mouth.

Sam laughs, a harsh, blunt sound. 'You want to—' he mumbles. 'Sure. I'll play along. Let's talk. What are you up to today?'

'Erm,' Efe begins. 'I've been painting today. I'll head back to my apartment later and—'

'You have an apartment?'

'You haven't been taking my calls. I had to do something. I don't know where we stand.'

'But why would you get an apartment? Are you gonna stay?'

'It belongs to one of Nanadwoa's friends. I'm only staying while she's away. I can leave any time.'

'What a cosy little life you have.' Sam says, and Efe feels herself shrinking, the sarcasm rolling off Sam in heavy waves.

She shakes her head. 'Can I talk to Liv? How is she?'

'I can't let you do that.'

'What? Talk to my daughter?'

'Efe, you made a choice. I'm not letting you drag her feelings all over the place. She's a kid. Someone has to protect her.'

Efe closes her eyes. 'Sam, I miss her. I want her to know I still care about her, even if I'm not there.'

There's a silence. 'Look, Efe. I need to go—'

'Just tell me you'll think about it. Please.'

When Sam speaks again, his voice is a little softer. 'Okay. I will,' he says and the line goes dead.

By the time Efe makes it back to the studio, the lights are off. She assumes everyone headed home for the night, but then she sees an orange dot flare in the darkness.

'You're sitting in the dark,' Efe says.

'Actually I'm lying down in the dark,' Lawrence corrects, his head turning towards her. Efe squints and sees he's lying on one of the rugs that are normally propped up in a corner by the sink.

'There's dumsor and the diesel in the generator is finished. I sent someone to buy some.'

'Did everyone go home?'

'They can't work with no light.'

Efe steps forward, slips off her shoes and bores her toes into the plush rug. It is cream with long woolly strands. Totally unsuitable for the climate and even less practical in an artist's studio, but it reminds her of snow. A moment later, Efe lowers herself to it. She crumples and rolls over onto her back, looking up at the dark ceiling. Lawrence is spread out too, their heads inches apart. Up close, thanks to the neighbour's lights along the outside wall, Efe can just about make out his reddened eyes, smell the tang of cigarette smoke on him. He catches her looking and half smiles, takes in a lungful of smoke and murmurs, 'Helps me think.'

'Can I have some?' she asks.

He passes it to her. Efe, who hasn't smoked in over fifteen years, not since she was a teenager, inhales and holds the smoke in her lungs until she feels her head grow foggy.

'What happened to you?'

'Huh?' Efe says.

'You disappeared and now you're back and sad.'

'I'm not sad. I mean. I am, but it's home stuff.' She runs her fingers through the rug fibres. 'What about you, huh? Why are you down here by yourself?'

'My mum called.'

'And?'

'She only calls to pressure me to get married. Today she saw two girls in her church and called to tell me to pick one so my father can finally rest in peace.'

'Oh.'

'Yeah, he passed three years ago and this is the only reason she calls now.'

Efe considers this, reaching up for the cigarette again. 'What are the women like?'

'Fine, I guess. She said one is Fante, a very fair-skinned lady. She owns her own business. The other one works in the doctor's office my mum visits.'

'Hmmm,' Efe says. 'Marriage isn't always what it's cracked up to be. You need the right person at your side.'

'I know.' He pauses, the quiet between them comfortable. A silent moment passes before he speaks again. 'I was in love before. Back when I was studying in Canada. Seven years. We still would be together if my father didn't die. I only came back for the funeral and all my mum could do, the moment I stepped off the plane, was talk about marriage and grand-children. Last year she told me not to visit her house if I'm coming alone.' He laughs, but the sound comes out wounded.

Efe lets out a long, low breath. 'I left someone behind too. We were happy.'

'So what went wrong?'

She thinks for a moment. 'I was trying to be someone else. Or at least I wasn't ready to be who he needed me to be. I couldn't—' She feels a pinch in her throat. 'And now it might be too late.' She wants to laugh and cry all at once.

Lawrence shifts until he is sprawled out on his side, head resting on his hand. 'Why are you still here?'

'I just—' Efe shrugs. She is grateful for the dark as tears begin to fall, carving a path from her eyes to her ears. Weeks have passed and she still doesn't have an answer to that question. All she has is a feeling within her. No longer a push, but a pull. She is no longer running away from her life, but has the sense that there is still something for her to discover. A horizon.

'You don't sound like you're over him.'

'He's my husband,' Efe says softly. 'I love him. I've known him almost twenty years.'

Lawrence nods. He takes a last, long drag of the cigarette and flicks it out into the road. His hand squeezes Efe's shoulder.

'Then do what you need to do here and get back to him. If I had the smallest chance in the world to be with the person I love, I'd take it.'

Two and a Half Months Before

Turning onto Gardenia Crescent, Sam double-checks the address and drives slowly. He edges the car up the road, past house after house, each large and detached with quaint sloping roofs and enormous bay windows. He parks outside number 117, a Tudor-style house with a double garage, set far back from the road, turns off the engine and looks over at Olivia.

'Daddy's here to do work, okay? So I need you to . . .'

'Be on my best behaviour,' Liv parrots.

'Which means?'

'No running. No shouting. Say please and thank you.'

'And?'

'Don't disturb you unless it's really important.'

'And I mean *really* important,' Sam says, stressing the word. 'I'll be as quick as I can.' Then he leans over the console and kisses Liv on the forehead, precisely where a strip of dark brown skin is visible at her parting, where he can still catch the faintest whiff of her baby scent.

'Okay,' Sam says, turning back to the house. 'Let's do this.'

Sam rings the doorbell and silently reminds himself how much he needs this gig. He's worked less since Efe left. Most days he struggles to drag himself to his laptop, to keep his mind focused on anything that requires more than an ounce of concentration no matter how many times he tells himself to snap out of it. Over the past few weeks, emails have been accumulating and new enquiries have been left unread. The evidence of his new, lax disposition is evident in their bank account, and the only reason he's forced himself to come here today is because the balance is teetering dangerously close to the red. He can no longer afford not to get paid.

Sam hears the click of a latch and a moment later his client flings the door open. He's a stout and grey-haired man, a broad smile on his lips as he reaches out to shake Sam's hand.

'Samson?' he says, still grinning. 'Nice to meet you.'

'Mark?'

'That's the one,' the man says before his gaze slinks to the left and he notices Olivia.

'Oh.' He hesitates. 'Who's this?'

'Tell him your name, Liv,' Sam says encouragingly, giving Liv a gentle prod in the back.

'Olivia,' Olivia murmurs, keeping her eyes low and shifting her weight to the other leg.

Mark looks perplexed. His brows draw together as he looks back at Sam, then past him, towards the empty driveway as if expecting a nanny to be waiting in the wings.

'Is she staying?'

Sam nods, trying to find the line between confident and apologetic. 'You won't even know she's here.'

Mark leads them through the house. Each room they pass is immaculately kept, stylish and suave, with muted blue cushions and lush creamy rugs, the type of furniture that's impossible to keep clean with a child in the house. To him, it feels more like a showroom than a home, right down to the large farmhouse sink, the pale pink peonies on the kitchen island and the bowl of perfectly ripe lemons on a dining table set for twelve.

Mark pauses a few feet into the kitchen. 'Sharon,' he calls. The patter of scurrying footsteps begin.

'The photographer?' a woman calls, stepping in through a side door. Sam guesses they're both in their late fifties, not too far from his dad's age. They have warm and genial faces that would make them fit right at home playing Father Christmas and Mrs Claus, and Sam hopes they're the type of people who'll overlook him bringing his four-year-old daughter to work.

The woman, Sharon, slips off muddy gardening gloves and unties an apron, looking from Sam to Olivia, a puzzled expression on her face.

'Your daughter?' Sharon asks, her voice rising at the end.

'Yeah,' Sam says. 'I don't normally bring her but it's the summer and my wife's . . . away.'

Olivia's head flicks towards him. He feels her eyes boring into him, but Sam leaves it at that. He only takes Liv to shoots when he absolutely has to, when there's no one else who can look after her. Sam notices she's trickier these days, worried every time he's out of sight and has basically become his shadow. She cries endlessly if he tries to leave her with anyone who isn't immediate family. She'd howled and clung on to his shirt and jeans the first time he'd tried to leave her with the childminder almost three weeks after Efe had left.

'This is such a beautiful house,' Sam says. 'Did you have any particular locations in mind?'

'I was thinking a few here in the kitchen,' Sharon says, gesturing to a brightly lit nook by the window. 'And a few in the garden.'

Sam pulls out his camera and follows, pausing to take a few test shots, adjusting the lights and his positioning when it isn't working. The whole time he can feel Olivia trailing a few steps behind.

'The dog is around here somewhere,' Sharon says ten minutes later as they step back into the kitchen. 'You're both okay with dogs, right?'

Sam glances at Liv.

'Yeah. We'll be fine.'

Three pairs of eyes go towards the door, watching as Mark strides back in wearing a freshly ironed shirt. 'Right,' he claps. 'Can I get either of you something to drink before we get started? We've got juice, lemonade, sparkling water.'

'Lemonade,' Liv says, nodding eagerly before remembering her manners. 'Please,' she adds.

'I'll have the same, thanks,' Sam says.

He watches as Mark pulls out a wide-based decanter and places two glasses on a tray.

'Do you have a plastic cup?'

Mark pauses and throws a quick look in Sharon's direction. She gives her head a quick shake.

'I'll just—' Sam says, rummaging through Olivia's bag even though he checked twice on the drive down and knows he forgot to pack her water bottle. He frowns and turns back to Liv. 'Two hands, okay?'

Sam's been doing this long enough to know his first job of the day is to make Mark and Sharon comfortable in front of the camera, so he starts off chatting with them while getting his camera properly set up.

'Did you say the photos were for an anniversary?'

At this Mark's chest swells with pride and Sharon places an affectionate hand over his. 'Thirty years,' she says, her gaze moving to Sam's wedding band.

'You?'

'Erm,' Sam begins, then finds he is no longer able to meet Sharon's eye. He preoccupies himself with the camera. 'Nine last month.'

'Ah,' Mark smiles warmly. 'The big one next year.'

'Did you do anything to celebrate?' Sharon chimes in.

The air thickens in Sam's throat. He runs a hand up the nape of his neck. 'She's out of the country at the moment – so – let's get started.'

They take a few shots beneath the oak tree and a few more by the pond. The whole time, Sam is half-watching Olivia out of the corner of his eye, her head bent over either a colouring book or Sam's work iPad. He's happy with how the photos have turned out so far. The clients are comfortable, laughing every few minutes and genuinely happy to be directed. 'That's it,' he says, inching closer.

A hand tugs his shirt. 'Daddy?' Olivia says quietly. 'I need the toilet.'

'Where's your bathroom?' he asks, turning to the couple, but Liv cuts him off.

'I want *you* to take me,' she whines, crossing her arms for good measure.

Sam sighs. 'Gimme one minute.'

The bathroom is opposite the reception, a gorgeous marble-walled room with a pristine, clawfoot tub.

'Wait for me,' Olivia says and leaves the door open a crack. Sam can hear her scurrying across the room. He pulls out his phone and sees a text message from Phoebe: So sorry. Completely forgot. Still happy to do Friday night.

Sam lets out a breath. The toilet flushes. A minute later Sam and Liv are striding back out into the sun-soaked garden, Liv peeling off and heading back towards the patio area and Sam returning to the couple. They seem stiff again. Sam puts on some music, pulling up the pre-prepared playlist of their favourite songs.

'Try one walking towards me, holding hands,' Sam suggests. And obediently, Mark and Sharon comply, looking more relaxed as 'Never Let You Go' reaches the chorus. Sam is so focused on getting the next good shot that he doesn't notice the dog approach. All he hears is Liv's high-pitched squeal a half-second before a glass smashes on the patio. The sound of the glass shattering seems to reverberate in Sam's ears. He's mortified, across the garden in an instant, tugging Liv out of the way and sending what looks like a small Pomeranian scampering.

There are slices of lemon and shards of broken glass all across the patio. Irrationally, Sam decides he has to fix this to salvage the shoot and make sure the journey out here wasn't for nothing. He groans and crouches down and reaches for the largest pieces of glass and piles them on the table.

'What happened?' Sam fumes. And Olivia, who has been frozen and silent for a full twenty seconds, crumbles, and starts to cry. Sam's anger dissipates.

'Are you hurt?' he asks, scanning her shins and palms for cuts or scratches.

Mark and Sharon head in their direction. 'It might be the shock,' Mark says.

Sam turns back to his still-wailing daughter and lets her wrap her thin arms around his neck and bury her face into his. 'Maybe,' Sam mumbles.

Later, when Sam is packing up for the day, far more tired than he should be after a half-day's work, Mark makes his way back over. He'd noticed Mark and Sharon's tense whispered exchange a few minutes before and the firm shove from Sharon that sent Mark in Sam's direction.

'Look,' Mark begins, driving his hands deep into his pockets. 'The glass your kid broke wasn't cheap. It's part of a set. Some luxury brand. I dunno, ask the Mrs.' He pauses. 'I'm not going to send you a bill or anything, but we really think you should take something off the top.'

Sam thinks of the mortgage payment that's due in ten days, the bills he's already had to move to credit cards. He sighs.

'Lemme see what I can do.'

A few days later, Sam drives to his dad's place, lets himself in and finds Liv and Phoebe in the kitchen. Both heads turn in his direction when he enters.

'Daddy!' Olivia beams, her tongue peeking through the gap where a tooth sat two days ago. 'Do you like my drawing?'

Sam steps closer and looks down at the paper flapping in Olivia's hands. He tilts his head one way, then the other. Whichever way he looks it's still a sausage with a smiley face on stilts. 'It's . . . beautiful. Best portrait I've ever seen.'

From the other side of the room, Phoebe says, 'It's a unicorn.'

'I can see that,' Sam says squinting.

'Thanks for watching her. How was she?' Sam asks.

Phoebe looks up from a bowl of Cheerios. 'She was great,' she says, then pauses, remembering. 'Actually she's been asking questions about you-know-who again – not details – just if she'll be back in time to go swimming on Friday. Stuff like that.'

'Oh okay.' Sam nods. He runs a palm over Liv's frizz and wonders where her bonnet got to.

'I heard you were a big girl last night and went to sleep without Bear-Bear,' Sam says, thinking back to the night before and driving all the way home before he spotted Liv's favourite teddy bear in the footwell.

'I had Plum,' Olivia says, reaching over to pull a dark-skinned doll in her lap. Sam looks at it curiously.

'Nice to meet you, Plum.' Sam turns to Phoebe. 'Who got this? You or Dad?' he asks, but Liv cuts in.

'Grammy gave it to me.'

Grammy? Sam thinks. In all the time he's known Maame, she has never been one to spend exorbitant amounts – or any amount – on postage. She is far more likely to lug two thirty-five-kilo suitcases through the airport than pay for postage.

'Who's . . .' he begins. Then it hits him. His stomach drops.

'Go get your things,' Sam says, and watches as Liv hops out of her seat and heads for the door. He is scowling. A hard tension settles in the air between him and Phoebe. He doesn't speak until he hears the sound of Liv's small feet stomping up the stairs and he is sure she's out of earshot.

He rounds on his sister. 'Are you serious?'

'I didn't invite her,' Phoebe says. 'She meant to leave the doll on the doorstep but we got home early and bumped into her.'

'You didn't have to introduce them.' Sam throws his hands in the air. 'You could've said she was a neighbour. One of Dad's friends. A delivery driver. You could've said anything. Anything.'

'I'm sorry, okay? It just came out.'

Sam had known Phoebe has been in contact with their mum for over a year now. He'd known when they started FaceTiming regularly and when they'd started meeting up in person. His dad has been a part of it too, more cautious at first, but eventually, he too let her back in. And, all this time, Sam has been careful not to ask about it. He kept his mum's reappearance confined to the peripheries of his mind while he focused on his marriage and raising his daughter. He was certain this would be another instance where his mum would blow in and out like an unwelcome storm, leaving all of them reeling and Sam to pick up the pieces. But a week had turned into a month, then two, six and suddenly fifteen months have been and gone and she's still here, living somewhere in the city.

'Why are you even trying with her? Do you not remember what she was like?'

'I remember that she was nice and fun and —'

'And she left us, Pheebs.'

'She sent postcards.'

'A dozen postcards over the years doesn't fix anything. It doesn't fix the missed birthdays and Christmases and parents' evenings and—'

'I can't change any of that,' Phoebe says. 'But she's here now. And I'd really like to have a mum for *once* in my life.'

Sam rests a hand on the plastic tablecloth, his fingers just grazing Liv's half-eaten bowl of Cheerios, the remaining cereal limp and bobbing on the surface.

'She asks about you,' Phoebe says, her voice soft now. 'You should just meet her.'

Sam shakes his head. He doesn't get it. He isn't sure he ever will. 'No,' he says firmly. 'I'm not letting her pull me back in, and I'm not about to let her do the same thing to Liv. It's bad enough with Efe gone.'

Phoebe swallows. 'Have you heard from her, Efe I mean?'

'Yeah,' Sam says. 'We spoke. Once.'

'That's a start.'

They lapse into a strained silence until Olivia skips back into the room. Ken trails a few steps behind her, hobbling. Residual weakness in his arm and a slight limp are all that remain of the stroke. He looks from Sam to Phoebe and back again, sensing the atmosphere in the room.

'Is this about the doll?' He gives his head a small shake. 'Don't blame me. I had nothing to do with it.'

Later that night, Sam is still thinking about his mum. He is annoyed at himself, wishing he could just let it go. His family is fracturing and it's playing on his mind. His thoughts won't quiet enough to let Sam fall asleep, and he's spent too many nights scrolling through his phone or staring at a blur of images flashing past the TV screen. All his life, Efe has been the only person he can talk to about this. It's after midnight when he calls her.

'Sam, hi,' she says, and Sam knows he's woken her up. He can hear it in her voice.

'Hey.'

'It's late. Is everything okay? Is it Liv?'

'She's fine. Well . . .' He opens his mouth to continue but doesn't know where to begin. 'She met my mum today – or yesterday – I'm not totally sure when it was.'

He hears movement in the background. The sound of a whirring overhead fan, the rustling of bedsheets. He imagines Efe sitting up, listening intently. 'I thought you didn't want to—'

'I didn't. It was an accident. Phoebe apologised.'

'And?'

'And now my mum wants to meet her. Properly.'

'Okay.' Efe waits a few seconds. 'What are you thinking?'

'That I don't want Liv to go through what Phoebe and I did growing up. She's a kid and it's so tough when someone you love just disappears.' He waits for Efe to respond, then realises. 'I'm not talking about you.'

'But it's the same.' She lets out a slow breath. 'I know I have the apartment now, but that's not keeping me here. I'm not pushing you before you're ready, but I want you to know I'd like to come back and work on us. I wanna speak to her and—' Her voice breaks.

'I can't think about that yet,' Sam says, lowering his head into his hands. 'Can we get back on topic?'

'Okay,' Efe says. 'It's up to you. The whole time I've known you, you've wanted to know why she left, why she didn't stay in touch, why she didn't show up to meet you when you were twenty-three. You've been holding on to so many questions for such a long time. Don't you want some answers?'

Sam considers this. He supposes she's right. Already, his thoughts are slowing. Settling. 'Can I ask you something?' he says in return.

On the other end of the line, Efe grows quiet. 'Okay,' she says softly.

'Don't you love her?' he asks.

She swallows. 'Of course I do.'

'Then why?' Sam says, hearing the desperate edge in his voice.

Efe lets out a long, low sigh. 'I can love her and still want something more for my life. Love and regret aren't mutually exclusive. I just –' she hesitates – 'I couldn't go back to the beginning. I couldn't let myself get stuck again.'

Sam is beginning to understand, but it still stings him, how easily she says this, how easily she's carried on without them.

'Is that how we made you feel, then? Stuck? Like we trapped you? I trapped you?'

'I'm just saying I always came last. I gave up my career, my body, five years of my life. I saw a glimpse at something close to happiness and I took it.'

AUGUST 2016

Two Months Before

Sam takes the train to Charing Cross. He arrives with five minutes to spare, but can't bring himself to walk straight to the restaurant. Instead he circles the surrounding roads, head lowered as rain falls like confetti. When Sam finally walks in, fifteen minutes late, he's managed to pull himself together enough to appear calm on the outside. The only thing that gives him away is a slight tremor in his hands.

The host makes his way over, dressed in a navy suit so suave Sam wonders if he should've dressed up for the occasion. 'Do you have a reservation?'

'I think it's under Rebecca,' Sam swallows. 'Rebecca Mensah.'

He shifts his weight to the other leg, watching the host run a finger down a thick, paper organiser. 'Uh-huh, right this way.'

Sam follows. He can feel his heart lurching and brings a hand up to his chest. Suddenly, Sam finds himself face to face with his mother. She springs out of her seat, her long earrings rattling, relief coming off her in waves.

'Sammy,' she says, a little breathless. She takes a half-step forward, arms lifting, but seems to decide otherwise when she sees Sam's stiff arms at his side. Instead, she gestures to the canary-yellow sofa on her left and Sam takes a seat. The restaurant is quirky, a mix between a cafe and a cocktail bar. Sam makes a quick scan of the room and notices people are sitting on an array of brightly coloured chairs, all of them mismatched, the walls around them navy, with fake grape-vines hanging overhead.

'Thanks for meeting me,' Rebecca says, clasping her hands in her lap. She looks nervous, earnest, a tight closed-lip smile on her face. It has been twelve years since Sam saw her last and over a decade before that. She doesn't look like a woman in her mid-fifties, but there are new wrinkles on her face, the skin around her neck is looser and her hair is thinner, a faint black shadow at her hairline where the dye has stained her skin.

'Phoebe wouldn't let it go so . . .' He trails off.

Without making a conscious decision, Sam has positioned himself at the far end of a sofa so low to the ground his knees are in line with his belly button. He shifts, stretching his legs out so they disappear under the coffee table.

'I ordered you a mocha,' Rebecca says. 'I remembered how much you loved hot chocolate as a kid, but then I thought you might want coffee. It's okay if you don't like it. I can get something else.'

'I can pay for my own coffee,' Sam says a little too forcefully.

His mum looks stunned, her mouth hanging open. 'Erm, I know that. Sammy, I wasn't trying to—'

'And no one calls me that. It's Samson or Sam.'

'Right,' she says, placing her hands in the hammock of her lap. Sam can feel himself making this harder than it needs to be. He feels uneasy and throws a few glances at the door, as if calculating what route he'd take if he had to make a quick escape.

His mum is perched on the edge of her chair, hands wrapped around a teacup, ankles crossed. She looks delicate, dressed in a long spotted dress that flows down her calves.

The atmosphere is tense when a waiter comes over, oblivious, and places a plate in front of each of them. Sam's eyes follow the movement, his breath catching in his lungs the moment he sees the cannoli. His mum looks startled.

Her eyes flick from Sam to the waiter and back again. 'Oh, you don't have to eat that,' she says. 'I asked your dad the type of things you like.'

Sam stills. He thinks of Efe and feels the sharp sting of tears in his eyes. A boulder settles in his throat. And he can feel his mum watching him, trying to unpick his reaction.

'It's fine,' Sam says at last, not meeting her gaze as he slides the plate closer. Then reaches for his mocha. 'Where have you been?' he says slowly. 'All these years?'

'All over.' His mum takes a deep breath. 'The whole time you were growing up I worked in offices, typing mostly, administrative stuff. But a couple nights a week I had a regular slot at this little jazz bar.'

'I remember that place,' Sam interrupts. 'You used to sing covers, and I'd sit in one of the booths taking care of Phoebe and doing homework until Dad's shift ended every day.'

'It wasn't every day,' she says firmly. 'It was once, maybe twice a week.'

'It was every day,' Sam grumbles, feeling like a twelve-year-old again.

'And one day after my set, Terrence Howe came up and asked me if I wanted to join a band. You won't remember him, but he was big in the nineties. A jazz musician. And their lead singer had just split up with Mickey on keys, and they needed someone to fill in. Your dad and I argued about it all week, but I went anyway.'

'And left us.'

'I was on tour. It was only meant to be six months. But then there was another tour after that, and your dad and I had spent so much time apart. I was so focused on singing, certain my big break was right around the corner. But years passed, and I was still playing in small clubs, back-up for big names. And soon so long had passed I didn't know how to find my way back.'

'Bullshit,' Sam says. 'Dad's lived in the same house thirty years and you suddenly forget where it is.'

'I knew where you were,' she says. 'But it wasn't that easy. I just couldn't face it.'

'You couldn't face your own family?'

'I couldn't face my life, Sam.' She sighs, her whole body arching forward. 'Being a parent is hard. Not everyone knows how to do it. I was barely nineteen when I had you. Can you imagine being a parent at nineteen? Suddenly you're in your thirties with two kids, wondering when your whole life passed you by.'

'Was it that bad, raising us?'

Rebecca pushes a hand out towards Sam, then thinks better of it. She lays it flat on the table. 'You're a parent now. Maybe you'll get it. I couldn't do anything right. I second-guessed myself. Worrying about every decision practically took over my life. You know how some people say the first few months are worst? Well for me, it didn't get better.'

Sam takes a sip of his drink, tightens his grip on the luke-warm ceramic.

'The only thing I could do well was sing.'

At this, Sam feels his head jerk up, his eyes narrow. 'But you were singing. Twice a week, right? Wasn't that enough?' But what he means is: *Weren't we enough?*

'I'm sorry it took me this long to come back,' she says softly. 'Truly, I am.'

'So why didn't you stay when I saw you? That was more than a decade ago. You had a chance then.'

She lowers her gaze. 'I'm not proud of it, but seeing you freaked me out. I'd only been back in the area twice since I left, and I guess I was –' she falters '– embarrassed. I'd been gone all that time, chasing different opportunities around the world, only to end up exactly where I'd begun. Twelve years ago, I still thought I had to prove myself.'

Slowly, Sam nods. He can see it then. A line that forever divided those who stayed from those who left and Sam, a stayer, would never fully understand.

'It doesn't matter now,' Sam says. 'I don't know why I brought it up.'

'I know this is upsetting and you probably feel like I barged my way back into your life, but I haven't barged into anything. Your sister and your father asked me to come back. They reached out to me.'

'And how long are you gonna stick around this time?'

'As long as they'll have me.' She pauses. 'And I'd really love to get to know you too. And, if it's okay, I'd like to meet your daughter.'

'You already met her.'

'She's amazing. Phoebe told me she's learning to read already, and so well spoken.'

'Yeah.' Sam nods. 'She's wonderful.'

'Is her mum still in the picture?'

Sam pauses, trying to judge how much Phoebe and Ken would've shared. 'We're working things out.'

'Good for you.' She smiles. 'And Phoebe too. She's incredible. You and your dad should be really proud of the way you raised her.'

'We had help,' Sam says, thinking back to all the people who stayed. He thinks of his dad, who worked twelve-hour shifts, six days a week, for twenty-five years just to keep the roof over their heads; and of how their next-door neighbour, Mrs Felton, had babysat Phoebe and Sam after school every day, never accepting money, just insisting they both got at least Bs in school, and in return Sam got all As and A*s; he thinks of his old manager at Blockbuster who gave Sam his first job when he was barely fifteen so he could help his dad out with the bills and start saving towards university; and all the other people who stepped up. Sam realises now he got it wrong. He'd wanted a family all his life, so badly at points that his whole body ached with longing. But maybe all this time he's had more family than he'd ever realised.

'I'm glad you had help,' his mum says.

'Me too,' Sam says. A moment passes. 'Could you do something for me?'

She looks confused for a second. 'What is it?' she asks.

'It's Phoebe. I need you to promise me you won't hurt her. Even if you don't stay or things don't work out with you and Dad. I need you to—'

'I promise.'

Sam nods. He looks down at his mocha and cannoli, both stone cold now. He stands, and his mum follows suit, the napkin fluttering from her lap to the floor.

'Can we do this again?' she says. 'I'll let you order your own coffee next time.'

'Sure,' Sam says, reminding himself he's not promising forever. Not promising forgiveness. Just another coffee. And as he leaves, Sam walks a little taller. For his whole life, since the day she left, he's felt a little off balance. And though he hates to admit it, something deep within him finally feels steady.

SEPTEMBER 2016

Six Weeks Before

Olivia is forgetting her. Sam realises this in the large Sainsbury's just off the high street. It's a Friday and the store is filled with slow-moving people, shuffling straight to the ready meals sections, tired from long hard weeks. Sam too walks slowly. List in hand, he pushes a trolley through an aisle lined with plastic-wrapped rice and pasta, ready-made sauces that glint under the fluorescent lights. Olivia strides ahead of him. One finger loops through the criss-crossing metal of the trolley, and she's chatting animatedly about her first weeks at school.

'. . . Miss Sing told Shawn two times. He won't stop talking so she put his name under the sad face.'

'Hmm,' Sam says and reaches for jars of pasta sauce. 'What happens when Miss Sing puts someone's name under the sad face?'

'You have to stay inside at playtime for two minutes. And Shawn's name is there two times.'

'So how many minutes did he have to stay inside?'

'Four.'

Sam smiles and pushes the trolley towards the packets of rice. 'And is Shawn your friend?'

'No!' Olivia says, this time turning to Sam, her voice thick with childish exasperation. She crosses her arms. 'He's naughty.'

Sam smothers a laugh with a cough, wonders where this confident spark of a person came from. He's proud of how

310

well she's settled in at school, of how well she's coping. 'So who are your friends?' he asks.

'My friends is Josiah, Nicky, Hayden . . .' Sam listens as she lists them off, counts each one on her fingers, and when they turn into the chilled dairy aisle, she's run out of fingers and is still going. He plucks a packet of cheese from the shelf. He thinks back to how for three days in a row she'd hesitated at the school gate, turned her anxious face up towards him, and Sam had crouched low and coaxed her into going in. Suddenly she's settled. *She's doing fine*, Sam thinks.

Coming down the aisle towards them is a woman with an overstuffed trolley. A boy in the same school uniform as Olivia shuffles beside her. In the time it takes Sam to turn to the shelf and scan the expiry dates on bottles of milk, she materialises beside them, stops inches away.

'Olivia, is this your dad?'

Sam's head turns towards her. They are miles away from the school. His brain takes a moment to place her.

'Oh, sorry. I never remember to introduce myself. I'm Nicola. I think I've seen you at drop-off.' She pushes a hand out and Sam shakes it.

'Sam.'

'And this is Jacob.' She gestures to the freckled kid tugging at grey shorts, his face half-hidden by fluffy brown curls. 'He's in Miss Branner's class. You might not've met her yet. She's the other reception teacher.'

'Oh, right,' Sam says.

'But you! You're hard to miss – we only ever see mums on the school run; dads are a rare sighting – like unicorns.' She laughs then, tucks a strand of hair behind her ear. Sam feels himself growing uncomfortable. A trio of teenage girls pass, the one at the back saddled with the basket loaded with popcorn, chocolates and fizzy drinks.

Sam turns back to Nicola. 'Yeah, Liv's mum is away.'

'Nothing bad, I hope.'

'No.' Sam shakes his head. He can feel Olivia's eyes on him and says the same thing he's been saying since she left. 'She's just staying with her parents for a little while.'

There's a quick movement, one Sam almost misses, as Nicola's eyes flick down to his left hand. When she meets his gaze again she smiles knowingly, like there's some shared secret between them. A muscle in Sam's jaw tightens. Her kid groans and turns his face towards the ceiling.

'Just a minute, Jacob,' she says, still looking at Sam. She continues, 'The other mums and I are planning to set up this WhatsApp group. Lots of us live in the area and thought it would be good for everyone to chat, get to know each other, pick up kids if someone's running late. You know, stuff like that. I can add you to it.'

For a second he thinks she's flirting with him and, as soon as he's thought it, the idea seems ridiculous. This woman – clothed in sporty leggings and an oversized jumper – is a PTA mum. She's just being kind. He recites his number.

'See you another time.' She waves and heads down the rice and pasta aisle. Sam moves the trolley on. It's ten minutes later when it happens. He's in the breakfast foods aisle. Cartoon characters line brightly coloured cardboard boxes. He reaches for the Rice Krispies and, when he looks up, Olivia's gone. His head spins in both ways down the empty aisle. His mouth dries up in an instant, thoughts spiral back to a grotty police station waiting room, the minutes that felt like hours while he had to wait.

'Liv?' he croaks, quietly at first. Then louder. He's running then, swerving round shoppers, mumbling apologies. He skirts around a trolley, looks down every aisle. Heads swivel as he calls her name. A sick feeling rises up in him and the world moves in slow motion. Then he catches a flash of red cardigan. It's over in less than a minute.

'Liv!' he shouts and she stops mid-stride and spins towards him, the grey pinafore puffing out a neat circle.

'What are you doing?' Sam says. 'How many times have I told you not to wander off? Why would you do that?' He kneels and pulls her close, rests his chin on her hair, waits for the pit-of-his-stomach feeling to settle. 'What were you thinking?'

'I saw Mummy.'

Sam draws back. He speaks softly. 'What? You just heard me say . . . She's staying with Grandma and Grandpa. Remember? I told you that.'

Olivia doesn't answer. Her bottom lip puckers and brows dip low in a familiar way, then she's crying. The heel of her hand comes up to her face.

'Listen. I'm not mad. You just can't run off like that.'

'But—' Her voice trembles and Sam pulls her into his arms again. He turns then and spots a woman at the far end of the aisle. She looks over and their eyes meet. Everything about her is wrong. She's too tall, her shoulders broader, her face longer and skin a shade or two lighter than Efe's. The only vague similarities are the nose and braids. Sam looks away and holds Olivia tighter.

'You're okay. You're okay,' he says. 'Let's get you home.'

That evening Sam texts Efe. Video call tonight? Liv needs to see you. He tosses his phone aside and prepares his usual dinner of something from a packet baked in the oven. In the last few weeks, when time allows, he's branched out into things that can be boiled on the stove and poured from a jar. Occasionally, he cooks meals he learned from Efe. Forty minutes later, Olivia is licking ketchup from her fingers when the phone rings.

'Here.' He passes her a piece of kitchen roll. 'Wipe your hands. Mummy's on the phone.' He answers and passes it over.

'Sam?' Efe says, just as her face flashes up on screen, then, 'Olivia! Hey, sweetie.'

'Mummy!' Liv exclaims.

Sam takes Olivia's plate and slips out of the room. He eats the last half of a fish finger, ignores the beans sitting in a reddish sludge. He can hear Efe's voice. 'It's so good to see you. Is that your uniform? You look so grown up!' She's gushing. They talk for twenty minutes. Delighted with a new audience, Olivia eagerly tells Efe all the stories Sam's heard already and lists off all the friends she's made since starting school. At 7.40 Olivia comes in and holds the phone out.

'Go get ready for bed, okay?' Sam watches as she scurries off, takes a deep breath before he looks at the screen. In the months since he saw her last, Efe's lost weight. She's visibly skinnier now, her face narrower, her cheekbones more pronounced.

'Hi,' he says.

Hi. Thanks for letting me talk to her.' She pauses. 'What changed?'

'My mum.'

'You met up with her?'

'Yeah.'

'Wow,' Efe says, then stops herself before she asks the question on the tip of her tongue. 'I'm glad you got to do that.'

'Me too,' Sam says and he leaves it at that, not quite ready to go into detail yet. 'How are the paintings coming along?'

'Good.' She grins. 'We're putting on an exhibition in a few weeks. I'm really hoping I have something to show by then.'

'Can you send me the details?'

For a second, Efe looks surprised, then she rights herself. 'I'll send them over now.'

Sam smiles. They drift into a comfortable silence. 'Hey, can I ask you something?' he says.

'Sure.'

'What was so bad about being pregnant? I'm trying to understand why you didn't want to do it again.'

'You mean besides carrying eight pounds and not sleeping for three months, a year if we're counting, after she was born?'

Sam exhales.

'Okay,' Efe says, her tone serious. 'Do you remember that year we visited Serwaa after Abena was born?'

'That must've been – what – 2009?'

'Yeah, September, I think. It was sometime in the autumn. Remember how she'd just go to sleep whenever you were holding her? With me, she was always so tense. Half the time she'd cry like I'd just pinched her, and I just wanted the floor to swallow me up.' She pauses. 'That's what it was like after Liv was born. All the time. With my own kid. I was trying so hard to keep it together and felt incredibly alone.'

Sam thinks it over. He knew he'd made mistakes. He remembers how often he'd let work come first. All the late nights, leaving Efe home alone with Liv, practically climbing the walls of the flat. He wonders what things would've been like if he'd taken the risk and thrown himself into full-time photography before Liv came along, back when Efe had first suggested it. He might've had both feet on the ground, a steady income, been able to decide his hours and been at home to support her when she needed him most. And he'd known she'd needed him. Even then. He sees now why she didn't want to go through that again.

Maybe, he thinks to himself, *this all could've been avoided*. He could've been the type of person who leaned in, instead of busying himself with work when his dad got sick or something else happened that he couldn't make himself face.

'I'm really sorry it was like that for you,' he says quietly, feeling a deep disappointment and frustration in himself. He understands it now, years too late. 'For what it's worth, I always thought you were an amazing mum.'

They speak again after that. She calls on Sunday morning, when Sam and Olivia are making pancakes, the counters sprinkled with sugar and overturned blueberries rolling in every direction. And they keep speaking throughout the week.

To Sam, it feels like they've been transported back to their university days, with him sitting on the kitchen counter, frowning down at food-smattered tiles, and her under the covers at Aunty Dora's flat, the phone cable stretched taut across the bedroom. Each conversation ends in a similar way and Sam feels a can of worms opening up inside of him. It's always after these conversations that the grief sneaks up on him. A week after they begin speaking, Sam spots a woman outside his office, her hands cradling a bump. He knows it can't possibly be Efe, but his feet still carry him four steps towards her before he stops himself.

SEPTEMBER 2016

One Month Before

On the front doorstep, Sam and Liv shiver. Autumn is ebbing away faster than Sam would like. Already, the grey is threatening to swallow up everything warm, gold and auburn. On the other side of the door, Sam can hear a faint step-and-drag pattern growing louder and louder until there's a low rattle of a hand on the latch and the front door swings open.

'Hey, Dad.' Sam smiles. They hug, lightly clapping each other on the back.

'Grandad,' Olivia says and slides her hand into his. She forgets Sam exists the moment her eyes land on Ken, and slowly they make their way into the living room, squeeze into the big armchair together. Sam closes the door behind them, pauses in the entryway to unwind his scarf.

'Hey, Liv,' he calls. 'Why don't you show Grandad what you learned at school today?'

Sam steps into the living room as Olivia slides a book out of her book-bag, runs a finger over the brightly coloured letters. She cobbles together three-letter words, looks up at Ken after each one.

'Isn't that something?' Ken murmurs, raising an eyebrow at Sam. 'I thought all they did was play.'

'So did I.' Sam makes his way into the kitchen. 'Liv, d'you want some water?'

'Juice, please!' Olivia replies.

'Dad?'

'You making coffee?'

'I can.'

Sam gives Liv a cup of juice then scrolls through his phone as the kettle boils, busies himself with the small stack of washing-up as the coffee brews. He clicks on Efe's page and sees nothing new in the four months they've been apart. He wasn't expecting to see anything, but a few minutes flicking through her photos causes his mind to quiet. When they'd last messaged she'd been talking about a painting she was starting over because she couldn't get it right. He messages to ask how it's going.

When he comes to, the coffee is velvety and a rich almost black. He pours two cups, adds a dollop of milk into one, and takes them through to the living room.

'This one's yours,' Sam says, passing the mug with milk to his father.

'I know – I'm trying.' Ken lets out a huff, the words gurgling up his throat.

There's a strained expression on Ken's face. Again and again, his arm lifts just high enough for his fingers to brush against the edge of the table. Sam puts the mugs down with a chink. 'Lift both arms up for me.'

Ken looks panicked now. Only one arm veers upward even though his face contracts with the effort. All the while Olivia sounds out 'cat', 'mat', 'sat'.

Sam reaches for his phone. 'I'm calling an ambulance.'

At the hospital, Sam paces. Slow laps around a bank of grey padded chairs while the overhead lights flicker and wane. Olivia is restless in her own way. Her small feet swing in too-big school shoes, arching high above the ground. *She's handling it all so well*, Sam thinks. Only once, as the paramedics wheeled Ken out to the ambulance, a quiet gurgle escaping his lips, had she tugged Sam's sleeve and asked, her voice trembling faintly, 'Is Grandad going to be okay?'

And Sam, remembering Olivia years ago, in a similar hospital, Ken in a hospital bed, had crouched low and said, 'You're too small to remember this, but he pulled through before. He'll do it again.'

Now, thirty laps later and no word from the doctor, Sam wishes he'd said, 'I hope so' or 'We'll have to see what the doctor says.' Something vague. Non-committal. Anything that means his daughter won't remember him as a liar if – he exhales, unable to finish that thought. He needs to think about something else and lowers himself into the seat beside Liv and slips his phone out of his pocket. Nineteen new notifications from the school WhatsApp group. Twelve new emails – probably junk. A couple of texts from Abbey, trying to get back in touch now she's back in London. He ignores them all. Each time he thinks back to it, he feels a red-hot slice of guilt and self-hatred cutting through him. Sam's thumb hovers over Efe's number. He knows he probably shouldn't call her, but also knows there's no one else he'd rather speak to right now. He presses the call button.

'Hello?' she says, picking up just as Sam thinks he's about to get her voicemail.

'Hey,' he says, his voice heavy with relief. 'I'm at the hospital.'

'Oh my God. Is it Liv? Is she okay?' Efe's voice is higher than usual, strained and breaking.

'She's fine. She's good. It's my dad.'

'What happened?'

'I— I don't know. We haven't seen the doctor yet, but it might be another stroke.'

'But his meds—'

'I don't know anything else,' Sam says, deflating.

'I'm so sorry, Sam.' Efe says. 'What can I do to help?'

'From Ghana?' Sam smiles wearily. 'Probably nothing. I just wanted to hear your voice.'

'Mr Mensah?' There's a stout, balding man standing over Sam, smiling a polite closed-mouth smile.

'Sorry, I've got to go,' he says to Efe.

'Yes?' Sam says, standing and shoving the phone into his pocket.

'I'm the neurologist treating your dad. The CT scan confirmed a clot on the left side of his brain.'

'Another stroke?'

The doctor nods. 'We've given him something to dissolve the clot, but we'd like to keep him in for a few days to monitor his condition.'

Sam nods, his breath catching in his throat. Outside this place, people are getting on with their days. A car rolls to a stop at a red light. People idly push shopping trolleys around supermarkets. Children play in playgrounds, clamber up climbing frames. In here, Sam finds himself face to face with the unimaginable.

Phoebe arrives after midnight, shuttled in on the late train from Edinburgh to London, leaving a work conference early and her disorganised manager to fend for herself. By the time she climbs out of the Uber, Olivia is tucked into bed at Aunty Dora's and Sam has contorted himself into an armchair that feels like a pile of bricks and is just drifting off when she draws back the curtain. He's half sleeping and hears the faint jingle as if in a dream. Then there's a sharp kick to the chair leg and he bolts awake. His eyes spring open, and the first thing he sees is the sad smile on his sister's face, the red-rimmed eyes and mascara clumping in places.

'You made it,' Sam says, yawning widely.

Phoebe brings a finger to her lips and makes a shushing sound. Sam follows her gaze to where their parents are, his mother in a chair by his father's bedside, her head resting on the bed frame, their hands interlocked. Sam hasn't met up with her again, but from time to time he hears how she's doing through his dad or sister, and silently wishes her well.

At first seeing such intimacy between them had shocked Sam, but as the evening's rolled on, neither of them have moved in hours and Sam's heard his mum whispering to him, seen her adjusting his oxygen tube. Twice, Sam had overheard her asking, 'Are you in pain?' both times her voice quivering. Sam rises, draping a blanket over her. He turns and follows Phoebe out.

'You look awful,' she says.

Sam stirs and yawns again. His mouth is dry. 'Who let you in?'

'One of the nurses. I had to practically beg her.' She wheels a slim suitcase behind her.

'Good to see you.' As they pass the lifts, Sam pulls her into a hug, feels the scratch of braids against his cheek.

'What did the doctor say?' she asks.

'Another stroke. They managed to dissolve the clot, but we have to wait and see how bad the damage is.'

She glances at her watch and draws herself up straighter. 'What are we looking for? Coffee?'

They make their way through the near-silent hallways, pass darkened wards and take the lift down to a brightly lit cafeteria. It's empty, the metal shutters drawn. In the corner they find a machine and slot in £1 coins until it churns out what looks like brown water. Under the fluorescent lights, Sam can clearly make out how crumpled Phoebe's clothes are, the puffiness and smudges of black around her eyes. Even her coat sags heavily at her shoulders. Everything about her is worn-down. She places the paper cup beneath her nostrils, pulls a face and takes a sip anyway. Still looking into the cup, she says, 'Do you think she'll stay?'

Sam considers this, learning to let things go. 'I dunno,' he says softly. 'But she's here today.'

Over the days that follow, Sam feels his life is getting further and further away from what he thinks it should look like. Days mush together in a bleary-eyed blur, with Sam bouncing from work to Liv's school and back to the hospital. Sometimes in the night-time hours, he heads back home to shower and try to catch a few hours of fitful sleep. The rest of the week passes with him and Liv surviving on nothing but cereal, hospital food and handfuls of crisps. This is what it must've been like for Efe, just with Liv on her hip or in the buggy, carting her back and forth to appointments, wiping drool from Ken's mouth. It is hard enough juggling it all while Liv is in school. He can't even imagine doing all of this with a baby in tow. Back then he'd only been to two or three of Ken's appointments, and he's ashamed to think about it now; how he couldn't face it and how he'd let Efe take over.

'There'll likely be some fatigue. He'll continue to struggle with motor function, difficulty controlling bowel movements. We recommend beginning physical therapy as soon as possible to give him the best chance at regaining function,' the doctor says, less optimistic about Ken's recovery each time Sam visits. They say they're planning to send Ken home in a wheelchair, so Sam spends his lunch breaks trying to find the most affordable way to install a stairlift in the house. When he realises that it can't be done, he starts coming up with a plan to move a bed into the living room and make the downstairs bathroom more accessible. He has a long list of medicines with unpronounceable names, a longer list of things to be on the lookout for – so much that could still go wrong – compounded by the knowledge that his mum could disappear at any moment, a volcano ripping through their already unstable lives.

And through it all, Sam puts on a brave face, but feels his eyes welling up each time he strides into the hospital room and sees his father wan and grey-skinned, tired. It is all too soon. Fifty-eight years of being indestructible in Sam's eyes, and now he is reduced into someone who chokes on spoonfuls of apple sauce and pureed vegetables, and Sam wonders just how long it will be until everyone is thwarted by life or their own body.

*   *   *

Sam is standing in the hospital stairwell when Efe's voice comes through the line. He's spoken to her daily since his dad was admitted, but today a faint worry is buzzing in the back of his mind, distracting him.

'You free?' she asks.

'Yeah,' he says. A pause. 'Where are you?'

'Heading back from the studio now.'

'How's the painting?'

'Almost there. I'm a little worried two of them won't be done in time for the exhibition.'

'I'm sure they're incredible.'

She laughs. 'You haven't even seen them.'

'I know you,' Sam says. 'And I believe in you.' A comfortable silence follows, then Sam – voice unsteady now – begins again, halting every few words. 'Actually, Efe. I need to tell you something about . . . that happened . . . with Abbey.'

He hears something shift and imagines her mind sprinting ahead, trying to make sense of it all. 'What about Abbey?'

'Well, erm . . .'

'You slept with her,' Efe says coolly.

'Just once. Back in the summer. A few weeks after we split up.'

Sam isn't sure what's happening on the other end of the line. He feels nervous, listening out for tears or the clipped sound of anger on the edge of her words. Instead, her voice stays flat and detached. 'Why?' she says.

Sam begins to speak, ready to run through all the reasons – being mad at Efe, wanting to hurt her, wanting to be happy, not wanting to be alone – but Efe isn't done yet.

'Don't you ever feel like we're making this so much harder than it should be? We could just be happy but we're ruining it. Damn it.'

Sam turns his face towards the window, through which he can see a half-full car park and a small circle of green-gowned patients smoking beneath a glass-roofed walkway.

His mind is grainy. And missing her. He hears himself say the words he should've said months ago.

'Let's start over.'

'What?'

'Everything. The last few months didn't happen. Let's talk, figure this out.' As soon as he says these words, Sam knows he'll say anything – do anything. Everything is between them, the good and bad swirled together, inseparable. The only way forward is stepping over it together, agreeing to leave it all behind. 'Okay?'

'Okay,' Efe says, sounding as nervous as Sam feels. He can hear a slight quiver.

'I love you.'

'I love you too.'

Two days before Ken is due to be discharged, Sam is back in the empty hospital stairway. Beyond the wall, Sam hears the ripple of voices, the rap of footsteps along the corridor. He leans against the railing. A glossy pamphlet hangs heavy in his fingers. It's for a rehabilitation programme and, when Sam opens it up, he sees an elderly patient flanked by two nurses in crisp white tunics, all of them red-cheeked and grinning. A space is available. They've been chasing Sam for an answer for the last two days, but each time Sam tries to sit down and think it through, the more he feels incapacitated.

The phone is already ringing by the time Sam realises he's called Efe. Hearing her voice on the other end of the line is a welcome relief and, for a few moments, Sam closes his eyes and lets her voice wash over him.

'Are you there?' she asks.

'Yes, sorry,' Sam says, slowly. Carefully. 'Just needed a second to catch my breath.'

'Okay,' Efe says softly. 'How is he?'

'Pretty much the same but a bit confused. I don't think he's totally with it.'

324

Sam hears her radio dip in the background. He imagines her with the phone pressed between her ear and shoulder, barefoot, still in pyjamas, her new apartment open and sun-filled.

'I wish I could do something to help,' Efe says. And Sam agrees.

'Come home,' he says. 'Not to help with Dad. I won't put you through that again. I'm not expecting anything. I just—' He drags a palm across his face. 'I need you. I need a partner.' The last few months have dulled his anger, eroded it away like a pebble worn smooth. He's cycled through so many emotions but now, everything in him is tired.

Efe grows quiet. 'I have a life here now. What about the exhibition?'

'Come after it. Or we can come to you and spend Christmas in Ghana. Celebrate or something. We can do whatever you want. I'm not asking you to give it up,' he says. 'We can do both. We can live in both countries. I could work remotely. We could rent out the flat the months we're not here and make it work.'

Efe lets out a quiet breath.

Sam adds, softer this time, 'You don't have to decide right now. Just think about it, okay? Promise me you'll think it through.'

'I promise,' Efe says. 'Maybe I can come after the show but before Christmas.'

'Whenever,' Sam says, already counting down the weeks.

He tries to pull his thoughts back, but his brain is telling himself stories of what it'll be like when she's back, how he'll get to experience all the things he's missed – her dewy fresh-out-of-the-shower sheen, the scent of the perfume she's worn for the last decade that's faded from the clothes she left behind. A sweet floral smell, with a hint of orange. The early morning lulls before the alarm goes off, when she'd rest her head on his chest and they'd talk about all their plans for the day, and he'd feel closer to her than he had to anyone else. He wants all of it back.

OCTOBER 2016

One Day Before

Efe lets herself in through the front door. She's not surprised to find it unlocked – she'd known it would be – but what does surprise her is the slight shaking in her hand as she reaches for the handle. Almost no one is here. She knows already that Paa has sent all the house girls off on long, unnecessary errands, and that he too has slipped out of the house. The only car in the driveway is Maame's.

Efe's footsteps echo as she makes her way along the empty hallway. She hasn't thought of this building as her home for decades. It is simply the house she grew up in. And walking beneath years-old photos hanging on the walls, she struggles to reconcile those frozen-in-time versions of her family with what her life has become. They're staring, serious-faced and unsmiling in all but the family portrait, taken a year before Efe and Serwaa left for London. In that one, Maame and Paa are seated in the centre, the girls standing behind them, their hands resting on their parents' shoulders. A picture-perfect family, captured mid-laughter. Yet Efe hasn't stepped foot in this house in months, not since the disastrous meeting with the elders.

Distant sounds are coming from the kitchen. Efe tries to keep calm as she drifts towards them. She rests a hand on the doorframe but doesn't enter. She hardly ever sees Maame cooking. Most often her cooking consists of supervising the house girls and scolding them for burning the pot. For just a few moments she watches Maame, standing with her back to Efe, bent over the sink and washing a few dozen tomatoes, humming along to a song on the radio. In the glittering sunlight, with her head bobbing and hair bouncing at her shoulders, she looks youthful and carefree. Efe holds her breath. She wants this moment to last forever. As soon as she thinks that, Maame's eyes flick up, and she turns around.

'Oh, it's you,' she says, then her gaze hardens. 'Who let you in? Paa!' she yells.

'He's gone out.'

Maame looks at Efe suspiciously. 'He didn't tell me.'

'He's gone out so we can talk.'

Maame kisses her teeth. 'So that's why he's sent everyone away and there's no one here to help me make this stew. You're plotting with your father now – what for – to ambush me in my own home?'

'He's only involved because you still won't speak to me.'

And it's true. Maame has spent months avoiding Efe, the rift between them ever expanding. They've only seen each other a handful of times since that meeting with the elders – all brief encounters, crossing paths at Serwaa's place, at the SHS graduation and once at the hospital after Nanadwoa's son was born. Every time Maame had made some excuse to leave the moment she saw Efe. For almost five months, she's been closer geographically to her mother than she has been in the decade before, but the gulf is only widening. Even now, she worries her mum will push past her and leave, that even this moment will slip through her fingers.

'Please,' Efe says. 'I just thought we could talk.'

Maame wavers. 'Don't just stand there. Peel and chop the onions,' she says.

Obediently, Efe washes her hands and gets to work. Above

the hum of the radio, the rhythm of chopping and water running are the only sounds in the room.

'Mum,' she begins, 'you should know I'm going back to London. To my family.' Even as Efe says this, she is struck again by how ready she feels to go back. Bewildered by her own willingness. But it finally feels right. She is returning to a life that she can commit to, something she actually wants. Sure, they still have work to do, but it will be easier because she's grown here; the months she's spent in Ghana, finally discovering her identity outside of them, have done her good. And the ground beneath her feet finally feels solid.

Maame laughs, a stark note that makes Efe wince and the knife in her fingers wobble. 'If he'll take you back,' Maame hisses.

'We've spoken it through. We're going to split our time—'

'Hmph, so he still wants you after what you've done?' she says with such force that Efe balks. She wasn't even sure Maame would acknowledge her abortion directly, but here it is, swift as a dagger whistling past her ear.

Efe groans, throwing her hands into the air. 'Now I'm the problem again. You don't even speak to Sam but you're insisting I go back to him. And now we're making it work and you're still mad. What is it with you?'

'Efe—'

'No,' Efe says, cutting her off. 'He's made mistakes too. I'm not saying either one of us is perfect.'

Maame dumps the tomatoes into a grinding bowl, settles down on a low stool. She reaches for the wooden pestle, brings it down on the tomatoes with a sludgy thump. 'I never told you to be perfect. I wanted you to have a good life. A husband that would take care of you. An easy—'

'None of this is easy. Nothing in this life. Motherhood isn't easy.'

'No, it's not.' Maame brings the pestle down hard. 'Being a mother is about sacrifice. Tough choices. Always thinking of your children before yourself.'

'And I didn't want that. I told you that I didn't want children and you . . . all of you forced me into this position.'

Maame jumps to her feet, drives a thumb into her chest. She looks at Efe, her expression twisted in anger. 'Me!' she says. 'Did I lie down to open my legs?'

'You don't get it.'

'Come on and explain then.'

Efe steels herself. 'Those first few years felt impossible. I didn't sleep for weeks. I can count on one hand how many times I had an hour or two to myself to sit in a cafe alone or grab a coffee with a friend. And God, the guilt you people made me feel for needing that. All that pressure and I was still screwing everything up. Sometimes I thought they'd be better off without me. You have no clue how often my mind would go there.'

Efe doesn't have the words to explain how she'd felt like her entire world had been overturned, and she was constantly losing pieces of herself for a full eighteen months after. How just before Liv turned one and Efe's parents had returned to Ghana, Efe desperately worried that she'd made the wrong decision in staying, crawled into bed and didn't get out for three weeks. And after those dark days, when Efe was still at her lowest, she would float, ghost-like, around the house and count all the pills she'd hidden, like a child hoarding sweets. Panadol. Ibuprofen. Paracetamol. Nurofen. Thirty-two pills Efe would spread out on their bedspread daily, wondering if it was enough.

She'd never told Sam this, but she was sure he'd sensed it. Maybe in the morning when he'd rub her back gently to wake her, he could feel the pull she had to leave. As always, her solution-minded husband had scoured the internet, and, after careful consideration, brought her the name of a therapist and talked her into seeing the GP, reassured her she wasn't making everything worse. And over the months that followed, Sam took over everything that needed doing in the house, and delicately pulled her back from the ledge.

Efe envies them. People like the Maames and the Serwaas of this world, people to whom mothering came so easily, would never understand. Efe knew they'd never spend days overthinking, wondering if their child's cough would turn into pneumonia, or worry about if a two-year-old still using a dummy would develop dental problems later in life. They somehow knew all the things she was second-guessing.

But Efe overthinks because she knows how easy it is to ruin a life. She knows that a series of small mistakes and pressure applied too soon can irrevocably change a person. People are malleable. Children particularly so. When it comes to mothering, she's always wanted to plan eight steps ahead and think years into the future, envisioning the person she'd like Olivia to be, praying she was giving her just enough space and guidance. Still, Efe knew how badly she could get it wrong, and the thought of that was paralysing. She doesn't have it in her. She tries to do her best, but knows it still may not be enough.

'How was I supposed to know?' Maame says.

'You didn't care. You were too busy forcing me to be this, this person I just can't be. You were so consumed with your idea of me that you couldn't see what it was doing to me.'

'Stop it.' Maame raises a hand. 'I said, "Stop it," Efe. Stop!'

Efe's panting now. 'You're the one who wanted to –' she falters '– you asked to hear the truth.'

Efe can see that Maame doesn't want to hear any more. She doesn't know what to do with her face. She runs the heel of her hand under her nose, scrunches up her mouth. She picks up the pestle again, murmuring to herself as she pounds.

Efe feels like a popped balloon. She starts crying now, noiselessly, and is glad Maame won't look at her.

'You think we didn't know you were unwell?' Maame fumes, driving the pestle into the bowl. 'I could see it. I could

330

feel it right here.' She lays a palm on her chest. 'I've always been able to tell. Maybe we should've come sooner, but we came. We wanted to bring you girls home. You think we didn't fight for you and pray for you every day? Every moment of every day, Efe. You are so ungrateful.' Maame thuds back into her seat, slams the pestle into the bowl with her full weight behind it. Quick furious jabs.

'That baby had done nothing wrong,' Maame says, and for the first time in years, maybe in Efe's whole life, they're two adults speaking to each directly.

Efe swallows, bites back the remainder of her tears. 'I know that.'

'Know whatever you want. You're still that child's mother.' She pounds with fury now. A sheen forms on her forehead and she keeps going, even when the tomatoes are a red slush, splattering up the sides of the bowl. 'I didn't know you could be so wicked. An innocent baby. God help you.'

What follows, Efe sees in slow motion. First, the bowl tips to the side. Maame tips with it. Liquefied tomatoes slosh over the edge. Second, Maame tries to right herself, drives her hand down. Slips. Third, the other hand, moving as if of its own accord, comes down. The end of the pestle meets her fingers with a crunch. The sound is nauseating. Maame howls, clutches her hand to her chest. Already, her fingers are turning a deep mauve, two of them twisted and the nail-beds darkening.

'Let me help.' Efe rushes forward. Maame snatches her hand away.

'Leave me,' she says. 'You've done enough.'

Then she pushes past. When her bedroom door slams, the whole house shakes, and Efe lowers her gaze. All that remains is the overturned bowl, pulped tomato seeping into the gaps between the tiles, and, in the midst of the mess, a thin gold band half-buried in red, broken clean in two.

* * *

331

Efe waits in the house. The hours pass slowly. She should be packing up her paintings and transporting them to the venue ahead of the show, but instead she shuffles past her parents' bedroom door a dozen times, presses her ear to the wood and hears nothing. She leaves a cold compress, painkillers and bandage outside the door and knocks gently, too afraid to try the handle in case it's locked.

The afternoon drags on. When Efe thinks to change the cold compress and leave a bottle of water outside the door, she finds the bandages untouched, painkillers unopened, the cold compress melted. Efe's still in the living room when the house girls return. Their chattering voices drift across the yard, move from window to window as they make their way round the house. They're laughing by the time the back light clicks on.

Paa arrives not long after. He is halfway across the hallway when he sees Efe, sitting in the dim, grey light, the curtains half-drawn behind her, turning her rings in circles.

He jumps. 'Efe,' he says. 'How did it go? Why're you sitting in the dark?'

Efe rises to her feet. The first tears begin to fall. Soon she is sobbing, not entirely sure why or who these tears are for.

'Oh, come here,' Paa says, and she walks into his open arms, presses her face into his chest. 'I'll talk to her,' he says eventually and pulls away, moves towards the stairs. Efe listens to the soft tread of footsteps overhead, the creak of a door opening, Paa's faint voice. She strains but can barely even hear the one half of the conversation, a murmur reverberating through all that empty space.

Paa reappears on the stairs, shifts his weight from foot to foot and sighs. 'She says she won't come downstairs if you're still here. What happened to her hand? I have to drive her to the hospital.'

'Oh.' Efe gestures in the direction of the kitchen. 'An accident. She was pounding tomatoes. I tidied it up.'

Paa winces, gives his head a brief shake. 'I'm sorry. Go home. Rest. I'll talk to her, okay?'

'Okay,' Efe says and gathers her things to leave.

Efe doesn't go to the studio. She lets herself into her apartment, still feeling frazzled by the argument with Maame. She knows she should wrap her pieces for transportation, but feels her awful mood would taint the space or somehow seep into the paintings she's spent months working on.

The weight of the day is heavy on her shoulders. She doesn't make it to her bedroom. Instead, she lugs herself to the sofa and drags a thin blanket up to her chest. There's a steady throbbing in her head now. She sighs and lets her eyes close.

When Efe next opens her eyes almost eight hours have passed. It's early. A dream sits heavy on her chest and the stillness in the flat around her feels tender. Outside the world is calm, the sky waiting for daybreak.

She rises, treading lightly on the cool tiles, feeling small pricks of gathered dust under her soles. In the bathroom, she washes her face and tries to focus. Mentally, she runs through all the things she has to do before her show tonight, but thoughts of Maame keep crowding in. She wants to talk it through with Serwaa or Sam, but knows it's still early and both of them will be asleep. Instead, she calls Nanadwoa.

'Did I wake you?' Efe asks, whispering.

When Nanadwoa speaks, her voice comes out groggy at the other end, the words muffled by a yawn. 'No,' she says. 'We were up already.'

Efe feels the corners of her mouth lift. 'How is the little king?'

'Ohene is good, but he's hungry. All. The. Time. I've never seen a child feed like this,' she says, but Efe can hear the smile in her voice. 'How did things go with your mum?'

Efe lets out a low breath. 'Awful. I don't know if we're gonna get there.'

'Don't say that.'

'No, really.'

'She'll come round,' Nanadwoa says. 'Didn't Sam? I don't know everything that happened between the two of you, but look at how far you've come. It will be the same again here. She's your mother.'

Efe feels unconvinced. She lets her eyes scan the bottles and tubs on the nearest shelf and picks up the cream Nanadwoa gave her. It had been days before Nanadwoa went into labour when Efe had visited to find Nanadwoa in her underwear, complaining about the heat, every fan and air-conditioning unit blasting. At the sight of her stomach, a perfectly round orb with not a single mark or blemish, not even a dark line drifting down from her belly button and disappearing beneath her knickers, Efe's mouth had fallen open. Since Olivia, her stomach has been riddled with stretch marks and sometimes she feels like a deflating balloon.

'It's all this cream, I'm telling you,' Nanadwoa had insisted.

Efe pulls the lid off, thinking of the tough, ugly scars still covering her back. She brings the tub to her nose, breathes in the tart chemical scent poorly masked by clove and peppermint. It makes her eyes water.

'What did you say was in this cream?' Efe asks.

Nanadwoa makes a sound partway between a laugh and a huff. 'I don't know but it works.'

Efe has to agree. She's used it once already and has noticed a slight improvement in the scars. She's sure the tough rivulets are softer under her fingers.

'If you're using it on your back, don't mind the instructions. You should leave it on for twenty or thirty minutes. Five isn't enough to break down scar tissue.'

Efe twirls the small pot, takes in the brand name and smiling Photoshopped faces, and sees instructions but no ingredients. She takes a deep breath.

'Let's see how it goes.' Nanadwoa stays on the line as Efe pulls her clothes off and lets them fall to the floor, presses her fingers into the neon-yellow liquid and spreads a thick layer along her scars. She sits on the edge of the tub as the paste dries and stiffens, the tingling sensation turns to burning, remembering a lifetime ago, how she'd sat on the rim of another bathtub, counting down three minutes, a sick feeling sloshing within her.

'Is it meant to hurt like this?' Efe asks twenty minutes later, biting down on her lip.

'Give it two more minutes.'

'Okay,' Efe says. 'Distract me. What else is going on with you?'

'Erm, Eric came to visit us yesterday.'

'Pastor?' Efe pauses. 'What did he say?'

'They're going to reinstate him, but he needs me to leave Accra.'

'Leave Accra? Do you want to go?'

'Maybe I don't have a choice. He's offered to find me a place in Takoradi. He'll visit every month and put money towards Ohene's expenses. Almost one thousand dollars every month.' She pauses. 'You should've seen him with the baby. It reminded me why I fell in love with him.'

Efe doesn't know what to say. She hadn't known it was love and Nanadwoa's admission shifts something in her.

'And is that enough?' Efe asks, not sure which part of Nanadwoa's statement she's referring to, the money or the love.

Nanadwoa sighs. 'It has to be.'

'But are you happy?'

A moment passes. 'Wherever I have my son is home to me. He'll be cared for. And Eric still loves me. I know it.' Over the phone, her voice sounds calm and resolute. 'People – even the ones who love you – can be a weight around your neck. You just have to choose which weights you want to carry. And I'm strong. This. This I can live with.'

Slowly, Efe nods. She understands. For almost two decades home has been a place shifting under her feet; she forever feels like she could take one step too far and the world could topple, her life shatter into pieces. It was all the same: school, university, relationships, motherhood. She can understand Nanadwoa wanting something steady. Maybe this too is brave.

'I wonder why we do that,' she says.

'Do what?'

'Measure a woman's strength by the amount she is able to endure?'

Efe only steps into the shower after thirty minutes, when the pain has become unbearable. Pale yellow water gathers at her feet. Skin comes off in flakes, the clumps like wet balls of disintegrating cotton. Not skin. Scars. When Efe climbs out she can see patches of new skin underneath, as pink and bright as a newborn's. Outside, a wind is whistling across the shutters. And when she looks up, she can see that dawn is coming – an orange blot pushing through a red-coloured sky, like a world set ablaze.

It is still early when Efe takes a cab from the studio to the gallery, her paintings wrapped in thick reels of plastic, stacked on the back seat. When she gets there, Efe sees her pieces are the last to arrive. She's set up galleries countless times before, but now it's her own work. She props the canvases up against the wall and walks through the space, judging the light and angles from different parts of the room, arranging and rearranging until she is satisfied. It takes longer than it should, but Efe reminds herself how much this matters, all the hours she poured into each piece.

She's feeling confident when she steps back outside. The show is supposed to start soon, but Efe knows it won't begin for hours. Only a handful of vendors have arrived. The staff are wrestling with folding tables.

In the car park, she spots the DJ unloading speakers from a car. Efe raises her hand. A red taxi comes to a stop, its saffron panels streaked with rust. And as they drive, passing only one taxi as they go, Efe reminds herself she has time.

Six Hours Before

Sam sleeps poorly on the plane. He wakes with his face pressed into the headrest, a ringing in his ears and a deep ache in his neck. They've just turned the lights back on, and he can see the flight attendants pushing metal carts down the narrow aisles, handing out paper cups of hot drinks and juices. He feels groggy and dry-mouthed. He guesses there's still an hour or so before their plane lands, and after that, they'll have to pass through customs and immigration, with its long spiralling queues, before they can finally collect their bags. Liv stirs, her head in Sam's lap, still dozing as the plane around them grows louder. Sam thinks about reaching over her, pulling up the blind to watch Accra come into view, but he looks down at his daughter and decides to let her sleep on.

It's after noon by the time Sam takes Liv's hand in his and wheels their baggage down the concourse. The forecourt is thick with people and buzzing with activity. It doesn't take Sam long to find a taxi. He knows how bad traffic in Accra can be, so plans to head straight to the venue. Even exiting the airport is a challenge, and though Sam asks the driver to avoid the main roads it's not long before they find themselves in one of Accra's notorious traffic jams – three lanes of almost stagnant traffic, the air filling with exhaust fumes.

A throng of people are walking towards them like a steady wave. Then the hawkers are upon them, sauntering between the cars, their wares held high on their heads. Shouts popcorn all around. 'Phone card!' 'Yo-ghat!' 'Pawpaw!' Accra's latest offerings. Today it is papaya, plantain chips, DVDs, imported cooking utensils and a back massager with 'Made in China' stamped on the smooth plastic.

At the sight, Olivia's mouth falls open and her face moves nearer the glass. Sam feels a laugh rise up in him. He remembers seeing this for the first time. The swell of people, seeing everything imaginable for sale drift by. Despite their best intentions, Sam and Efe have only visited Ghana as a family once since Liv was born – and that was when she was too young to remember – so Sam sits back and tries to see it through her eyes. She is looking at the car beside them, watching two boys hover by a sleek black Mercedes. '*Sah?* English? You want newspaper, *sah?*' the older boy calls. '*New Vision? Daily Guide?* This one very nice—'

Without looking in their direction, the driver shoos them away. Opposite, a woman in a dark Toyota winds down her window. She throws her voice into the din. 'Wah-ta, *mepaakyɛw*,' she calls, projecting every syllable. The cry is picked up, funnelled from person to person. Heads turn. The call echoes, jumps over the idling cars until one of the hawkers comes running.

The gallery is off a wide street in the looming shadow of a church the size of a stadium. The driver slows, carefully manoeuvring around the jutting rocks and sprawling ditches. The event is due to begin in twenty minutes, but the street is calm. All but two parking spaces are empty. The only other vehicle they pass is a red and yellow taxi going the opposite way. Two men are lugging large speakers across the road. To Sam, it feels hidden. Quiet. Before they get out of the taxi, he double-checks the event poster Efe sent over to make sure he's at the right location.

'Thanks,' Sam says, handing over 60 cedis, still crisp from the bureau de change.

They walk to the entrance, Liv's hand in Sam's, the suitcase carving grooves into the burnt-orange ground. The only people Sam can see are the staff and a couple of American tourists wandering around the grounds while the vendors set up. He looks over to the gallery and sees the doors are still closed. Sam and Liv settle down at a picnic table.

He texts Aunty Dora to let her know they've landed safely, remembering how hastily she'd agreed to drop them off at the airport when Sam had asked. The whole journey she'd been humming to herself, barely able to hide her smile. The second text he sends to Phoebe, knowing she checks her phone more than both of his parents combined and will pass the message on, the three of them inseparable these days. Happy. Sam is coming round too, little by little.

He sits and waits.

Sam notices when the artists begin to arrive. They're spread across the grounds, standing stiffly, throwing equally relieved and anxious looks at the milling crowd. Sam has stowed the suitcases at reception. He and Liv are near the front when the gallery owner makes a short speech. Waiting for the event to begin, he scans the crowd, looking for Efe. He can't see her and toys with the idea of calling her, either to wish her luck or let her know they're here. Instead, he decides to keep it a surprise.

The doors open. People begin to file into the building. Sam moves through the gallery, trying to work out which pieces are Efe's. He's certain she's been painting but he isn't sure if she'd meant portraits on canvas, or if she'd been painting something else, so he spends a little while looking at the brightly painted sculptures near the entrance, looking for some hint of Efe there. The next three pieces are large. Long strips of blue-black fabric suspended in ten-foot strips on a piece of wood hanging down from the ceiling. A portrait is etched in thick red paint. An old man's face on one side. A woman's face on the other.

'Can you see that?' Sam says, pointing it out to Olivia, showing her the way the painting changes depending on where they're standing.

He's about to move on when he sees something out of the corner of his eye. He doesn't remember consciously telling his feet to move, but he finds himself pushing through the crowd until he's standing beneath them. Seven canvases. Three months of work right here. Each painted in various shades and hues of a colour in the rainbow. The first is reddish-orange, a painting of the two of them based on a photo taken on the night Sam had proposed. He hasn't looked at the photo in years and is shocked by how young they look. How happy and giddy they are, even though he remembers how nauseated he'd felt the day it was taken. He hadn't been sure if it was from nerves or the boat's constant rocking. There is one of Efe, painted in shades of navy and paler blues. She's holding a tiny newborn Liv, the baby snuggled into her chest, a tired smile on her lips. Sam recognises their bedroom mirror and dressing table, both painted in a dusky blue, fading into nothing.

Someone bumps into him. Sam takes two stumbling steps forward and finds he's so close to the painting he can see something he didn't see the first time. At first he thinks it's a leftover pencil outline, but then he realises it's intentional, paint as thin as a strand of hair. There's another version of her face there, the eyes closed, lips puckered like she's letting out a long, low breath. Sam would've missed it if he hadn't been standing this close or didn't know to look for it. He looks to the left and sees the same thing in the painting of them at the beach. And again in one with just the two of them in matching pyjamas, copied from a photo taken a year ago on Christmas Day. He sees it now, all the feelings she'd never been able to articulate right here in front of him.

Sam comes back to himself then. He's aware of how full the gallery has become, the people ambling around the room, the warm night air seeping in through the open windows and the DJ blending one song into the next. His breath feels sluggish and thick in his throat. He misses her intensely then. Suddenly. Deeply. Like when she'd first gone, before he'd known about the baby. He pats his pockets down, looking for his phone, and when he has it in his hands his fingers are shaking.

'So the two of you fly all this way and don't let anyone know?'

Sam turns and sees Serwaa standing a few feet away, her expression apologetic and warm all at once.

'Aunty Serwaa,' Liv says, letting go of Sam's hand for the first time and crashing into Serwaa, her arms wide open.

She looks up. Sam swallows. 'Hi, Serwaa,' he says.

'Efe didn't say you were coming.'

'I wasn't. Well –' he pauses '– she doesn't know. I wanted to be here for opening night. She talked so much about it so . . .' He trails off.

Serwaa nods, the air between them still uncomfortable. Both of them remembering the last time they were face to face.

Sam looks towards the door. He can see other artists standing by their work and more people are arriving each minute, but none of them are her. 'Is she here? Have you seen her?'

'No, not yet.' Serwaa falters, wringing her hands around the handle of her handbag. 'Can I ask – does this mean you're—'

'We're gonna make it work.'

She nods, her eyes glistening with tears, 'I'm really happy to hear that, Sam. And I'm sorry for my part in this mess.'

'You're ringing.'

'I'm what?'

'Your phone.'

'Oh,' she says, laughing, digging around in her handbag. Sam thinks it over while Serwaa is on the phone. He is

341

learning to throw away his plans, to let himself get swept up in all the unexpected parts of this life. He's learning to be happy despite everything that's happened. And that this could be enough.

OCTOBER 2016

Three Hours Before

Efe steps back into her apartment around the time the show should begin. She knows she should be hurrying into the shower and getting ready to go back out, but she pauses in the living room, taking in the almost-empty space. Ever since she booked her ticket home, Efe has started to pack. She's filled the two suitcases that wait by the door. She plans to leave no trace of herself in the space. What she hasn't packed, she will give away, but she is still baffled by how little she has acquired over the last few months, and as she moves from room to empty room, she realises just how easy it is to leave a whole life behind. Again. She does one last loop of the rooms. The walls are bare. The cupboards empty as she's known they would be.

She thinks of all the things she has to do over the next couple of days: pick up the tailormade outfits for Sam and Olivia, visit Nanadwoa, meet up with a friend of Aunty Dora's to collect some jewellery flown in from a recent trip to Dubai. Say goodbye to the other artists. There's a knock. The sound is louder than it should be and Efe's head spins towards it.

'Dad,' she says, swinging the door open. They hug and she glances over his shoulder, looks both ways down the desolate walkway.

Paa purses his lips and gives his head a little shake, answers the question on the tip of Efe's tongue. 'She means well,' he says.

'Right.' Efe tries to smile but only manages to pull her lips up slightly before they fall.

'Give her time.'

They move from doorway to sofa. 'You want something to drink?' Efe asks.

'No, I'm not staying long.' Paa claps his hands together, wraps an arm around Efe's shoulders. 'I just wanted to wish you luck before your show.'

'You're coming?' Efe says. She hadn't expected much when she sent the invite to her family WhatsApp group, but smiles properly now.

'Yeah, I can drive you, but I've got to do a few things first.'

'Don't worry, it's fine, I'll take a taxi,' Efe says. 'The gallery has asked each artist to give a short speech about their work, so I can't wait.'

'See you there,' Paa says, standing to go.

The taxi arrives not long before dark. Efe hears the thrum of the engine, the crunch of gravel as it rolls up the driveway. Outside, there's the whine of an opening car door. The taxi driver – a thin man with a smooth, bald head – greets her kindly and opens the car door as she approaches. Softly, Efe closes the front door behind her. She steps out into the night and feels the first drops of rain. She lifts her face and watches it sputter. Wordlessly, the driver clicks the engine on. Efe fastens her seatbelt and stares at the road ahead. The rain picks up until it's coming down in slabs. Efe cranes her head to look and is certain that the sky has split. The wipers swish furiously.

As they drive down the motorway, Efe starts envisaging all the elements of her life blending together. She imagines seeing Sam again. Their reunion would not be dramatic, but simple and hopeful – walking into each other's arms and adjusting until they fit together. She imagines it like finally taking a deep breath after a multitude of held breaths. She'd see the look in his eyes and know she'd hurt him – hurt both of them – and that in saving herself she'd dragged her family through dirt, left them scraped raw and bleeding. But raw and bleeding things are still alive.

The rain comes swiftly. Soon the cars are pushing through grey-brown water that ripples outwards in wave after wave. Efe lets her eyes close as they near the bridge. She's tired. Lately she's been dreaming of falling, crumpling, and the ground rushing up to meet her. Vivid, feverish dreams where she's never quite sure if she falls or jumps or is pushed. All she knows is that her toes teeter over the edge of a precipice, and when she feels the wind pick up and dance around her ankles she leans into it.

Suddenly, Efe is awake. A jolt. Her heart in her throat. There's the sound of screaming metal and she hears the blare of a passing lorry. The driver is yelling, the door beside him crumpled inwards like balled-up paper. His hands grasp the wheel even as the car spins off course. There's a deafening boom – the smack of bumper against metal barrier. Efe is blinded by the sharp snap of pain across her chest, her neck. It knocks the wind out of her. She sees stars, watches, wide-eyed, as the car's bonnet curls skyward. Smoke billows. For a fraction of a second, the barrier holds fast. Then it buckles. The view through the windscreen veers sideways. The car tips. Below them, the river is in spate. Fast flowing. She hears two voices screaming, is certain one is hers.

Time slows as they're falling. She thinks of Olivia. Her parents. Serwaa. Kobby. Abena. Afia. Aunty Dora. Sam. His face crystallises in her mind. She sees him at seventeen: a flash of his furrowed brow over a pile of textbooks; twenty-two: his eye winking from behind a camera; twenty-six: the breaking of a wider than wide smile as his fingers reach for her veil; thirty: his lips meeting Olivia's forehead for the first time. These are the things she thinks of. Then they hit the water.

OCTOBER 2016

One Hour After

Sam and Serwaa are talking when it happens, sitting on blue fold-out chairs behind a plastic picnic table. Quietly the clouds have been gathering. A thin drizzle begins and thickens until people begin to move under the shelters. The kids are still playing in the rain, Abena leading Liv round the grass, Liv shooting Sam looks every minute or so, trying to keep him in her eyeline.

It's another hour before Serwaa gets the call.

'Accident?' Serwaa says, one hand covering her ear so she can hear over the music. 'Is she okay?'

They pile into the car. On the drive to the hospital, Sam's heart is beating faster than he thought possible. In the back seat, the children lurch from side to side. There is traffic everywhere, but Serwaa takes the turns too quickly to avoid it, surges onto the roundabout and cuts off a silver SUV.

Twice, they hear the news reports coming in. There are fragments of the story on every station, rumours that the emergency services took thirty minutes to arrive. A crowd is at the site. A group are praying on the roadside. Radio presenters blame the flash flooding, poor visibility on the roads, irresponsible drivers. They claim the man driving the lorry was asleep at the wheel. They talk about potential fatalities. At the sound of this, Serwaa presses harder on the accelerator. Sam can hear her muttering a prayer under her breath.

When they get to the hospital, Sam runs ahead, Serwaa bundling up the children and following a few steps behind. She stops the first nurse she sees. 'Please,' she begs. 'I need help. The accident—'

A police officer rises to his feet and pulls his hat off. Beneath it, his hair is streaked grey. 'Mrs Addo,' he says, addressing Serwaa. 'I'm the one who called you.'

'Is she okay?' Serwaa says, breathless.

'You're the sister?' the police officer asks. 'And this is?'

'Her husband,' Serwaa says softly, and the officer nods. 'Please. This way.'

'Sam, you should go. I'll stay with the kids.'

Sam follows the police officer away from the reception. They walk in silence, along long corridors, to a dim part of the hospital with crumbling, unpainted walls.

Let it be someone else, Sam says in his head. *Let it be a mistake.* He tells himself that someone stole Efe's bag, or that this officer has mixed Efe up with another Efe, confused the Owusus with another family. It's a common name. He tells himself it won't be Efe, that she's at her apartment or the exhibition. He tells himself that she's fine.

At the end of the hallway, the officer reaches forward and rings a buzzer Sam didn't notice. He tries to focus on each breath but they're all coming out laboured. He's dizzy.

The sound of the buzzer is startlingly loud. And when the door swings open, Sam can hardly breathe. There's a damp, stale smell in the air. A hint of salt. The room is windowless. Grey. It isn't a ward. Two bodies lie under sheets at the far end, and a man in a black polo shirt is looking at them, a silent question behind his gaze. His eyes flick from Sam to the police officer.

'This is the husband,' the officer says and Sam hears the words like a far-off whisper. He feels his feet carry him forward. There's a film over his eyes. He blinks it away until he sees clearly. Then he watches his own hand reach for

Efe's. Already, her skin is cold, her knuckles battered, hand bloodied, two fingernails clawed off trying to break out of the taxi. He feels like vomiting, but focuses on Efe. Her skin is shrivelled and sallow, face puffy. Litres of river water have settled in her lungs.

Sam is too late. At this thought, he feels his legs weaken. The sobs come like a low tide rising.

Sam doesn't know how he manages to leave the morgue. He feels like he's watching himself, tracing a path back through the dim hospital corridors, and suddenly, unexpectedly, stepping out under a deep, navy sky. It's disorienting. He can see Serwaa's kids running back and forth over a grassy bank not far away. He hears their laughter, including Liv's excited shrieks, he's sure of it.

'Sam?' It's Serwaa.

Through his eyelashes, Sam can see her vague shape coming towards him, but he can't bring himself to look at her. She calls again – more concerned now, a nervous edge to her voice. Sam focuses on each shuffling step. He's trembling. Then there are just a few metres between them. Finally, he lifts his eyes to meet hers. She knows.

'No.' It's a whisper at first, her hands on her cheeks. Then louder: 'No, no, no, no, no.' Suddenly, she's doubled over, sobbing and gulping for air. The scream that follows is deafening.

Eight miles away, in a house covered in flowering trellises, the phone rings. One of the house girls answers, but can barely make out the words Serwaa is shrieking. She runs upstairs to get Maame.

Maame is sitting stubbornly in her room, ignoring Paa's messages asking if she's heard from Serwaa, saying he's at Efe's show but hasn't seen either one of them, urging her to come down to the gallery. She has no plans to leave the house. She has no plans to do anything for Efe let alone speak to her. Her mind is already on the week ahead, the one hundred and fifty girls she is responsible for, the teachers she encourages daily, the petty squabbles she puts to bed. She's proud of what she's done, the children she's raised.

She thinks of her own daughters next. Back when they were little, she loved them so fiercely she could feel it in her body. A pang of pain before Serwaa ran inside crying. She could tell a lie from the curve of a lip. She alone discovered the lengths and depths of Efe's silences and interpreted every head movement or glance after their hasty return to Ghana, when Efe, just turned six, was so affected by what those kids had done to her she could not speak. She still loves them just as fiercely, but the connection has frayed over the years. It's slowed and quieted over the thousands of miles and an infinity of oceans. And now that her girls are fully grown with children of their own, one of her girls is dead and she doesn't even know it.

When the house girl bursts in, Maame can hardly make sense of her words. It comes out in a rush, bits and pieces that she is slowly putting together. Then Maame hears it, and her whole body goes numb.

Her vision blurs. She stumbles to the right.

'Madame?' She hears the house girl's nervous voice, uncertain what comes next. Maame is trying to remember the last thing she said to Efe. She realises now it's been months since they did anything but argue. She thought there'd be more time. That Efe would come to her right mind, apologise to the elders and spend the rest of her days praying for forgiveness. Maame knows what it's like to want a child so badly. She remembers how much she'd wanted Efe. And now . . . now . . . Maame can't think straight. When she throws herself on the floor, the wailing will be so intense, so inhuman, the neighbours will come running.

One Month After

Their bedroom still looks like she could walk into it tomorrow. Sam rifles through a dresser topped with bottles of her perfume, lotion, a small bowl of jewellery. In the bathroom, he digs through the cupboards, skim-reads the backs of leave-in conditioners, curling custards and gels. He pops the lid off one he recognises, brings it to his nose, and feels a deep ache rumble through him. The scent – sweet, like mangoes in the summertime – stirs up a memory. It's as sudden and vivid as a flare in the night: Efe months ago, the end of a headscarf falling into her face, rubbing hair cream into her scalp when she'd spotted his reflection in the mirror and grinned. When Sam comes to, he's trembling. He reminds himself to hold it together in front of Liv, but sometimes the grief is so thick he feels he could choke on it. Now, he blinks back the tears and steadies himself.

'What do you think?' Sam turns to Olivia, holds the tub aloft.

She nods. 'That's the one Mummy uses.'

'Let's get to it.'

In the living room, Sam swings a towel over Liv's shoulders, like a barber's cape. He parts her hair diagonally twice, an X, and smooths her dripping curls into four ponytails. He twists each one. It's a style he remembers little black girls wearing when he was a child, one he's watched Efe do countless times. He moves slowly and carefully, wraps the twists in red and purple bobbles. After, he holds up the mirror and Liv swivels round and hugs him hard.

'Thanks, Daddy,' she breathes. And Sam feels the prick of tears in his eyes. *Efe should be here today*, he thinks, his mind flashing through all the things she'll miss. Liv learning to ride a bike. Her first day of secondary school. Exams. Prom. Sending her off to university. For all the years to come, it will be Sam and Liv alone. *Efe won't see any of it*, Sam thinks, feeling himself breaking.

People begin arriving at noon. By then, Sam has changed into smart, black trousers and a dark jumper. The bags under his eyes are fading. He helps Olivia into a long-sleeved black dress, woolly black tights. Nate, Sam's old schoolfriend, is one of the first to arrive. Sam hasn't seen him in years.

'I'm so sorry, Sam,' Nate says. 'Anything you need, anything at all.' He sniffs.

'Thanks.' Sam lowers his eyes to the floor. A lump forms in his throat. He feels stupid standing up here without her, like the most important piece of himself is missing. 'Help yourself to food and drink. It's all on the dining table.'

When Efe's family arrive they keep to themselves mostly. Maame is wan, her old joints acting up in the cold. She moves slowly, Paa's arm slung protectively over her shoulders. Serwaa, Nanadwoa and Aunty Dora bring up the rear, the shared loss of Efe the gravity that brings them all together.

'Thank you for coming,' Sam says, hugging each of them in turn. And in that way, they support each other.

The upstairs neighbours come. Other friends from school and university that Sam hasn't seen in years. A handful of Efe's clients. Her old colleagues. Parents from Olivia's school who've never even met Efe. Sam doesn't know how they heard about this or how they got his address. 'How're you coping?' 'I'm so sorry for your loss,' 'Let me know what I can do to help,' he hears on repeat until the flat is full and the guests blur into an indistinct mass.

So these are all the lives she touched, he thinks. There are no speeches planned. It's enough that they're all here together, having quiet conversations and sharing stories.

Sam squeezes into the kitchen an hour in. Phoebe pulls him to the side, holds out a plate. 'Eat something,' she says so firmly Sam takes the plate. He hasn't asked them to bring food but they do anyway. Foil trays and plastic tubs stack up on the surfaces. There's so much of it. Sam peeks at each dish. Limp egg and cress sandwiches sit beside cheese crackers and celery sticks.

'She'd hate the food,' Phoebe says, noticing the downturn of Sam's lips. 'What was that thing she always said? Oh yeah. She's used to food that tastes of something.' They're both laughing now.

Sam blinks back a tear. 'Where's the real food?'

'There's jollof and chicken in the oven.'

Sam comes back with mac and cheese, jollof rice and a spoonful of roasted vegetables.

'Where's Liv?' he asks. 'She should eat too.'

'She's with Aunty Dora.'

A few moments pass. Sam feels the weight of pitying looks and pushes food around his plate. He skewers a carrot, holds it to his lips. Phoebe shifts, watching him. 'Have you spoken to Mum?'

'Not today,' Sam says. 'I've got a lot on my mind.'

Phoebe nods, turns to face her brother head on. 'She's trying. I think you should give her a chance.'

Sam exhales. He knows she's trying. He can see it for himself. Since the stroke his mother has spent every day at Ken's side. She's been the one to bathe him and dress him, read him the news highlights and plump the pillows behind his head. She's memorised his physio exercises, and they work through them together, two wilting bodies taking back some of the time they've lost.

Sam puts the plate down. All of a sudden he wants everyone out. He needs air, and storms into the hallway.

'I have to go,' Sam says. It's the wrong thing to say but all he can manage. He pushes past, shrugs on his coat in front of slack-jawed guests.

'Where are you going?' Serwaa asks, appearing as Sam's hand rests on the latch.

'Downstairs. There's just—'

'Okay.' Serwaa nods. Sam watches as she steps back into the living room, places a hand on Paa's shoulder and says something in a low murmur. She's beside Sam not thirty seconds later, reaching for her coat. Whatever Serwaa says makes its way through Efe's family circle, then the other mourners, because by the time Sam and Serwaa make it to the bottom of the bare, concrete stairwell, there's a small procession following, all drawing zips as high as they'll go or wrapping scarves around their necks.

The grass squelches beneath Sam's feet. A plane streaks across a flat grey sky. He feels steady, Serwaa's arm looped in his. To Sam, the sky seems lower than it usually is, and for a second he wonders if it's always been like that and he's simply spent his whole life not noticing. It's cold for November. In a month or two the pavements will be dusted with snow, but today beads of condensation mist at his lips.

Sam and Serwaa wait for an opportunity to cross the road to the stamp-sized park behind the bus stop. The gate creaks open. A few steps in, he pauses to take a few deep breaths, waits for his heart to steady.

There's another creak as the gate opens behind him. Maame and Paa. Aunty Dora, Liv and Nanadwoa. The other guests filing in behind them. Above them, the wind is howling through the bare tree branches. Maame is the first one to look up, and he hears the little gasp that escapes. Serwaa's eyes move heavenward too.

'Sam,' Serwaa says, but falls short. 'Oh my goodness . . . did you . . .?' She can't find the words, but Sam nods. When Sam turns her palms are steepled over her mouth, her eyes wide in awe. Sam went through every roll of film he could find. One hundred and eight rolls, plus all the digital files. Every photo is Efe. He's laced them through trees, tacked them up to fairy lights. Almost twenty years of photos, from that very first year Sam had known her until now. Everywhere they look is her.

APRIL 2017

Six Months After

Sam is here because he made a promise. On the long ride over with Efe's parents, he reminds himself of this. The car jostles and the warm afternoon air surrounds them like a shroud. Every so often he catches Paa's eye in the rearview mirror and each time Paa smiles. It's a nervous smile, like he's worried Sam will throw open the car door and disappear into the bush with Olivia. Maame too has the house girls under strict orders; she acts like she's afraid the slightest upset will send them running back to London. Both of them are different now. Skittish. Withered. Everyone treads carefully.

'Okay, we're here,' Paa says, and all four of them climb out of the car at Efe's parents' house. Olivia is at Sam's side in an instant. That happens now. Since Efe's passing, he finds that if he steps out of the room for more than a minute or veers too close to the door, Olivia's head jerks up, swings from side to side until she sees him. They're inseparable these days.

Maame leads the way inside, Paa shuffling close behind her, bowed beneath a weight no one can see. Sam pulls Olivia onto his back and they step inside. Some days he feels hollowed out, or the pain fresh and cutting deep like it did when they first lost Efe. Doubts reign. He worries he can't get through the next hour. But the time passes anyway. The days keep coming. They build themselves into weeks and months almost without him noticing. Six months gone. Their lives splintered into before and after. The therapist says this is normal. They've both been having weekly sessions – him and Olivia – and it's helping in big and little ways.

'Are those hers?' He points down the hallway to where the family portraits have been replaced with tall, thick canvases.

Paa nods. 'These are just the ones that were unsold on the night.'

Sam opens his mouth to ask another question but he's drowned out by the long blare of a car horn. They make their way round to the front of the house and find Serwaa's car parked beside Paa's, her and the children climbing out. They greet each other warmly.

'Want some?' Serwaa extends a cut of sugarcane towards Olivia. Olivia throws a cautious glance at the other sticky-fingered children and accepts.

'Okay, go play,' Serwaa says. Kobby sprints in the direction of the garden, Afia tottering behind, but Abena hesitates, holds a hand out for Olivia. Liv brings a foot up to her calf, rubs the back of her leg with a sandal. She glances up at Sam, communicates a silent question.

'It's okay,' he urges. 'I'll be right here when you get back.' And what he means is, *Don't worry. I'll always be here.*

Carefully, Liv puts her hand in Abena's. Then they sprint after Liv's other cousins, run to the end of the garden, where the grass is tall and trees are dripping with fruit. A bird flits above them, flutters from one tree to another. Moment by moment its roots grow deeper. Sam feels his eyes close, tilts his face to the sun. He hears the sound of the children's laughter drifting up towards the sky, like a long-forgotten song lyric in a distant memory, coming back to him like all the things he's forgotten – all that he's lost. And he's right where he needs to be.

Acknowledgements

For a long time I've known that writing a novel is a group effort, but I couldn't have imagined how many incredible people would play a role in bringing *Rootless* to the world.

I'd like to begin by thanking my phenomenal agent, Juliet Mushens, everyone at Mushens Entertainment, and Jenny Bent at The Bent Agency for championing this book right from the start. I'd also like to thank my extraordinary editors, Carla Josephson and Chelcee Johns, who fell in love with Sam and Efe's story and helped me see what it could be.

I'm thankful for Caroline Young and Elena Giavaldi for designing my gorgeous covers, as well as Kimberley Young, Sarah Munro, Fliss Porter, Alice Gomer, Sarah Shea, Abbie Salter, Amber Ivatt and Susanna Peden at Borough Press. I'm also thankful for Sydney Collins, Kara Welsh, Jennifer Hershey, Kim Hovey, Ted Allen, Jennifer Backe, Pam Alders and Alexis Capitini at Ballantine for all you've done. Thank you to the team at Signatuur for taking *Rootless* to the Netherlands.

I'm grateful for the brilliant staff at the London Library, particularly organiser extraordinaire Claire Berliner. To my peer group and the rest of the 2020-2021 cohort, thank you for showing up at the perfect time. Before the Emerging Writers Programme, there were other writing groups, teachers, seminars, workshops, cafes and retreats that gave me the space and confidence needed to write. Thank you to Charlie at Urban Writers' Retreat, for being an utterly lovely human, and everyone at The Novelry, for being the most amazing bunch of people I've ever had the pleasure of working along-side. Workshop Wizards: Elaine Frost, Jyoti Patel, Rajasree Variyar, Zainab Omaki, Harriet Cummings and Peggy Lee, you are all wonderful. I could not appreciate your feedback and friendship more.

I'd also like to thank the exceptional authors who came before me. I couldn't possibly list you all by name, but your books changed my life. Thank you for making my journey to publication that much easier and for gifting the world with your words.

Rootless certainly wouldn't exist if not for the amazing friends and family who joined me on this journey. My thanks go out to Becky Watson, Alice Dawes, Simran Sandu, Anna-Joy Coulter, Naomi and Joel Catchatoor, Sarah Waterman and Antonia and Jeff Blege. I'd also like to thank Sarah Lewney, Ellen Ahn, Hanna Berhanusdotter, Shanice Bailey and Beth Elwis at the House of Dreams. I also need to apologise to Beth because Dash the hamster did not make the final cut – sorry! Deborah Atuahen, thank you for being the very first person (other than me) to read *Rootless* the whole way through and vehemently being Team Efe from the very first chapter. A special thanks goes out to my sisters, parents and cousins, and extended family. You know who you are. Thanks for your support and for celebrating the milestones with me.

My final acknowledgement is for my nieces. Firstly, I hope you all become readers and realise how life-changing books can be. Secondly, I hope you learn to block out the noise, stay true to yourself and be brave enough to follow your dreams.